"Come, Alusair Nacacia Obarskyr," the orc crooned, matching the cadence of the song rising behind him. "Be my bride before you become my meal. I will do you that honor!"

The orc chieftain's laughter rose like roaring thunder around her, and Alusair reeled, hoping she'd have enough strength left to run. Perhaps after she screamed.

FORGOTTEN REALMS

The Cormyr Saga

Cormyr: A Novel
Ed Greenwood & Jeff Grubb

Beyond the High Road
Troy Denning

Death of the Dragon
Troy Denning & Ed Greenwood

August 2000

DEATH OF THE DRAGON

The CORMYR SAGA
Book III

Troy Denning
&
Ed Greenwood

DEATH OF THE DRAGON

Cover art by Matthew Stawicki
First Printing: August 2000
First Paperback Printing May 2001
Library of Congress Catalog Card Number: 00-103751

9 8 7 6 5 4 3 2 1

UK ISBN: 0-7869-2614-7
US ISBN: 0-7869-1863-2
620-T21863

U.S., CANADA,
ASIA, PACIFIC, & LATIN AMERICA
Wizards of the Coast, Inc.
P.O. Box 707
Renton, WA 98057-0707
+1-800-324-6496

EUROPEAN HEADQUARTERS
Wizards of the Coast, Belgium
P.B. 2031
2600 Berchem
Belgium
+32-70-233277

Visit our web site at www.wizards.com/forgottenrealms

To our fair Filfaerils, who'll kill us if we do this again.

Acknowledgments

The authors would like to thank their editor, Phil Athans, for his many valuable contributions; Mary Kirchoff for putting forward the idea of a collaboration; Jeff Grubb and Kate Novak for letting us play with their toys; Steven Schend, Julia Martin, and the entire FORGOTTEN REALMS® group for their advice; and most especially, Andria and Jen.

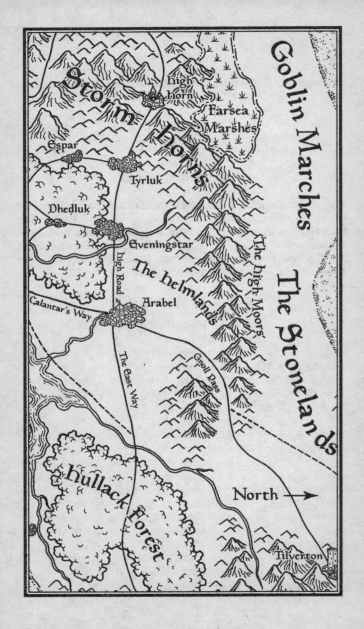

Goblin Marches

Storm Horns

Highhorn

Farsea Marshes

Espar

Tyrluk

Dhedluk

Eveningstar

high Road

The helmlands

The high Moors

The Stonelands

Calantar's Way

Arabel

The Elast Way

Gnoll Pass

North →

Hullack Forest

Tilverton

Prologue

I hate having to guess so boldly," Alusair told the first clear hoof print she'd found in three days, "but these snortsnouts aren't giving me much time to do it the proper way."

Something dark moved on the crest of the ridge behind her. Alusair snarled an oath and trotted into the nearest copse of trees. Two days at least, now, the orcs had been following her. It had been two nights that she'd dared not sleep. She was talking to herself more to keep awake than to measure her weary thoughts.

Her bold guess as to which valley Rowen had chosen had been right again, but gods blast this, it was sloppy tracking. Rowen had ridden Cadimus here, or someone had. The marks of the hooves where the war-horse crossed soft mud were deep enough to tell the Steel Princess that Cadimus had willingly carried a rider, heading as straight north as the land allowed.

Three days had passed since Alusair had left her sister Tanalasta and the sage Alaphondar and set off to rescue—

1

or learn the fate of—her scout Rowen. The scout—a Purple Dragon ranger—was an outlawed Cormaeril, but the father of Tanalasta's unborn child. Cormaeril or not, the wedding was lawful. The babe, if it lived, would be the rightful heir to the throne of Cormyr.

"Gods above and below, but father will be furious," she murmured, ducking her way through a stand of young shadowtops. "I don't know which I'd rather not be—Tana or Rowen!"

A wry smile plucked at the corners of her mouth, then vanished in an instant as her eyes fell on the moss ahead. There was a break in the trees, and Cadimus had passed through it. Tracks led up a mossy slope and away from the open valley floor, where in wet weather a creek meandered and the rest of the time open turf made for swift and easy mounted travel. Why leave that open ground? To camp?

Alusair caught herself yawning again. She slapped her own thigh with the flat of her sword to rouse herself. Gods *damn* these persistent orcs. The Steel Princess threw back her head and drew in a deep breath. She was too tired to do this properly, she was—

Suddenly very awake, with her skin crawling. She could feel the creeping, all over her, that meant her hair was rising. Something was wrong here, very wrong . . . but, by all the gods, what?

The trail went around the man-high, rotten stump of a long dead duskwood. She hefted her sword. From where she stood, as far as the eye could see, the trees ahead—an entire stand of them, dozens and dozens—were waiting. Silent, and yet not silent, there was a menacing, watchful heaviness hanging in the air.

Alusair peered grimly up into still branches and past mighty trunks, seeking a living, lurking foe but seeing nothing. The trees stood thick enough that there could well be a beast larger than a man—or even a score of such—ahead, where she could not see. The Steel Princess cast a quick glance behind her, listening intently for sounds of orcs scrabbling up the trail, but heard nothing. Her pursuers had never bothered to strive for stealth in their gloating eagerness.

After a moment, she shrugged and strode forward, sword tip tracing a ready circle at her feet, half-expecting a root to leap up and try to ensnare her. There was something unhealthy about the trees.

Alusair stopped again and studied the nearest one, almost fancying that it had moved slightly, but no. Her weary eyes were playing tricks on her.

It was a duskwood, and an old one. Some long ago lightning had left it misshapen, as gray and as gnarled as the convulsed gauntlet of a buried giant, its bark scaled where there should be no scales. No, not scales . . . runes.

The bark was engraved with a spiral of sinuous, somehow menacing glyphs. The runes seemed new, powerful, and—not good. The roots of the tree were exposed in all their tangles by a crude and recently dug burrow. The loose earth was simply flung aside as if a huge dog or hunting cat had dug swift but clumsy paws into the soil and torn at it. The hole was a ragged oval, just large enough for a man to crawl down. Alusair stepped back, then to one side, peering in. Every tree bore similar runes, and a hole had been dug under each of them.

Heavy breathing and the scrape of boots came at last. Orcs were ascending the mossy trail behind her. Alusair rolled her eyes and strode quickly forward, following the clear path Cadimus had left for her.

The trail continued to climb and the dark, recently disturbed earth now began to display strange treasures for her inspection. There was a metal scepter of swirling, clearly elven design, yet dead and dark as no elf would have made it. Stones that should have been gleaming gems were dingy and clouded, and the metal itself was as dull and gray as forge lead. Beyond the scepter was a sword, also of splendid shape. It too seemed somehow . . . drained.

That was it. There were more blades beyond, and a coffer and a quiver, then something that must have been a staff of great magical power or ornate ceremonial significance. Everything was gray, dull, and lifeless, as if all power and beauty had been stolen out of them.

The Steel Princess frowned down at them as she hurried

on. Had this been an elven burial ground or a treasure cache? What manner of creature would know where to find, or dare to despoil, either?

"Gods," she whispered aloud to herself, "Cormyr was such a simple place when I was a child. When did it grow so many unfolding mysteries?"

As if in reply, and startling her with its suddenness, a voice sang out of the trees ahead. Haunting and mournful, the liquid but sometimes harsh song was that of an elf maiden who was neither friendly nor gentle as she shaped words Alusair could not understand.

If there'd been no orcs right behind her, the Steel Princess would have backed swiftly away from that sound. As it was, the iron taste of fear was suddenly in her mouth, and she felt again that eerie stirring of hair rising all over her body. Well, at least she was fully awake now.

The song swelled, and she made out a few of its words. There was the name Iliphar, then the word *shessepra*, which humans had mangled into "scepter," and something that sounded like *haereeunmn*, which was in several old elven ballads sung by master bards when they visited the court, and meant, more or less, "all things of elves."

It was repeated. Something of a refrain, then, about Iliphar's scepter giving him power over all things elven. The voice was unearthly, achingly beautiful, yet as menacing as the hiss of a serpent. Alusair found herself shivering in time to its soaring.

Her hurrying feet brought her around a bend, and face-to-face with more than a hundred orcs. These were black, hulking snortsnouts of the most powerful sort, with battle-rings on their tusks and a cruel welcome glittering in their porcine eyes.

Their leader, a mighty orc almost twice as tall as the sort of tusker Alusair was used to slaying in the Stonelands, whose much-battered breastplate was studded with grinning human skulls, was grinning at her as one large, grubby finger rubbed along the glyphs of the largest tainted tree Alusair had yet seen. The song was coming from the runes the orc was touching, each one

4

flickering ever so slightly at the chieftain's touch.

"Well met, Princess," the orc hissed. The scuffle of boots told Alusair that her pursuers were coming up behind her. "Or should I say, my next meal!"

The orc chieftain's roar of laughter rose to join the eerie song as the Steel Princess snarled and sprang to one side, snatching at the magic she carried at her belt. She was going to die here, horribly, if she didn't—

Almost lazily the orc chieftain moved one arm, dark muscles rippling, and a blade as long as Alusair stood tall flashed end over end across the space between them.

Alusair ducked away, but the blade seemed to follow, curving down.

A sudden sharp, clear pain pierced her shoulder like fire. She'd taken an arrow in that shoulder once and had managed to forget just how sickening it had felt. This was worse. She set her teeth and twisted away from the tree the orc's foul blade had pinned her to. Alusair staggered away, retching.

Behind her, the pierced tree was making horrible gurgling sounds, as if it were choking around the orc's blade. Alusair stared at it, wondering what new horrors her next breath could bring.

"Come, Alusair Nacacia Obarskyr," the orc crooned, matching the cadence of the song rising behind him. "Be my bride before you become my meal. I will do you that honor!"

The orc chieftain's laughter rose like roaring thunder around her, and Alusair reeled, hoping she'd have enough strength left to run. Perhaps after she screamed.

1

he world vanished, and Tanalasta's stomach rose into her chest. A sudden chill bit at her flesh, and there was a dark eternity of falling. She grew queasy and weak and heard nothing but the beating of her own heart. Her head reeled, a thousand worried thoughts shot through her mind, then she was simply someplace else. She was standing on the parapets of a castle wall, choking on some impossibly acrid stench and trying to recall where in the Nine Hells she was.

"Teleporter!" yelled a gruff voice. "Our corner!"

Tanalasta glanced over her shoulder and saw a small corner tower. In the arrow loops appeared the tips of four crossbow quarrels.

"Loose at will!" yelled the gruff voice.

As the weapons clacked, Tanalasta threw herself headlong down onto the wall walk. The quarrels hissed past and clanged off the stones around her, then ricocheted into the smoke-filled courtyard below. She looked after them and found the enclave filled with kettles of boiling oil, barrels

6

packed with crossbow bolts, fire tubs brimming with water. At the far end of the enclosure stood a sturdy oak gate, booming loudly under the regular crash of a battering ram. A constant stream of women and children ran up one set of stairs and down another, ferrying buckets of crossbow bolts and pots of boiling oil to the warriors gathered along the front wall. Though a few of the men wore only the flimsy leather jerkins of honest woodsmen, most were armored in the chain mail hauberks and steel basinets of Cormyrean dragoneers.

The sight of royal soldiers finally cleared the teleport after-daze from Tanalasta's mind, and she recalled that she was in the Cormyrean citadel at Goblin Mountain. She would have preferred to enter by the main gate, but there happened to be a host of orcs hammering at the portcullis with an iron-headed ram.

Behind her, the tower sergeant's gruff voice called, "Ready your bolts!"

"Wait!" Tanalasta fished her signet ring from her pocket and spun toward her attackers, holding the amethyst dragon high above her. "In the name of the Obarskyrs, stay your fire!"

There was a pause, then the tower sergeant hissed, "By the Black Sword! That's a woman—in a war wizard's cloak!"

"It is." Tanalasta dared to raise her head and saw a heavy-browed dragoneer peering out of an arrow loop. "And that woman is Crown Princess Tanalasta Obarskyr."

The sergeant narrowed his eyes. "You don't look like any portraits I've seen, *Princess*." He spoke to someone inside the tower, and a freshly loaded crossbow appeared in the arrow loop next to him. He turned back to Tanalasta. "You won't mind if we come down for a closer look."

"Of course not," Tanalasta replied. "And bring some ropes—long ones."

"One thing at a time," the sergeant said. "Until then, don't move. We wouldn't want Magri here to spike the crown princess, would we?"

Tanalasta nodded and remained motionless, though doing so made her fume inside. The sergeant was right to be cautious, but she had more than a dozen companions rushing across the valley toward the citadel. If she did not have ropes waiting when the haggard band arrived, the orcs would see them and trap them against the rear wall.

The tower door opened, and three dragoneers in full battle armor stepped out. Two of the soldiers flanked Tanalasta and leveled their halberds at her, while their heavy-chinned sergeant took the signet ring from her hand.

He eyed the amethyst dragon and its white gold mounting for a moment, then hissed a curse in the name of Tempus. "Where did you come by this?"

"My father gave it to me for my fourteenth birthday." Tanalasta craned her neck back so she could glare into the soldier's eyes. "According to *Lord Bhereu's Manual of Standards and Procedure*, part the fourth, item two, I believe the proper procedure now is for the sentry to demand the royal code word."

The sergeant's face paled, for Tanalasta's command of anything written in a book was well known throughout the kingdom. "M-may I have the code word please?"

Tanalasta snatched her signet back and said, "Damask Dragon."

The dragoneer paled, then stooped down to take Tanalasta's arm. "Highness, forgive me!" He pulled her to her feet without awaiting permission, then remembered himself and turned the color of rubies. "Your face ... er, I, uh, didn't recognize you. I beg your forgiveness."

Tanalasta grimaced at the thought of what she must look like. She had been traveling hard for nearly two months now, and the last few hours had been the most difficult by far.

"No offense taken, Sergeant," she said. "I must look a fright."

Along with her companions, she had crawled the last mile with her face pressed into the mud to avoid being stung by wasps.

"Now fetch those ropes, and some strong fellows to man them. My company is in a dire state, and there's a ghazneth close on our heels."

At the mention of a ghazneth, the dragoneer's face went

from pale to white. He spat a series of orders to his subordinates, then all three men rushed off to do the princess's bidding.

The orcs continued to batter the portcullis, and an iron bar finally gave way with a deep clang. The sound was answered by an astonishing flurry of crackles and sizzles from the war wizards in the small gatehouse. The tempo of the pounding slackened.

Tanalasta stepped over to battlements and peered through an embrasure into the valley behind the castle. Below was a vast wooded glen with a broad, meandering river and precipitous granite walls. The princess needed several moments to locate the line of figures scrambling through the trees toward the citadel. She could glimpse no more than two or three men at a time, some limping and some struggling to carry wounded fellows, but her heart fell. No matter how patiently she watched, she never counted more than ten forms, and there should have been fifteen.

The jangle of approaching soldiers rang along the rampart, and Tanalasta turned to find a sturdy officer of about forty winters leading a dozen dragoneers toward her. Four of the warriors carried a large iron box. The rest were armed with crossbows and iron swords. A pair of anxious war wizards accompanied the group, one at each end of the iron box.

The officer stopped before Tanalasta and bowed deeply. "If I may present myself, Highness," he said. "I am Filmore, Lionar of the Goblin Mountain Outpost." He motioned to the eldest wizard. "And this is Sarmon the Spectacular, master of the war wizards King Azoun sent to meet you."

Sarmon stepped forward and also bowed. Though his weathered face looked far older than the lionar's, his hair and long beard remained as dark as that of a youth of twenty. "At your service, Highness. We have been expecting you for the past several days." He extended a hand to her and said, "The king has commanded that we teleport you to Arabel the instant of your arrival."

"When my friends are safe." Tanalasta ignored the wizard's hand and pointed into the valley, where her companions were now struggling up the wooded hillside below the citadel. Several hundred paces behind them, a hazy cloud of insects was drifting across the river after them. "Alaphondar Emmarask and High Harvestmaster Foley are still out there, and the ghazneth is close upon them, as you can see."

Sarmon and Filmore peered over the wall, then arched their brows in concern. The wizard turned back to Tanalasta and said, "Truly, Princess, the citadel is in enough peril from the orcs alone." He reached for her arm. "My assistant will see to the safety of the Royal Sage Most Learned and your friend from Huthduth, but I dare not let you risk your life—"

Tanalasta pulled away before he could touch her. "*You* are not risking it—and don't you dare teleport me without my permission. You have told me what the king commanded, but there are things he doesn't know."

Sarmon's eyes betrayed his surprise at her commanding tone, but he nodded and said, "Of course, Majesty."

The tower guards returned with four long ropes. Tanalasta instructed the sergeant to secure the lines to the merlons and drape the ends over the wall, then appointed four of Filmore's burliest dragoneers to help the tower guards hoist her companions. The lionar assigned the rest of the company to battle the ghazneth when it came over the wall.

A loud crack sounded from the gate, followed by a muffled round of guttural cheers. The wizards in the gatehouse unleashed a tempest of lightning bolts and blasts of fire even greater than before, and again the tempo of the battering ram slowed. Tanalasta glanced over and wondered if her friends would be any safer inside the citadel. A large vertical split had appeared in the gate, and even Sarmon's war wizards seemed unable to repel the attack.

An anxious murmur broke out beside Tanalasta. She turned to find the cloud of insects swirling up the slope behind her companions, who were finally breaking into the cleared area near the rear wall. There were only ten of them, and three of those were being carried by others. At least Owden and Alaphondar seemed to be all right.

As Tanalasta watched, one man stopped and kneeled at the edge of the woods. He placed the man he was carrying on the ground, then pulled off his black cloak and slipped it over the fellow's shoulders. A second man stopped beside them. He placed a second figure in the arms of the first and pointed toward the corner where Tanalasta stood. The man in the cloak managed a weak nod, then he and his companion simply vanished.

A sharp noise sounded between the princess and Sarmon, and in the next instant two men, stinking of blood and gore, appeared. The pair collapsed in a heap of flesh and armor and lay groaning on the stones, their faces so swollen and blotchy that Tanalasta recognized only the one in the cloak—and even then only by the sacred sunburst hanging around his neck.

"Owden!"

Tanalasta dropped to her friend's side. The man in his arms was already dead, his throat ripped out and his steel breastplate dented by the ghazneth's claws. Owden himself was in little better condition, with a fist-sized wound in his left side and two ribs protruding from the hole. One elbow was coiled around his burden's leg so that he could reach the weathercloak's magic escape pocket. Tanalasta pulled the arm free, then allowed a dragoneer to drag the dead man from the priest's arms.

"Owden, can you hear me?"

The priest's only reply was a muffled groan.

Tanalasta motioned to Sarmon's assistant and said, "Teleport this man to Arabel at once. His life is to be saved, and I don't care if the queen must order the High Hand of Tymora himself to resurrect him." When the wizard hesitated, Tanalasta added, "I think you should hurry. This was the last man to see Vangerdahast alive."

"Alive?" demanded Sarmon. "What do you mean?"

"I thought you would have heard by now," Tanalasta said. "After the loss at the Farsea Marsh, the royal magician vanished."

Sarmon eyed Tanalasta as though she had been trying to besmirch Vangerdahast's reputation. "There was nothing in

Her Majesty's message to imply Vangerdahast might be dead. The queen said only that he had disappeared while giving chase to one of the Cormaeril traitors."

Tanalasta felt the heat rise to her face but resisted the urge to make a sharp reply. "Not all Cormaerils are traitors," she said mildly. The wizard could hardly have meant to offend her, for he could not have known about her recent marriage to Rowen Cormaeril. The ceremony had been performed deep in the Stonelands, and so far her trail companions were the only ones she had told. "But when Vangerdahast disappeared, he *was* chasing Xanthon Cormaeril. Now Xanthon is chasing us."

Sarmon's face fell at the implications—both for Vangerdahast and for the citadel itself—then he gave his assistant a curt nod. "Take the good harvestmaster to the palace at once."

The wizard nodded his obedience, then took Owden in his arms and uttered a single mystic word. The pair vanished with a distinct *pop*, leaving a huge pool of crimson blood where the harvestmaster had been lying. Tanalasta stared at the blood for a long time until Sarmon stepped to the wall beside her and peered over the side. Too exhausted to run even in such desperate circumstances, the rest of her companions were plodding up the steep slope toward the rocky cliff upon which the citadel sat. Behind them, the insect swarm was beginning to boil out of the woods and drone after the haggard company.

"If Xanthon is chasing you, am I to take it he is also a ghazneth?" asked Sarmon. "I thought the ghazneths were supposed to rise from the spirits of *ancient* traitors to Cormyr."

"In most cases, yes," said Tanalasta. "Xanthon is the one who dug them out of their graves. He also seems to have found a way to become one."

The insect cloud began to obscure the men below. They broke into a weary trot and started to slap and curse. The one in the magic weathercloak pulled the hood over his head and looked up at the citadel. Tanalasta caught a brief glimpse of white hair and pale skin, then the figure raised a hand to his throat clasp.

The wrinkled face of Alaphondar Emmarask appeared in Tanalasta's mind. With sunken eyes and hollow cheeks, the old man looked almost mad. He scowled angrily, then his rasping voice sounded inside her head.

Tanalasta! You're smarter than that. Go to Arabel this instant! You carry Cormyr's future in your belly.

Tanalasta started to bristle at the sharp tone, then realized the Royal Sage Most Learned was right, as always. Though she was barely a month pregnant, that did not diminish the importance of the child growing inside her. With the realm on the brink of war and King Azoun IV a few winters beyond sixty, the worst thing a crown princess could do was risk her life or that of her baby. In such precarious times, either of their deaths might well mean the end of the Obarskyr dynasty—and perhaps of the kingdom itself.

I'll wait down in the bailey, Tanalasta replied, speaking to Alaphondar with her thoughts. *Don't be long!*

As soon as she finished, the sage's image vanished from her mind. There was no chance for him to argue. A weather-cloak's throat clasp allowed the user to exchange only one set of thoughts per day, and even then the messages had to be brief.

Tanalasta stepped away from the wall, then turned to Sarmon and said, "Filmore and his men seem to have matters well in hand. I'll wait for you in the bailey."

Sarmon's brow rose. "Of course, Princess," he replied. "There is no sense putting yourself at any greater risk." A hint of disdainful smile danced at the corners of his mouth, and he pointed across the courtyard at the door of the opposite rear corner tower. "That will be a safe place to hide."

"I will not be *hiding,* Sarmon," Tanalasta said. "I will be staying out of the way."

The wizard's expression turned unreadable. "Of course, Highness. Do not take offense at my poor choice of words."

Though the insincere apology galled her, Tanalasta bit her tongue and descended the corner tower's musty stone stairs. The comment irked her only because of the truth in it. No matter the reason, she was retreating to safety

13

while Alaphondar and her other companions remained in danger, and that made her feel like a coward.

Tanalasta stepped out of the tower into a smoky miasma of acrid odors and coppery-smelling blood. Several dozen wounded dragoneers lay in a groaning row along the back wall, attended by two grim-faced clerics and a dozen qualmish women. Apparently, word of Tanalasta's presence had already spread through the citadel, for the soldiers saluted as she passed and the women curtsied. One of the priests went so far as to offer a healing spell for her face. She sent the persistent little man away, telling him graciously but firmly that he had better things to do with his prayers.

By the time Tanalasta reached her assigned place and turned back toward the rampart, Filmore's men were already hauling four of her companions through the embrasures. Exhausted, bloody, and groaning, the men were in little better condition than Owden had been. Even from down in the bailey, she could see their armor hanging in tatters and their tunics dripping blood. As the rescuers untied the knots around their chests, Tanalasta began to feel hollow and guilty inside. Those men had risked their lives that she might escape.

A cloud of insects came boiling over the battlements. Filmore's dragoneers began to curse and slap at their faces, and several soldiers leaned through embrasures to fire their crossbows down the cliff face. The bolts were answered by a mad cackle of laughter, then the air blackened with insects. The men howled, dropped their weapons, and stumbled back from the wall.

Sarmon was the first to recover his wits. The wizard raised his hands and bellowed out a spell, calling up a steady wind that tore across the courtyard and swept the insect cloud out across the forest. As soon as the swarm was gone, the soldiers began to reload their weapons, the rope haulers tossed their lines back over the side, and Filmore shouted orders.

At the front of the castle, the head of the orcish battering ram began to show through a split in the heavy oak.

A company of purple-clad dragoneers poured down from the wall to gather in front of the widening breach.

The rope haulers pulled another of Tanalasta's companions through an embrasure. Though battered and bloody, the man was strong enough to stand by himself. He freed himself from the ropes with a quick slash of his dagger, then began to drag his wounded fellows out of harm's way.

Sarmon's wind spell faded abruptly, and again insects started to pour over the battlements. One of Tanalasta's companions screamed, then his rope went slack. Half a dozen dragoneers leaned out through embrasures to fire down along the wall. Whirling spheres of wasps gathered around their heads, stinging them in the eyes and ears, making it impossible to fire their weapons. They stumbled back from the wall, screaming, and in their agony began to batter themselves about their own heads.

A second shriek echoed up the wall, and another rope went slack. Tanalasta's heart fell. Though Alaphondar's voice had not been one of those that screamed, she could not help fearing that he was already dead. Only one line remained over the side, and the rope haulers were not even pulling it up. She could only hope that the old sage did not need the rope. He had obviously been wearing one of the magic weathercloaks when he sent the thought message to Tanalasta, and if he was wearing a cloak, he could simply teleport into the castle.

Filmore leaned out to shout an order. His head disappeared into a black swarming cloud, then he screamed once and vanished over the wall. His men began to rush back and forth, stretching through the embrasures to hack at something with their iron swords. The cloud of insects grew so thick Tanalasta could barely see what was happening.

The orcs' battering ram finally splintered the gate with a tremendous crash. A deafening chorus of guttural cheers reverberated through the citadel, then the ram withdrew. A stoop-shouldered orc stepped into the breach and was met by a hail of crossbow bolts. He died standing in the hole.

In the rear of the citadel, Sarmon cried out suddenly and stumbled back from the wall. A tall, gangly silhouette scrambled onto the merlon beside him. The figure was naked and gaunt, with a ragged tuft of beard and a cloud of insects whirling about his body. Tanalasta needed no more to identify him as Xanthon Cormaeril, youngest of the ghazneths and cousin to her husband, Rowen. He had been hounding their trail for several days now, and she had seen more than enough of him to know him by sight.

Xanthon dropped into a crouch and lashed out with one hand after the other, catching a pair of dragoneers by their throats. There were two sickening pops, then the soldiers' heads simply came off in his hands, leaving their bodies to take one last step before collapsing in limp heaps.

Sarmon pointed at the intruder and began a long incantation. The ghazneth spun off his merlon, turning his back on the wizard and spreading a pair of rudimentary wings across his shoulders. The appendages were thin and square, with ragged edges and a dusty gray color that gave them a distinctly mothlike appearance. As soon as Xanthon landed on the wall, he backed toward the wizard, taking care to keep his wings between him and his foe. The cloud of insects moved with him, giving him a vaguely ghostlike appearance. Sarmon's voice cracked and rose an octave, but he continued his spell at the same droning tempo.

A trio of brave dragoneers leaped to the attack, their iron swords arcing toward the ghazneth's back from three different angles. Xanthon's foot shot up behind him, crumpling the steel breastplate of one soldier and sending another man tumbling off the rampart with a lightning fast hook kick to the head. He stopped the third attack with a simple wrist block that snapped the poor fellow's arm and sent him spinning over the battlements.

Sarmon's voice finally fell silent, and a bolt of gray nothingness shot through the insect cloud to strike Xanthon square in one wing. The ghazneth stumbled forward and dropped to one knee, head shaking and wing glowing brilliant silver. Sarmon's jaw fell, and a croak of astonishment rose from his throat—as well it should have. Tanalasta had recognized the spell as a bolt of disintegration, one of the most powerful in the arsenal of Cormyr's war wizards, and it had done little more than stun the ghazneth.

The tower sergeant barked an order. Half a dozen drag-oneers rushed forward and surrounded the ghazneth, their swords falling in a flurry of hacking iron. Xanthon let out a raspy snarl and exploded into a flurry of slashing claws and thrashing feet. He ripped the first soldier's leg off at the knee, then hooked the dismembered ankle behind the man's remaining foot and jerked it out from under him. The second and third dragoneers screamed and went down when he smashed the gruesome club into the side of their knees. Xanthon was up, driving his naked claws through a fourth man's throat and shouldering a fifth off the rampart.

Sarmon raised his hand and uttered a single mystic syl-lable, blasting a fist-sized meteor into the side of the ghazneth's head. The impact sent Xanthon cartwheeling down the rampart, spraying blood and bone everywhere. A dozen paces later, he finally tumbled over the edge and crashed into courtyard below, his ever-present cloud of insects trailing down behind him.

When the ghazneth showed no sign of rising, Sarmon waved the surviving dragoneers over the edge and shouted, "Do you want him to kill the rest of us? Get him in the box!"

The tower sergeant enlisted the aid of two more drag-oneers and shoved the box off the rampart onto the ghazneth's motionless body, then lowered himself over the edge after it. Sarmon simply stepped off the rampart, rely-ing on the magic of his war wizard's weathercloak to lower him gently into the insect cloud.

As the wizard descended, Alaphondar's bony shape appeared on the carnage strewn walkway. The old man was clutching his side with one bloody hand and slapping at his wasp-stung face with the other, shaking his head in confu-sion as he tried to overcome his teleport after-daze.

"Sarmon, above you!" Tanalasta yelled. "Alaphondar!"

The princess could not make herself heard above the clamor at the front gate, where a hundred orcs were squeal-ing in agony as they poured through the splintered gates. Despite the rain of death pouring down on them through the gatehouse's murder holes, the orcs were slowly forcing their

Troy Denning and Ed Greenwood

way forward, and Tanalasta knew it would not be long before they came pouring across the courtyard. She closed her weathercloak's magic throat clasp and pictured Sarmon's face in her mind.

The wizard's brow rose, and she spoke to him with her thoughts. *Alaphondar is on the rampart above you. Get him, and let's go to Arabel.*

Sarmon glanced up, then looked across the bailey and nodded. *As soon as we box the ghazneth. Perhaps we can learn of Vangerdahast's fate.*

"Box it?" Tanalasta cried, too astonished to care that her clasp's magic was gone for the day and Sarmon could no longer hear her. "Have you lost your wits?"

Heart rising into her throat, Tanalasta opened her throat clasp to deactivate the weathercloak's magic, then pulled her battle bracers from her pocket. She stopped short of slipping the bands onto her wrists. Putting them on would activate their magic, and the last thing she wanted when Xanthon recovered was an aura of magic. Ghazneths absorbed magic the way plants absorbed sunlight, and they could detect dweomer for miles around.

To Tanalasta's astonishment, the dragoneers were able to do as the war wizard asked, scooping Xanthon into the box and slamming the lid before he recovered. Sarmon stepped over to the box and reached for the iron bolting bar.

A muffled squeaking erupted from the rear corner tower, and the wizard glanced reflexively over his shoulder. That was all the opportunity Xanthon needed. The box lid flew open, slamming Sarmon so hard that he fell and tumbled backward across the courtyard. The ghazneth sat up, his arm flashing up to swat aside the iron sword of an alert dragoneer, then looked across the courtyard toward Tanalasta. Through the swirling cloud of insects, she saw a strange wedge-shaped face and a pair of red, oval eyes, then a dragoneer blocked her view.

The man's sword slashed down once, then he screamed and clutched at his belly. In the next instant, a dark hand wrapped itself around his neck and gave a sharp twist.

Holding her battle bracers ready, Tanalasta backed

18

toward the corner tower behind her. Though she had not yet spoken with Xanthon Cormaeril face to face, she knew of his hatred for the Obarskyrs and had no doubts about what he would do to her—and her unborn child—if he caught her alive. With Sarmon still lying in a heap where Xanthon had knocked him, she would have to climb up to the rampart and flee to the gatehouse, where there would be no shortage of war wizards ready to teleport her back to Arabel.

As Tanalasta stepped through the door, she was greeted by the same squeaking sound that had distracted Sarmon earlier. Something scratchy brushed past her ankle, and she looked down to see a blanket of rats pouring across the floor beneath her. One stopped to sniff at her leg.

Tanalasta bit back a scream and started up the stairs, then heard a pair of feet whispering across the stony floor behind her. A powerful hand grabbed her by the hair, snapping her head back and jerking her off her feet. She landed flat on her back, still clutching her battle bracers in one hand. When she raised her hand to slip the bands on, she found a beady-eyed rat clinging to the cuff of her cloak. This time she did scream.

A naked black foot swung across her body, pinning her arm to the floor and trapping the bracers in her hand.

"I think not, Princess."

Above Tanalasta appeared a black, chitinous face that seemed more insect than human. The brow was broad and smooth, the nose long and slender, the mouth lined by a ridge of jagged cartilage. Though Sarmon's spell had left a fist-sized crater in the side of the thing's head, the edges of the wound were already closing.

Little clawed feet started to tug at Tanalasta's weather-cloak, and the rats swarmed over her body, gnawing her clothes, hair, and flesh. Xanthon reached out with a spindly arm and slammed the tower door shut, then slipped the heavy lock bar into place as though it were a mere stick.

"Sentries!" Tanalasta yelled. "Down here!"

The ghazneth smiled. "So it *is* you, Highness." With his northern accent and dry huskiness, Xanthon sounded so much like Rowen that Tanalasta could have sworn it was

19

her husband talking. The ghazneth chuckled brutally, then said, "I fear your face is so swollen that you are no longer recognizable to your loyal subjects."

"Swollen as it is, at least it remains human," Tanalasta said. "Whatever you have made of yourself, it was a poor trade."

A metallic clamor began to echo down the stairs. Xanthon glanced toward the sound, and the rat swarm poured up the stone steps. The men started to curse and yell, then one screamed and a tremendous crash reverberated down the spiraling passage.

Hoping to take advantage of the distraction, Tanalasta screamed for help, then shot her free hand across her body and slipped a bracer onto her wrist.

Before she could put on the second, Xanthon caught her arm and plucked the bracer from her grasp. "You are too kind, Princess."

The luster of the metal faded at once, and the gruesome wound in Xanthon's head healed before Tanalasta's eyes. He discarded the band and grabbed the other one. As he pulled it off, he gave Tanalasta's arm a vicious twist. She felt the bone snap, but heard only the briefest crack before her scream drowned out the sound.

A pair of guards stumbled out of the stairwell cursing and trying to kick the rats off their legs. The first lowered his halberd and drove it into Xanthon's ribs, pushing the ghazneth off Tanalasta and pinning him against the wall. The blade did not penetrate, however, for it was made of steel and only weapons of cold-forged iron could wound a ghazneth.

Xanthon slapped the halberd aside, then grabbed the dragoneer by the back of the helmet and smashed his unarmored forehead into the tower's stone wall. There was a sickening crack, and the man went limp. Xanthon finished the second soldier with even less trouble, blocking the attack with one arm, then catching the man beneath the chin and simply tearing his jaw off.

Tanalasta's gorge rose with pain and revulsion. Clutching her broken arm to her chest, she pushed her way through the rat swarm and braced herself against the wall.

A series of deep thumps reverberated through the tower as warriors outside began to hammer at the door, but Tanalasta knew better than to think they would break through the thick oak. She thrust her good hand into her cloak, trying desperately to slip her shaking finger into her commander's ring.

Xanthon ignored the hammering at the door and stepped across the room. He squatted and pulled her hand from her pocket, then plucked the ring from her grasp. The wound in his head was almost completely healed now, and the scalp grew back as he drained the magic from her ring.

"Do you know who is doing this to you?" he asked. "It is important that you know who is killing you."

Tanalasta nodded. "Xanthon Cormaeril." She tried to keep the fear out of her voice. Whether or not she was going to die, she did not want to give him the satisfaction of seeing her terror. "I know. Your cousin was a traitor, and you are too. May the both of you rot in the nine-hundredth pit of the Abyss."

Xanthon grabbed her jaw. "I was no traitor until your father stole our lands." He squeezed until a bone snapped, and Tanalasta nearly fainted from the pain. "But we Cormaerils have never been ones to hold grudges. Vengeance is so much sweeter."

Something cracked in the door, and the hammering began to intensify. Xanthon glanced over his shoulder, then pulled Tanalasta up by her broken jaw. He reached around to grab the back of her neck with his free hand, and she realized he meant to rip her head from her shoulders.

A loud crack reverberated through the room, and the hammering at the door grew louder and faster. Xanthon's fingers dug into Tanalasta's neck, and she knew she would never survive until the thick oak splintered. A sudden calm came over her. She closed her eyes and began to pray, begging the Great Mother to watch over her soul and that of her unborn child.

"Open them!" Xanthon hissed.

Tanalasta croaked out something she meant to be *What?*, then was struck by the irony of Xanthon's vengeance. Bitter

21

laughter began to boil up from deep within her, racking her battered body and grating at the ends of her broken jaw. The pain flowed through her like water. Her mouth fell open, and she laughed in Xanthon's face, fully and hysterically. His grasp tightened until Tanalasta thought her neck would snap, but still she laughed. She could not stop.

"No!" Xanthon shook her, and the pain meant nothing to Tanalasta. "Stop!"

"How can I?" she mumbled. "You're killing a Cormaeril!"

"Liar!" Xanthon squeezed so hard that his fingers broke her skin. "You're no Cormaeril."

Tanalasta shook her head. "I'm not, but Rowen is." She managed to stop laughing, then added, "I'm carrying his baby."

"Never!" Despite his reaction, Xanthon's jaw fell, and his gaze dropped to her stomach. "He's a low-born dog, hardly worthy of the Cormaeril name."

"Still my husband—still your cousin." Tanalasta mumbled only the words she needed to. Now that her hysterics were passing, she saw a slim hope of forestalling her death, and with that hope came pain. "A Cormaeril could sit on the throne . . . could have not only your lands, but all of Cormyr."

The gamble failed. Xanthon's eyes flashed crimson, and the sinews of his dark arms rippled as he jerked on Tanalasta's jaw. A terrible aching pain filled her head, but she fought to stay conscious, determined to defy her enemy until the end.

But her head did not come free. Despite the pain it caused, her neck remained solidly intact, and Tanalasta found herself staggering from one side of the room to another as the ghazneth tried to pull her head off her shoulders.

Xanthon's ovoid eyes grew wide and scarlet. "Liar!"

He forced her to kneel and tried again. Tanalasta's hearing faded and her vision narrowed to a mere tunnel, but the ghazneth's doubt seemed to have sapped his strength. To keep from losing consciousness, she opened her mangled mouth and screamed.

The pounding at the door stopped, and a muffled voice began a spell. Xanthon glanced over his shoulder. For a moment his fading humanity was visible in the profile of his heavy brow and long nose, then he looked back to Tanalasta with a hatred more human than ghazneth burning in his eyes.

Tanalasta tried to say it was true, that if he killed her he would be robbing the Cormaerils of the first Cormyrean monarch to bear their blood, but she was too weak—and in too much pain.

All she could manage was a pompous smile and a short nod.

That was enough. In Tanalasta's delirium, the shadow seemed to leave Xanthon's body. Suddenly, he began to resemble little more than a naked man with hate-filled eyes and a bitter soul.

"Harlot!" Xanthon spat, and reached down for the sword of a dead guard.

Before he could pull it, Sarmon's muffled voice fell silent. A loud boom reverberated through the tiny room, and the tower door came apart in a spray of shattered planks and twisted hinges. The explosion caught Xanthon full in the back, hurling him across the chamber but shielding Tanalasta from the worst of the blast. Armored soldiers came clanging through the door instantly, coughing and choking on sulfurous fumes.

Xanthon rolled to his feet and hurled himself down the stairs, disappearing into the musty depths beneath the tower before the dragoneers had taken two steps. A moment later, Alaphondar rushed through the door, Sarmon the Spectacular close on his heels.

"Tanalasta!" cried Alaphondar. "In the name of the Binder! No!"

The old sage collapsed to his knees and cradled her head in his lap. He started weep and rock to and fro, causing the ends of Tanalasta's broken jaw to rub against each other. She moaned and reached up, clamping her fingers onto his arm to make him stop.

"By the quill! She's alive!" Alaphondar pulled her higher into his lap, wrenching her broken arm around painfully, and waved Sarmon over. "Teleport us to Arabel—*now!*"

2

o," the oldest tracker said flatly, "no horse willingly gallops along bare rock when there's soft turf to be had, unless the rider it's obeying guides it so. If Cadimus went along here—as he must have done, to leave no trace for so long, and not having wings—then you can be sure someone was riding him."

"His master?"

The tracker shrugged. "Who else?" Suddenly mindful that he was answering an anxious king and not an ignorant recruit, he added awkwardly, "Mind, Majesty, riders don't exactly leave tracks of their own that we can follow, if ye take my meaning, but . . ."

"I understand," Azoun said, lifting a reassuring hand. "You do good work, Paerdival—continue. The fortunes of the realm may depend on the trail you find for us."

In reply, the tracker silently lifted a bushy pair of eyebrows for a moment, then bent over again to study the southern end of the bare shoulder of rock. In a matter of moments he'd given the impatient wave of his hand that

24

meant he'd found signs left by the passage of the royal magician's war-horse, and the army moved on.

The brief horn call that blared a breath or two later brought the army to an abrupt halt, and hundreds of heads turned in haste. A man was running from the rear guard, waving his hands as he came.

"To arms!" he cried. "Orcs behind us—thousands of them!"

The king did not hesitate. "Up this hill—everyone!" he bellowed. "Form a ring, spears to the fore, all with bows within and readying them. *Move!*"

The swordlords and lancelords around him began relaying the orders as Purple Dragons surged into motion, rolling up the hill in a vast, gleaming wave.

"I'll be needing a foray force," Azoun called to the lords Braerwinter and Tolon. "Gather forty men at most—men who can move swiftly and have good eyes, but none of the scouts. They deserve a rest."

As he spoke, the horns that would call in the far-flung scouts sounded, and the first men reached the crest of the hill. In involuntary unison they turned and peered in the direction the rear guard had indicated for the orcs.

"Move, Tempus-damned sheep!" a swordcaptain bellowed at them. "Time for sightseeing later—there's a war on, and we're in it!"

Several mock bleats came as a reply as dragoneers moved hastily into a ring, grounding their spears and looking for their accustomed officers.

"*Move*, I said!" the swordcaptain growled at a lone, motionless figure, then fell silent, realizing he'd just bawled an order at the king.

Azoun spun around and clapped him on the shoulder reassuringly. "Keep right on doing that," he murmured. "You never know when you might save a royal life. Just be assured that most of the time, I'll ignore you."

They traded grins—albeit a rather sickly one on the swordcaptain's part—and took their own places. The officer stepped into the ring, and the king stood beside the two nobles who'd wisely selected some veteran officers to lead the force rather than trying to claim glory for themselves. They were standing with about twenty men. The king nodded approvingly.

"I'll be needing some swift swords to seek out the enemy," he told them. "If anyone is footsore or slowed for any reason, say so now. Your lives will almost certainly depend on being fleet in the field."

He looked again at the hill from where the rear guard's warning had come and stiffened.

A lone figure was running toward them, stumbling with weariness. It was a warrior, armor covered with dust, but seeming somehow familiar—a Cormyrean, to be sure.

Orcs were streaming up over that hill now, close behind the running knight. They were going to catch him and slay him right under the king's nose, in full view of all the royal army.

Azoun's mouth tightened. It would be foolish to abandon a strong defensive position to go down there to swing blades with so many orcs, but the last thing he wanted was to stand idle and watch a man he might have saved get hacked apart while he did nothing.

It was also something he didn't want Purple Dragons to see and remember. The lone figure might be them, next time. What good is a king who stands heartless when a subject is in need?

"Foray force—down, and defend that knight! The rest of you charge when the hilltop is covered with orcs!" he roared, and set off down the hill.

"Majesty!" a lancelord protested, and another cried, "This is madness, good king!"

Azoun turned without slowing and cupped his hands around his mouth. "I can only hear officers who run with me," he called. "If one man dies while I stand idle, what kind of king am I?"

He heard the approving murmur from the warriors in the ring, and the officers heard it too. No more protests came to the royal ears as the King of Cormyr, and his strike force raced down the hill, angling their charge so as to come between the foremost orcs and the lone fleeing figure.

Gods, but it *was* a horde. Hundreds of tall, hulking orcs, fresh and eager, loped along with their blades out and their tusks gleaming, howling as they saw the humans rushing to meet them.

The two running forces crashed together in a sudden mass of shouts, ringing blades, and thudding bodies. Azoun pointed at the lone, gasping knight they were trying to rescue to make sure no orc slipped through the fray. He saw that Tolon and Braerwinter were leading four dragoneers to form a ring, then he crashed into a knot of struggling men with the old, quickening eagerness for the fray. The king drove his sword half through an orc's forearm. The beast screamed and tried to shake the steel free. Azoun barely heard an unexpected shout through its noise.

"Father! *Azoun!* Father!"

It could only be Alusair, but her voice was a raw sob. The king fell back from the fray, raising his ring. "Alessa? Lass?"

"Majesty!" Braerwinter's voice arose like a trumpet, and Azoun realized that the exhausted, fleeing knight had been his daughter.

He sprinted across the field, hearing the mighty roar of his main army behind him as it charged down the hill to slay the orcs. He ran to where the small ring led by the lords stood around a lone, shuddering form.

The Princess Alusair was sitting, her mouth wet from the healing potion Braerwinter had already forced down her throat, her face streaked with dirt and rivulets of sweat. Her eyes were dull with weariness, and she was shuddering between gulps of air.

He might have stood on a hilltop and watched orcs butcher her—one of the best warriors in the realm.

"Lass," he said fervently, dropping his sword and putting his arms around her in as gentle a cradling as he could manage. Her own embrace was fierce, and she put her face against his armored chest for only a few heaving breaths, never letting the men standing watchfully around them hear a single sob.

"I . . . found a grove of those twisted trees . . . 'Twas full of orcs . . . Been running since . . . Spent all the magic I had fighting and running . . . Ring wouldn't take me to you . . . How came you here to my backlands?"

The battle was rising around them in earnest now, men and orcs shrieking and shouting as they died, their cries almost lost in the incessant ringing of steel.

"Alessa," Azoun said, rocking her slightly in his arms, reluctant to let go of what he'd come so close to losing, "I'm looking for the man who always knows what to do, no matter how much you two have crossed swords down the years. I need his counsel now, more than ever. Vangey's war-horse came this way. We've been following the trail, hoping to find him alive."

Alusair shook her head. "Cadimus was carrying someone else on this ride. Vangerdahast was—*is*—missing."

"What? Vangey wasn't in the saddle?"

Alusair shook her head again. "I fear he is truly lost," she whispered.

The king threw back his head as if someone had slapped him, paying no heed to the battle raging close around them now. The endless orcs were slowly driving back the men of Cormyr.

The king closed his eyes and shook his head grimly. "No," he muttered. "Gods, no."

He let go of her and walked away, as if alone in a fog. Alusair and the lords exchanged startled glances, then sprang to their feet and followed. The Steel Princess scooped up her father's forgotten sword.

"I'm no good at riddling my way out of prophecies!" Azoun told the air around him despairingly.

"Father?" Alusair slapped the blade back into her father's hand and shook his shoulder, imploring, "King Azoun—speak to me!"

"Vangey's wisdom lost to me, when I need it most?" Azoun murmured. "After all these years . . ."

He whirled around and snapped, "It cannot be. The old wizard's off on some quick work of his own. Something he hasn't told us about, as usual."

"And if he's not?" Alusair almost whispered.

Her father looked at her grimly, then said almost calmly,

as if he were noticing the weather out a castle window, "Then the gods have truly turned their backs on me."

A horn call rang out, bidding the army of Cormyr to try to return to their hilltop. The sound was almost lost in the derisive roar of a new wave of orcs.

3

angerdahast sat atop the highest step of the grandest goblin palace in the great goblin city, holding his ring of wishes in one hand and his borrowed mace in the other, staring out over the black expanse of the central goblin plaza into the great goblin basin where a pair of scaly golden membranes lay furled along opposite rims of the pool, giving it the slitlike appearance of a giant reptilian eye watching him watch it watch him watch it and so on so on to the end of all things, like a mirror mirroring a mirror, or an echo echoing an echo, or a man pondering the depths of his empty, empty soul. A wizard could lose his mind in a place like that.

Perhaps a wizard already had. The plaza around the pool seemed to be turning scaly and red, save for a long chain of giant white triangles that bore an uncanny semblance to teeth. Vangerdahast could also make out the shape of a sail-sized ear and the curve of a bridge-length eyebrow, and even the arcs of several lengthy horns sweeping back from the crown of the head. Taken together, the features gave him the uncomfortable feeling of looking at the largest mosaic of a dragon he had ever seen.

Probably, Vangerdahast should not have worried about failing to notice it earlier. At the time, he been fighting for his life, trying to capture Xanthon Cormaeril and force him to reveal the exit to the goblin city. There had been flashing spells and gruesome melees and hordes of droning insects, and it would have been normal for even the most observant of combatants to miss the mosaic.

But Vangerdahast was no mere combatant. He was the High Castellan of the War Wizards, the Royal Magician of Cormyr, the First Councilor to the King, and he did not over-look such things. He could not afford to. Everyday the life of the king and the strength of Cormyr depended on his powers of observation, and he kept his senses honed keener than the blade of any dragon-slaying knight. He perceived all that passed before him, heard every whisper behind his back, smelled any kind of trouble the moment it formed, and still he had not noticed the mosaic until—well, until sometime earlier. Days had no meaning in this place. The only way to mark time was by the steady shrinkage of his ample belly, and he had already taken in his belt two notches before he began to notice the mosaic. Either he was hallucinating or the thing had begun to form before his eyes. He would not have liked to wager which.

A pair of yellow membranes slid across the pool, coating the surface with a fresh layer of black sheen, and slowly retracted again. Vangerdahast had seen the pool blink before, long before the dragon appeared, so perhaps the blinking had nothing to do with the mosaic. Everyone knew mosaics could not blink.

Vangerdahast slipped his ring on, then descended the stairs, moving slowly to keep himself from blacking out. The goblin city contained nothing but stone and water, and he could not eat stone. He had long since passed the stage of hunger pangs and a growling stomach, but his dizziness was almost constant.

Near the bottom, his strength failed. He dropped to a stair, where it was all he could do to brace his hands against

31

the cold granite and prevent himself from sliding the rest of the way down.

"A meal you need." The words were deep and sibilant, and they rumbled through the lonely city like an earthquake. "A nice roast rothé, and a big flagon to wash it down."

Vangerdahast leaped to his feet, his strength returning in a rush. He peered into the murk beyond the plaza, searching for a pair of glinting eyes, or a skulking black silhouette, or some other hint of the speaker. Seeing nothing but murk, he considered hurling a few light spells into the darkness but quickly realized he would find nothing. His hunger had finally gotten the best of him, and now he was hearing things as well as seeing them. There was no sense wasting his magic on hallucinations. Magic was too precious in this place, where even spells of permanent light seemed to burn out like common torches.

The pool continued to stare, and it seemed to Vangerdahast that the darkness in its heart had swung around to stay focused on him. He crept down to the bottom stair and crouched above what would be the crown of the dragon's head. There was a definite rise where the skull swelled up out of the ground, and he could feel a rhythmic shuddering in the steps beneath his feet. Vangerdahast reached out and ran his hand down the nearest scale. It was the size of a tournament shield and as warm to his touch as his own flesh.

"I've lost my mind," he gasped.

"Yes, you have lost something, but not your mind," the voice rumbled. Ten paces beyond the eye, the row of white triangles moved in time to the words. "You've lost only your big belly—and soon your life, too, unless you eat."

Vangerdahast scrambled up the stairs, but grew dizzy half a dozen steps later and had to stop. He rubbed his eyes with the heels of his hands. When he looked again, the dragon face remained, the eye in the basin still staring at him.

"Why have you less faith in your eyes and ears than the doubts of a spent and weary mind?" asked the dragon. "I am as real as you. Touch me and see."

"I'd rather, uh, trust you about that."

Vangerdahast remained where he was, his mind whirling as it tried to make sense of what he was seeing. Insanity still seemed the greatest likelihood, save that he had always heard the insane were the last to know of their illnesses— but down here, he *would* be the last to know. He had been trapped in the goblin city for . . . well, for some while. In the eternal darkness of the place, time had no meaning. The only way to mark hours was by the duration of his spells, which all seemed to fade far too quickly.

When Vangerdahast remained quiet, the dragon spoke again. "You don't believe in me, or you would ask my name."

The admonishment jarred Vangerdahast back to a semblance of his senses. Concluding that if he was going insane he had already lost the battle, he decided to treat the dragon as though it were real. He gathered up his courage, then sat down on the step and addressed the dragon.

"I'm interested less in who you are than what," he said. "If you are some chimera manifested by my guilty soul to abuse me in the lonely hours before death, I'll thank you to spare me the nonsense and get down to business. I know the evil I've done, and I'd do it again, fully conscious of the costs to myself and others."

"Fully conscious?" the dragon echoed. "That *is* impressive."

"Cyric's tongue!" Vangerdahast cursed. "You *are* a phantasm! I suppose that's my reward for letting Alaphondar and Owden prattle on about symbols and meaning."

"Meaning has power," answered the dragon, "but I am nothing of yours, I promise. I am a true dragon."

"Dragons are hatched, not . . ." Vangerdahast paused and glanced derisively at its emerging figure. ". . . not . . . formed."

"And hatched I was, in the days when rothé ran free and elves ruled the woods." The dragon's eye shifted from Vangerdahast and stared at a magic sphere of light fading above it. "But now I am a prisoner, and more than you."

"A prisoner, you say?" As Vangerdahast spoke, he was doing a quick set of mental calculations. The dragon's accent and its reference to rothé—the extinct buffalo that once roamed the forests of Cormyr—placed its age at well over fourteen hundred years. Even for such an ancient wyrm,

33

however, it was too large by far. The distance from its eye to the last white fang had to be sixty feet, which would make the length from snout to tail somewhere in excess of six hundred feet. "I doubt that. The wizard has not been born who could cage such an ancient wyrm."

"Nor the warrior who could imprison a mage so great as yourself," replied the dragon. "Yet I have seen you casting your spells—teleporting here, plane-walking there, dimension-dooring all places between, sending thought-pleas to anyone who might hear—and yet you remain here with me. It was no wizard who caught me, or you. We were trapped here by our own folly and pride, and prisoners we will stay."

Vangerdahast rolled his eyes and stood. "If you're going to talk like that—"

"Oh, yes, go and starve to death!"

A tremendous boom resounded from the dragon's one visible nostril, and a fireball the size of an elephant went sizzling into the darkness. It crashed into a distant goblin manor, spraying blobs of melted stone in every direction.

Vangerdahast cocked a brow. "I won't be stepping in front of you, I think."

A scaly red lip drew away from the dragon's teeth, creating a snarl as long as some streams Vangerdahast had seen. "Die if you like, but leave your wishes for me."

Vangerdahast folded his hands behind his back, concealing the ring he had been contemplating earlier. "Wishes?"

"In the ring." A wisp of yellow fume streamed out of the dragon's distant nostrils. "Everything else you have tried, but the wishes are too dangerous. You don't understand this place, and if you wish wrong . . . puff, no more wizard!"

Vangerdahast frowned. "Have you been reading my mind?"

The dragon broke into a raucous chuckle, and clouds of boiling sulfur hissed into the plaza.

Vangerdahast waited until its mirth died away, then said, "Your point, I suppose, is that you *do* know the nature of this place?"

The yellow membranes closed over the basin in a sort of

reptilian wink. "A long time I have been here," it said, "but you—even if there was food, humans do not live so long. If you are to leave, I think it must be with me."

Vangerdahast studied the beast for a moment, considering the kind of havoc he would unleash by helping such a creature escape. If the thing truly was as old as it appeared, its magical abilities would rival his own—and he had already seen what its fire breath could do. On the other hand, Cormyr was doomed without him, especially with the ghazneths loose and Princess Tanalasta still infatuated with that lowly ranger she had met—kin to the traitorous Cormaerils, he was, and a ground-splitting Chauntea worshiper as well.

Vangerdahast unclasped his hands and started down the stairs. "I suppose you have a name?"

"I do," replied the dragon, "but no human could understand it. You may call me Nalavara."

It was all Vangerdahast could do to avoid falling again. The name came almost directly from a chapter of Cormyr's earliest history—and not a very proud chapter at that.

"Something is wrong, wizard?" rumbled Nalavara.

Vangerdahast looked up and saw he had stopped moving. "Not at all—just weak with hunger." Hoping that Nalavara had not been reading his mind, he started down the stairs again. "But I would like to hear your full name, if I might."

The dragon's huge eye membranes drew closer together. "Why?"

"Human translations are so graceless." Vangerdahast reached into the component pockets inside his weathercloak and withdrew a pinch of salt and another of soot, then rubbed them between his fingers and uttered a quick little spell. "My understanding of Auld Wyrmish might surprise you. I have a special fondness for the beauty of the language."

"Do you?" Nalavara's eye remained narrow, but her long lips twisted into a crocodile's smile. "Very well."

She rattled off a long series of rumbling growls and firelike crackles that Vangerdahast understood perfectly as *Nalavarauthatoryl the Red.*

"So, human, do you like my name?" asked Nalavarautha-toryl the Red.

"Sorry, didn't understand a word." Actually, Vangerda-hast understood better than he would have liked. The name wasn't Auld Wyrmish at all but ancient Elvish. The phrase meant something like "the maiden Alavara, betrothed of Thatoryl, painted in blood." He forced a stupid smile and added, "The human ear can be a bit flat."

"One fault among many," Nalavara agreed. "And you are called . . . ?"

"Elminster," Vangerdahast replied, lying through his teeth. "Elminster of Shadowdale. Now, how do we get out of here?"

Nalavara's eye widened to its normal proportions, which was to say about as broad and long as a spacious work table. "First, Elminster, you must wish for something to eat. You will need a clear head for the work to come."

"Work? You must be jesting," Vangerdahast scoffed. "That's why I have a ring of wishes—and I'm not about to waste the last one on a pot of porridge."

An angry shudder shook the stairs, then Nalavara rumbled, "One wish only?"

"Only one, so be certain of yourself."

Vangerdahast was not exactly lying. The truth was he had no idea how many wishes remained to the ring. It had been handed down to him through a long line of royal magicians, and if any of them had ever known the number it contained, the secret had died long before it reached Vangerdahast.

"Tell me what to wish," the royal magician said, "and I'll have us out of here."

A long ribbon of flame snorted from Nalavara's distant nostril. "A fool I am not," she rumbled. "Come and bind your-self to my horn, and I will tell."

Vangerdahast did as he was asked, but the horn was as large as a tree trunk, and even his over-large belt was not long enough to reach. He explained this to Nalavara, then wrapped his arms around the horn and said, "I give you my word I won't let go."

Nalavara snorted angrily, then said, "Be warned—if you try to leave me behind, the wish will not work."

"Leave you behind?" Vangerdahast echoed. "Never. My word is as good as my name."

"That is less of a comfort than you think, Elminster," the dragon rumbled. "Know that if you try to cheat me—"

"Yes, yes, I can imagine," Vangerdahast said. "You will look me up in Shadowdale, and I shall forever after have reason to regret my perfidy. Now, are we going to cast our wish or not?"

"Very well," grumbled Nalavara. "The secret is not to wish us out of the city, but to wish the city back in time. You must call upon the ring to fill it again with goblins."

"Goblins?"

"The Grodd Goblins," Nalavara said. "That returns the city to the time when goblins ruled the land. From there, we must use our own spells to travel to our own times—have you a time-walking spell?"

"No," Vangerdahast grumbled. "Though it hardly matters."

He released the dragon's horn and jumped off her head, then started down the plaza filled with disappointment and despair. Had there been any real chance of the spell working, Nalavara would certainly have insisted on holding him in her mouth—then she'd bite him in two once the wish was made.

"Wait!" Nalavara boomed. "Without me, the spell will work not!"

"And not with you either," he called back. "Whatever you want, Nalavara, it isn't to be free of this place. Red dragons are not so trusting."

To Vangerdahast's great surprise, Nalavara did not explode into a fit of anger. Instead, she began to chuckle, shaking the plaza so violently he lost his footing and had to sit.

"Come now, *Elminster*," she rumbled. "You know I am more than a dragon, and I know you are not who you claim to be."

Seeing that the virtues of deception had long exhausted themselves, Vangerdahast also began to laugh, a deep, mad laugh begot more of weariness and despair than humor—but a laugh nonetheless. He was one of only two men living who knew the name Alavara and what it meant to Cormyr, and it struck him as absurdly funny to find himself trapped alone with her in a deserted goblin city.

Lorelei Alavara was an elf maiden, quite beautiful by all accounts, who had lived in the Wolf Woods when the first humans began to intrude. She had been betrothed to Thatoryl Elian, a handsome young hunter foolish enough to argue with a band of human poachers over whose arrow had killed a bear. The argument ended only when Thatoryl became the first Wolf Woods elf to be murdered by human hands. Lorelei Alavara's grief knew no bounds, and she plotted constantly with King Iliphar to make war on the humans and drive them from the land. It was she who organized the slaughter of Mondar Bleth in the days before Cormyr was a kingdom, and who slew a thousand humans more before her own kind grew weary of her obsession with vengeance and, a century after the first murder, finally banished her to the Stonelands.

That much of the story was told to every member of the royal family as soon as they reached the age of majority, but there was more, passed only from royal magician to royal magician and told only to the ruling monarch since the founding of the kingdom. Thatoryl Elian's murderer had been Andar Obarskyr, brother to the founder of Cormyr, Ondeth Obarskyr, and uncle to the first king, Ondeth's son Faerlthann.

According to the story passed down to Vangerdahast, Andar had escaped retribution by virtue of good luck, having been tending to nature's call deep in the woods when the elves came to avenge their kinsman's death. Though the massacre had left Andar too frightened to ever again set foot in elven territories himself, he had told his brother many times of the bounty of the Wolf Woods, and those descriptions were what convinced Ondeth to build a new home beyond the frontier. That Cormyr's birth had resulted from such a miscarriage of justice had been the kingdom's most jealously guarded secret for more than fourteen centuries

38

now, and Vangerdahast could not help chuckling at the thought that the dragon had actually hoped to make him the instrument of its divulgence.

"Alavara the Red," he said. "I should have thought even your thirst for vengeance long quenched."

"It is not vengeance I seek, only justice," answered Nalavara. "Though I know a different appetite sustains the mighty Vangerdahast."

As Nalavara spoke, the sphere of magic light floating above her head grew dim. A black circle appeared on the dark ground between Vangerdahast's feet. He cried out in astonishment and scrambled away, then began to feel cowardly and foolish when he saw that the thing was not moving.

"Take it," urged Nalavara. "There is no reason to be afraid."

Vangerdahast exchanged his ring of wishes for a simple commander's ring from the royal armory, then whispered, "King's Light."

A halo of golden radiance rose from his hand and illuminated the ground in front of him, revealing a simple crown of iron.

"What's that?" he demanded.

"You know," answered Nalavara. "Your whole life have you craved it, and now it is yours. All you need do is wish."

"Wish?" Vangerdahast kicked the crown away, then stood and began to hobble off into the darkness. "If I were to wish for anything, it would be that you never existed."

"By all means," Nalavara chuckled. "Any wish will do."

4

The horn call rang out a second time, and Alusair glanced over at her father. To her astonishment, the king was smiling.

He caught sight of her and said, almost exultantly, "Magic still serves the crown in some things, lass!"

The Steel Princess lifted an eyebrow, overjoyed to see the King of Cormyr out of his dark mood but somewhat puzzled as to why.

"You didn't expect Dauneth to meet us here?" she asked, glancing around at the familiar cliffs and crags of Gnoll Pass. "You told me yesterday how sorely we needed the reinforcements he'd bring, and now his obedience seems to be a cause of . . . Are things in Arabel worse than I'd heard?"

"No, no, lass!" Azoun chuckled. " 'Tis what he's brought with him that's a cause of . . . I'll tell all later. For now, let us claim yonder hilltop and there raise the tent I hope young Marliir's also brought along."

"Tent? Father, are your wits addled at last?"

"Have a care for treason of the tongue," a lancelord snapped from behind the Steel Princess. "You speak ill of the king!"

She whirled around with sparks fairly spewing from her eyes and snarled, "Dare less with your own speech, soldier! Obarskyrs speak freely and thereby keep the realm strong. Learn that well, if you learn nothing else about fighting under the Purple Dragon banner."

"You chided the Steel Princess?" someone muttered, just loudly enough for Alusair to hear as she turned to stride after her father. "Man, are *your* wits addled at last?"

A smile almost rose to the lips of the princess at that, as she hastened down loose rocks and slippery tussocks of clingvine and grass to where Dauneth Marliir was kneeling before his king.

"All is as you requested, Your Majesty," the High Warden of the Eastern Marches was saying earnestly. "The poles-crew await your orders. The mages stand there, with the cage. As you can see it is wrapped to hide its true nature, just as you instructed."

"Wrapped to hide—?" Alusair murmured, coming up to stand beside her father's shoulder. "What by all the unslain orcs of the Stonelands is . . ."

"Tell me now," Azoun was asking, "what was the look on Elemander's face when you brought him my orders, and showed him the royal ring?"

"Total astonishment," Dauneth said with a smile, "but it soon slipped into disgust about the time I began describing the massive cold iron bars. 'Beneath my skills,' he sniffed, and snatched the ring from my fingers to make sure I wasn't playing him false. He cursed—I can't remember all the words even if Your Majesty cared to hear such foulness, and I doubt there even is such a thing as the 'blind-flying spawn of a love-slave-slapped, dung-sucking donkey'—then he took the suit of armor he'd been working on from its stand and hurled it the length of his shop."

The king exploded in laughter, slapping his thighs then dealing Dauneth a blow across the back that sent the young warden staggering. "Wonderful!"

"Will someone," Alusair asked with silken politeness, "kindly tell me what this matter of royal armorers fashioning crude cold iron cages is all about?"

"Lass," her father said jovially, indicating the hilltop and giving Dauneth a nod to tell him to send the poles-crew on its way, "we're going to catch ourselves a ghazneth—and if need be, trade its freedom in exchange for our lost royal magician!"

"Oh," Alusair replied with deceptive mildness, "just like that? Well, now that you've told me, I'm sure everything's going to go off without a hitch. It certainly sounds plausible enough, hmm?"

Azoun lifted an eyebrow at her tone, murmured something under his breath that might have been, "Just like your mother," and swung around to point back behind them. "Surely you've had enough of fleeing from floods of orcs?"

"Gods, *yes*," Alusair growled as fervently as any Purple Dragon veteran sick of long marches and given a chance at sitting idle instead might.

"Well, with Dauneth's reinforcements guarding our flanks, we're going to turn around and strike right back at them. They've been howling at our heels for long enough now that they don't expect anything else from us except grim retreat. We're giving them a despairing last stand right now, on the other side of that last hill behind us. The moment that tent is up, we're going to break ranks and run back here. They'll pour after us to enjoy the rout and slaughter, and we'll send Dauneth's troops looping out and around them like a long arm, taking them from behind while the war wizards Dauneth's also brought with him hurl spells at them from the tent."

"So the slaughterers will become the slaughtered," Alusair said calmly. "I'm with you so far. Just how, exactly, are we to deal with the ghazneths who'll inevitably come soaring in at us when we start this hurling of spells?"

"Wizards will cast visible defensive magics—harmless faerie fires—on the tent," the king told her, "then scuttle inside when the ghazneths swoop down. The cage will be lined up with the tent mouth, and Purple Dragons will be standing inside with weapons of cold iron raised and ready to transfix any ghazneth bursting in."

Alusair shook her head, then suddenly shrugged and grinned. "In other words, you're just pitching in, running wild, and hoping," she said. "Well, why not? We've tried everything else."

"I knew you'd be ready for a little striking back," her father replied, "because, by all the sheep who've ever drunk from the Wyvernwater, *I* certainly am!"

* * * * *

Three young war wizards stood in the dark mouth of the tent on the hill, their faces tight and pale with fear. Fireballs and lightning bolts streamed from their hands, flashing into the heart of the howling orcs surging up the slope then recoiling from the line of hard-thrusting Purple Dragon spearmen. Orc bodies arched in agony or were flung, broken, through the air only to be caught in the blast of the next spell and hurled anew.

It took only the space of a few breaths for the first of the expected ghazneths to streak in, flying low and hard from the south.

"Gods above, but they're fast," Alusair murmured at the king's shoulder. She glanced over at the three war wizards—Stormshoulder, Gaundolonn, and Starlaggar, that was his name, Mavelar Starlaggar—and saw them, to a man, pale-faced and trembling with fear. "Are you sure our war wizards are up to this?"

Azoun followed her quizzical glance in time to see one of the young mages convulsively lose his last meal onto the ground. The king lifted his shoulders in a shrug and said, "We all have to face our first battle sometime, and I can't hold the realm if only old, grizzled veterans know how to stand and fight for Cormyr."

"Old, grizzled veterans like the king?" Alusair said with a smile.

"Exactly," Azoun snarled back, and sprang forward. "Here comes a bolder bird now. . . ."

Troy Denning and Ed Greenwood

The second ghazneth to appear over the hilltop wasted no time in the circling and shrieking that its fellow was engaged in. Without pause it swooped at the tent.

One war wizard moaned in fear and fell over his nearest fellow mage in his haste to escape, causing them both to topple over into the tent. The third one stood desperately trying to roll them out of the way as the ghazneth—a large, powerful one with a bald head and the shoulders of a large and imposing man—plunged down at it.

With seconds to spare, War Wizard Lharyder Gaundolonn got his two companions out of the way and threw himself over their bodies into the dim interior of the tent. The ghazneth raced in behind them like a laughing bolt of black lightning whose swift flight ended in a crash of splintering bones and reluctantly rolling cage that shook the entire hilltop.

A swordlord threw the slide that locked the cage, thrust the two iron spikes that would hold it from moving into place, and waved forward the spearmen whose weapons would keep the captured ghazneth away from them. "Well, majesty," the swordlord said, "you've got your caged bird—faster and cleaner than I'd feared it'd come to us, too . . . and now?"

The king shrugged and said, "We only have the one cage."

He looked out over the tumult of bloody battle where Purple Dragons were slowly advancing to meet each other, hacking down the orcs trapped between them, then up at the—three, by now—ghazneths who were swooping down to claw off a head here, and rake open a face there.

"Enough," he said. "Dauneth, is the senior war wizard ready?"

"Majesty, he is," the warden replied, and gave a chopping hand signal to a man the Obarskyrs couldn't see.

A long moment later, a small foundry of cold iron daggers, arrowheads, and spear points appeared as a midair cloud above the nearest swooping ghazneth and fell on it like pelting rain.

Its shriek was raw and deafening as it fell helplessly into the heart of the hacking fray. Long before it rose, flying raggedly, and fled low over the raging battle, the other two ghazneths had flown away.

"That worked well," Alusair said admiringly. "Now all we have to do is hold off another few thousand orcs while you go and horse trade with a wounded, furious ghazneth. Blood of Tempus, look at them coming down the hills. How can any orc tribe feed so many mouths?"

"Horse trade indeed," the king said with a smile. "By the looks of him, we've landed the worst of them after Boldovar, too. It'll be Luthax, I've no doubt, once second only to Amedahast among the war wizards of his day."

Alusair shook her head ruefully and said, "You never did believe in doing things the easy way, did you?"

Azoun's grinning reply was lost in the fresh howls of orcs, charging furiously up the hill on all sides.

5

he rat bites had withered to little red puckers, leaving Tanalasta's pale breasts and belly strewn with star-shaped scars and oozing abscesses. Though her head throbbed and her joints ached with the remnant of a fever, she felt remarkably alert and rested and—finally—safe. Owden Foley, looking pale and battered but alive, sat at the edge of her bed. His eyes were closed in concentration and a healing hand was pressed over her womb. The corridors outside her chambers were guarded by an entire troop of dragoneers. Two war wizards sat in her anteroom, just a short yell away. Even her windows had been double-secured, being both barred by iron and sealed with mortar and stone.

Owden opened his eyes, but left his hand pressed to Tanalasta's naked abdomen. She could feel the goddess's mending heat flowing into her womb, making her loins tingle and ache in way that was not entirely unfamiliar and a little bit embarrassing. Tanalasta let the sensations wash over her and tried to accept what she felt with no shame.

46

Such stirrings were a gift from Chauntea, and private though they were, no worshiper of the Great Mother should deny them.

By the time the High Harvestmaster's gaze finally drifted toward Tanalasta's face, she could bear the suspense no longer. "What of the child, Owden?" The princess found it difficult to speak. Though a healer had obviously worked his magic on her broken jaw, it was sore, stiff, and bound by a silken scarf. "Has it been injured?"

Owden's eyes flickered away before answering. "You have had no pain or bleeding?"

Icy fingers of panic began to work up through Tanalasta's chest. "What's wrong?"

"We don't know that anything is," Owden said. He did not remove his hand from Tanalasta's abdomen. "It's only a question."

"One you must know I can't answer." Tanalasta had awakened only a short time earlier, and the first thing she had done was send for Owden. "How long have I been asleep?"

"Half a tenday . . . or so they tell me." Owden raised his free hand and absentmindedly rubbed the cloth over his own wound. "I awoke only yesterday myself."

"And Alaphondar?"

"In the palace library. Seaburt and Othram are also here, but I'm afraid the others . . ." He shook his head, then said, "The orcs came in too fast."

Tanalasta closed her eyes. "May their bodies feed the land and their souls blossom again," she whispered.

"The goddess will tend them." Owden clasped her arm. "They were brave men."

"That they were." Tanalasta glanced down between her bare breasts to the harvestmaster's other hand, still pouring its healing warmth into her womb and asked, "Now, what of the child? I trust you are not just enjoying yourself."

The joke drew a forced smile from the normally jovial priest. "With all those guards out there? I think not." He glanced toward the anteroom door, then shook his head and told her, "The truth is, I have no way of knowing. I could ask

47

the royal healers if there have been any signs, but they'd know at once my reason for asking."

Tanalasta considered this, then shook her head. "Let's avoid that. We need no rumors sweeping the realm, at least not until the nobles have accepted that I am married."

"And to whom," Owden added pointedly.

Tanalasta flashed him a frown of irritation, one of those rare glowers she reserved for the few people who would not interpret them as some subtle message by which whole families were made and unmade.

"Would knowing the signs make any difference to the child?"

Owden thought for a moment, then shook his head. "Either you are still with child or you aren't," he said simply. "If you are, all we can do is keep pouring Chauntea's blessings into your womb and pray they are enough to counter the corrupting influences of your association with the ghazneth."

"Would you please call it a fight?" Tanalasta asked dryly. "'Association' makes it sound like we were . . . trysting."

Owden winced at her objection, but the anteroom door banged open before he could apologize. Jerking her bed gown down over her breasts, Tanalasta looked over with an angry rebuke on her tongue and found her mother striding into the room.

Queen Filfaeril was, as always, strikingly beautiful. Tresses of honey blonde hair streamed behind her, and blue eyes glared at Owden's hand, which continued to rest over Tanalasta's womb. If the harvestmaster felt any embarrassment, his face did not betray it.

"Mother," Tanalasta mumbled, so surprised that she strained her aching jaw. "You might have had someone announce you."

Filfaeril continued toward the bed, her stride growing more assertive and forceful. "I came as soon as I heard you had awakened." She stopped at the base of the bed and continued to glare at Owden's hand. "I'm glad to see you feeling so well."

Tanalasta felt the heat rising to her cheeks, but took her

cue from Owden and refused to take the bait. "To be truth-ful, I'm not quite sure how I feel." She waved at Owden and said, "You remember Harvestmaster Foley?"

"How could I forget?"

The expression in Filfaeril's eyes would have wilted a lesser man, but Owden merely stood and bowed without removing his hand from Tanalasta's abdomen. "As radiant as ever, your majesty."

Having failed to intimidate Owden, Filfaeril turned to Tanalasta and said, "A bit old for you, don't you think?"

"That is hardly to the point, Mother," said Tanalasta. "Harvestmaster Foley is tending to my health—as I am sure you know."

Filfaeril's expression remained icy. "The royal healers are not to your satisfaction?"

"I prefer Owden." Though her feelings were fast growing as icy as her mother's glare, Tanalasta forced herself to smile. "Surely, even a princess may choose who lays hands on her own body without the matter becoming the latest political crisis?"

A hint of shame flashed through Filfaeril's eyes, but she quickly regained control of her expression. In a slightly warmer voice, she said, "I suppose that is hardly too much to ask, and I really did not come here to discuss the matter of your royal temple anyway." She turned to Owden and graced him with a queenly smile. "So, how does our patient fare? I wasn't aware that she had suffered any injuries so far . . . south."

"She is a hale woman, majesty." Owden raised a querying eyebrow at Tanalasta—ever so slightly—and received the merest shake of a head in response, then continued without missing a beat. "She had some pain in her intestines, but I'm sure it is merely a matter of lying in bed too long . . . nothing a long walk won't cure."

As subtle as the signals between Tanalasta and Owden had been, they did not escape Filfaeril's notice. Her queenly smile grew cold enough to freeze a bonfire. "A walk, you say?" the queen asked. "Your Chauntean remedies are certainly more forward than those of our royal healers. They have warned me not to let her leave bed for the next tenday."

"A tenday!" Tanalasta pushed herself up. "Not on their—"

Owden motioned her back down and said, "The royal healers have not had occasion to observe the princess as closely as I over the past year. Trust me, the exercise will do her more good."

"*I* trust you," said Tanalasta. "That's all that matters."

Thankfully, Owden's healing hand finally cooled against her skin. He withdrew it, allowing her to lower her bed gown the rest of the way.

Filfaeril continued to glare at the priest so icily that even he began to grow uncomfortable.

He turned to Tanalasta and said, "If you are feeling well enough, perhaps I will withdraw and see to my own wounds."

"Of course, Owden, and thank you—for everything."

Owden bowed to her and the queen, then left. As soon as the anteroom door closed, the queen's attitude softened. She took the priest's place on the edge of the bed.

"I really didn't mean to intrude, my dear." She took Tanalasta's hand. "It's just that when I heard you were awake, I couldn't wait a moment longer to apologize."

"Apologize?" Tanalasta regarded her mother warily, as surprised now as at their parting less than two months earlier, when the queen had berated her so ferociously for wanting to establish the Royal Temple of Chauntea. "Truly?"

Tanalasta's astonishment seemed to take Filfaeril aback. The queen looked confused for a moment, then let slip an uncharacteristic snort of laughter.

"Not about the temple, my dear! You're still going to have to forget *that* idea before your father will feel comfortable dying and leaving the throne to you." Filfaeril tried a diplomatic smile and saw it fail, but continued unabashed. "What I am sorry about is the way I handled you."

"*Handled* me, Mother?"

"Yes, Tanalasta, *handled* you." Filfaeril's voice had grown stern. "We are both women of the palace, and the time has come to acknowledge that. It doesn't mean that we don't love each other, or Azoun and Alusair—"

"Or even Vangey," Tanalasta added.

The queen's eyes darkened noticeably, but she nodded. "Even Vangerdahast—and he is the worst handler of any of us. We all have our own aims that inevitably set us against each other, and the only way to stay a family is to acknowledge the fact."

Tanalasta regarded her mother as though meeting her for the first time. "All right . . ."

"So what I am sorry about is misjudging you. I was frightened by the change in you after Huthduth, and I thought you weren't ready to be queen." Filfaeril paused to blink away the tears welling in her eyes, then continued, "I thought you never would be, and I told your father to name Alusair in your place. I did everything I could to persuade him, but Vangerdahast wouldn't have it."

"*Vangerdahast?*" Tanalasta began to wonder what her mother was playing at. Vangerdahast had made a living hell of her life over the last year, constantly trying to bully her into becoming the kind of queen he expected to sit on the throne of Cormyr. Finally, the situation had grown so bad that Tanalasta had rebelled and told him to take what she was or start bullying Alusair into shape. "You aren't saying that just because he's gone, are you?"

"No," Filfaeril said. She shook her head vehemently, and now the tears did begin to spill out of her eyes. "It's the truth. He never doubted you, but I did. I apologize."

"Don't," Tanalasta said. "There's no need to apologize. There was at least one time when you were right. When Gaspar and Aunadar tried to poison Father, I couldn't have been less ready. I'm far from sure if I am now, but that hardly matters at the moment. With the ghazneths running loose, Cormyr is on the verge of disaster."

"It is no longer on the verge, I fear." Filfaeril wiped her eyes dry, then rose to her feet, assuming her familiar regal air. "The blight has destroyed every crop in the north, and it's working its way south by the day. There are wildfires everywhere, whole villages are going mad, and others are dying of the plague, the orcs have massed in the north and . . ."

"And the Seven Scourges are upon us," said Tanalasta.

"Blight, Madness, War, Pestilence, Fire, Swarms."

"That's only six."

"The seventh is 'soon to come,' and when he does . . ."

" 'Out come the armies of the dead and the legions of the devil made by itself,' " Filfaeril finished, quoting Alaundo's ancient prophecy. "What then?"

Tanalasta could only shake her head. "We can't let it come to that." She threw her covers back and swung her legs out of bed, then looked toward the anteroom door and barked, "Korvarr!"

Filfaeril took Tanalasta's arm. "What are you doing?"

"I did something in Goblin Mountain that weakened Xanthon," she explained, all but dragging her mother to the wardrobe. "It may be that I've stumbled onto something."

"What?" Filfaeril asked.

"I don't know yet. It's going to take some research."

Tanalasta pulled her bed gown off and tossed it aside, then flung the wardrobe open—and discovered it to be empty.

The anteroom door slammed open, and Korvarr Rallyhorn, the lionar of her guards, burst into the room with a dozen men at his back. They all skidded to a halt, then nearly fell over each other in their rush to avert their eyes and retreat.

"I . . . I b-beg your forgiveness, Princess," stammered Korvarr. "We thought you called."

"I did."

Filfaeril snatched the bed gown off the floor and thrust it at Tanalasta.

"Find Alaphondar and tell him to meet me in the library," Tanalasta said, draping the bed gown more or less over her breasts. "And send me something to wear."

"As you command, Princess."

Korvarr did his best to escape the room without looking at Tanalasta.

As the door shut, Filfaeril turned to her daughter and said, "My, you *have* changed."

Tanalasta smiled and draped her arm over her mother's shoulder. "And you have not seen half of it—which reminds me, I have only heard half the news. What of Father?"

"And Dauneth, perhaps?"

Tanalasta rolled her eyes. "If you must, but I warn you, I have less reason than ever to interest myself in the good warden."

"What a pity. You'd make such a handsome couple." Though the pout Filfaeril feigned was playful, there was a serious element to it. The queen and king had yet to hear of Tanalasta's marriage to Rowen Cormaeril—or her pregnancy. Filfaeril raised her hands as though to forestall her daughter's ire. "I'm not goading—"

"Only 'handling,' perhaps?"

"Perhaps." Filfaeril smiled briefly, then grew more serious. "The last I heard, your father and Alusair—"

"Alusair?" Tanalasta gasped. "Then she is safe?"

"Yes," Filfaeril said. "Your father came across her in the Stonelands. As I was saying, they were to meet Dauneth and his army in Gnoll Pass—"

"Was Alusair alone?" Tanalasta demanded. After Vangerdahast's disappearance at the battle of the Farsea Marsh, Rowen Cormaeril had somehow come into possession of the royal magician's horse and set off to warn King Azoun about the ghazneths. Unfortunately, Tanalasta and Alusair had come across his trail a few days later, heading north into the Stonelands for some reason they could not understand. Alusair had set out alone to track Rowen down, and that had been the last Tanalasta heard of either one. "Did she find Vangerdahast's horse?"

"As a matter of fact, Alusair did send a message for you—how silly of me to forget." The queen's sly smile made clear that she had not forgotten. "She said to tell you 'the king has Cadimus, but your favorite scout is still on the prowl.'"

Tanalasta retreated to the bed and sank down, suddenly feeling weary and weak.

The queen came and pulled the cover up around her shoulders. "Tanalasta, I'm sorry," she said. "I had no idea this would upset you."

"It shouldn't, I suppose," Tanalasta replied. "The mountains have grown so dangerous, and I was hoping for something a little more . . . certain."

Filfaeril leaned down and embraced her daughter. "I know. If I could even count the times I have wondered after your father's safety . . . and often as not he was off with the daughter of some minor noble."

Tanalasta shook her head. "Rowen wouldn't do that—even if there *were* noble daughters in the Stonelands."

"Rowen?" Filfaeril stood up again and frowned. "The only scout named Rowen I know is Rowen *Cormaeril*."

Tanalasta nodded, then patted the bed beside her. "You'd better sit down, Mother. I have something to tell you."

6

hey'll draw off now," Alusair said with some satisfaction, "and wait for the dark. Just make sure we've gathered brush enough for a good, big ring of fires."

The royal army stood wearily leaning on well-used swords, atop three hilltops somewhere in the northern marches of the realm. They watched orcs beyond counting growl and hiss and snarl their way down the hillsides, leaving their dead heaped in spilled gore behind them.

The fray had been long and bloody, the tuskers rightly not believing that such a paltry few humans could stand their ground—even high ground—against charge after charge of tested and eager warrior orcs. The slaughter had been frightful, awing even gray-haired veterans among the Purple Dragons. If the orcs had been able to muster just a little more boldness, they might have forced their way past tired human sword arms and cleared the hilltops of human life, reaping a king and a princess among their kills.

The ghazneth had exhorted them with harsh Orcish cries

and barked orders, shaking its iron cage in its eager fury, but to no avail. The attacking orcs, so far as Alusair's experienced eye could tell, had mounted no special effort to reach the imprisoned creature.

In the eerie silence that had fallen on the heels of the retreating orcs, the Steel Princess and her father watched the first cautious forays of dragoneers and noble blades move out to gather brush, then turned to face each other.

"Time to learn what we can of the fate of Vangerdahast," Azoun muttered, taking care to turn his shoulder between his lips and the watching ghazneth.

"Do you still have the tracing dust Vangey gave you to find wayward, rebellious princesses?" Alusair asked, arching an eyebrow.

Azoun nodded and said, "I'd not forgotten it. I yet retain the firefending magic he laid upon me, too."

Alusair's eyes fell to the wands hanging from her father's belt, and settled on a certain one marked with a red rune. "Bait?" she asked simply, and the king nodded again.

"Let's be about it," he said tersely, and beckoned a lancelord to his side, to deliver the orders for everyone to stand back—a good twenty paces back—from the cage.

The ghazneth laughed harshly as the Cormyreans backed warily away, not sheathing their blades or taking their eyes off it for long. The deep, rumbling laughter grew as the two Obarskyrs strode forward to approach it.

"Made bold by your iron bars, paltry excuse for a king?"

"Well met, Luthax," Azoun replied evenly. "Found your way out yet?"

The ghazneth who had once been the second most powerful—and in a brief, dark moment, perhaps *the* most powerful—war wizard in Cormyr hissed and rattled long talons along the bars. He could draw those talons right back into his fingers, Alusair noted, taking care to keep just out of reach of those corded black arms.

"Seeking to supplant the rightful royal magician of today?" the king continued, almost playfully.

Luthax threw back his bald head and laughed, the broken fringe of beard around his jaw giving him a truly bestial appearance. "Is that fool's fate your most pressing concern? O blind King, you've *far* worse troubles to worry about right now. There's the survival of your throne and kingdom, for instance."

The ghazneth leered at Alusair through the bars, and asked, "How much for this she-wolf, Azoun? I have need of a spirited apprentice—or a breeding wench for the steed I plan to birth wrapped in truly powerful spells. Care to try your best mages against me?"

"Not particularly," Azoun said, strolling around the cage with a humorless half-smile flickering at the edges of his mouth. "My duty is to preserve the lives and well being of my subjects as much as I can—even subjects such as you—not throw them away in pointless spell hurlings."

"I'm not your subject!" Luthax spat. "Go find Vangerdahast, if it's the fawning kisses of tame, groveling wizards you want."

"And just where would I find him?"

"Oh, no," Luthax taunted. "You must be used to crossing verbal swords with *very* dull-witted courtiers, Azoun. Think you to worm one word out of me that I don't care to let fall? I'm Luthax, a mage the likes of whom you've never seen and can't, brute-wits that you are, even hope to understand. Cormyr seems infested with ghazneths just now, doesn't it? Enough of us—*more* than enough of us—to hold one feeble old Vangerdahast where neither you nor any other man will ever find him."

"Think *you* so?" the king replied softly. "The royal magician's magic has already told me otherwise."

" 'Otherwise'?"

"The hold of a ghazneth," Azoun said casually, "seems far less sure than at least one ghazneth presumes it to be. Certainly less powerful than these crude iron bars. I wonder, now, just how much more of the vaunted powers of ghazneths are mere bluff and arrogance?"

The dark creature in the cage roared in fury and laid hold of the bars, shoulders rippling. The cage shook with its straining, but the bars held fast, and the creature hissed and snatched its hands away, holding them curled and trembling as if it had been burned.

"Starved for magic?" the King of Cormyr murmured. Azoun waited until the ghazneth's angry eyes were fixed on his, then brought into view the wand he'd drawn from his belt and held hidden behind his back as the ghazneth vainly tried to tear apart its prison. "I am prepared to make a little trade."

He stepped back, and watched the ghazneth that had been Luthax struggle with rage, then several other emotions in turn, before he wheeled and asked in a deep rumble that was once more calm and cunning, "A trade of what for what?"

"This untrapped, operating wand of fireballs—" Azoun paused, watching the ghazneth's fiery eyes flicker "—for complete and accurate identification that I can understand and deem sufficient as to the wizard Vangerdahast's whereabouts, and any traps or guardians upon him or on the way to reaching him."

Luthax seemed to freeze, sitting hunched in silent thought for a time that stretched longer than most men would have found comfortable, but the ghazneth and the king might have been two statues, so patient and still did they both remain. The bald head in the cage suddenly stirred, and its owner rumbled, "You have a trade, King. Approach."

Azoun took a step closer to the cage then halted with a smile, holding out the wand crosswise. Both he and it were still well outside the ghazneth's reach.

Luthax's eyes flickered again, but he said merely, "Some seven hills southeast of yonder ridge is an abandoned stead: a house dug into a hillside, a privy, and a collapsed barn. There is a well between the house and the barn, and your prized wizard is at the bottom of it, yoked and weighted, wet but safe. He cannot speak, see, or move his hands, and from his shoulders rise two rings that a ghazneth—or you, with rope and hooks and a little patience—can draw him up by. He is well, if you'll excuse the pun, but probably far from amused."

"No traps?"

"None—unless you consider the uncovered, unmarked

58

well hole a trap. I don't suppose a wizard would be improved by having a Purple Dragon in full battle armor crash down on top of him."

"This is all I should know?"

"By our bargain, all. Give me the wand, if kings yet have honor."

"*Kings* still do," Azoun told him dryly, and drew out the locking pins that held the sliding hatch lock shut. He threw back the heavy hatch with surprising strength for a lone man of his age, and hurled the wand into the cage.

The ghazneth snatched it out of the air, howled in glee, and boiled up into the air like a serpent striking at the sun. His wings beat in a ragged blur as blue lightning raged around the wand, became a burst of light, and sank back into Luthax's now empty hands as he spat. "I've not forgotten all my old spells," Luthax said. "Lose a wand, and gain a meteor swarm!"

Balls of fire raced out from the ghazneth's mouth, followed by bellows of wild laughter, straight at the king. Azoun stood his ground, shouting, "Everyone—get back and get *down!*"

On the heels of Azoun's cry, the hilltop exploded in flames.

Hooting with laughter, the ghazneth tumbled backward through the air, flapping his wings exultantly. "A little warmer than you expected, Azoun? Ha! What an idiot! What a fool! *This* was the best the Obarskyrs could give the realm?"

The ghazneth circled the blazing hilltop once, roaring with laughter as the warriors below cowered away from him with their vainly upthrust swords bristling like blades of grass. Luthax flew away.

There were gasps of awe from the warriors as the King of Cormyr strode out of the raging flames, apparently unharmed, and snapped at the nearest swordlord, "Waste no time searching for fictitious wells or abandoned steads—a quarry I once lost a horse in lies seven hills southeast of yonder ridge."

"Whither then, Majesty?"

Azoun Obarskyr pointed at the ghazneth in the distance.

Troy Denning and Ed Greenwood

"Clever and arrogant war wizards gone bad may be—but they aren't quite confident enough not to check on their captives, once the seed of doubt is planted."

He smiled a tight smile and reached for the hilt of his ready sword.

angerdahast crested the last flight of crooked stairs in the great goblin palace and knew he had finally, certainly, lost his mind. The grand corridor was steeped in a savory, rich aroma—the same savory aroma that had drawn him into the murky warrens of the palace in the first place. A strange chorus of chittering voices echoed down the corridor from the left, where the expanse of dark wall was broken by a cockeyed square of yellow light. The voices were entirely alien to him, but the odor he recognized. Rabbit. *Roast* rabbit.

He plucked one of his eyelashes and encased it in a small wad of gum arabic from his pocket, then whispered the incantation of his invisibility spell. His hand vanished from sight, leaving only a halo of light emanating from his unseen commander's ring. He slipped the ring off, then on again, suspending its magic radiance, and crept down the grand corridor. Though the hallway was the largest he had seen inside any goblin building, he still had to crouch to almost half his height. Grand goblin

61

architecture expressed its majesty in the horizontal and more or less ignored the vertical.

As Vangerdahast neared the yellow light, it resolved itself into a lopsided doorway, with one side taller than the other and neither perpendicular to the floor. He began to pick out distinct speakers among the chittering voices, and the aroma grew deliciously, irresistibly overpowering. He had not been conscious of his hunger as such a palpable force for some time, but the smell of food—or the illusion of the smell—filled his mouth with saliva and made his stomach rumble. Knowing the despair that would come over him when he rounded the corner and found an empty room, he almost turned back. His belt was wrapped around him almost double now, and he suffered regular blackouts and periods of weakness so severe he could not stand. Discovering this wonderful aroma to be mere illusion might be enough to kill him.

But of course Vangerdahast did not turn back. The smell drew him on, and the sound, also, of voices other than his own—no matter how strange and alien. Soon he stood hunched over the little door, craning his neck around to peer under the sill at a candlelit table laden with the steaming carcasses of ten plump skunks and several dozen crows.

They certainly looked real enough. The skunks had been fully dressed and spit-roasted, then served on their own fur. The birds had been prepared just as elegantly, having been baked *enfeather* with shelled walnuts in their beaks and silver root grubs in their eye sockets. Vangerdahast wondered what kind of sick trick his mind was playing. At any other time, the mere sight of such a banquet would have disgusted him to the point of illness. Now, it made his hands tremble and his mouth water.

Squatting on their haunches around the table were more than thirty goblins, well dressed in brightly colored loincloths and pale tunics girded with leather sword belts. Rather husky and short for their race, they stood at most three feet tall. They were also the wrong color. The eyes and hides of most goblins ranged in hue from yellow to red, but these had pallid green skin and pale blue eyes the color of Queen Filfaeril's.

To Vangerdahast's amazement, the goblins' manners were as eloquent as the creatures themselves were strange. A dozen white-cloaked waiters stood stationed around the table at equal intervals, using bronze carving utensils to cut the meat into bite-sized chunks. Whenever a diner chittered at one of the servers, the server would flip a tasty morsel in its direction, which the creature then endeavored to catch by moving its open mouth beneath the food. There seemed to be something of an art to process, with diners being careful to remain on their haunches and keep their hands tucked securely behind their knees until the food arrived. Whenever a guest caught a morsel that had been flipped a particularly long distance, behind the back, or through a flickering candle flame, the others would break into a burst of appreciative hissing. Only once did Vangerdahast see a diner miss, and the others quietly averted their eyes while the embarrassed goblin pressed its face down to snap the morsel off the dirty floor.

So polite were the goblins that Vangerdahast suspected he might win a dinner invitation simply by casting a comprehend languages spell and introducing himself. With a somewhat smaller mouth than the hosts, however, he suspected his manners would not measure up to their standards, and he really did not fancy eating his crow off the floor. In fact, he had never liked the idea of eating crow at all, and he was not about to start now—not when there was tasty, whole-roasted *mephitis mephitis* to be had instead. Vangerdahast raised an invisible hand toward the nearest skunk, then turned his palm up and made a lifting motion.

As he whispered his incantation, a soft rustle sounded from the head of the great staircase. He spun around and thought he glimpsed a pair of pearly dots at the mouth of the corridor. The goblins broke into a cacophony of astonished chitters and alarmed snarls. He looked back into the banquet hall and found his skunk hovering just above his invisible hand, filling his nostrils with an aroma that, if it was a hallucination, was at least the sweetest hallucination he had ever experienced.

63

The goblins were staring at the floating skunk less in fear than wide-eyed amazement, as though waiting for the fang-filled mouth of some unseen god to materialize out of the darkness and gulp the thing down whole. Happy to oblige them in the best way possible, Vangerdahast pulled his invisible dagger from its sheath and cut a morsel off the carcass, then popped it into his mouth. It certainly tasted real. In fact, he could not remember ever before enjoying a piece of meat so much, not even from the kitchens of Suzail Palace.

The banquet room erupted into a tumult of chattering and chiming as the goblins jumped up and began drawing little iron swords from their little bronze scabbards. Vangerdahast reached into his pocket and tossed a pinch of diamond dust into the doorway, booming out an incantation even as they turned to rush him. A shimmering curtain of force flickered into existence across the cockeyed portal. The first goblins slammed into it at a dead sprint and bounced back into their companions.

Vangerdahast broke a length of rib bone off the skunk carcass, then illuminated it with a quick spell of light and tossed it down the corridor. A tall, manlike silhouette ducked quietly down the great staircase, and a chill ran down the wizard's spine. The thing looked far too robust and human to be Xanthon, but there had been no hint of a tunic or cloak covering the smooth outline of its shoulders—and the wizard was all too certain of what that meant. Ghazneths could not wear clothes, for their bodies caused fabric to rot almost instantly.

The skunk suddenly lost its taste, but Vangerdahast forced himself to cut another piece and eat it. He was going to need his strength.

The goblins hurled themselves at the wall of force for only a few moments before concluding they could not get at their invisible thief through the doorway. They posted four guards in front of the portal and retreated to their table, then fell into a heated discussion. Keeping a watchful eye in both directions, Vangerdahast remained where he was and cast a spell to eavesdrop on their conversation. With a ghazneth lurking somewhere in the palace, he did not want to move until he had eaten his fill and recovered some of his energy.

"This thief we must find," rasped one goblin, a particularly broad fellow in a crimson loincloth. "The Grodd Palace he must not have the run of."

To Vangerdahast's great dismay, it sounded to him as though the goblins were speaking some corrupted dialect of the same ancient Elvish in which Nalavara had spoken her name.

"One jill it is only," said another. "Let the sneak have it and choke. Later we will smell him out."

"Nay, later there will be more." This speaker seemed to be female, and the others remained respectfully silent when she spoke. "Has the Iron One not spoken of these human things? If one is abided, a thousand come. We must smell him out before others follow, or the way of Cormanthor will we Grodd go."

"As Otka commands." The male who had spoken pointed toward a door in the back of the room. "Ghislan and Hardy, through the kitchen with your companies, and the alarm sound. Pepin and Rord, at the wall with yours."

With chilling efficiency, Pepin and Rord gathered twenty of the diners and began to chink at the powdery mortar in the walls. Ghislan and Hardy took the rest and rushed off through the kitchen, leaving only Otka and the white-cloaked servers standing alone in the center of the banquet hall. Vangerdahast had no idea whether Ghislan and Hardy or Pepin and Rord or their subordinates were male or female. The only hint of their sexes he had been able to identify was their voices, and now they were too busy working to talk.

Vangerdahast managed to wolf down only half of the skunk before he heard the companies of Ghislan and Hardy charging up the great staircase. Deciding this particular tribe of goblins was too efficient to toy with, he wrapped the remaining carcass in its fur and stuffed it inside his cloak, then cast a spell to help him see in the dark and scuttled away down the corridor.

At the first intersection, Vangerdahast turned down a small side passage, circling toward a secondary staircase he had seen at the rear of the palace's great foyer. The skunk meat sat in his belly like lead, though he suspected this had more to do with the condition of his neglected stomach than the Grodds' skills as chefs. This particular tribe was unlike any he had ever seen before, being much more organized and—it made him shudder to think such a thing—civilized. His thoughts leaped to the forlorn keeps scattered throughout the Goblin Marches, but he could not see how the Grodd were related to those ancient structures, which had stood abandoned long before there was a Cormyr. Of course, he did not see how he had failed to notice Otka and her band earlier, and yet here they were in the grand goblin palace. Both mysteries, he suspected, had more to do with Nalavarauthatoryl the Red than he would have liked.

When Vangerdahast finally started down the final passage toward the stairs, he was dismayed to find a reddish, manlike silhouette crouching atop the landing. The head and body remained distinctly human, but the thing's pearly gaze shone with the same faint light the wizard had seen in the eyes of Xanthon Cormaeril and the other ghazneths. Moreover, the figure was definitely naked, and he was peering across the foyer toward the skunk bone Vangerdahast had illuminated earlier. Though only a few minutes had passed since the spell was cast, all that remained of the magic was a faint yellow aura.

Vangerdahast cursed silently, then burped under his breath and retreated back up the corridor. He was already feeling stronger—but not yet strong enough to battle a ghazneth. It would be better to take his chances with the goblins.

He had scuttled nearly to the front of the palace when the soft hiss of sniffing goblins sounded around the next corner. Quietly, he retreated to the previous corner and started up another passage. This corridor was the smallest yet, so cramped he had to crawl on hands and knees. Had his life depended on it, he could not have turned around. The first goblins, silent save for the snuffle of their noses, passed the corner behind him. When none of them sounded the alarm, Vangerdahast breathed a silent sigh of relief and kneeled on his haunches, peering back beneath an arm to watch the rest of the group pass.

The sigh came too soon. The line had almost passed when a goblin stopped and squinted into the cramped passage, then chittered in excitement. With a sinking feeling, Vangerdahast dropped a shoulder and craned his neck to look down along his back. Where he should have seen nothing but darkness, he glimpsed a faint patch of blue. Like all magic he cast in the city of the Grodd, his spell of invisibility was wearing off prematurely.

Vangerdahast started to reach for a fire wand, then had a terrible thought. If his magic was not lasting as long as it should (and it was not), perhaps that meant something was draining it. If that something was what he feared, the last thing he wanted was to start spraying magic bolts around like arrows. Deciding his brain was starting to work again now that he had something in his stomach, he shoved the wand back in its sleeve and scurried down the passage as fast as his hands and knees would carry him.

The goblins quickly began to close the gap. Given the choice of being spitted on an iron sword or using another small bit of magic, the wizard allowed himself a single wall of stone. The goblins hit the barrier at a sprint, then bounced away into the murky warrens to find another route to their quarry.

They must have known the labyrinth far better than Vangerdahast. It was all he could do to reach the front of the palace and crawl out onto a tiny balcony before the little warriors caught up. The first one rushed out after him, nearly piercing a kidney before the wizard hurled himself over the balustrade into the darkness.

Vangerdahast experienced a flash of pain as his weather-cloak's magic triggered itself, and he began to flutter toward the ground as slowly as a feather. The wizard allowed himself to descend slowly, secure in the knowledge that there had been no time for the goblins to fetch crossbows, then he felt his stomach rise as he began to fall faster.

He rubbed the commander's ring on his finger and said, "King's light."

Troy Denning and Ed Greenwood

A sphere of purple light sprang up around Vangerdahast, revealing the startling fact that he was not only picking up speed, he was drifting away from the Grodd Palace. He twisted around to look toward the center plaza and was even more startled to find Nalavara's huge eye rearing up before him, slowly blinking and still bearing a strong semblance to the dark basin it had been when Vangerdahast arrived in this strange city.

The spell failed entirely then. The wizard plummeted to the ground and hit hard, then rolled to his knees and found himself looking up at Nalavara's reptilian jaw. As he shook his head clear, the dragon pulled another two neck scales out of the ground, and Vangerdahast knew he had guessed right about what was happening to his magic.

"Shrew!" he yelled, furious at being used in such a manner. "I'll die in hell before I free you!"

"As you like." Nalavara's voice seethed from her throat like hissing steam. "But were I you, I would mind my wishes. Remember the ring."

A terrific chittering broke out in the entrance to the Grodd Palace. Vangerdahast looked up and saw a company of goblins starting to spill down the stairs. He hoisted himself to his feet, but when he turned to run, his ribs were too sore and his legs too weary.

"Even strong and fresh, you are too old for that," Nalavara chuckled. She raised her head far above, her horns gouging great tufts of spongy substance out of the city's dark ceiling. "You have only the choices I give: die by the hands of my goblins, or take up their iron crown and rule in my name."

Vangerdahast glanced up toward the palace and saw how right Nalavara was. The leading goblins were already halfway down the stairs, with more than a hundred of their fellows close behind. It would have been an easy matter for a wizard of his power to slay them all, of course—but only with a lot of magic, and he could see for himself what that would mean to Nalavara. The dragon's head was already free, and every spell he cast only liberated more of her.

Better to die, then—save that the goblins would capture his magic and no doubt turn it over to Nalavara, all of the wands, rings, clasps, and amulets he carried hidden inside his secret pockets—not to mention the weathercloak itself, and even his tiny traveling spellbook, which relied on magic of its own to enlarge itself whenever he needed to read it. Dying would be worse than fighting. Dying would instantly give her all the magic she needed to free herself.

Vangerdahast did not even consider the iron crown, of course. Quite aside from any mystic powers Nalavara might have instilled into the circlet, to don the crown would be to declare himself a subject of the dragon herself, and he knew better than to think she would lack the means to enforce his liege duties. That left him with only one choice.

The goblins reached the bottom of the palace stairs and started across the plaza. Vangerdahast pulled a dove's feather from his cloak and tossed it into the air.

"This is it," he swore, spewing out the incantation of a flying spell. "This is the last magic you get from me!"

8

re you hurt, your majesty?" several warriors growled in rough unison, charging forward with swords raised.

Azoun gave them a mirthless smile and said, "Not unless my men refuse to follow me. Lass, have you chosen?"

"These who stand with me," Alusair replied, spreading her hands to indicate a burly swordlord, a lancelord, a war wizard, a dozen or so noble blades and dragoneers, and the lords Braerwinter and Tolon.

"We've left a command here in the field?" the King of Cormyr asked, indicating the army spread out around them.

Alusair gave her father what some were wont to call a "dirty look."

Azoun grinned openly before turning his head to watch the ghazneth who'd once been a lord among war wizards streak away into the sky. "Then let us be away," he said calmly.

"You go to try to recapture the escaped darkwings?"

a swordcaptain asked excitedly. "Take me!"

The king spun around. "No, loyal warrior. A few only are needed for this foray. The ghazneth did not escape—we let him go, that he might lead us to its lair."

"But . . . he's gone, beyond our sight."

"The royal magician gifted me with a magical trick," the king explained, raising his voice so that many could hear. "It's a dust I used to taint that which the ghazneth snatched. I can trace it for some days—which I hope will not be needed. Expect our return forthwith, but do not hesitate to move on from here if battle demands it. We go!"

Without further ado, the small force went, shaping itself around the king like a gigantic, wary shield. Azoun seemed sure of the ghazneth's direction and led them without pause over a hill into a place of stony slopes.

"Think you there're orcs ahead?" a Purple Dragon growled to his companion.

"Undoubtedly," that veteran warrior replied, hefting his sword. "In fact, I'm counting on it."

"Why is it," Lancelord Raddlesar inquired of the world at large, "that so much of fighting consists of hurrying through the wilderlands, chasing something that's well beyond the ends of our swords—and possibly beyond our powers to slay?"

"That's not just fighting, warrior," the war wizard told him quietly. "That's life."

Some stealthy things that might have been orcs scurried out from behind rocks and away as the king led his small strike force over several hills into an area where the land was riddled with breakneck gullies and rock outcrops, cloaked in stunted trees. They were probably only a few miles from the main army, but they might as well have been several kingdoms away, in land that—save for the occasional sheep's skull—looked like men had never set foot on it.

A shrill cry rang out from a ridge ahead as they struggled up a thorny slope to a knife-edged crest.

"A sentinel," Alusair said warningly. "Expect trouble ahead, and keep low—beware of arrows."

Trouble was indeed waiting for them when they reached the ridge. A line of impassive, hulking orcs in black leather armor with well-used axes and swords in their hands stood ready.

"Strike, then withdraw at my horn call," Alusair snapped. Men looked to the king for guidance. He merely nodded and indicated the Steel Princess, so they inclined their heads to her and made ready their swords.

The fray was brief and brutal, the king's men keeping close together so that two or three of them could face— and swiftly fell—a single orc. With the safety of both the king and a royal heir at stake, there was no "fairness" to hold to. Two dragoneers fell before Alusair sounded her horn and the panting Cormyreans drew back, leaving behind twice their number of twitching or motionless orcs to the flies.

"Did you see—?" the lancelord gasped.

"Not yet," the Steel Princess snapped, "but I'm watching. Look there." A dozen orcs—no more—came up the hill to join the few survivors along the ridge. "If there are many more ahead, they want us to advance. I see no messengers hastening away to call any others."

The king nodded. "So into the waiting jaws we'll go," he said. "I'm tired of wandering around these hills waiting to be attacked by a foe who seems to dwell or rest nowhere. It's time, and past time, to lash out."

Heads nodded agreement as the Steel Princess raised her hand and looked around. "Ready all?" she asked.

A breath or two later, she brought her hand chopping down. "Then forward!"

The orcs seemed to melt away like smoke before the wind of their charge. The Cormyreans broke through a small thicket onto a ridge that overlooked a small, deep bowl valley. Its depths held a mud castle akin to the ones many in the force had seen before.

"Gods!" one of them swore. "How is it that these things can be built in our own marches, and us not know?"

"A fortress!" another growled in disbelief. "A bloody tusker castle!"

Orcs in plenty could be seen on the slopes of the valley and on the spiraling ramparts of the mud tower, which was gray wherever it wasn't a sickly fresh dung color. It rose untidily out of a muddy moat, rock rubble strewn around it. The tower might have been raised the day before, or might have been older than the king.

"Has anyone among us traveled these hills before?" Azoun asked, almost absently.

He was answered only by uneasy silence, until his daughter growled, "What does it matter? We know what we have to do."

As if her words had been a signal, the ghazneth that Luthax the War Wizard had become circled the mud tower almost lazily, slipping out of one of the structure's many gaping, arched windows to plunge back into another. It was almost a taunt.

"I've no love for these mud fortresses," the king said flatly, "but a lair we came seeking, and a lair we've found. Let our swords strike for Cormyr!"

"For Cormyr!" came a ragged shout in reply.

The small force trotted down into the valley, steel rang on steel, and again the slaughter began.

9

t was what had become a typical morning in the courtyard of the Arabellan Palace. Walls rumbled to the sound of passing plague wagons, the air was laced with smoke from the wildfires outside the city, and cobblestones rang to the bark-and-clang of drill sergeants training recruits to meet the orc menace in the north. Beyond the lowered portcullis women begged gruel for hungry children, madmen trumpeted the world's end, and clouds of flies droned over carts of food spoiling faster than it could be shared. The scene was much the same across all of northern Cormyr. If the ghazneths ran free much longer, Tanalasta felt sure, the entire kingdom north of the High Road would be reduced to a scorched, diseased wasteland.

With some difficulty, the princess turned from the gate and looked to her small entourage. Save for herself and the queen, all of the guards, wizards, and companions carried only one small satchel of personal effects. Even Filfaeril and Tanalasta had packed their belongings into a single trunk each.

"Is everyone ready?" When no one reported otherwise, Tanalasta nodded to Korvarr Rallyhorn. "You may proceed."

"As you command, Princess." The steely-eyed lionar bowed stiffly—almost resentfully, Tanalasta thought—then turned toward the front of the group. There, two war wizards stood, each one linking arms with four burly dragoneers. In their hands, the dragoneers held bare iron swords. "You may proceed. We will follow in a hundred-count."

The wizards spoke a magic command word and vanished with a distinct *blat*, taking their eight dragoneer escorts along. Korvarr began to count aloud, slowly and audibly so everyone in the remaining half of the party could hear and understand.

Tanalasta's mother leaned close. "You know what this looks like, dear."

"That can't be helped," Tanalasta replied. "The research I need is in Suzail."

"People will think we're fleeing to safety," Filfaeril continued. "It hardly inspires confidence."

"I am not confident," Tanalasta replied. "We understand Xanthon, but what about the other ghazneths? The Arabellan library doesn't have the answers. If we want to stop them, I must return to the Royal Archives."

"And knowing why these traitors forsook Cormyr will help us *how*?" Filfaeril asked pointedly.

"You know how. I've already explained what happened to Xanthon when he learned that I had married Rowen." Tanalasta spoke even more quietly than before. Together, she and Filfaeril had decided it would be wisest to let Azoun announce her marriage so it would appear the king approved. "Learning the reasons the other ghazneths betrayed the realm is just a matter of enough study—and studying is what I'm best at."

"You are also an emblem of Cormyr," Filfaeril reminded her. "If the people think we are fleeing, they will lose hope."

"Then you may stay to reassure them, Mother," Tanalasta said. "But I will do what I think best for Cormyr."

Korvarr's count reached ninety, and Sarmon the Spectacular stepped up and offered them his arms. Tanalasta slipped her hand through the crook of the wizard's elbow, then cocked a querying eyebrow at her mother.

"I am coming," Filfaeril sighed. "For me to appear braver than you would undercut your station—and I am done costing you prestige."

"One hundred," Korvarr announced.

Sarmon uttered his spell, and Tanalasta's stomach rose into her chest. There was that timeless interval of numb, colorless falling in which she knew only the wizard's fingers around her wrist and the roar of silence in her ears. Now she was somewhere else, standing in a different courtyard, attempting to blink away the teleport after-daze and recall where she was.

The dull clamor of clanging iron rang off the bailey walls, and the air reeked of battle gore. The stones beneath her feet reverberated to the erratic thud of tramping feet and falling bodies, and there were armored men and black shapes flashing past in every direction. Sarmon had teleported them into a battle, and for the life of her, the princess could not recall why.

A dark silhouette whirled back toward her, and Tanalasta glimpsed an eerily familiar shape streaking toward her on black wings. The thing had gangling arms and hands with ebony talons, a skeletal torso with naked female breasts, coarse black hair that framed smoldering scarlet eyes.

"Ambush!" cried Korvarr Rallyhorn.

The lionar's armored body struck Tanalasta sidelong, slamming her into Sarmon and Filfaeril and driving all three to the ground. Suddenly, Tanalasta recalled where they were supposed to be. They were supposed to be in the inner bailey of the Suzail Palace, but Sarmon seemed to have bungled his spell and teleported them into one of the terrible battles raging in the north.

A loud clunk sounded above Tanalasta as the ghazneth's talons struck Korvarr's armor and tore him off her. Trying to fathom how the lionar's escort had bungled a teleport spell in exactly the same way as Sarmon the Spectacular, the princess rolled off the pile. She pulled the wizard off her mother and shoved him toward Korvarr.

"Help the lionar!" she ordered.

Even as the ghazneth dragged Korvarr bouncing and skipping across the cobblestone pavement, the lionar somehow managed to pull his iron sword and start hacking at the creature.

"And Sarmon—try not to bungle your spell this time," Tanalasta added, not bothering to conceal her anger at the wizard's incredible mistake.

Brow rising at her sharp tone, Sarmon pulled something from his weathercloak and tossed it in the lionar's direction. As he started his incantation, a familiar drone rose behind Tanalasta. She spun around to find herself looking through a swirling fog of wasps and flies at the looming spires of the Dragon Keep, which stood well inside Suzail Palace.

As Tanalasta struggled to digest the fact that they *had* teleported on destination, the lanky figure of Xanthon Cormaeril emerged from the droning haze and started to fight his way through the royal bodyguards. He was carrying a ten-foot halberd in each hand, leaping and spinning and whirling the ungainly polearms like a pair of windmills. The dragoneers countered bravely, charging in behind their purple bucklers to hack at his legs or thrust iron-headed spears at his heart, but they were no match for the ghazneth's speed. He batted their attacks aside one after the other and continued toward the crown princess.

Filfaeril grasped Tanalasta's arm and pulled her in the opposite direction, following Alaphondar, Owden, and half a dozen dragoneers toward the Purple Barracks. Their escape came to a sudden halt when a squat little ghazneth with a pot belly and a filthy black beard dropped out of the sky and blocked their way. He fixed his crimson eyes on Queen Filfaeril and started forward, using his powerful wings to bat aside fully armored soldiers as though they were little children.

"Boldovar." Filfaeril gasped the name so softly that Tanalasta barely heard it. "No!"

"Faithless harlot!" Boldovar hissed, wagging his red tongue at the queen. "I love that in a woman."

Filfaeril shrank back, then turned and would have run, had Tanalasta not caught hold of her arm. Owden stepped forward, placing himself squarely between the queen and her tormenter. Boldovar sneered and spread his wings in readiness. Instead of raising his iron mace, the harvestmaster pulled the sacred flower amulet off his neck and thrust it toward the ghazneth.

"In the name of the Great Mother, return thee to the grave and surrender thy body to the good soil."

Boldovar's eyes grew as hot as flames. He began to curse and gnash his teeth so furiously that a bloody froth spilled from his mouth, but he veered away from the holy symbol and tried to circle around—not to Filfaeril's side but to Tanalasta's. Owden cut the ghazneth off and stepped forward, pushing the amulet to little more than an arm's reach of the ghazneth.

"Owden, don't be a fool!"

Tanalasta caught the priest by the back of the cloak, then glanced in the direction of the first ghazneth. The creature was knee-deep in mangled dragoneers and also struggling to reach her. It was hindered by a trio of warriors whose armor and iron halberds had suddenly turned flaky and orange with rust, and by a short chain of golden magic wrapped around both legs. At the other end of the chain lay a feeble old wizard bearing a fatherly semblance to Sarmon the Spectacular. One arm was buried to the shoulder beneath the cobblestones, and he was screaming in anguish as the ghazneth struggled to pull free.

There was no sign of Korvarr, unless he was the green hummingbird darting in and out to plunge his pointed beak into the ghazneth's scarlet eyes. The bird seemed to be having more effect than any other attacker. Every time it struck, the ghazneth screeched and used its powers to heal the injured eye, then flailed about madly trying to knock the tiny creature from the sky. As quick as the dark fiend was, however, the hummingbird was quicker. It dodged, darted, then zipped in to strike again.

A cloud of wasps and flies arrived in a boiling, stinging swarm. Tanalasta looked back to see Xanthon less than five paces away, tearing into her last two bodyguards. Behind him, the palace garrison was streaming into the bailey from all directions, but the princess had noticed the pattern of the ghazneths' attacks and knew the guards would never arrive in time to save her. Even Boldovar, who had held Filfaeril captive for nearly a tenday, and in his madness still considered her to be *his* queen, was circling toward Tanalasta instead of her mother. Clearly, the time had come to reach for her escape pocket and count herself lucky.

Instead, Tanalasta turned to face Xanthon. It alarmed her to find him here, as powerful as ever, and perhaps even more so. His wings were now large enough that the tips rose above his shoulders. Had her theory about how to defeat the ghazneths been correct, he would be no more than the sniveling traitor who had fled Sarmon at Goblin Mountain, but the princess was not about to give up her idea so easily. If her theory was wrong, she would at least understand why.

Xanthon trapped one dragoneer's iron sword in the head of a halberd and began a tight loop, preparing to fling the weapon out of the warrior's grasp. Tanalasta raised her chin haughtily and stepped toward the battle, dragging her mother along and ignoring the wasps and flies descending to attack their faces.

"How now, Cousin?" Tanalasta called. "Is a Cormaeril on the throne no longer vindication enough?"

The loop of Xanthon's halberd stopped short, and the dragoneer managed to free his sword from the trap.

"Don't talk of thrones to me, shrew! You are no more married to Rowen than you were to Aunadar."

"She's not?" Filfaeril cried. She pulled free of Tanalasta's grasp and placed a hand over her breast. "By the Lady's Fiery Tresses, that's good news! I didn't know *how* I was going to explain it to the king. Imagine! A Cormaeril as the royal husband. What *would* the Silverswords do?"

Xanthon's eyes flashed crimson, and he gasped, "She told *you*?" He grew so distracted that he was barely quick enough to deflect the next few attacks. "Then it's true?"

"I should hope not!" Filfaeril stepped toward the ghazneth. "If it is, take me now and end my shame."

Troy Denning and Ed Greenwood

The shadow seemed to fade from Xanthon's face, and the hatred in his eyes took on the more human aspect Tanalasta had witnessed at Goblin Mountain. She caught her mother's arm and jerked her back, beginning to fear that perhaps the queen's reaction was not really an act.

"That's quite enough, Mother." Tanalasta had learned all she needed—perhaps even more than she would have liked. She nudged Alaphonder toward Owden, who was still facing off Boldovar, then spun away from Xanthon and reached for her weathercloak's escape pocket. "We'll discuss this further in my chambers."

A dark door opened before Tanalasta and she stepped through, dragging her mother along behind her. There was that timeless moment of falling, then she was back in the familiar confines of her own chamber, not quite sure why she felt so disoriented or why she was holding hands with the queen. In the next instant, Alaphondar arrived with Owden Foley in tow, then Tanalasta heard the battle clamor out in the bailey, and it all came rushing back to her.

She opened the door to her anteroom and shouted, "Sentries! Alarm!"

"And bring your irons!" added the queen. "We have ghazneths."

Tanalasta could not help smiling as she heard the startled cries echoing down the halls. Though she had not been home in well over a year, she was glad to see some things never changed. She listened for a moment to the astonished guards relaying the news of her return, then turned back to her mother.

"I hope that act was for Xanthon's benefit," she said.

Filfaeril smiled too sweetly. "Of course, my dear. I couldn't be happier for you."

Without awaiting a reply, the queen crossed the bedchamber and peered out between the draperies. Tanalasta followed close behind and took the other side. Out in the bailey, Boldovar and the other winged ghazneth—it had to be either Suzara Obarskyr or Ryndala Merendil, since they were the only two female ghazneths—were little more

80

than specks in the sky. Still lacking wings large enough to lift him, Xanthon Cormaeril was clambering up the outer wall like a huge spider, now fully reverted to his full ghazneth self.

Shaking her head in frustration, Tanalasta stepped away from the curtain and turned to her mother. "It's my turn to apologize. Apparently, I was wrong."

"You—wrong?" Filfaeril let the curtain drop and gave her daughter a doubtful look. "Why do I have a hard time believing that?"

"Because she wasn't." Alaphondar stepped between the two women and cautiously peered out between the draperies. "Had Tanalasta been wrong, I doubt the ghazneths would have set this trap for her."

"A trap?" echoed Owden. He and Alaphondar exchanged meaningful glances, then he looked away and did the same with Tanalasta. "You don't suppose they could have been worried about something else?"

"I don't see what," Tanalasta said quickly. Though enough time had passed for the princess to be certain she remained with child, she had not yet told her mother—partly because she feared the queen's reaction, and partly because of her own irrational desire to shelter the child by keeping the pregnancy secret as long as possible. "But we shouldn't congratulate ourselves yet. We've been able to weaken Xanthon twice now, but he has also recovered—and in fairly short order. I don't think my theory is going to destroy the ghazneths."

"Not yet, but it is a start," insisted Alaphondar. "If not, why would the ghazneths be worried?"

The sage's question caused Filfaeril to cock her brow. "A much more interesting question, I think, is why they were worried at all."

Owden and Alaphondar frowned, but Tanalasta, who was more accustomed to her mother's shrewd political thinking, was quicker to understand her meaning. "And how they happened to be waiting when we arrived."

Alaphondar's old chin dropped. "By Oghma's eternal quill!"

81

Troy Denning and Ed Greenwood

Only Owden, unfamiliar with the duplicitous life at court, did not understand. "I can't believe they're that smart. To surmise that we might come to Suzail is one thing, but to guess when . . ."

Tanalasta laid a silencing hand on the harvestmaster's thigh. "It wasn't a guess, Owden. They have a spy."

10

he brisk, muffled tramp of a goblin company on the march rumbled up the crooked lane, and Vangerdahast snuffed the candle by which he had been studying. The goblins were chittering a cadence, slightly off the beat as usual, slapping their palms against their iron breast armor to make their numbers sound greater. They were definitely coming in his direction. The wizard closed his traveling spellbook, then let it shrink back to carrying size before slipping it back into his cloak pocket.

Without the candle, his world grew as black and tight as a crypt. The cavern's spongy ceiling hung somewhere above, a full arm's length away, yet as musty and pressing as a coffin lid. The single opening was the small third-story window through which he accessed his crude hammock, and even that led to a cramped little room where he could barely stretch his arms.

Vangerdahast rolled to his stomach, ready to cast a spell into the pitch darkness below. He had no reason to believe there would be need. More than a hundred patrols had passed beneath him already, and the closest thing he had heard to a goblin alarm was a goblin sneeze. He knew that would change eventually. Every time he woke, there seemed to be more Grodd living in the city. They materialized out of nowhere, simply appearing as though they had been living there all along. Twice now, Vangerdahast had been forced to move farther from the central plaza after nearby buildings became suddenly inhabited.

Despite his vow to use no more magic, Vangerdahast was occasionally forced to cast a spell after the goblins caught him stealing food or filling his waterskin. Once, while using an enchantment to eavesdrop on his pursuers, he heard the goblins refer to the command of the "Iron One" that he and his ring be captured. Though Vangerdahast felt certain they were referring to Nalavara, and that the ring she wanted was his ring of wishes, what he did not understand was why.

During their first meeting, Nalavara had tried to trick him into wishing the then empty city full of goblins—a wish she had apparently not needed his ring to fulfill. Had she merely been trying to trick him into making any wish, so she could absorb the spell's powerful magic and be freed? Or had she been trying to keep him from wishing himself out of the city—or perhaps from wishing *her* out of existence? Vangerdahast had pondered the question and pondered it—he had little else to do—and still he could not decide. He was beginning to fear the matter would come down to simply trying an option and seeing what followed. This was a means of escape he was disinclined to attempt, given the high price of guessing wrong.

The tramp of the first company had barely faded before the sound of another one followed. The wizard listened carefully and heard several more companies coming in his direction. This was no simple scouting party. This sounded like an entire legion. Vangerdahast pulled an agate from his pocket and held it to his eye, whispering the incantation that would allow him to see in the dark. He did not know how close Nalavara was to freedom—every time he went to the plaza to see, he was discovered by an entire cohort of goblins and forced to use even more magic to escape—but something important was happening, and he had to find out what.

By the time Vangerdahast finished his spell, the second company of goblins had passed down the lane and vanished around a corner. He did not have to wait long for a third. By the magic of his spell, which enabled him to see via radiant heat instead of light, he beheld a file of red-glowing forms marching single file behind a bronze-armored standard bearer. Their centurion followed half a dozen steps behind, jaw snapping as he barked the cadence. Like the goblins behind him, he wore a heavy field pack on his shoulders and a short sword on his hip. Instead of the iron javelins they carried against their shoulders, however, he cradled an ivory baton in the crook of his elbow.

As the company passed by fifteen feet beneath his hammock, it was all Vangerdahast could do to remain motionless. He had been lurking on the fringe of the occupied warrens for some time now, quietly trying to follow a hunting party to wherever they killed their crows and skunks—presumably somewhere outside the city, since he had never seen signs of any such creatures in its vast darkness.

His efforts had met with no more success than his attempts to teleport, dimension door, or plane walk out of his prison. The hunting parties always seemed to disappear a thousand paces beyond the occupied portions of the city, sometimes vanishing after they rounded a corner and other times simply fading into the darkness at the other end of a long, straight corridor. Nothing Vangerdahast tried had ever enabled him to trace their route, not even magic.

This time it was no mere hunting party. This was an entire army, and armies did not vanish into thin air—not even goblin armies.

The present company had barely rounded the corner before Vangerdahast heard the next one coming. He gathered his possessions and scrambled through the window. Before descending to the bottom floor, he cast a spell to make himself invisible. Goblins seldom looked up, but they were extremely aware of matters at their own level and would certainly notice him if he did not take precautions.

Once the company had passed, Vangerdahast slipped out the door and started down the alley after them. He had no trouble keeping up for the first quarter mile or so, until the goblins entered a series of low passages running beneath the tenement buildings' second stories. He dropped to his hands and knees and quickly began to fall behind. Somewhat reluctantly, Vangerdahast cast a flying spell so he could keep up without making too much noise. It was the nineteenth spell had used since he came to realize that his magic was freeing Nalavara.

By the time the company reached its destination, the magic had been drained from all three of Vangerdahast's spells. He cast each spell again—the twentieth, twenty-first, and twenty-second since he had vowed to use no more magic—then followed the goblins into an open space covered by an immense domed ceiling.

With jagged boulders littering the floor and stalactites hanging from the ceiling, the area had the look of a natural cavern. In the center of the vast space, a set of crooked timber stairs ascended an equally crooked scaffold and disappeared into the darkness above. A full legion of goblins—more than a hundred companies—stood before the structure in tidy ranks. Their attention was fixed on the first landing, where a handful of high-ranking goblins in iron armor stood staring out over their growing army.

Heart pounding in excitement, Vangerdahast ducked behind a nearby boulder to plan his next move. There was a time when he would have been arrogant enough to slip invisibly through the ranks and ascend the scaffold at once, but he had long ago learned not to underestimate the Grodd goblins.

Another dozen companies entered the marshaling ground and took their places at the rear of the legion. Finally, when the last warrior had taken his place and posted his javelin in front of him, a tall goblin in a red robe stepped forward. He raised both arms, and a curt, deafening cheer rose from the legion.

Twice more the goblin raised his arms, and twice more

the legion gave its cheer. The red-garbed figure pressed his fingertips together and gestured toward the legion, then stepped back. Another goblin, this one in white, took his place and began to speak.

Vangerdahast cast his twenty-third spell.

". . . Iron One has spoken," said the goblin. The voice was that of Otka, the female whom Vangerdahast had seen giving orders in the Grodd Palace. "Now is the time. To the Wolf Woods you go!"

Otka flung her arm up the stairs and stepped aside. The first company started up the stairs three abreast, leaving Vangerdahast to curse the waste of his magic. Even the dimmest of Azoun's high nobles would not have needed magic to guess the meaning of such a short speech.

Seeing no reason to wait in line—even in the city of the Grodd, royal wizards were entitled to their privileges—Vangerdahast stepped out of his hiding place and launched himself over the heads of the goblins. He landed three-quarters of the way up the tower, on a platform fully thirty feet above the leading company, and started up the cockeyed stairs. He ascended rapidly but cautiously, being careful not to stomp or slap his soles on the stair treads or make any other noise that would alert the goblins to his invisible presence. Unfortunately, there was nothing he could do to keep the scaffold from shaking and swaying beneath his weight. The Grodd had many strengths—especially for goblins—but construction was not one of them.

Upon reaching the next landing, Vangerdahast looked up and saw the stairs ascending into pitch darkness. The wizard climbed to within arm's reach of it, then looked down and decided to cast one last spell before departing the goblin city. He pulled a small handful of sulfur and bat guano from his cloak and began to roll it into a sticky ball—then saw the glowing eyes of a ghazneth watching him from the mouth of a goblin tunnel.

One pearly eye vanished and reappeared. Vangerdahast stopped rolling his fingers. The thing had *winked* at him. Forgetting about the spell components in his hand, the wizard bounded up the last few steps in a dead sprint—and crashed headlong into the cavern's spongy ceiling.

The surface parted and yielded ever so slightly, then suddenly stiffened and forced his head downward, so that he found himself staring at the goblins below. The ball of sulfur slipped from his fingers half-combined and plummeted groundward. He feared for an instant that he would follow, but the ceiling held him fast, spread-eagled forty feet above the legion.

Vangerdahast lost sight of the sulfur ball, then heard a dull ping and saw a goblin centurion drop to a surprised squat. The soldier pulled his helmet off and craned his neck to look—of all directions for a goblin to look—up.

Even then, Vangerdahast thought he might remain undetected. He was, after all, forty feet in the air, invisible, and camouflaged in a black weathercloak, but the goblin's eyes grew round and white . . . and vanished into pitch darkness.

The wizard dared to hope he was being drawn through the ceiling into the Wolf Woods—known in his own day as Cormyr—when a high little voice began to chitter far below, and the scaffold began to groan and sway beneath the trammeling of little boots. Vangerdahast realized that the spongy barrier holding him fast was also drawing the magic from his spells. He could no longer see in the dark, nor—in all likelihood—fly.

Vangerdahast glanced toward the tunnel where he had seen the pearly eyes and found nothing but darkness. Having no doubts about what the thing would do next, he reached for his weathercloak's escape pocket and found his arm stuck fast to the ceiling. Shrill goblin voices began to chitter below, not more than ten feet away.

Knowing he could never teleport out of the cavern—he had tried it a dozen times before and never found himself anywhere but the immense goblin city—Vangerdahast elected to try something simpler. He closed his eyes and spoke the incantation of a blink spell.

There was a fizzle and a hiss, then a dozen tiny hands clutching him from below, tugging at his lapels and jerking the throat clasp from his collar, fishing through his pockets and pulling out wands, potions, and rings, little bundles of dried toad tongue and chopped rock lichen and powdered newt eye of no use to anyone but him.

A pair of shining pearl eyes appeared in the darkness below, more or less where Vangerdahast remembered the corner of the scaffold to be. The goblins began to shriek and yammer madly. The eyes grew steadily, rapidly larger. The ghazneth was coming.

Finally, a goblin leaped up and caught hold of Vangerdahast's sleeve, then began to work its way hand-over-hand toward his wrist. The wizard's heart rose into his throat. He closed his eyes and tried one more time to decide whether Nalavara needed his ring of wishes or was frightened of it.

When the goblin grabbed hold of his wrist, he still had not decided. He closed his eyes and began, "I wish—"

A deafening clap of thunder interrupted the command. Vangerdahast's eyes were pained by a brilliant flash of light, and the goblin's weight vanished from his arm. A smell like scorched rabbit permeated the air.

"Do not!" growled a raspy voice. "As it is, you have nearly freed her!"

After squeezing his eyes open and shut several times, Vangerdahast was finally able to see a small cascade of flames licking the scaffold below him. The goblin leaders were chittering angrily and pointing at the flames. A moment later, several brave goblin warriors hurled themselves into the conflagration, using their own bodies and bare hands to beat out the fire.

Vangerdahast ignored their selfless display and stared into the ghazneth's gray eyes. "Do I . . . know you?"

"No," came the answer. The ghazneth pulled his shadowy body onto the landing beneath Vangerdahast, then plucked a pair of wands from a squealing goblin's wrist and began to absorb the magic. "Nobody knows me."

"You're lying," Vangerdahast said. Though the voice was far raspier than any he knew intimately, there was something familiar in its dry huskiness and crisp northern accent. "Where have we met?"

"Nowhere but here in this hell."

Troy Denning and Ed Greenwood

The ghazneth spun away and began to knock goblins off the scaffold, crying out when one little warrior managed to thrust an iron javelin through his abdomen. Vangerdahast watched in astonishment, at first confused as to why the phantom had come to his aid, then growing more frightened as the obvious answer occurred to him. He was a magician, and ghazneths needed magic the way vultures needed death.

After clearing the immediate area of goblins, the ghazneth spun around to point down the stairs. As the phantom turned, Vangerdahast glimpsed a dark but handsome face with reasonably human features and a grotesquely cleft chin. Before the wizard could see more, a torrent of water shot from the ghazneth's hand and blasted twenty goblins off the scaffold. The spray doused the fire they had been fighting and plunged the cavern back into darkness.

A powerful hand reached up and pulled Vangerdahast out of his wizard's cloak, then turned to throw him off the tower.

"Wait!" Vangerdahast cried, finally putting the chiseled face and northern accent together. "I do know you!"

"No longer," said the voice. "Now, go back to your nest and do not make me sorry I saved you."

The ghazneth pitched him into the darkness, and Vangerdahast barely had time to picture his snug little hammock before he heard himself shout the syllables of his teleport spell.

11

hese tuskers are so ugly," Lancelord Raddlesar grunted, as his blade ripped apart a fat-bellied orc's belly from its crotch to its breastbone, "that you'd think orc mothers'd soon lose interest in mothering more of them, hey?"

"They never do, Keldyn," another lancelord replied mournfully. "They just never do."

Those were the last words he ever uttered—a black blade burst through his helm and cheek and out his mouth in a red froth, and Lancelord Garthin toppled into the blood-churned mud without a sound, his dreams of settling his sweetheart in a grand house in Suzail swept away in one bright and terrible instant. His fall went unseen by his fellows in the frantic, hacking tumult.

"I've slain at least thirty," a swordcaptain gasped, bringing his blade around in an arc that struck sparks and rang shrieks of protesting weapon steel from a dozen orc swords.

The endmost orc reeled back from that clash of arms, and Swordcaptain Thorn's blade darted in like the fangs of a

91

springing rock viper, in and out of a fat tusker's throat so swiftly that one might have been forgiven for not seeing the slaying stroke—at least until the blood started to jet, and a fat, dirty body staggered helplessly back.

"Is that all, Thorn?" Lord Braerwinter called, over the surging shoulders of two orcs that were hacking an already dead armsman to the ground. "Whatever have you been *doing* all this time?"

The swordcaptain chuckled. "Sharpening my steel," he roared back, trading deafening blows with a snarling orc captain larger than he was. "And tempering it—"

Both combatants swung as hard as they could, blades cleaving air until they clashed together numbingly, spraying sparks. Tortured steel screamed around their ears. As one, orc and man staggered back, shoulders shaking helplessly from the force of their meeting blades.

One of the gigantic snortsnout's elbows struck a dragoneer's helm, sending the man flying. The warrior fighting beside the downed man gave the reeling orc a look of disgust, whirled despite an orc blade seeking his own ribs, and drove his dagger hilt-deep behind the tusker's ear.

"—in orc blood!" Theldyn Thorn roared, drawing back his warsword in both hands and smashing it forward through the staggering orc's guard with such force that both of his boots left the ground—and the huge, hairy jaw, breast, and ribs beneath all shattered. They fell together, rolling in the mud, sweeping the legs out from under the orc trying to slay the dragoneer.

Someone else fell atop that orc, screaming in raw agony, and two sword blades burst through the tusker's body inches from Thorn's nose, almost blinding him with hot, dark gore. As he shook his head frantically in the stinking darkness, the screaming above him ended abruptly.

The swordcaptain blinked and heaved and spat his way up from under, finding his feet somehow in the muck. When he could see once more, he found he was in a little space clear of living orcs, facing staggering and blood-spattered Purple Dragons across heaps of the dead. He gave the dragoneer a dark look and snarled, "Slay your *own* orcs, boldblade!"

"Well," the dragoneer growled back, kicking his way free of bodies that were still leaking bright blood, "I *humbly* beg my lord swordcaptain's pardon. My hand must've slipped."

"No doubt," Thorn grunted, setting his shoulders to hack his way forward through a squalling tangle of blood-streaked orcs whose blades were caught in the armor of the Purple Dragon they'd spitted together. "No doubt."

In the heart of the fray, Swordlord Glammerhand and the lords Braerwinter and Tolon were grimly hacking and par-rying, trying to keep orc blades away from two fellow war-riors who refused to be protected: King Azoun and his daughter Alusair. The Steel Princess was leaping and twist-ing like a mad thing in the heart of knot after knot of snort-ing, screaming tuskers, hurling herself into danger as if she were eager to die. Black orc blood dripped from her helm and chin, and her blade leaped like a flickering flame amid the gore, rising and falling tirelessly.

Ever Alusair struck boldly forward, and ever her father followed her, hacking and stabbing with cool efficiency as he sought to deal death to any orc who got between him and his daughter and thus necessarily around behind Alu-sair's back.

Orcs a head taller than she was snorted in anger as they put their shoulders down and rammed forward, together. One paid for his lowered guard with his life, his gorget cut away and the throat beneath opened in a hot flood—but the other sent Alusair staggering and chopped sidearm with his blade like a forester hewing down a sapling.

She grunted—it was more of a sob—as his blade bit home, and almost fell. An orc blade had drawn royal blood!

Roars went up from both sides as orcs shouted in tri-umph, and Cormyreans bellowed their fervent need to reach and rescue the Steel Princess.

"*Die*, tuskers!" Swordlord Glammerhand shouted, almost beheading an orc with a terrific cut. "Get thee to death and save us this trouble!"

Azoun's eyes narrowed as he caught sight of dark limbs and wings waving almost tauntingly in the shadows beyond the orcs. A few more desperate thrusts and slashes brought him to where he could stand over the shuddering Alusair. He slapped a vial of healing elixir into her hand and growled, "Drink, reckless idiot!"

Alusair coughed, on her knees in the mud between two sprawled bodies, neither of them an orc. "Th-thanks, father," she said thickly, spitting blood. "Always there when I need you."

"Get up, lass," he snapped. "I need your thoughts now, not your blade."

"How so?" she gasped, reeling to her feet as the lords Braerwinter and Tolon took up stances on one side of the royal pair, blades raised and ready, and Swordlord Glammerhand and Lancelord Raddlesar stood guard on the other.

"Look you," Azoun gasped, pointing through the slaughter with his blade. "We chase and chase this ghazneth, and it retreats, never crossing claws with us—is this the usual way these beasts war with us? And all we ever see is one and the same ghazneth. Where are the others?"

"We've been lured away," Alusair said quietly, holding her side where the orc blade had bitten into her, and bringing her fingers away sticky with her own blood. She lifted her head and shot glances like arrows around the fray, stopping when she found the war wizard who was never far from the king. Arkenfrost was the mightiest mage out in the field with the royal army. "How many of your fellow wizards remain with the troops, Lord Mage?"

"Eight or so, if one counts untried apprentices," Arkenfrost replied calmly through the tumult, "and three who've spells enough to make a difference in battle."

"If they try," Azoun snarled, "ghazneths galore will be down on them like hungry vultures. We've been duped—again!" Gods, he missed Vangerdahast's foresight and sarcastic calm . . . but this was one war the King of Cormyr was just going to have to win without his royal magician.

He looked around at Purple Dragons heartily hacking down orcs, then back at Arkenfrost. "If we leave you, can you bring these men out into the sunlight again and back to rejoin us?"

Arkenfrost shrugged. "We fought our way in here, Majesty," he replied calmly. "I daresay we can fight our way out."

The king nodded curtly, caught hold of Alusair's hand, and snapped, "We go. Guard yourselves."

Alusair opened her mouth to say something, but Azoun made no move to halt his will. His ring flashed once as the vast blue falling seized them both—and when it cleared they were out under the sun again, the royal standard Azoun had sought to return to was fluttering beside their ears, and they were staring into the frightened eyes of three men in robes whose hands were leveled at the Obarskyrs, and whose wrists were crackling with the awakened lightning of battle magic.

"Strike not your king!" Alusair roared, her voice as deep a snarl as any swordcaptain's. "How goes the battle? Did you face any ghazneths?"

The foremost man sketched the briefest of bows and stammered, "N-none, Royal Lady. Ah, Eareagle Stormshoulder, loyal mage of the Crown, at your service. Uh, your majesties." He drew in an unhappy breath, and said stiffly, "We face a sea of orcs—tuskers everywhere, like a cloak on the hillsides all around. We dare not use much magic, for fear of the darkwi—the ghazneths."

"Prudent," the king said, nodding, "but use what magic you must. To let men die while you stand idle is to give a ghazneth a victory it hasn't even taken the field to earn." He shot the other two mages a steely glance. "Has Stormshoulder seen the fray correctly?"

"Ah, he has, your majesty," one wizard said awkwardly, while the other stammered, "He has." Then they both seemed to remember whom they were addressing, and found their knees with almost comical haste.

"Loyal Mage Lharyder Gaundolonn, O King."

"Loyal Mage Mavelar Starlaggar at your service, Crowned Lord of Cormyr."

Azoun waved these formalities aside with a growl that became the command, "Follow me! I'll have these orcs swept from my land even if I have to slay each and every last one of them myself! For Cormyr and victory!"

Holding high his warsword as if it were a flaming brand sent down by the gods, the king charged forward. Alusair snatched up the royal standard and followed, snapping a quiet, "Come!" to the open-mouthed war wizards.

Helmed heads were turning to look at them as they trotted forward. The king's army was facing a host of orcs that covered the hills ahead for as far as they could see, but a great shout went up as the Obarskyrs surged forward to the line where men and orcs were hacking at each other in the sunlight with a sort of grim resignation.

"For Cormyr and victory!" a thousand throats shouted in unison.

"Death to all orcs!" a swordcaptain called back, and the reply rolled out deafeningly, "For *CORMYR AND VICTORY!*"

And as the royal army raced forward with renewed vigor to hew down orcs, slipping and sliding in the black blood of the tuskers who'd already fallen, not a man there spared a glance into the sky for a ghazneth. There were orcs to kill, and too little daylight left to down them all.

"For Cormyr," Azoun shouted happily, shouldering his way past a startled lancelord to lay open the face of a snarling orc, "forever!"

"Gods, yes," Alusair murmured, from somewhere near his left shoulder, "let it be forever."

12

analasta stood on the Amethyst Dais of the Royal Audience Hall, feeling small and lost in the soaring grandeur of the golden chamber, yet also very glad for the concealing bulk of her Purple Robe of State. She was beginning to thicken around the middle, and it wouldn't do to have this particular pack of wolves speculating over the cause. There were nearly two hundred of them clustered at the base of the stairs, droning quietly in their little cliques even as Lord Emlar Goldsword addressed the crown.

"These ghazneths are proving a nuisance, Highness. Already, a rather stubborn blight has taken hold in my vineyard, the flies have made a maggot barn of my stables, and I have had to dismiss several servants who spoke harshly to Lady Radalard."

The complaints differed only in detail from the litany of grievances to which Tanalasta had been listening all morning. A fissure of molten rock had run down the middle of the Huntcrown country estate, swallowing the mansion, Lord

97

Tabart's favorite stallion, and a dozen good gardeners. A quarter of the ships in the Dauntinghorn merchant fleet had developed sudden cases of dry rot, forcing the family to leave whole shiploads of foodstuffs moldering on the docks. For no reason anyone could name, the young men of the prolific Silverhorn family had developed a sudden hatred of the Hornholds and initiated a deadly blood feud that had already cost both families their firstborn heirs.

Most of the speakers were united in implying that Tanalasta had brought this plague of calamities with her when she came down from the north, and in suggesting that had she had the foresight to seek refuge elsewhere, perhaps they would not have been so inconvenienced. She listened to each lord politely, interrupting only to clarify a point or to ask a description in the rare event that the speaker had actually joined his guards and gone out to do battle when the ghazneth came. What the princess heard convinced her that all six of the creatures were now plaguing southern Cormyr.

It also convinced her that most of the nobles before her were not worthy of the name. Why was it, she wondered, that the highborn of a family so often turned out to be selfish cowards, while the lesser cousins proved true and brave? That had certainly been so among the Cormaerils. She could easily picture Gaspar or Xanthon there before her, complaining about the inconvenience of having the kingdom assaulted by the scourges of Alaundo's prophecy while their lesser cousin Rowen was off actually trying to do something about it.

Tanalasta forced herself to focus on Lord Goldsword. She did not know whether it was her condition or her growing concern about Rowen's long absence, but she found her attention wandering to her husband at increasing intervals. It had been three months since King Azoun had found the ranger's mount riderless and alone in the Stonelands, and she had heard about the blood on the saddle and the likelihood it had come from a festering wound. The conclusion was obvious, but Tanalasta could not bring herself to believe it without a body, especially not when she had heard nothing from Rowen himself. He had been wearing a royal ranger's cloak, which had the same magic throat clasp as a war wizard's weathercloak. Had he lain slowly dying somewhere, Tanalasta knew his last act would have been a sending to say good-bye. He would never be cruel enough to simply die and leave her in doubt—not Rowen Cormaeril.

"Highness?" asked Lord Goldsword.

Tanalasta found herself looking past the pate of Emlar's shiny bald head and realized she had been staring off into space again. With much-practiced poise, she kept her gaze fixed on the ivory dragon at which she had been staring and did not allow her face to betray any shock.

"You were saying that some of your servants had gone mad and insulted Lady Radalard," Tanalasta said. "Was there anything else?"

"Only the matter of the hounds, Highness," he said.

"Ah yes, the hounds." Tanalasta let her gaze drop to the lord's face. This time she did not try to disguise the irritation she felt at being petitioned about vineyards and hunting dogs while the ancient prophecy of Cormyr's doom came true before their eyes. "What do you intend to do about it, milord?"

Goldsword looked taken aback, and the drone of the half-whispered conversations around him fell suddenly silent. "*Do*, Majesty?"

"Yes, Emlar," said Tanalasta. "What do you intend to do about the ghazneths? They are the cause of all these troubles—or haven't you heard?"

Emlar's eyes flashed with irritation. "Of course I have heard, Highness." His voice assumed that silky tone nobles liked to use when they tried to manipulate some fact or half truth to their own advantage. "Everyone knows how you brought them—"

"The princess did not *bring* them, Lord Goldsword," said Queen Filfaeril. She rose from her throne, where she had been quietly working on a silken needlepoint depicting her rescue from Mad King Boldovar. "If you will recall, they were waiting when we arrived. The princess was very nearly killed—and I, for one, would like to know how that came to be."

Troy Denning and Ed Greenwood

The color drained from Emlar's jowly face, as it did from so many faces when the queen spoke in that icy tone. "I beg the princess's pardon." He continued to look at Filfaeril and bowed more deeply than he had to Tanalasta. "I meant only to say that these ghazneths are a matter for the crown. The nobles can hardly be expected to muster their household guards—"

"And why not?" demanded Tanalasta, glaring at the lord even more harshly than he deserved. Though her mother had been careful to stop a pace behind her, the princess would rather the queen had remained in her throne. Even the mere demonstration of support for Tanalasta's leadership implied that it was needed and weakened her in the eyes of the nobles. To regain their respect, she would need to be more stern than before. "While I was in Huth-duth, did the king release the nobles of their liege duties and neglect to inform me?"

"Of course not," replied the lord, "but the king is not here."

"The king is always here," Filfaeril began.

Tanalasta raised her hand ever so slightly. As subtle as the movement was, such things seldom went unnoticed in the cagey world of lordly politics, and the gesture drew an astonished gasp. Lord Goldsword looked to the queen, clearly expecting her to put Tanalasta in her place and take over the audience. Instead, Filfaeril merely inclined her head and retreated to her throne, leaving the nobles to ponder the new structure of royal power.

Tanalasta stepped to the top of the stairs. "The king is in the north fighting orcs, as are most of Cormyr's armies." She looked away from Goldsword and ran her gaze over the other nobles. "If the south is to be defended, it will not be by Purple Dragons."

The expected murmur had barely begun when a husky voice called out from the back of the crowd, "Perhaps I may be of some service in that regard, Majesty."

Tanalasta looked toward the speaker and saw a broad-shouldered man with dark hair and darker eyes stepping out of a small circle of Rowanmantles, Longthumbs, and other merchant families. The fellow's foppish feathered hat

100

prevented the princess from seeing his face clearly, but as he bowed she caught a glimpse of swarthy cheekbone and a proud cleft chin. Her heart began to pound so violently that she feared the nobles could hear it down on the chamber floor. Though she could not imagine what Rowen would be doing in the garish silks of a Sembian merchant, the similarity of their appearance was too great to overlook.

Tanalasta extended a hand and could not quite keep the excitement from her voice as she said, "The gentleman in feathers may rise and present himself."

The enthusiasm in her voice prompted a louder murmur than the last, and even Lord Goldsword turned to see what stranger had prompted such a reaction from their taciturn princess.

The newcomer removed his hat with a flourish and bowed even lower, then answered in an almost comically thick Sembian accent, "As you command, Majesty."

The man stood and started forward, and Tanalasta's heart fell a little. The distance was too far to see his face clearly, but his hair was shorter than Rowen's and more heavily styled. Still, hair could be cut and trained, and if her husband had some reason for coming to her in the guise of a foreigner—and she could not believe any true Sembian would speak with such a thick accent—it would behoove him to be certain his hair supported the disguise.

Tanalasta's curiosity could not wait until the man reached the base of the stairs. "Tell us your name, good sir."

The man stopped and bowed again, and even Queen Filfaeril grew curious enough to leave her throne and step to Tanalasta's side.

"That would be Korian Hovanay," said the man. "Ambassador of the Consortium Princes of Saerloon, Selgaunt, and all of Sembia, at your service, Majesty."

Filfaeril glanced at Tanalasta and cocked her brow, but the princess paid the gesture no regard and motioned the man forward again.

"Come along, *Ambassador* Hovanay," she said, playing along. "We are discussing serious matters here. We do not have all day to wait on your bowing and scraping."

Troy Denning and Ed Greenwood

Korian quickly rose and started forward again, and Tanalasta's heart sank a little further. The man's face was fleshier than her husband's, and it lacked the chiseled, weatherworn aspect that had attracted her to Rowen in the first place.

Still, Sembians liked to eat well, as though the number of a squid tails and octopus legs a man could afford to choke down were a measure of his acumen as a merchant. Two months of such rich, heavily buttered food would fatten the cheeks of even the hardiest royal scout.

Now the Sembian began to speak as he walked. "I apologize for keeping Her Majesty waiting, and will endeavor to be brief. Cormyr's many and growing troubles in the north and elsewhere having come to my masters' attention, they have bade me come to Suzail and offer their every assistance."

"Assistance?" Tanalasta echoed, finding it difficult to concentrate on the man's words instead of his face. "What kind of assistance?"

"The kind the crown of Cormyr finds to be mutually agreeable." The ambassador stopped at the base of the stairs and started to bow again, then caught himself and simply continued. "At this moment, my masters have an army of ten thousand sellswords commanded by our own Sembian officers on the march toward Daerlun."

"Ten thousand?" Filfaeril gasped.

Tanalasta barely heard her mother, for she saw now that this handsome ambassador could not be her Rowen. Though hardly fat—especially by Sembian standards— the merchant's softness clung to him like a blanket, and his mannerisms had the smooth, practiced air of an accomplished liar.

"Ten thousand sellswords?" Filfaeril repeated, this time more into Tanalasta's ear than toward the ambassador. "That is not help. That is an invasion."

Korian raised his hands in denial. "Nothing of the sort is meant. My masters only wish me to convey that the army is advancing to the Swamprun for our own protection. And since it will already be close, they thought—"

"They might as well claim southern Cormyr," Tanalasta said. Now that she had discovered the error of her assumptions, the princess's amiable disposition toward the man was replaced by an unreasonably terse anger. "Ambassador Hovanay, you may return to your masters with our thanks—and this warning: While their armies remain on Sembia's side of the Swamprun, our countries remain at peace."

The ambassador's eyes widened in a practiced show of surprise. "Majesty, I fear you misinterpret my masters' intentions."

"And I fear I do not," replied Tanalasta.

"And *I* fear you are being too hasty," said Lord Goldsword. He dared to place a foot on the bottom stair of the dais, prompting Korvarr Rallyhorn and a dozen more of Tanalasta's bodyguards to grab the hilts of their swords and flank him.

Goldsword remained where he was. "You said yourself that our own armies are occupied in the north, and I'm sure I speak for every noble here when I say we have our hands full enough just trying to keep these ghazneths off our lands."

He glanced around the chamber and received an enthusiastic round of *hear, hears.* Only Giogi Wyvernspur, Ildamoar Hardcastle, and a handful of other dour-looking loyalists remained silent.

A terrible anger welled up inside Tanalasta and she descended a single step toward Emlar Goldsword. "Are you a coward, sir?"

Emlar's jaw dropped, and his face turned stormy and red. "I beg your pardon?"

Tanalasta descended another step, ignoring Korvarr Rallyhorn's startled head shake. "I believe my question was clear enough, Goldsword. I asked if you were a coward."

Emlar's face turned the color of Tanalasta's royal robe. He started to ascend the stairs to meet the princess—only to find the tip of Korvarr's dagger pressed beneath his chin.

"What—" Emlar was so furious he had to stop and lift his shaking jowls off the dagger before continuing. "What is the meaning of this?"

103

Tanalasta descended another step, bringing her to within arm's length of the quivering noble. "The crown demands to know." She reached out and slapped the man. "Are you such a coward that you'd rather sell your realm than defend it?"

"I—I—I ought to—"

"Careful." Korvarr pricked his dagger beneath the man's chin. "You're speaking to the throne."

Emlar glared at the princess. "You . . . are . . . not . . . the . . . king."

"No, I am the crown princess acting in his absence." Tanalasta looked to Korvarr, then said, "If that is all Lord Goldsword cares to hide behind, let us see how brave he really is. Korvarr, stand back and let him go."

The lionar's eyes flashed in alarm, but he sheathed his dagger and backed away as ordered. Tanalasta stepped down another stair, so that she was now standing eye-to-eye with Goldsword.

"Well?"

Goldsword's body began to shake so violently that Tanalasta thought he would drop dead. His hand drifted toward his sword belt, and a series of sharp chimes echoed through the chamber. Giogi Wyvernspur and a few others drew their own weapons. That was enough for Emlar, who backed off the step and turned to leave.

"Lord Goldsword!" Tanalasta snapped.

Emlar stopped, but did not turn around. "What now, Princess?"

"Now that you have answered my question, you are free to go."

Emlar paused, then started toward the door at a brisk, overly dignified march. As he passed, the other nobles looked away and said nothing.

Tanalasta waited until his steps had grown distant enough not to compete with her voice, then said quietly, "Anyone else who would rather trade our land than fight for it may join him."

She paused a moment to see if anyone would accept the offer, and Ambassador Hovanay started to leave as well.

"Not yet, Ambassador. There's something I want you to understand."

Hovanay turned. "I think you have made your point clearly enough."

"Humor me," Tanalasta said. She looked to Giogi Wyvernspur, who, having heard the audience was to be a council of war, had come to the audience dressed in a gleaming suit of steel plate. "Lord Wyvernspur, may I take it that you and yours stand at the crown's service?"

Giogi raised his sword in salute. "You may."

"Then you are to prepare an army and hide it well in your Hullack Woods," said Tanalasta. "Should even one of those sellswords cross the Swamprun, you are to visit upon Sembia all that the ghazneths are visiting upon Cormyr."

This time, Ambassador Hovanay's eyes grew genuinely wide. He glanced toward Queen Filfaeril and, finding no support there, looked back to Tanalasta. "I assure you, Princess, that won't be necessary."

"Good," Tanalasta said. "Because it angers me that I must even consider the possibility during our current troubles. You are dismissed."

Hovanay bowed rather more shallowly than he had before, then left. Tanalasta watched him depart with a growing heaviness in her heart, and not because she feared any trouble Sembia might cause. Whatever their aspirations in Cormyr, Giogi would see to it that they found the price too dear to pay.

Once the ambassador was gone, Tanalasta looked back to the nobles below. "Giogi Wyvernspur has declared himself ready to serve the crown. Who will stand with him?"

Ildamoar Hardcastle, Korvarr Rallyhorn's father Urthrin, and a handful of others stepped forward to declare their readiness to sacrifice life and fortune on behalf of Cormyr. Most of the other nobles, however, remained ominously silent. Tanalasta surveyed them silently, pausing on each lord just long enough to be sure they knew she had noted their reluctance, then came to the one true surprise, Beldamyr Axehand.

"Lord Beldamyr?" she asked. "The Axehands are not ready to defend Cormyr?"

Beldamyr's face reddened, but he did not look away.

"We are ready," he said. "When the *king* calls."

Though the refusal struck Tanalasta like a blow, she tried not to show how much it disheartened her. Even had she been given to self delusion—and she was not—Beldamyr's refusal could not be attributed to cowardice. His family was one of the few that had remained steadfastly loyal to her father during the previous year's attempt on the throne, and Beldamyr's reluctance to commit now could only be attributed to his lack of confidence in her.

Tanalasta held Beldamyr's gaze and simply nodded. "Then I will try to keep the realm together until he is able. Be ready."

She ascended the dais again, then turned to face the nobles. "Between most of us, there is little more to say. I respect your decisions, even if I am disappointed in them, and stand ready to accept your help when you are ready to fulfill your liege duties. Until then, honor me in this much: The crown hereby forbids all non-royal use of magic south of the High Road, on pain of confiscation, imprisonment, or death—depending on whether it is we who find you or the ghazneths."

There were a few grumbles, but most of the lords understood either the sense of the edict or the wisdom of keeping their objections to themselves. Tanalasta waited until the chamber fell silent again, then dismissed the assembly with a wave.

"I will hold a war council in one hour," she said. "The royal chamberlain will make messengers available for dispatches for those who attend. Korvarr, you will prepare your men for a noon departure."

The lionar bowed his acknowledgement and turned to issue the orders, and it was Queen Filfaeril who asked the obvious question.

"Departure? Where are we going?"

"Not we, Mother—me," replied Tanalasta. "I'd like you to stay with Alaphondar and continue the research in the royal archives."

Filfaeril folded her arms. "And what are *you* doing? Leading the ghazneth hunt?"

"Someone must," said Tanalasta, "and I am the one who knows them best."

ods, but he'd missed the wild, rolling northern marches of the realm.

Azoun looked out over miles of sheep-studded hills with stone-rabble and tanglestump fences, broken here and there with dense stands of trees. A lone hawk circled high in the cloudless blue sky.

Turning his head slowly, the King of Cormyr could see the rising purple and gray bulk of the Stonelands on one hand and the distant green and gold of the tilled fields nigh Immersea on the other. It had been years since he'd ridden these backlands with no more cares cloaking his shoulders than keeping word of his worst exploits from his father's ears.

A sudden thought made him turn his head to look at his younger daughter. Alusair's gaze was fixed on his face, a curiously gentle expression in her often stormy eyes. Over the last few years, the cares of the Steel Princess had been just the same as those of her young and carefree father. Azoun wondered just how much the war wizards who watched over her omitted from the reports they sent back to the king. A lot, if he knew anything about wizards.

"Gods," he murmured to Alusair, leaning his head toward her to make his lowered voice carry, "but I begin to remember, from my younger days, the real reasons you spend so much of every year out here, riding with your sword drawn and your men around you."

"Prettier perils than at court, eh?" the Steel Princess murmured back. "Though truth be told, my nobles treat me to a petty, bickering little traveling court that's all their own."

"I suppose so," Azoun agreed, eyes still on the rolling beauty of this corner of his realm. "And with all of that riding with you, why ever seek the dust of Suzail for pomp, feuding, and intrigue?"

"Why indeed?" Alusair echoed, as they shared a smile.

Azoun shook his head. Gods, but Alusair reminded him of himself—the younger, more rebellious self who'd chafed over formalities and ceremony and preferred flirtations to feasts. Why, for half the coins in his—

"My King!" a lancelord he did not know called out. "There's a man come to us who demands audience with you. He gives his name as Randaeron Farlokkeir and says he brings urgent word from court."

Azoun frowned and exchanged glances with the Steel Princess. Alusair gave him a half-smile and a gesture that said clearly: "Your trials, and you're welcome to them."

"Consider yourself in command for the next few breaths, ere I return," he told her with a wry smile.

"Urgent word from court" always meant "trouble." Moreover, the lancelord was obviously suspicious of the messenger. When armies go to war, many men ride with their suspicions held ready before them like a drawn sword.

"I will speak with him," Azoun told the officer. "Conduct me to him without delay."

It seemed like only a passing breath or two before Azoun found himself looking down at a travel-stained man in plain leather armor who lay gasping on his back on an untidy heap of blankets. His weapons had been taken from him, and he was ringed by the glittering points of many drawn swords.

"My King," he panted, trembling with weariness. "I am come from the Wyvernspurs with pressing news intended for your majesty's ears alone."

"Withdraw," Azoun murmured, lifting a hand without bothering to look up. "I know this man."

In truth, he'd laid eyes on the ranger only once or twice before, and had never known his name, but if Cat Wyvernspur trusted a man, that was good enough for the King of Cormyr.

Shuddering with exhaustion, Randaeron was now trying to roll to a kneeling position. Azoun put a hand on his shoulder to stop him—and to induce the more suspicious Purple Dragons to put away their blades and step out of hearing.

"How came you here?" the king murmured.

"R-ran, my liege. The Lady Wyvernspur . . . used her magic . . . to teleport me to a watchtower, well south of here. A ghazneth came and circled it before diving at me. I . . . I fought it off and ducked into ditches and ran until it flew away. Then I met with goblins . . . and fought and ran more."

"Goblins," Azoun nodded. Thus far they'd encountered only orcs. The king took note of this, then asked, "What news?"

"The Crown Princess faces troubles at court. Though her words are firm and fair, some nobles openly refuse to obey her, vowing to follow only you, sire. The Dragon Queen is similarly ignored by those who choose to do so . . . and they are many."

There came a stirring among the men standing around, a muttering without words, but Azoun never looked up from the laboring lips. The ranger coughed weakly and went on. "The situation is . . . not good. Sembian interests seek a breach in our armor, many factions at court rise like restless lions to renew old plots, dismissing the war in the north as a ploy of the crown to empty their coffers and keep their sons as royal hostages . . . and the old whispers of rebellion— Arabel and Marsember, hidden royal blood heirs, and all— are heard again in the passages of the palace and the back rooms of the taverns. The Wyvernspurs fear the Obarskyr hold on the Dragon Throne will be lost—and Cormyr itself split over warring noble ambitions—despite the real foes that threaten the realm here. All it will take, Cat says, if I may be so bold, sire, is one blade through the wrong hot-headed noble's guts, and the bloodshed will begin. You are needed, Majesty, and better you come surrounded by loyal and ready knights, in strength, to slay any thoughts of daggers in royal backs or ceilings spell-sent down onto crowned heads."

The king nodded, allowing the wry ghost of a smile to touch his lips. "I can tell there's more, yet. Speak."

The ranger let out a deep and unhappy sigh, then said in a rush, "Princess Tanalasta looks unwell and—not content, yet she seems determined to personally destroy the ghazneths. The more they're seen, the more she rushes to cross blades with them."

He and Azoun stared into each other's eyes for a long, shared breath, both of them keeping their faces carefully expressionless, before the ranger added quietly, "I, too, have a daughter left alone in this, sire. The Wyvernspurs are not the only ones who fear that Cormyr may soon lose its heir."

"So it would be best," Azoun murmured, "if I reached the ghazneths before the princess does." Another smile twisted his lips before he added, "And even better if I had some sort of plan in mind for defeating them when we do meet."

"Majesty," Randaeron agreed carefully, "it would."

Azoun nodded. "You've done well. Stay in the field with the Princess Alusair, I charge you, as I take the men we can best spare here and head south in haste to hold my kingdom." He strode away, murmuring, "And if the gods really smile upon me, perhaps I'll even win myself a little rest. Old lions, however stupid, deserve to lie down once in awhile."

Randaeron knew he wasn't supposed to officially hear that last royal remark, so he let his eyes close and kept silent. Silence is often the best court policy.

14

he echo of a distant splash rolled down the river behind Vangerdahast and faded into nothingness. The wizard turned and looked toward the sound. The water was as black as the foul air, and the air was as black as the contorted walls, and the walls were as black as a chimney flue—save that instead of soot, they were covered in some black scum that seemed half moss and half stone. Circles of the stuff floated on the water just a few inches beneath Vangerdahast's chin, stinking of must and mildew and some ancient filth he did not dare consider, given that he was in a tunnel just one level beneath the city of the Grodd.

The cavern remained ominously quiet, but at the last bend behind Vangerdahast, the scum circles were rising and falling ever so slightly on the river surface. The wizard looked at the tiny crow leg hovering above his palm, which he was holding above the water more or less at eye level, and saw that it was still pointing forward. The ghazneth remained somewhere ahead—so what was behind?

Visions of albino sharks and cave-dwelling anacondas began to fill his head, but Vangerdahast dismissed these fears as unfounded nonsense. Such creatures needed a steady diet, and the goblins—the only substantial food source he had found in these caverns—had repopulated their city only recently. It seemed more likely that a patch of scum had simply fallen off the ceiling and made the sound as it landed. Much more likely.

Vangerdahast continued down the passage, following his makeshift compass down one fork of a three-way intersection. If he was right about the ghazneth's identity—and he sincerely hoped he was not—the thing was Rowen Cormaeril, the handsome young ranger whom Princess Tanalasta had found so unfortunately infatuating. The wizard had last seen them together in the foothills of the Storm Horn Mountains, when the pair had pulled free of his grasp to avoid being teleported back to Arabel. At the time, Vangerdahast had been furious with the pair, but now he was—well, now he was scared to death. If Rowen had become a ghazneth, he could not bear to think what had happened to Tanalasta.

The water grew a few inches deeper, and the wizard tipped his chin back and slipped his feet carefully along the bottom. Holding the torch so high tired his arm, and he wondered whether it might be wiser to cast a spell of light on the crow's foot. With both hands full, he would have a difficult time defending himself if there *was* something behind him, and there was a very real possibility of stepping into a hole and dousing the flame anyway.

But casting a light spell would mean feeding Nalavara more magic, and he was worried about how close he had come to freeing her already. A few hours after his near capture at the goblin tower, Vangerdahast had taken advantage of his pursuers' lingering confusion to return to the great plaza and sneak a peek at Nalavara. To his horror, he had found a dragon fully six hundred feet long, with the remains of his weathercloak, wands, rings, and other magic items lying dull and drained of mystic energy around her head. Though she was still attached to the ground along one flank, writhing in the air were four tree-sized legs, a wing large enough to shade the Suzail Palace, and a spiked tail half the length of the Royal Parade Ground. The sight had frightened Vangerdahast so greatly that when the inevitable cohort of goblins found him out he very nearly allowed himself to be captured rather than cast another spell. Only his determination to track down the ghazneth and find out what had happened to Tanalasta had convinced him to flee.

Another splash sounded in the cavern behind Vangerdahast, louder and more certain than the last. The noise was followed by a hissed chitter, and for a moment the wizard could not grasp what he was hearing. It could not be goblins—not when the water was so deep it soaked his beard to the chin. He listened and heard a soft, rhythmic purling, and his disbelief changed to dismay. They had followed him—and his own nose told him how. Though he had grown accustomed to the acrid stench of his torch, the smoke it produced was heavy and rancid and must have seemed like a beacon to the goblins.

Vangerdahast glanced one more time at the crow's leg in his palm, then thrust the butt of his torch into a small wall crevice. The flames began to lick a loose sheet of black crust, and almost instantly the edge began to smolder, sending plumes of ghastly smelling smoke rolling along the ceiling. Chuckling quietly at the thought of what the bitter stench would do to the goblins' sensitive noses, the wizard set off into the darkness.

A few minutes later, the goblins seemed to realize what was happening and filled the tunnel with angry chittering. Though Vangerdahast was already feeling his way around the next bend, he paused long enough to look back down the passage into what had become a flickering ring of fire. The goblins were paddling into view on rough-hewn logs, sitting three and four to a raft with their legs dangling in the water and using crudely shaped paddles to propel their craft forward. As they approached the burning wall, they squealed and pressed their faces into their elbows, trying to shield their heat-seeing eyes from the flames.

The first log hit the wall and spilled its passengers into the water, and it became apparent that goblins could not swim—at least not in bronze armor. The second log seemed to be staying on course, so Vangerdahast backed around the corner and turned into the darkness—then let out a cry when he saw a pair of pearly eyes shining down on him from above.

The cry elicited a cacophony of chortled commands and sloshing paddles from the goblins, but Vangerdahast had no time to react before a hand grabbed him by the beard and hauled him onto a small rock ledge.

"I am growing tired of saving you, Old Snoop," said the same husky voice he had heard earlier. A powerful hand caught Vangerdahast's wrist and plucked the enchanted crow's leg from his palm. "Were I you, I would not rely on my good graces again."

Vangerdahast's heart sank, for there were only a handful of individuals who knew him by Tanalasta's favorite nickname—and Rowen Cormaeril was one of them.

"Stay here, old fool." Rowen dropped off the ledge and slipped into the water as silently as an owl slips into the air.

"Rowen, wait!" Vangerdahast rolled to his belly in the darkness and began to feel for the edge.

The goblins' voices rose in a sudden panic, then a tremendous wind roared through the passage, stirring the water into a splashing frenzy and threatening to tear the wizard from his perch. Vangerdahast pressed his face to the ledge and dug his fingers into the dirt, working his hand cautiously forward until he came to a loose rock.

When the wind finally slackened to a mere tempest, he sat up and rubbed his fingers over the stone's slickness, casting a spell of continual light upon it. He would have preferred to give himself the ability to see in darkness, but that particular enchantment required either an agate or a pinch of dried carrot to activate it, and he had lost most of his spell components when Rowen pulled him out of his weathercloak at the goblin tower.

A deep glow arose within the rock, flooding the passage with magical light and illuminating the ghazneth at the bend of the passage. Though the wind was roaring past his head and the water crashing against him in waves, Rowen stood upright without any hint of effort, his long hair hanging to his collar motionless, straight, and utterly undisturbed.

Finally, no more sounds were heard from the goblins, and the wind slackened to a mere bluster. Rowen glanced back once, then looked away and started around the corner without causing the water to ripple or purl even slightly.

"No you don't, Rowen Cormaeril!" Vangerdahast swung his legs over the lip of the ledge and dropped into the water, then splashed down the passage after the ghazneth. "Come back here, coward! Stand and present yourself!"

Much to Vangerdahast's surprise, he rounded the corner and found himself looking up into Rowen Cormaeril's murky face. With a sturdy brow, prominent cheeks, and cleft chin, the scout's features were still chiseled and handsome. They were also more gaunt and pronounced than Vangerdahast remembered, so that the overall effect was one of power and domination.

"Do I look like a royal scout to you?" Rowen's hand seemed to twitch. Vangerdahast found his wrist locked in the ghazneth's grasp. "The time when I must take orders from you is long past."

"No one has released . . ." Vangerdahast had to swallow to wet his dry throat. "No one has released you from your oath. I am the king's Royal Magician and superior to every soldier in the land. You will do as I as command . . . unless the blood of all Cormaerils runs treasonous."

Rowen's eyes grew white with anger. His grasp began to tighten, and Vangerdahast's fingers came open of their own accord. The ghazneth glared at him for a long moment, perhaps debating whether to continue squeezing, then plucked the glowing stone from Vangerdahast's hand and began to absorb its magic.

"For someone reputed to be the most cunning man in Cormyr, you are certainly the fool," said Rowen. "I would think you would know the consequences of using magic by now."

Vangerdahast began to breathe easier. "I do, but you have made yourself difficult to reach. It was the only way to find you."

"You have found me now." Rowen absorbed the last of the light from Vangerdahast's rock, then dropped it into the water. "And I pray you are done mocking me. Do not be so bold again."

Ignoring the menace in the ghazneth's words, Vangerdahast reached out blindly and caught his arm. The flesh was firm and cold and as slimy to the touch as that of an eel.

"I did not come to mock you," the wizard said. "To kill you, perhaps—or to ask your aid, depending."

Rowen's eyes continued to glow white. "Depending on what?"

"On what became of Tanalasta," Vangerdahast said.

The anger faded from Rowen's gaze. He turned away, plunging the cavern into total darkness.

Thinking his quarry was slipping silently away, Vangerdahast sloshed forward—and ran headlong into the ghazneth's back.

"I left her with Alusair," said Rowen. "I was leaving the company to find you, and they were on their way to Goblin Mountain. That was the last time I saw her and knew it to be certain."

" 'And knew it to be certain?' " Vangerdahast echoed.

Rowen grabbed the wizard by the shoulder and led him up the passage, guiding him onto a slick incline that climbed up onto the ledge where he had been earlier.

"It was perhaps a day after the battle at the Farsea Marsh," Rowen began. "Your company lay floating and bloated in the water, and the orcs were still looting the bodies. I discovered a note in Alaphondar's spyglass charging whoever found it to report to the king that the scourges of Alaundo's prophecy were awakened. I took the note and was about to start for Goblin Mountain when your horse, Cadimus, broke out of hiding in some willows at the edge of the marsh.

"As Cadimus crested the hill, the ghazneths noticed him and left their keep. It was all I could do to get mounted and into the woods before they were on us. They hunted me the rest of the day. One even ambushed me as I crossed a clearing and latched its talons into my shoulder before I dragged

116

it into a tree. That night, I decoyed the monsters by activating my cloak's throat clasp and sending it downstream on a log. I slipped away and was no more than a day from Goblin Mountain when I heard her."

"Tanalasta?"

There was a pause in which Vangerdahast could imagine the ghazneth nodding, then Rowen continued, "She was screaming and begging me to kill her, and . . . and I couldn't bear it. I knew Alaphondar's message to be even more important than Tanalasta's life, but I was in love, and I went after her.

"The ghazneths turned northward and started to play games, scraping her along the treetops above my head, landing on the other side of a meadow and making her beg for death until I used my escape pocket to reach her, then snatching her away and flying off before I came out of the after-daze. By then, I knew they didn't want to kill me. They were just luring me northward into a trap, but what could I do? I was too exhausted to think straight and terrified of letting her suffer. Even if I had turned back they would have killed me on the spot."

"No doubt," said Vangerdahast, trying not to sound unsympathetic. "But what of Tanalasta?"

"I . . . I don't know," Rowen said. "Before I knew it, we had crossed to the north side of the Storm Horns again. The last I saw her, King Boldovar had her on the far rim of gorge, and he was . . . he was doing something unthinkable to her. I went mad and used my escape pocket to reach his side of the canyon. But when I came out of the after-daze, she wasn't there—only my cousin Xanthon, laughing and holding me over the canyon by my collar, threatening to push me in after Tanalasta."

Though he was already in the dark, Vangerdahast closed his eyes and whispered, "Very good."

"Very good?" echoed Rowen, sounding less surprised than he might have. "Then it *was* a decoy?"

"Our own trick used against us," Vangerdahast confirmed. "Boldovar can create illusions. He did the same thing to us at the Farsea battle, and it nearly cost Alaphondar his life."

"It has cost me more than that, I fear," Rowen continued. "I slipped my iron dagger out and managed to plunge it into Xanthon's stomach, then held on as he stumbled back from the edge of the rim. Boldovar started after me, then the others appeared, and I took Cadimus and fled into a grove of the largest trees I can ever recall seeing.

"The ghazneths stopped at the edge and stood there hurling the vilest curses I've ever heard, and I couldn't understand why they didn't come after me until I looked around and saw the elven glyphs. They were similar to the glyphs we found on those twisted trees over the tombs Boldovar and the others came from—except these trees were not twisted and diseased. They were all beautiful and healthy, and when I ran my finger along the letters, the songs made me cry. Even the ghazneths fell quiet until the music was done."

"A whole copse of Trees of the Body?" Vangerdahast gasped.

A Tree of the Body was a sort of memorial created by the ancient elves who had inhabited Cormyr before men. According to Tanalasta—and the princess was known for being well read on such things—when an esteemed elf died, his fellows sometimes inscribed his epitaph on the trunk of a small sapling and buried the body beneath the roots. Vangerdahast did not understand all of the subtleties of such commemorations, but he had never before heard of even two of the majestic trees being found in a single location, much less a whole copse.

"You are sure they were Trees of the Body?" Vangerdahast asked.

"Later I became sure," Rowen said. "There were hundreds of them, and the ghazneths kept me trapped among them for nearly a tenday. They watched me constantly and were there waiting every time I tried to leave. One night, I decided the time had come to die or escape, and I was riding out when the ghost of a handsome elf lord rose from the ground before me. He wore a three-spiked circlet set with a single purple stone, and in his hand he carried a golden staff with the haft twisted in a ropelike pattern, and he spoke to me harshly.

" 'Nine days have thou forsaken thy duty hiding here, human, and nine days have we sheltered thee, but ere thou leave, know thy death atones nothing. To undo thy betrayal, a greater amends must thou make at a cost greater to thee than death.'

"I did not need to ask what betrayal, for I still carried Alaphondar's letter close to my heart and knew well how I had failed. I had let my love for Tanalasta blind me to my duty, and I knew that Cormyr would pay dearly for my failure. What could I do but bow my head and reply, 'Milord, I would redeem myself. My only question is how.'

"The elf warned me again of the terrible cost, and again I told him I would gladly pay. The elf smiled then and took Cadimus's reins from my hand. He whispered something in the horse's ear that caused him to nicker and nuzzle me on the cheek, then turn and flee to the far side of the grove.

"The elf spoke again. 'Know, human,' he said, 'that I am Iliphar, King of Scepters, and this grove is my burial place, where a thousand treasures have lain hidden for more long ages than I can count. Follow me that I may bestow on thee the greatest of all, the Scepter of Lords.'

"King Iliphar led me to the center of the grove, where stood an ancient oak the size of a castle keep. The ghost pointed at the base of the tree and said, 'Take my scepter and give it to thy king. Tell him that when wielded with compassion, it has the power to smite any elven-spawned evil—but only given that all the wrongs that spawned that evil in the first place have been set right. By surrendering the scepter to a human, I am righting the first. It will be for he who wields this weapon to right the other.'

"And that was all King Iliphar said," said Rowen. "He stepped away and faded back into his tree. I drew my dagger and began to dig where he had pointed. No sooner had my blade touched the soil than the ghazneths screeched in triumph and streaked in to attack. I thought for a moment they had deceived me again and tricked me into dispelling the grove's magic protection—which I am sure now was their entire purpose in luring me north in the first place—but if so, the last trick was on them. An army

119

of elf ghosts rose from beneath their trees to meet the ghazneths, and the trees wove their branches into an impenetrable net of protection. The ghazneths tore into the limbs with fire and blight, and the ghosts tore into them with sword and club. I concentrated on my digging, and it was not long before I had wormed my way well down among the roots.

"But even the elves could not hold on forever, and it seemed the deeper I dug, the weaker they grew. By the time I finally broke into Iliphar's treasure chamber, the great tree branches behind me were cracking and snapping as the ghazneths tore through. I pulled my commander's ring and activated the light spell, then cried out at all the treasure I saw heaped beneath the tree. There were hills of it, glowing with magic and crusted with enough gems to dazzle the eyes of old Thauglor himself.

"A loud rumble rolled down the tunnel from outside, then all the trees started to sing at once. I rushed into the chamber and began tearing through the treasure heaps. There were wands and staves and rods of every ilk. Any one of them and none of them could have been the Scepter of Lords, and I despaired of ever finding the right one.

"Then a terrible rasping broke out in the tunnel behind me. Thinking to bring the roof down on my pursuer, I grabbed a silver sword and rushed toward the mouth—and that is when I saw it, resting in the crooks of two roots, with a thin circlet of gold hanging from its haft."

"The Scepter of Lords?" Vangerdahast asked.

Rowen's pearly eyes rose and fell in the darkness. "It was a golden scepter fashioned in the shape of sapling oak, with finely wrought branches sprouting off at odd angles and a huge pommel of amethyst carved in the figure of an acorn. It was the most beautiful treasure in the chamber, and there was no mistaking its power.

"I snatched the scepter off its hooks and stepped off to the side of the tunnel, still fumbling with the crown on its haft as I cocked the thing back. The crimson eyes of a ghazneth appeared in the tunnel mouth, and I threw my weight into a mighty strike.

120

"But as I brought the head down, a hellish curse came from the tunnel and spilled out into the room in billowing black fumes. The ground shook and cracked beneath me. The floor gave way, and I fell into this horrid abyss, and I have been no more able to leave than you have."

"What of the scepter?" Vangerdahast's heart was pounding so ferociously he could barely hear his own question. "Tell me you didn't lose the scepter!"

"Of course not." Rowen's fingertips crackled with tiny balls of lightning, illuminating the ledge in twinkling bursts of silver. He reached behind him and produced a small, triple-spiked circlet with a pale amethyst set in the center. "Nor the crown that went with it."

Vangerdahast snatched the crown from the ghazneth's hand. It was as dull as lead, all the golden magic gone from it.

"You didn't!"

"I'm afraid I did, before I realized what I was turning into," said Rowen. "On the other hand, it was a useful lesson. The Scepter of Lords is still full of magic and hidden safely away—someplace where Nalavara's goblins will never find it, and where it hasn't been a constant temptation to me."

"That's something." Vangerdahast flipped the leaden crown in his fingers, silently bemoaning the loss of such ancient magic. He could have learned much by examining it—almost as much as he had by listening to the tale of its recovery. He patted Rowen warmly on the knee—then instantly regretted the gesture when it elicited a shudder of revulsion from the ghazneth. "You've done well, Rowen. We can make this work for Cormyr."

"How?" The ghazneth waved his crackling fingers around the cavern in despair. "How can we make this work for anyone?"

Vangerdahast smiled. "Nalavara went to a lot of trouble to trick you into breaking the power of Iliphar's burial ground. She wouldn't have done that unless she was worried about the scepter—a weapon you've kept out of her hands."

Rowen's expression brightened considerably. "We're going to kill her?"

Troy Denning and Ed Greenwood

"Not us," said Vangerdahast. He was thinking of the ancient secret that he and the other royal magicians had helped their kings keep for so many centuries. "Azoun will do it. If the scepter is to work, I fear it must be wielded by a king."

15

ears of Chauntea!" Azoun swore. "Even if they raid so savagely and so unopposed as to strip the land bare, fair Cormyr's northern reaches can't *feed* this many goblins! Where are they all coming from?"

The grim, weary officers around him didn't bother to answer. After hacking a bloody way through two walls of goblins already this day, the king's army had crested another hill to find the rolling country ahead awash in hooting, chittering goblins. The little humanoids waved their banners tauntingly at the sight of the royal standard, but held their positions as if they were the claws of a well-disciplined foe, rather than charging in their usual wild flood. The way south, it seemed, was blocked by several thousand sharp and waiting goblin blades.

"Hold ranks!" a swordlord snapped, as some of the men ahead surged forward, armor clanking.

"To Talos with orders and ordered formations now!" a nobleman roared, raising his blade. "In at them, and slay—for Azoun and for me!"

Others took up the cry. "For Azoun *and for me!*"

The king watched them charge to their deaths with frustration and pleasure warring behind a tightly expressionless face. He couldn't afford swift-tempered, disobedient idiots of nobles here in the field—or, for that matter, flourishing anywhere in the realm—but it did feel good to hear that battle cry, and see the excitement around him as men joined in, waving their blades but holding their positions under the watchful gazes of growling swordcaptains and cold-eyed lancelords.

"Let no true Cormyrean leave this height without orders to do so!" a swordlord roared, and Azoun doffed his helm to let the eyes he knew would be turning his way clearly see him nodding in agreement. He needed capable swords, not glory-seeking corpses. He also needed a way south to Suzail that would be swifter and less bloody than carving his way through all of these waiting goblins.

The war wizards had already agreed grimly that wild nursery tales notwithstanding, the army was much too large to teleport. Not even by draining all their magic items and trying a combined spell, even without ghazneths racing to pounce on any significant use of magic, could they guarantee to pluck more than a few hundred men south. Their best efforts, therefore, could only serve to scatter the army and even slay a few men with the roiling energies of the translocational magic. Even that was assuming nothing at all went wrong, and something would, they all knew. On battlefields, something always did.

There had to be another way. Even if he'd had time and men enough to march wide to the east, his Purple Dragons couldn't outrun eager goblins, or avoid running into the barrier of the Wyvernwater. That left only the forest. It would be something of a shield against spying eyes and a deadly maze for both his men and any goblins who plunged into it in search of them.

Unless, of course, he had a guide as expert as the foresters who accompanied him on his rarer and rarer stag hunts. That meant finding Duskroon's, or one of the other dozens of foresters' cottages, along the edge of the forest. Feldon was a local man. . . .

He turned to the lancelord standing nearest and said crisply, "Swordcaptain Feldon to me, at once!"

The man scurried to obey, and it seemed like the space of only two long, goblin-surveying breaths before Feldon's familiar ragged mustache was bobbing before him. "Your Majesty?"

"Good Feldon," he said, "I need the nearest royal forester of skill brought before me, well guarded and in a trice."

The swordcaptain's weathered face split in a broad smile. "Would the Warden of the King's Forest do, my liege? He's staying at Ildulph's stead, not three bow shots west."

"With all his family? In the very teeth of all these goblins?"

Feldon's smile disappeared. "Well the way of it's like this, your majesty," he muttered. "Lord Huntsilver and Goodman Ildulph are both of the mind that the royal writ is a shield for all loyal men. If the goblins aren't there by the king's will . . ."

"Then before all the gods, the goblins just aren't there," Azoun completed the sentence calmly. "Or at least they dare not attack or despoil save by royal leave."

Feldon nodded, and Azoun smiled slowly and said, "Fetch them both." Before Feldon could more than open his mouth to reply, something occurred to the king. "Bid the warden bring his family. Let the ladies be ready to march—*without* two warrior-loads of jewels and finery each."

As Warden, Maestoon Huntsilver saw to the state of all the game in the King's Forest, and all of the royal foresters, too. He was one of the few Huntsilvers capable of doing the crown so useful a service as guiding the royal army through the heart of the forest. Moreover, he was one of the few who probably would want to.

There had been many marriages between the Huntsilvers and the Obarskyrs down the years, but there were Huntsilvers who'd probably laugh to see Azoun IV laid in his grave. Maestoon's last surviving son, Cordryn, was one of those nobles exiled and disinherited for conspiring with Gaspar Cormaeril in his plot to seize the throne.

Maestoon himself, however—or so Vangerdahast had sworn, after a little covert magical spying—was genuinely ashamed of that, and anxious to return to the royal good graces. Soft-spoken and even effeminate, he was that rare thing: a forester who knew wildlife and how to encourage their breeding. He was also a courtier so skilled with his tongue and so watchful as to always say the right thing in any awkward situation at court.

Maestoon had at least two more troubles than the tendency of his sons to get themselves killed or mired in treason. He had a wife and a daughter.

His lady Elanna, much younger than her husband and a Dauntinghorn by birth, was an ash blonde of thin, sleek, devastating beauty whose dancing had been known to make watching men growl with lust—and who knew her powers only too well. She amused herself by toying with almost every noble she met, setting some against others and all to doing ridiculous tasks and pranks, purely in hopes of tasting her favors.

Maestoon's daughter Shalanna was a very different bad apple. She played her own pranks, knowing just enough magic to be malicious and dangerous to those she dared to turn it against. That one was fat and sullen, resenting her mother for being beautiful and the war wizards for not making fat Shalanna the beauty she deserved to be, and all young noblemen for courting her for her riches and standing when she knew she disgusted them . . . and everyone else, Azoun supposed, for seeing her as she truly was, both inside and out. Azoun didn't know which she-viper was worse.

Half his kingdom was under the sway of folk worse than these—the kingdom he was fighting to preserve and would someday die fighting for. Yet it was the only realm he had, and his home, and Azoun knew he'd not trade it for another if his own queen and all the other women in it were Elannas and Shalannas.

Right now, he wished Maestoon joy of them, and hoped he'd not have their blood on his hands a few days from now. He'd hate to give that sort of cold reward to so good and loyal a man.

There came the warden now, smiling eagerly at his king and bustling in his haste to serve.

Azoun watched him come and drew in a deep breath. Yes, there were a lot of good and loyal men in Cormyr he'd not want to hand the cold reward of death to, in the days ahead.

And a few others who must be stone cold insane to want the Dragon Throne for themselves.

16

hough the summit of Jhondyl's Ridge stood well hidden beneath an ancient forest of giant hawthorn and oak, the west side fell away in a steep scarp that overlooked all Cormyr south of Gray Oaks. From her camp table beneath the spreading boughs of an old ironbark, Tanalasta could mark the location of each ghazneth by the particular devastation following in its wake. Luthax's wildfires gushed smoke along the Starwater, Suzara's blight browned the fields between Calantar's Bridge and Marsember, and Xanthon's locusts boiled northward along the Way of the Dragon. The ghazneths were easy enough to locate—but what could she do to stop them?

So far, Tanalasta's campaign to save the south had been little more than a meaningless string of hard rides and costly battles. After spying a ghazneth's depredations, she and a company of handpicked soldiers would teleport to the scene to keep the phantom pinned in place until the rest of the army arrived to destroy it. Inevitably, they caused the area a lot of inadvertent damage, then finally suffered too many casualties to prevent their foe from escaping. That the creatures always seemed to appear a good half day's ride from her army struck the princess as more than coincidence, especially since she was taking precautions to keep the force hidden, but she also knew that her suspicions might be little more than the frustration of trying to catch up to a winged enemy.

A loud rustle sounded from the woods behind Tanalasta, and she turned to find Korvarr Rallyhorn leading Filfaeril, Alaphondar, and a small company of bodyguards toward her table. Hoping her black weathercloak would be enough to conceal her growing bulk from the queen's discerning eye— Tanalasta still had not found the right occasion to mention her pregnancy—she spread her arms and went to embrace her mother.

"You had a safe journey, Majesty?"

"No journey is safe these days, Tanalasta, but it was without incident." Filfaeril returned her daughter's embrace, then stepped back and eyed her up and down. "I see the hardships of the trail have not affected your appetite."

Tanalasta launched instantly into the response she had planned. "We do a lot of waiting. Sometimes it seems there is nothing to do but eat." She stepped away from her mother and embraced Alaphondar. "And how are you, old friend?"

"As well as I hope you are." The sage pressed his mouth to her ear. "Tell her soon, my dear. You are running out of time!"

Tanalasta laughed lightly, as though at some jest. "Alaphondar, that is not a very nice thing to say to a princess!" She released him and glanced over to the war wizards in her mother's party. "Sarmon the Spectacular could not attend?"

"Still too old," Alaphondar said. "The royal priests have not yet learned how to reverse the ghazneth's aging effect."

"Pity," said Tanalasta. "Perhaps Harvestmaster Foley will have some thoughts on the matter when we return."

She guided the pair to her camp table, where Owden Foley sat poring over maps and dispatches. As they approached, the priest stood and bowed to Filfaeril, who returned the gesture with a polite if unenthusiastic smile, then stepped away from his chair to embrace Alaphondar like the old friends they had become.

Tanalasta waited while one of her bodyguards pulled a chair for the queen, then sat next to her. "What news from Alusair and the king, Majesty?" She did not ask about Vangerdahast. Nobody asked about Vangerdahast any more.

"Still nothing about your friend, I'm afraid," said Filfaeril. They both knew what the princess was really asking, for the question was always Tanalasta's first on the infrequent occasions they spoke. "Alusair seems to be holding her own against the orcs. Your father is on his way south to help with the ghazneths."

"Of course." Though Tanalasta's heart sank, she tried not to show her disappointment. The mere presence of her father would draw the rest of the nobles into the fray and spare Cormyr much suffering. That it would also undo what little progress she had made in winning their respect really did not matter. The destruction of the ghazneths was too important to let concerns about prestige interfere. "I am sure the king will bring the situation quickly under control."

Filfaeril took her daughter's hand. "That's what he's best at, Tanalasta, and what he loves. You are to be commended for taking the field in his place, of course, but everyone knows that your strength lies . . . closer to the palace."

Tanalasta withdrew her hand. "Is that why you arranged this rendezvous? To fetch me home?"

"Actually, I was the one who suggested a meeting." Alaphondar took a seat across from Tanalasta, drawing her gaze away from the queen, and drew a roll of parchment from inside his robe. "I have made some progress in our research, and I thought it might be of use here in the field."

Tanalasta accepted the parchment but glanced back to her mother. "Then I'm not being recalled to the palace?"

"As much as I would like to, the decision is not mine to make," said Filfaeril. "It will be for your father to decide

130

when he arrives. Until then, all I ask—no, command—is that you be careful."

"Command accepted."

Tanalasta smiled and unfurled the parchment. It was a catalog of the six ghazneths they had identified so far, along with notes on their demonstrated powers and speculations on their motivations for betraying Cormyr. It also included suggestions as to what might satisfy the desires that had caused them to become traitors in the first place.

"This is good work, Alaphondar, they're all here," Tanalasta said, scanning the list. When she came to King Boldovar's name, she could not help glancing at her mother, whom the ghazneth had kidnapped in the early days of the crisis.

" 'King Boldovar, Scourge of Madness, master of darkness, deception, and illusion,' " the queen quoted, guessing which entry had caused Tanalasta to stop reading. " 'He loves the pain of others, and their fear. To win power over him, one must surrender.' "

"Boldovar was the only one I could not figure out," said Alaphondar. "Your mother's experience was most useful on that account."

Tanalasta let the parchment furl itself into a roll. "Mother, I had no idea."

Filfaeril merely looked away. "When you faced the other ghazneths, I am sure your own distress was just as great."

Though Tanalasta suspected it had not been, she knew better than to argue the point. Her mother had avoided speaking of the experience before and showed little inclination to do so now.

It was Alaphondar who filled the uncomfortable silence. "The list names the weaknesses of all the ghazneths, but it remains lacking."

"You have not discovered why Xanthon's powers return?" asked Owden.

"I fear not." Alaphondar shook his head drearily. "Until we understand that, I fear we must assume that any advantage we gain over the others will also be temporary."

"Well, this is a good start," said Tanalasta, tucking the scroll into her cloak. "At least it will help the advance

131

company detain them until the rest of the army arrives."

"What will?" asked a young voice at the fringe of the tree boughs. "Have we discovered something good?"

Tanalasta looked up to see Orvendel Rallyhorn, Korvarr's guileless younger brother, approaching with a tray of drinks. A squinting youth of about seventeen, he was as pale and awkward as Tanalasta had been at that age, which no doubt accounted for the sisterly affection she bore him. When the queen's bodyguards crossed their iron glaives in front of the boy, he cast a crestfallen look in Tanalasta's direction.

"I thought the Royal Sage Most Learned might like a refreshment."

Korvarr gasped at his brother's slighting of the queen, and Filfaeril herself looked rather surprised, but Tanalasta could not help chuckling. It was just like the bookish youth to be taken with Alaphondar and oblivious to the royals. She nodded to the guards and motioned the youth forward.

"Alaphondar Emmarask, may I present Orvendel Rallyhorn." She waited for Orvendel to set the tray on the table and bow to the royal sage, then said, "If aptitude and ardor count for anything, he will be Master of the Royal Libraries one day."

Orvendel's eyes grew wide. "When?"

"One day, Orvendel," growled Korvarr. Clearly embarrassed by the youth's naivete, he stepped to his brother's side and motioned to Filfaeril. "Perhaps you would like to bow to the queen, Orvendel?"

If Orvendel realized his mistake, his face did not show it. He bowed quickly to the queen and turned back to Alaphondar. "What do you think of Luthax? Because I was thinking—"

Noticing the horror-stricken look on her mother's face, Tanalasta caught Orvendel by the sleeve. "Don't you have some supplies to see to?"

Orvendel merely shook his head. "That's done."

"I think the princess is saying we would like some privacy," said Alaphondar, gently shooing the youth toward Korvarr. "If you are going to be a sage, you must start

132

paying as much attention to what people do not say as to what they do."

A cloud came over Orvendel's face, but he finally seemed to realize that his presence was something of an intrusion and backed away. "That's all right, I'll come back later." He reached the circle of bodyguards and turned, saying, "Maybe when the king gets here."

Tanalasta sent Korvarr after the boy with a flick of her eyes, then looked to her mother.

Before she could apologize, Filfaeril asked, "That boy is part of your army?"

"Not really," Tanalasta explained, "but he knows these woods better than the wolves do. He leads out the supply trains, and quietly keeps Korvarr in good ale."

A rare frown creased the queen's brow, and she looked pensively after the boy.

"Really, Mother," said Tanalasta. "You can't be thinking that Orvendel—"

"How could I?" interrupted Filfaeril. "I didn't know about him until now, but Korvarr is still on the list."

"Korvarr?" Tanalasta rolled her eyes. "That's not possible. You saw what he did when Sarmon turned him into a hummingbird."

As Tanalasta finished, the ewer and mugs Orvendel had brought began to shake. Suddenly sharing in her mother's suspicions, the princess leaped up and swept the tray off the table. The ewer shattered on a stone and spilled nothing but red wine onto the ground.

The whole ridge started to shake and rumble, and an alarm horn sounded in the top of the oak—once, twice, then something crashed into the branches and it came to a strangled halt. The queen's bodyguards and war wizards started forward, as did the princess's, and something long and green dropped to the table between Tanalasta and her mother. The princess was still trying to identify it when the thing twined itself into a coil and raised its head to strike at the queen.

"Ghazneths!" Tanalasta screamed.

Tanalasta lashed out and caught the serpent by its coil, jerking the thing away from her mother even as it unfurled

133

itself to strike. Filfaeril cried out and pushed away from the table, tumbling over backward in her chair. The snake's head hung in the air above the queen, swinging back and forth for just an instant, then shot around in a half circle and planted its fangs high in Tanalasta's breast.

A torrent of liquid fire gushed through Tanalasta's chest and spread slowly outward. The arm holding the snake grew weak and numb and dropped limp at her side. She croaked out a surprised cry and staggered back two steps and fell.

The ridge was shaken by a tremendous eruption. Pieces of slope began to slough off the escarpment and crash into the valley below. Tanalasta barely heard the roar, for a terrible ringing had filled her ears. She looked toward the sound and saw a fissure of magma opening down the spine of the ridge, spewing clouds of sulfur-stinking smoke and curtains of churning fire high into the air. The great oak listed across the fiery gap, and its trunk burst instantly into flames.

The heat made Tanalasta feel queasy and confused. She tried to roll away and found herself too weak. She managed to turn her head, then saw a dark silhouette swooping down out of the smoking boughs above her. She recognized the wedge-shaped face of Xanthon Cormaeril—those red, ovoid eyes were hard to overlook, even with a head full of fog— then saw a flurry of crossbow bolts catch the ghazneth in the side, peppering him with so much iron that he veered over the escarpment and sank out of sight.

A distant crackle came to Tanalasta above the ringing in her ears, then there was a red flash and the anguished voices of burning dragoneers. Her vision narrowed and began to darken, and somewhere far away Korvarr began to shout orders and curses.

Owden Foley appeared above her, then she felt something rip free of her breast. It was a pair of fangs. How could she have forgotten the snake? Owden's rough hand slipped under her weathercloak and ripped it free, exposing her from her collarbone to her swollen waist. He slashed the bite open with his dagger and began to squeeze the blood out, all the while calling upon Chauntea to neutralize the poison and protect her from its effects.

A circle of war wizards rushed up and stood gaping down at her. At first Tanalasta could not imagine why they looked so surprised, then she recalled her enlarged breasts and swollen belly, and the dark line running down the center of her abdomen. Owden placed his hands over the snake bite and chanted his spell, and Chauntea's healing magic began to warm her chest and surge through her veins behind the snake's poison.

A dozen dragoneers appeared next, gaping over the war wizards' shoulders and gasping at the obvious signs of the princess's pregnancy. Head clearing, Tanalasta reached for her torn robe, but found herself still too weak to pull it across her abdomen. Alaphondar appeared at her side and began to shove the circle back, chiding the gawkers for neglecting their fellows who were busy fighting the battle.

As the chastened crowd backed away, Queen Filfaeril finally broke into the circle and saw Tanalasta lying on the ground. Her eyes grew as large as saucers. She looked from Tanalasta's face to her belly, back to her face again, then to the thin pink blood dribbling out from beneath Owden's hands.

"Why is my daughter still here?" Filfaeril demanded, speaking to no one in particular. She grabbed the nearest war wizard and shoved him toward Tanalasta. "Back to the palace—at once!"

17

The cavern reminded Vangerdahast of what starry nights once looked like, save that these stars hung down around the height of his belly, winking and blinking in the radiance of the ball of lightning dancing atop the ghazneth's finger. The ghazneth—Vangerdahast still found it difficult to think of him as Rowen Cormaeril—had brought him into a strange warren of narrow passages and soaring chambers packed with thousands of small, goblin-sized iron racks. The racks looked eerily like goblin scarecrows, with anywhere from one to a dozen crooked iron arms hung with jagged scraps of metal, broken spectacles, brass buttons, bits of colored glass, anything that might glitter or gleam. No paths or trails twined through the peculiar little legion, which stood in such close array that Vangerdahast could not thread his way through without constantly stopping to unsnag his tunic hem.

The ghazneth seemed to suffer no such difficulty. He slipped through the jagged hordes swiveling his hips to and fro, sidestepping and pivoting past the little scarecrows so quickly that it was all Vangerdahast could do just to keep up. Presently, the foul stench of rot and mold began to fill the air, and the scarecrows grew so thick that even Rowen could not slip through the host without dislodging a chain of brass buttons or knocking a string of tin scraps to the slimy floor. Whenever this happened, he paused to return the object to its place, arranging it more artfully than before. Vangerdahast tried to move more carefully, but said nothing about the long string of displaced trinkets his own passage had left strewn behind.

Finally, they came to a dark clearing, and the stench grew so overbearing that Vangerdahast had to cover his nose. The ghazneth stopped at the edge and put out an arm to prevent Vangerdahast from going farther.

"Can you jump across, old man?"

"Across?" Vangerdahast glanced down and saw that he was standing on the edge of a foul-smelling pit. "By the wand!"

Rowen raised his hand, and the lightning ball expanded until Vangerdahast could see the far side of the pit, perhaps four paces away. "Can you jump that far?"

"When I was twenty," said Vangerdahast. "Now it would take magic."

"Not wise," said Rowen. He took Vangerdahast's arm and clasped it above the wrist. "Grab hold."

Vangerdahast eyed the distance and frowned. "Why don't we just work our way—"

The wizard's suggestion dissolved into a cry as the ghazneth sprang, jerking him out over the reeking pit. Vangerdahast caught a glimpse of sheer, irregular walls caked with a thick layer of brown . . . something, then his knees buckled as he and Rowen crashed down on the opposite rim.

Rowen pulled him to his feet and said, "You're the one who asked for my help. Do not insult me by refusing to trust me."

"That might be a little easier if you let go."

Vangerdahast cast a meaningful glance at his wrist, where the ghazneth's hand was sliding down toward the ring of wishes. Rowen let go so abruptly that Vangerdahast nearly fell and had to catch hold of a bauble rack.

"Let's go." Rowen backed away, his dark brow arched in horror, then started through the scarecrows again. "Once you have the scepter, we are done with each other. Take it and hide someplace I won't find you."

"I'm not going to do that. I can't." Before following, Vangerdahast allowed the ghazneth to advance a few extra steps. "Our chances are better together."

"Until my hunger grows too strong." Rowen was moving so fast that Vangerdahast began to fall behind. "Then I will steal your ring and drain the scepter. When that's gone, I'll turn on you."

"You won't," Vangerdahast said. "I can feed your hunger."

"But never satisfy it," said Rowen. "The more you fill it, the more it will grow. It is like your thirst for the crown."

Vangerdahast stopped and stared at the ghazneth's back. "My *what*? I have no thirst for the crown."

"No? Then you did not claim to be king when Boldovar wounded you?"

Vangerdahast was too astounded to reply. He had told Rowen about being wounded by the mad king but not what he had hallucinated—the wizard barely remembered that himself.

A few steps later, Rowen stopped and turned to face Vangerdahast. "It was a guess." His tone was gentler now, almost sympathetic. "But not a terribly hard one. We all have a dark seed in our hearts, and it is from that seed that a ghazneth's power sprouts."

"And what was *your* seed?" Vangerdahast demanded huffily.

"Fear," Rowen said. "Fear of never seeing Tanalasta again."

Vangerdahast was not nearly as astonished by the admission as he was by his own reaction to it. During their travels together in the Stonelands, he had considered Rowen's affection for Tanalasta a danger to the crown and done everything he could to discourage it. Now here he was, relying on that same affection to insure a ghazneth's loyalty and protect himself from feral hungers he could only guess at. The irony was not lost even on Vangerdahast. He knew the real monster between them.

Vangerdahast laid a hand on Rowen's shoulder and said, "You'll see Tanalasta again. We both will."

"And that is what I fear now." Rowen shrugged the wizard's hand off. "This is not how I want her to remember me."

"She won't," said Vangerdahast. "What is done can always be undone. I'll see to it when we escape."

"*If* we escape, wizard. Be careful of your arrogance."

Vangerdahast started to object that it was confidence, not arrogance, then thought of how long he had been in the city already. "Good advice. *If* we escape, then."

Rowen nodded, then started forward again. "And if you do escape, you must never tell her what became of me."

"If I escape, I pray you will be there to tell her yourself."

Vangerdahast's reply was careful, for there was a danger in making promises even a royal magician might find impossible to keep. He followed the ghazneth across the immense cavern, past another dozen pits—at least judging by the smell and the irregular crescents of dark clearing—and untold thousands more iron scarecrows. The chamber narrowed to a small passage crammed full of racks and baubles, with a long sliver of a black pit running along one wall, then opened into an immense room where the scarecrow legion stood even thicker.

The ghazneth threaded his way through the darkness into the center of the chamber, then stopped at the edge of another pit. This one was so large that the far side remained swaddled in darkness, even after Rowen doubled the size of the lightning ball on his fingertip.

"Down there." Rowen pointed into the rancid hole.

Vangerdahast dropped to his knees and peered down. The wall dropped away more or less vertically, though it was hard to be certain beneath the thick layer of brown gunk clinging to the sides. Somewhere below—he could not tell how far in the flickering light—lay a tangled mass of what looked like . . . sticks?

"Do you see it?"

139

"Not without better light," Vangerdahast said. "I can't be sure what I'm seeing."

Rowen dropped to one knee and thrust his arm down into the pit to illuminate the bottom, plunging the rest of the cavern into darkness.

A loud chime rang out behind them, as though the sudden murk had caused someone to stumble into an iron scarecrow.

Rowen extinguished his lightning ball at once.

"Goblins?" Vangerdahast whispered.

"Not here," came Rowen's soft reply. "Not following us."

Scraps of tin and glass began to tinkle as the unseen stalker broke into a rush. Vangerdahast snatched a stone off the floor and started a light spell. He had not even reached the second syllable when Rowen shot a ball of silver lightning into the cavern roof.

In the brilliant flash that followed, Vangerdahast glimpsed a sinewy woman with flaming red hair dodging through the scarecrows toward them. Though her skin was fair, she was as naked as Rowen and far more powerfully built, with scaly red wings unfurling behind her back and a pair of fiery, diamond-shaped eyes glaring in their direction.

"She's free!" As the cavern sank back into darkness, Rowen pushed Vangerdahast away from the pit. "Go!"

But Vangerdahast had a better idea. He turned and flung himself into the pit. He gave himself a single heartbeat to vanish over the edge, then spoke a single word that slowed his fall to that of a feather. Seeing no reason to avoid magic now that Nalavara was free, he pulled a crow's feather from his pocket and spoke a long series of mystic syllables, then swooped down to snatch one of the sticks off the pit bottom.

Vangerdahast pulled into a steep ascent, flying blindly into the pitch darkness above. He pictured the scepter Rowen had described earlier, a long golden staff carved into the semblance of a sapling oak, then plucked a few hairs from his woolly beard. Leaving the direction of his flight to chance, he rubbed the hairs over the length of the stick and quietly uttered the twisted syllables of a little deception spell.

The first clue of his enchantment's success came in the form of the heavy pulse of Nalavara's wings, approaching from straight ahead and rapidly growing louder. Vangerdahast veered left and narrowly escaped a roaring cone of flame, which splashed against the far wall and brightened the entire cavern. The wizard glimpsed the scaled figure of a two-hundred-foot elf woman changing into a giant dragon, then again fell sightless when she closed her mouth and the flames vanished.

Vangerdahast cast a spell of light upon the stick in his hands, revealing what appeared to be an oak sapling of pure gold, with an amethyst pommel carved into the shape of a huge acorn. The wizard swung the staff to his side and saw Nalavara's huge mouth, all fangs and tongue and now completely reptilian, swooping into the light. He dived beneath her, then nearly lost control of his flight as her jaws boomed shut behind him.

Flying beneath the dragon seemed to take forever. He passed between her first set of legs without incident, for Nalavara was still smacking her jaws and did not yet realize she had missed him. Her scales were the size of tournament shields and as thick as doors, and when Vangerdahast came to her abdomen, the heat of the fire burning in her belly was enough to sear his flesh. Had he spread his arms and held the staff out to its full length, he would not have spanned half the breadth of her body. As he passed beneath her wings, the turbulence nearly knocked him from the air, then a pair of taloned feet appeared in the light, reaching forward out of the darkness to slash at him blindly. He steered dead center between the huge claws and still had an arm's length to each side.

Knowing better than to risk her thrashing tail, Vangerdahast plunged groundward and turned toward the narrow passage by which he and Rowen had entered the chamber. If he could lure her out of the cavern, he would send his counterfeit scepter streaking off on its own and teleport back to recover the real one.

Nalavara wheeled around, glancing off the wall and filling the cavern with an enormous crash. Knowing his light spell would draw her eye like a beacon, Vangerdahast dropped to within a foot of the iron scarecrows, making wide erratic turns in both directions. The ploy failed miserably. As he neared his goal, a stream of fire shot past overhead and filled his escape tunnel, forcing him to dodge to one side and duck into a nearby hole.

For a moment, Vangerdahast dared hope it would not matter. The passage was as narrow as the first and packed even more densely with the same iron scarecrows. He streaked twenty paces forward—then was forced to pull up short when he came to a gray dead end.

The ground rumbled, and the wizard knew Nalavara had landed behind him. He dropped down among the iron scarecrows and jerked one out of its base, then thrust it toward the entrance and began a spell.

Vangerdahast had barely started the incantation before Nalavara's snout blocked the mouth of the passage, her nostrils already boiling with fire. He rattled off the final syllables, sighed in relief as a thick wall of iron sprang up before him—then shrank away as the dragon's fiery breath crashed into his magic barrier.

The roar continued for what seemed like several minutes. An orange circle appeared in the middle of the wall and slowly spread outward, pouring so much heat into the tunnel Vangerdahast thought he would burst into flames. The iron began to melt and drip out, and long tongues of flame poured through the hole, licking at the tunnel's end and turning the bauble racks white with heat. Vangerdahast pressed himself to the side of the passage and crept closer to the iron wall, where he would be more sheltered from the flames.

Finally, Nalavara's breath gave out, leaving a huge circle of white-hot iron between the wizard and his foe. He remained pressed against the wall, confident as ever that he would survive but trying desperately to find some way to turn this to his advantage.

"Sir Magician?" rumbled Nalavara's voice.

Vangerdahast thought about remaining silent, then decided he would be better served by confidence. He took a deep breath and stepped in front of the hole.

"Still here, Nalavarauthatoryl." He tipped the counterfeit Scepter of Lords briefly into view. "I understand you have been looking for this? Feel free to come and get it."

A ghastly chuckle rumbled through the cavern outside, then Nalavara tipped her head, blocking the mouth of the passage with one of her huge eyes.

"I think not, wizard. You have proven more . . . challenging than I thought."

"Shall I take that as a compliment?" Vangerdahast asked. Seeing no sense in allowing his foe more of a chance than necessary, he tipped the scepter out of sight. "Or have you decided to surrender?"

Again, Nalavara chuckled. "You are not that stupid. But you are dissatisfied. I could satisfy you."

"I trust your proposition is not a carnal one?"

"Hardly. You know what I have planned for Cormyr, so your dream of ruling that particular realm is impossible."

"I see you have been eavesdropping."

"More than you know, wizard." Nalavara's eye was replaced by a half open mouth filled with teeth as tall as men. "But there will be a realm left when I am through—a realm free of men but in need of a ruler nonetheless."

"How very generous of you," Vangerdahast said. "So you intend to give Cormyr to a bunch of goblins? No wonder Iliphar's ghost rose against you."

"The Grodd will defend the Wolf Woods!" Nalavara hissed. "They will not yield it to a band of murdering humans." Her voice grew calmer. "And you . . . you will be their ruler."

"I will?"

"If you give me the scepter."

"And if I don't think that's a very good idea?" Vangerdahast asked.

"Then destroy it yourself." The dragon lowered her eye, again blocking the passage. "It is all the same to me."

"All I need do is pick up the iron crown?"

"It is waiting for you in the palace," Nalavara said. "Wear it, and you are master of your own kingdom."

"A kingdom of goblins?" Vangerdahast stepped back behind the iron wall. "I think not."

Nalavara remained ominously silent. Vangerdahast closed his eyes and pictured himself standing beside the pit where he had left Rowen, then hissed his teleport spell. There was that instant of colorless, timeless falling, then he found himself lying on his side gasping for breath, staring up into a dark fissure between two teeth the size of wagon wheels. In his teleport after-daze, he could not imagine how he had managed to shrink himself to the size of a rat and end up in a terrier's mouth.

"Magic? With me here?" rumbled a deep voice. "You are not as smart as I thought."

Finally recalling the situation, and recognizing by the scaly lip above what had happened, Vangerdahast smashed the golden scepter against the dragon's teeth.

The staff broke in two, and Nalavara flinched, jerking her head around and flinging the wizard across the dark chamber. He crashed down among the iron scarecrows, then rolled to a painful halt and found himself staring at his hand, watching the glow fade from the stump of a broken little thigh bone. Though recovered enough from his teleport after-daze to recall that the scepter in his hand had been counterfeit, he couldn't think of why he should be holding a goblin's femur.

Nalavara's head swung in his direction, then disappeared from sight as she spat out the top half of the thigh bone. "Fraud!"

Vangerdahast rolled away before the stub could strike him, then found his escape blocked by a dozen iron scarecrows and began to think the situation more serious than he had imagined.

"Rowen?" he called. "Help?"

A bolt of lightning crackled up from the opposite side of Nalavara and silhouetted her immense snout against the black vastness. Her head swung away and disappeared into the darkness. There was a booming crack as her jaws came together, and Rowen howled in agony.

Vangerdahast knew what he had to do. "I wish Nalavara out of existence!" he cried, rubbing his ring of wishes. "I wish

144

Nalavarauthatoryl the Red out of existence! I wish Lorelei Alavara out of existence!"

The cavern went suddenly quiet, then a familiar flickering glow began to illuminate the scarecrows fifty paces distant.

"Rowen?" Vangerdahast called.

"Aye, wizard, it's me." The ghazneth stood and tried to walk, then doubled over backward and collapsed. "But why in the Thousand Hells did you not make your wish *before* she bit me in two?"

ery good progress, Your Majesty," Warden Huntsilver confirmed. "We can judge how far we've come by certain trees that mark the distance along the trail. There's one of them: Velaeror's Oak, named for the swordcaptain buried there, after his valiant death fighting brigands, by your great, great—"

Azoun. The voice in his mind was warm and familiar, yet sharp with an urgency he'd seldom heard before. It took a lot to break Filfaeril's outward calm. The king put an imperious hand on Maestoon Huntsilver's arm, and the quick-witted and sensitive warden of the King's Forest fell silent, instantly devoting his attention to guiding the silent Azoun smoothly along the root-studded trail, so that the king need not even look down . . . or anywhere.

Faery, I am here, he replied silently, fumbling behind his belt buckle for the little catch that would release what he might need. To the gods' dark places with all ghazneths! He was king in this land, and he'd use his ring if it seemed needful. *What ill?* Another three identical rings tumbled into his hand. The only spares he possessed—perhaps all that still existed. He held them ready to touch to the one on his finger, not caring, just now, if he burned all the magic in the royal treasury.

Gods, but he'd missed Faery's voice—even if it did now bring dark tidings.

Tana has been wounded, and—as many now know, though she keeps secrets well—is pregnant.

Azoun was more amused and pleased at his eldest daughter's spirit than angry, though he knew he should be furious at the keeping of a secret that could so endanger the crown. *Do you approve of the father?* he sent to his queen, not hiding his feelings, as he touched one of the rings to the one he was wearing, and it flared up with a bright pulse that they felt in their linked minds like a racing line of fire.

I have not yet met the father, she replied tartly, *so it is difficult to—*

Her touch faded. Hastily Azoun thrust another ring against the first. In an instant, it blazed up and was gone. Gods, would all magic prove so fleeting?

Come to me, my lord love. Filfaeril's voice was stronger now, almost pleading. *Whatever Tana says or does, I need you. More than that, Cormyr needs you here, if only briefly.*

I come in all commanded haste, Azoun sent wryly, ending the contact with the wordless rush of emotion that they used in lieu of a kiss across the miles between their lips.

"Warden," the king said smoothly, shaking the ashes of a crumbling ring off a blistered finger and sliding his last replacement onto it without heed for the pain, "affairs of state call me away, perhaps for a short time, but more likely for longer. You are to obey Swordlord Ethin Glammerhand as you would me, and guide all here safely and swiftly through this my royal forest. The good Swordlord is . . ."

Azoun turned to find and identify Glammerhand, only to find him walking right behind them. "Here, my liege," the swordlord said promptly. "I have heard, and will obey. Your needs now?"

147

"Halt and rest the men, but speedily send to me the Lord Mage Arkenfrost."

Glammerhand bowed his head and turned to give the orders. Remaeras Arkenfrost was the ranking war wizard accompanying the army, and a calm, shrewd diplomat to boot—eminently suitable for teleporting himself and his king into the midst of a possibly tense court confrontation. He was also, as it happened, carrying many healing potions and other beneficial magics brought along to safeguard the king and officers. Azoun disliked many of what he liked to privately call "Vangey's Brood" because they were arrogant, ignorant of the real world, openly ambitious and overeager, or suffered from all of these faults at once, but there were exceptions—mages he liked on sight and respected increasingly the more he saw of them. Arkenfrost was one such mage.

Azoun felt a rush of warmth now as he saw the man hastening toward him in response to the subtlest of hand signals from Glammerhand. Ever-tired eyes like those of a hangdog hound, pepper-and-salt beard, well-tailored but dark and plain robes worn over warrior's boots . . . what a war wizard who served Cormyr before his own interests should be. Perhaps they could say and do the right things to rein in the more fractious nobles and set things to rights at court, then return to this army soon.

"Your Majesty?" the wizard asked, kneeling as if he was an oath-sworn warrior. Some of Vangey's Brood never knelt, even at the most formal state occasions.

"Good Lord Mage," Azoun greeted him, clasping the mage's work-hardened hands firmly and drawing Arkenfrost to his feet, "I've urgent need to be at court, at the side of my queen. How soon can the two of—"

Something blotted out the sun overhead. Something dark and large. Very large.

Almost instinctively Azoun drew in under the shading boughs of the nearest tree as he peered up at the biggest red dragon he'd ever seen.

Just above the treetops it hung, gliding more slowly than he'd thought the lightest bird could manage, its sharp eyes fixed on the warriors of Cormyr. Dragoneers and lionars suddenly erupted into a whirlwind of shouting, trembling, and vomiting. Some men drew their swords and hacked wildly at those nearby, or at the empty air. One man stared fixedly ahead and began to foam at the mouth, while another sank down drooling something yellow from his blackening, bloated face. Others began to scratch feverishly, whimpering, and Azoun saw a bristling green mold spreading over the limbs of one such victim, coating armor and flesh alike with horrifying speed.

"They come for us! They come!" one man bellowed, attacking the nearest tree with such insane force that his sword bent under the force of his blows. A swordcaptain beyond him started to howl like a hound.

"Swordlord," Azoun said evenly, "are *your* wits still about you?"

Ethin Glammerhand was sweating like a river, and a muscle was working on one side of his jaw, rippling in endless, uncontrolled spasms, but his voice was steady enough as he replied, "I-I think so, my liege."

The king drew his sword and said, "Bring all of the mages and priests to me, speedily if you think they are as stricken as these men here. Use any officers you can trust to disarm and truss those doing harm to others. Worry not about chasing those who flee into the forest."

"Forthwith, Your Majesty," the swordlord snapped, and leaped away into the confusion of shouting, staggering men with a stream of bellowed orders. The sound of his voice seemed to steady some of the demented, but Azoun had eyes only for the war wizard standing beside him, and the point of his blade was raised and ready.

"Arkenfrost?" he barked.

The Lord Mage smiled thinly. "I believe my wits are unaffected, Majesty," he said. "In answer to your query, we can be standing beside the Dragon Queen in the space of two breaths. If I must now use magic to heal or quell maddened or injured clergy or mages, it will of course take longer to be elsewhere."

Azoun grimaced rather than grinning. "You're as sound as any of us, I guess."

149

Glammerhand was already trudging back toward them, head swinging constantly from side to side as he shot glances around at the tumult of men among the trees. "If any of the holy men or the mages were affected, Majesty, they've recovered speedily and thoroughly enough to conceal their afflictions entirely from me."

"Can you handle those affected without us?"

"With all respect, Your Majesty," the swordlord growled, "I can do so better if I need not watch and worry for the king's safety."

"Get gone, then?"

Ethin Glammerhand's frowning face split in a real smile. "Eloquently put, my liege."

Azoun gave him an answering smile, sheathed his blade, and turned to the waiting lord mage. "Arkenfrost?"

The war wizard inclined his head, and reached forward his hand to touch Azoun's wrist. "To the queen," he murmured and cast his spell.

The world was suddenly a place of blue roiling mists, shot through with lightninglike flickers of brighter, lighter blue, through which Azoun was endlessly falling . . .

. . . but suddenly on solid ground—or rather, somewhere that moved underfoot, as warm and fetid as a slaughterhouse charnel pit, all rotting meat and damp rushing air. Somewhere slippery.

Shaking his head to clear his eyes of the after-daze, Azoun clung to the reassuring firmness of the sword in his hand, and crouched low, trying to listen, and keep his balance. He seemed to be somewhere dark and warm that was rapidly getting darker.

Abruptly he realized that the dark bulk immediately in front of him was a gigantic tooth, long and sharp, and that it was one of a line of teeth. He was in the mouth of a huge creature, standing on a tongue that was rising under his boots like an inexorable wave, to hurl him forward into the reach of those clashing fangs! Arkenfrost was already tumbling ahead of him. Gods preserve—they were in the mouth of the dragon!

The fangs drew back, Azoun's world suddenly brightening,

150

and an instant later the King of Cormyr was plunging helplessly forward, borne on the reeking wind of the dragon's
breath. In a moment those cruel teeth would clash down,
and he'd be cut in two or crushed.

Shuddering, the Most Royal Flower of the Obarskyrs
kicked out hard against the slippery tongue, tumbled
crazily forward until his boots struck a fang, and sprang
away. Teeth crashed down, someone screamed, and the
king was suddenly in utter darkness and awash in stinging
fluid—fluid that seared like flame, and swiftly acquired the
iron reek of fresh human blood. Arkenfrost was probably
now dead.

The dragon's teeth parted again, light flooded in around
the king, and Azoun flung himself between them, out into
the brightness beyond.

He was falling, tumbling away beneath the huge red
dragon as it flew on over the forest, its jaws working—not,
it seemed, having noticed his escape. His weathercloak's
featherfall magic would save him from a smashed-bones
death when he reached the ground . . . if, of course, the
dragon didn't see him and come flying back to bite and
swallow.

The King of Cormyr watched the wyrm dwindle into the
distance, and wondered grimly how Arkenfrost's spell had
taken him into the red dragon's maw. A twisting of magic on
the dragon's part or the act of some unknown foe . . . or the
treachery of Arkenfrost himself?

No sane man seeks his own death, but . . . Azoun
Obarskyr had been wrong when judging men a time or two
in his life before.

Yet not, he thought, this time. It was all too easy for any
king to start to see conspiracies in every shadowed chamber
and deceit in every word that fell from any lips. And to what
purpose? If every man's hand is raised covertly against the
king, what profits said monarch from acting differently?
How does it help the realm, or keep a royal head on its accustomed shoulders for a breath or two longer?

The dragon, it seemed, was not coming back, and this was
undoubtedly the King's Forest beneath him, the tops of its

thick-standing trees approaching swiftly now. It was a long fall, cloaked in the magic that would save him from a killing landing ... too long a fall. Goblins had bows, and many forest beasts had keen eyes and the habit of looking aloft for approaching trouble. Or meals.

Azoun drew his sword and devoted himself to peering all around and down at the trees rising to meet him. If nothing threatened, he might as well enjoy the view of his realm ... perhaps the last look at it he'd ever have time enough to enjoy.

Or perhaps not. Something was streaking at him from the south, coming low over the trees, and coming fast. A small, dark fleck against the blue sky, rapidly becoming a larger dark spot, with wings.

Aye. A ghazneth. Azoun swallowed, finding his mouth suddenly dry, and licked his lips grimly, raising his blade and slapping at the hilt of his nearest dagger to be sure of just where it was.

Gods, but they were fast! The leathery black wings were almost a blur as the ghazneth swept up to the slowly descending king. Azoun saw two thin arms, two crooked legs, a lanky but unmistakably female body trailing long brown hair, and a face whose eyes glittered with hatred and the rising fire of the hunter eager to slay. Her fingers had become impossibly long talons—hooked, cruel claws whose needle-sharp tips seemed cloaked in clinging drops of dark liquid. Poison? Or the blood of her last victim?

The ghazneth climbed in the air as she closed with her drifting target, and Azoun steadied his blade, holding it in both hands. On and down she came, with a wordless shriek of anger. Azoun waited, his sword held low and a little behind him, for just the right moment to strike. The ghazneth beat foul wings in a flurry to slow then swoop then slow again, trying to fool him but sacrificing the sheer power of a swift pounce.

She twisted at the last moment, banking past him to claw and scream, and Azoun swung his blade in a hard, round-house slash, cutting mainly air and feathers but biting into something as the ghazneth flapped strongly away and dipped one wing to loop around. She was trying to come at him from behind as he fell, turning uncontrollably in the wake of his swing and her strike, and Azoun snarled silently in determination and twisted, trying to throw himself around to meet his foe.

He was only just in time. The ghazneth was gliding right at him, talons raking the air so as to present him with a whirling wall of death. He ducked his head to protect his eyes and slashed the air, chopping hard and swiftly to keep her from getting inside his reach.

A talon got through, cutting a line of fire across his head. The ghazneth trying to blind him with his own blood. A second talon just caught his cheek as he twisted his head back and away and drove his blade solidly through a flailing wing and into the back and thigh beneath.

The ghazneth screamed, a raw, rough cry of anger and pain. Azoun found himself in the blind heart of a dark flurry of stinking wings that buffeted him like the winds of a spell-spun tempest he'd once been caught in. The fury ended only when she twisted away from his blade and spun in the air, the magnificently-muscled line of her naked back momentarily only a foot or so from his nose, to strike at him face to face.

His sword, its everbright enchantments gone at her touch, was behind or beyond her wings and useless, but the King of Cormyr was ready. As her talons swept up and she drew back her legs to kick, she met his dagger, hard and full into her breast.

Azoun grimly set aside the fact that this was a weapon-less woman and his own blood-kin, and kept stabbing, pumping his arm and keeping his legs drawn up to protect himself. She spat blood at him, breast heaving under his blade, but her shrieks and squalls soon became coughs, and she faltered in the air and drew away without striking home with a single talon.

Where she had struck earlier, though, Azoun felt a sickening weakness, and a trembling was beginning. Her wounds were closing as he watched, while his own were festering—no, worse than that. As the weakness spread, his

153

skin was withering and the flesh beneath it was rotting, a dark and spongy blight that was spreading swiftly. Soon he'd not be able to hold his sword. He had to end this quickly or have it ended for him.

Bringing his sword back in front of him like a leveled lance to keep her at bay, he felt in his codpiece for the magic he'd hoped not to have to waste this soon in the defense of Cormyr. He sought to distract his foe with the taunting, polite purr, "And whom, Dark Lady, have I the pleasure of slaying today?"

Her reply was a scream of bubbling rage out of which he could only just discern the name "Suzara" before she plunged in again.

The king was ready. He swung his sword aside and threw the small iron globe in his hand full into Suzara's face. If only its explosive magic persisted long enough to work, in the face of the magic-starved ghazneth's draining of dweomer . . .

It did. In a flash of raging radiance the sphere burst apart in leaping hoops and bands of cold iron that swung out into the air, dimming and flickering as Suzara flung back her head and gasped in unmistakable pleasure. The iron bands shrank in with lightning speed to tighten around the fell creature.

Gods be thanked! They were crashing through branches together now, Azoun and his monstrously transformed ancestor, and already the iron bands were crumbling away to white flakes and gray ashes as the ghazneth greedily drank their magic, but as they tightened the bands of cold iron burned Suzara, lacerating her limbs. The king saw her trapped wings spasm and writhe in pain as she tumbled past the last few boughs and smashed into a dark, stagnant forest pool.

Its waters danced away from the crippled ghazneth, then slid back over her like an eager blanket, leaving no trace of her but a few bubbles that soon slowed, then stopped.

Not dead, Azoun knew, just down out of battle for a time . . . and probably not a long time. He'd best be away from here in haste, and without using more magic than he had to, either, not with a dragon gliding along just above the trees sniffing for it.

Healing was needful right now, though he probably required more than he was carrying. Azoun drained the two steel vials that rode in his boots, hefted his no-longer-magical blade, and set off through the damp green depths of the forest in the direction of the army he'd left behind such a short time ago.

The King of Cormyr felt surprisingly cheerful, despite the small concerns of a ghazneth behind him, a dragon lurking somewhere above, his kingdom hanging in the balance as orcs and goblins raided, the very real possibilities of meeting with a forest predator or just failing to meet with his troops in the vast and trackless trees ahead—and, of course, the danger that the rotting brought on by the talons of the ghazneth would claim him before he reached any aid, or leave him staggering when he did find a foe.

The very thought brought a fresh spasm of weakness in his cooling, trembling limbs and sent him staggering sideways against a tree. His smile, however, was a real one as he concentrated on Filfaeril's image, bringing his queen to mind as he liked to remember her best, arching to meet his chest a-bubble with laughter, lusty fingers tugging at his hair . . .

He felt the wry warmth of her awareness as she shared and appreciated that memory. *Faery*, he said silently into her mind, *I've been, as courtiers say, unaccountably delayed—but I'm alive, I'm coming, and never doubt*, dying to see you.

155

19

s Vangerdahast circled down into the pit, a fork of lightning cracked across the cavern ceiling, illuminating the host of spear-shaped stalactites overhead. An instant later, the chamber was dark again, and a soft drizzle began to fall, deepening the stench of rot and decay that rose from below. Vangerdahast stopped his descent and hovered in place, looking up toward the rim of the pit, where Rowen Cormaeril sat watching.

"Do you mind? This place smells bad enough as it is." Vangerdahast lowered his light and saw that the tangle of "sticks" he had glimpsed earlier were in fact small bones. "What the devil is this hole, anyway?"

"A goblin grave," Rowen replied.

A handful of mold-covered lumps that might have been fresh bodies came into view. There was also a glint of gold, buried well down among the skeletons.

Rowen continued, "When goblins become a burden on their clan, their children give them an iron tree. They bring it here, string all their treasures on it, and jump."

Vangerdahast nodded. "Very practical of them. I take it that's the reason they never come here?"

"The reason they never leave," Rowen corrected.

The ghazneth raised his face to the drizzle and closed his eyes in concentration. Though it had only been a short while since Nalavara had bitten him apart, all that remained of his wound was a pale scar across the top of his abdomen. After collapsing to the ground in two pieces, Rowen had pulled himself together and asked Vangerdahast to start pelting him with magic. The wizard had blasted him with magic missiles, lightning bolts, and any other spell he could cast with the components at hand. Some of the magic did stun the ghazneth for a moment, but most of it he simply absorbed and used to regenerate himself. It was the most frightening thing Vangerdahast had ever seen, at least until he recalled the other six phantoms wreaking havoc on Cormyr at that very moment.

The drizzle did not stop, and Rowen opened his eyes. "I can't stop it." He shook his head. "All that magic . . . I'm out of control."

"Ah, well . . ." Vangerdahast wanted to say something comforting, but could think of nothing the boy would not recognize instantly to be a lie. "A little rain never hurt anything."

"A little *rain*, no, but we both know it won't stop there. You should kill me now, before I become the Seventh Scourge."

"We'll have no talk of that kind," Vangerdahast said sternly. He felt at more of a loss than he had since Aunadar Bleth had managed to poison Azoun on that fateful hunting trip. "I doubt I *could* kill you. To become a ghazneth in the first place, you had to betray your duty to Cormyr *and* rob an elven tomb. Do you think I can just wave a hand and undo that?"

Rowen considered this a moment, then shook his head. "I suppose not. It is the darkness of my betrayal that makes me a ghazneth, and a ghazneth I will stay until that betrayal is forgiven."

"If that were so, you would be a ghazneth no longer. Your betrayal was small enough as such things go." Vangerdahast did not add that he himself had made worse mistakes for less cause and still not turned into a ghazneth, but he had never opened an elven tomb either. "I, for one, have already forgiven you."

"But *you* do not wear the crown of Cormyr." Rowen let his chin drop. "That will be the hardest part of this—to admit to Tanalasta that *she* was the reason I betrayed my oath." He remained silent a moment, then turned his pearly eyes back to Vangerdahast. "You should have let Nalavara kill me."

"I couldn't. The realm still has need of your services," said Vangerdahast, hoping he had finally hit on a way to lift Rowen's despair. "We must get the scepter to Azoun."

"But you wished Nalavara out of existence," said Rowen, as always too observant for his own good. "Three times. I heard it."

"And she no longer exists here, wherever *here* is." Vangerdahast raised his hand and displayed the ring of wishes. "Unless this damned thing worked better for me than it ever has for any of my predecessors, Nalavara remains a force to be reckoned with, and you may be our only way of getting the scepter to Azoun."

"Me?"

"When the change takes you," Vangerdahast explained. "Xanthon could come and go at will. As you become more of a ghazneth, presumably you will, too."

"And you think you'll be able to trust me?" Rowen asked. "With the scepter in your hand?"

"That's the reason I risked what I did, yes," said Vangerdahast, "though you may have to leave alone if it proves impossible for me to go with you."

Rowen laughed bitterly and stood. "If I must leave alone, I think it would be wiser for you to kill me." He began to back away from the edge of the pit, and said, "What good will the scepter be to Cormyr if I have drained all its magic?"

20

lusair let her arm fall and nodded in grim satisfaction as the banner beside her dipped for the last signal.

Obediently, at the head of the valley, a banner dipped in answer.

"Positions," Alusair murmured almost absently, her eyes on that distant height.

Men moved to their bows and the bristling "flowers" of arrows standing ready in the turf, the few hopeless shots taking up bills and pikes behind the archers. They'd step forward only when the charging foe were mere paces away.

It seemed to take only a few quick breaths before the first smoke drifted up. Alusair smiled grimly.

"Welcome to *our* cookfires, you eaters of men," she said aloud, reaching for her own bow. It shouldn't take long now.

Orcs had no more love of smoke than men and could no more resist ready food and water. Alusair's men had driven the few stray sheep they'd found down to the ponds in this valley the day before, setting the perfect lure.

Like stupid beasts the orcs had plunged down upon the prize. They even fought among themselves over who'd get mutton for evenfeast. They were down there now, and Alusair had made ready their next meal: massed volleys of arrows, right down their throats.

Smoke was rising in dark clouds now, the breezes driving it right down the valley.

"Waste no shafts," Alusair murmured, repeating the order she'd given rather more forcefully some time ago. "Fire only at tuskers you can see."

There came a snarling out of the smoke, then its cause. Orcs were running hard, some with unlaced armor bouncing askew, but all with weapons out and ready. Red eyes glittered with rage and smoke-smarting pain, seeing the doom to come and knowing there was no way to escape it.

All around Alusair bows twanged and death hummed. The Steel Princess chose a target, sighted, and let fly. She plucked up another shaft from the sheaf standing ready even before her victim threw up its hands to claw at the air, her shaft standing out of its throat, and fell over on its side in the dust. It rolled under the running feet of orcs who stumbled and fell, but kept coming—only to sprout swift thickets of arrows and fall in twisting spasms of pain.

A barricade of writhing orc bodies was growing across the mouth of the valley. The slaughter was as impressive as it was swift. Unless they dared to tarry among the vultures for other orcs to kill while they tore free their shafts to use again, Alusair's warriors would have very few arrows left to loose at later foes. Not that arrows were much use against the dragon she expected at any moment. Lord Mage Stormshoulder had hazarded a spell to warn her of what it had done to her father's army, and she had seen it winging across the horizon not long after setting this trap.

As if that grim thought had been a signal, a dark and sinuous shape appeared over the hills on the horizon. Alusair cursed and cried out, "Into the trees! Break off battle and *run!*"

Some did not hear her through the screams and whistling of arrows and the clang of blades rising from the few places where orcs had managed to stagger through the storm of shafts and reach the waiting line of Cormyrean pikemen, but a horn echoed her order, and the warriors of the Forest Kingdom started to move.

That was when Alusair saw the first dark line of orcs stream over a nearby hilltop, then more, over the next hilltop. Gods, but there must be a thousand thousand of them!

"Move, gods *damn* you!" she raged, waving her blade. The dragon was growing in size with almost breathtaking speed.

It was going to catch her army on the hillside well shy of the trees. They were right in the open, as helpless as the sheep she'd left for the orcs.

Alusair saw some of her swordsmen scrambling in among the arrow-bristling heaps of orc bodies across the mouth of the valley, and others staggering as they gasped for air in their haste. She saw a few turn and ready their pikes or bows in vain but valiant defiance as the dragon's dark shadow swept down.

A shadow that was abruptly banished by fire—a long, blinding torrent of flame, unhampered by trees or rock barriers or a dragon harried by spells or wounding weapons—a deluge of searing flame that blackened and laid bare half the hillside, and gave the men on it no chance to even scream.

Alusair could have sworn that the roaring sound coming out of the dragon as it swept past, its belly low enough for her to touch if she'd leaped high, was mocking laughter.

Dark red death swooped up into the sky, wheeled, and came down again. Alusair raised a blade she knew was useless and watched the dragon come.

It spread its huge wings above and behind itself like two huge sails that cupped the air and slowed its racing bulk. Alusair heard the air rippling over them with its own roar in the instant before the dragon pounced.

It snatched up two huge clawfuls of men in its talons and squeezed, reducing the men to bloody bonelessness even as it crashed down on vainly running warriors and rolled, crushing hundreds more with its great weight and flailing, smashing wings. It bit at men as it rolled playfully, twisting to and fro on its back like a gigantic dog. Alusair snarled at it in futility, never slowing her race for the trees.

161

She half expected the great red dragon to rear upright and start plucking up clawfuls of trees like a petulant child tearing up flowers from a garden. Instead it roared out its triumph in a wordless bellow that rang back from the hilltops and was echoed by orc throats on all sides, before it sprang into the air and flew away, looping and wheeling in the air almost as if it was taunting the surviving humans below.

Alusair crashed into a tree with bruising force, reeled away, and shook her head to clear it of images of horses and their riders bitten in two with casual cruelty and great talons tearing men to bloody shreds of meat.

In the space of a few breaths victory had become disastrous defeat. With a vicious snarling the foremost orcs reached the trees, raising their blades. Alusair shouted to rally her men and moved to meet them almost eagerly. To have a foe she could reach and smite and have any hope of felling was suddenly a wonderful thing.

Snarling, tusked mouths screamed as her blade bit down, and growling orcs were suddenly all around her, black blades singing out. She ducked and hacked and sprang, rolling and twisting like a young girl at play, alone among her foes. Black blades crashed together, skirling past her ear, and one bit sudden fire along her flank, cleaving armor with the force of its strike.

Cormyrean swordsmen were hacking their way to meet her, crying her name. The Steel Princess saw one man— Faernguard, that was his name—take a blade in the stomach and fall to his knees, spilling out his guts in a steaming, bloody flood. He'd barely drawn breath to scream when an orc cut his throat, jerking the head around with brutal ease.

Gods above! And what if the dragon returned? What then?

Alusair stared in horror at the men dying all around her, some of them crying her name. Men she knew—some of them men she'd bedded or gotten drunk with—died in bloody horror. They were protecting her with their own bodies . . . and their lives.

21

analasta woke feeling like someone was kicking her from the inside and discovered it was so. There was some little creature down in her abdomen, punching and pushing and trying to find its way out of her of belly. She wanted it out, too. Groggy and confused, she pushed herself up in bed and found herself looking down at a swollen belly that could not possibly be hers and saw little ripples working their way across the tight-stretched skin and tiny bulges rising where the thing was trying to push out through her skin.

"Guards!" she cried. "It's alive! In the name of the Flower, get it out!"

"Tanalasta, it's all right. Nothing is wrong." The voice was male, kindly, and vaguely familiar. A dark, work-weathered hand appeared from beside her and gently forced her head back to the pillow. "Stay down a moment. You've been asleep."

"Asleep?" Tanalasta asked, growing calmer but continuing to stare down at her belly. The thing looked more familiar now, though she still could not understand how it had grown so huge—or why it was jumping around so. "How long?"

"Not long." A weathered face with gray, close-cropped hair leaned into view, and Tanalasta recognized the man as her friend and spiritual mentor, Owden Foley. "Only a few days."

"Only a few?" Tanalasta gasped. She frowned at her swollen belly. "What happened?"

"Happened?" Owden asked, sounding as confused as she was. He followed her gaze, then chuckled heartily and laid a hand on her stomach. "Nothing bad. Your baby has learned to kick, that is all."

"My . . . baby?" Tanalasta repeated. She noticed the soreness in her breasts, and the scabs where the snake's fangs had pierced her skin, and everything that had happened came flooding back to her. She stared down at her writhing belly and suddenly felt tired and frightened and guilty. "In the name of the goddess! How could I have forgotten?"

"Forgotten, my dear?"

Tanalasta felt something wet and warm rolling down her cheeks, then realized she was crying. The fact surprised her, for she had considered herself long past tears—and far, far above the station where such luxuries could be permitted. She used the edge of a silk blanket to wipe the drops away, but they reappeared instantly, running down her face in such a torrent that they cascaded from her jaw and soaked the blanket.

A muted clanking drew Tanalasta's attention to her anteroom door, where Korvarr Rallyhorn and one other guard stood watching their crown princess sob like some delicate little girl who'd skinned her knees. Tanalasta wiped her eyes again and willed herself to stop crying, but her tears flowed all the more, unleashed by her embarrassment and a sudden appreciation of the risks she had been taking with the life of her unborn child.

Seeing that the princess's eye had fallen on him, Korvarr bowed cautiously. "The princess called?"

Tanalasta started to order him away, then realized that doing so would only compound Korvarr's concern and send a flurry of concerned whispers fluttering through the castle halls. She started to blubber an excuse about a bad dream but made it only as far as "I was having . . ." before she realized that reacting so strongly to a nightmare would make her appear even weaker. Tanalasta let the sentence trail off unfinished.

Korvarr's dark brows came together. "Yes, Highness?"

When Tanalasta could think of nothing to say, Owden came to her rescue by furling her blanket back and proudly pointing to her swollen stomach.

"The princess's child is quickening," Owden explained happily.

Korvarr looked rather confused and did a quick scan of the room, no doubt trying to fathom whether there was some secret meaning to the priest's words. When he found nothing amiss, he gave Tanalasta an uncomfortable smile.

"That is very good news, I'm sure." His gaze shifted to Owden. "Thank you for informing me."

This drew a snort of amusement from the priest. "Relax, Korvarr. No one's saying you're the father."

"Of course not! I would never do such a thing to the princess."

Owden cocked his brow. "Truly?" He looked to Tanalasta, then drew the blanket back over her. "I don't know how you should feel about that, Princess."

Korvarr's face reddened. He began to stammer an apology, then seemed to lose his way and settled for simply clamping his jaw. The lionar's embarrassment drew a deep chuckle from Owden, and the humor proved catching. Tanalasta found herself laughing and crying at the same time, then crying with laughter, then finally just laughing. She motioned the lionar over and took him by the hand.

"Don't be embarrassed, Korvarr. I may be your princess, but I'm also just a woman," she said. "A woman and a friend. Never forget that."

This seemed to put the lionar a little more at ease. He smiled stiffly, then bowed. "Thank you, Highness."

Owden rolled his eyes, then said, "Korvarr, perhaps you should inform Queen Filfaeril that her daughter has awakened. As I recall, she can be touchy about that."

"She did leave instructions to be notified," said Korvarr. Despite his acknowledgment, he made no move to leave. "But it may be some time before she is available."

"Really?" Owden looked doubtful. "I would want to be certain of that, were I you. The last time, Queen Filfaeril seemed most eager—"

"As she is this time, I assure you," interrupted Korvarr, "but she is occupied with a matter of state."

The slight furrow in the lionar's brow did not escape Tanalasta's notice. "*What* matter of state?" she asked.

The lionar glanced in Owden's direction, clearly appealing for help and receiving none.

"Lionar, I asked you a question," Tanalasta said. "Where, exactly, is the queen?"

Korvarr arched his dark brow at Owden one more time, then sighed and said, "She is in the Audience Hall with the Lords Goldsword and Silverswords, and some others."

Tanalasta threw her covers back and swung her legs out of bed. "Discussing what?"

This time, Korvarr knew better than to hesitate. "You, Highness, and what should be done."

"Done?" Tanalasta stood, then nearly fell again when her head grew light and her vision blackened.

Owden caught her by the arm and braced her up. "I know you're concerned, Princess, but you must not rush. You have been in bed for days. Go slowly."

Tanalasta paused long enough to let her vision clear, then looked back to Korvarr. "Done about what?"

"About Sembia's offer, Highness," said Korvarr. "Ambassador Hovanay has repeated it, and Emlar Goldsword has been working hard to convince the more conservative nobles that the, uh, *uncertain* paternity of your child—"

"Uncertain!" Tanalasta fumed. Practically dragging Owden along, she started across the room toward her wardrobe. "Didn't anyone tell them?"

"I'm afraid not," said Owden. "Given your previous discretion, the queen thought it best to keep the matter secret."

Korvarr scowled in confusion, but was too much the soldier to ask the question on the tip of his tongue.

166

Tanalasta answered it anyway. "There is nothing *uncertain* about the parentage of my child, and I think it's time we made that clear to Lord Goldsword and his ilk."

Korvarr mustered the courage to follow her toward the wardrobe. "I beg the princess's pardon, but I may have put the matter too delicately. It is the child's legitimacy they are complaining about. That your first born should be misbegotten—"

"It is not 'misbegotten,' Korvarr." Tanalasta could sense the disapproval in the lionar's voice, and it was all she could do not to whirl on him. "It was 'gotten' by my husband."

Korvarr stumbled over his own feet and nearly fell. "Husband?"

"Rowen Cormaeril," Tanalasta said. "And I think it is time the realm knows it—before Lord Goldsword and his cronies sell our kingdom to the Sembians."

22

he King of all Cormyr took a cautious step forward on the damp forest moss, then froze. Overhead, through the dappling of many green fingers of leaves, the light had changed. Azoun Obarskyr knew all too well what that meant.

The source of the stolen sun flashed past overhead, beating dark wings. The dragon—a red dragon as large, or larger, than any he'd ever seen—was heading south in a hurry. Azoun grimly watched it go.

Something fell in its wake, something that had spun out of its jaws to hurtle to the ground forgotten.

Something that was plummeting down so close to Azoun that the dragon's forgetting it was a very good thing.

Azoun stood as still as any tree as the something crashed into the damp leaves, bounced once, then fell still. A little dust trailed away from where it had landed, but not enough to conceal from intent royal eyes what the forgotten detritus was. It was the bloody remnant of a human leg, still encased in a boot—a boot of the sort well-to-do Cormyrean courtiers wear when they must take to the country.

The king wondered which of his subjects this grim remnant had belonged to—and if a swift, but brutal death now was going to turn out to be a fortunate thing for a Cormyrean. An instant later, he was very glad he'd kept still and silent. Hoots and hissing chuckles—goblin mirth, without a doubt—arose from just ahead of him. The sound came from at least three sides, mingled with cries of "Nalavara!" and "*Ardrak!*" That last word, he knew, was "dragon" in some goblin tongues.

No lad or lass of Cormyr over about four winters of age thinks of the deep green forests as empty, private places. The tales they're told leave them in no doubt that the woods are more alive than even barley fields with no hawks or owls about to keep the mice down. They also know that if one is not to become hunted on any woodland journey, one must have stealth, wary alertness, and ready weapons. Yet in all but the most northerly reaches of the Forest Kingdom, goblins were a woodland rarity. Azoun allowed himself a soundless curse of astonishment. A sizeable band of the scuttling vermin must be just in front of him, *very* close by. They could only be in the woods on some sort of stealthy business ... and that business, of course, could only be an intended ambush of the king's army.

Azoun Obarskyr had not played at being a forester since the most daring and pranksome days of his lass-chasing youth, but he sank down onto his knees in the soft forest moss as slowly and gently as any veteran woodsman. The lives of many Purple Dragons depended on how careful he was now. To say nothing of the life of just one Azoun Obarskyr IV.

Moreover, goblin noses and ears were keener than those of the human guards and others he'd fooled when he was younger, bolder, and more agile. He was, he hoped, just a little wiser now, so he waited until a good ten breaths after he heard the faintest rustling moving away from him before he followed. Then he crawled.

The rotting caused by the ghazneth was feeble now and would kill him as surely as a goblin blade if this took too long. Well, it would take as long as it took, that was all. The King of Cormyr wore caution like a cloak during the eternity of stealthy creeping that ensued, moving along with infinite care so as to keep the stealthily advancing goblin battle band always ahead of him.

Ahead, finally, to a place where he could hear the murmur of human voices, occasional heavy footfalls, and even the ring of an incautiously drawn blade. The goblins had led him back to his army . . . so that he could save it, if he handled this just right. Slowly, like a vengeful shadow, he drew himself to his feet, standing upright and throwing his head back to draw in the breath he knew he'd need. With but a single chance, this must be done *just* right.

"*Araga?*" a goblin throat hissed, not far away to his left. That, if his memory served, meant "Ready?"

Azoun decided not to wait for the answer. Filling his lungs, he roared as loudly as he could, "We've got them surrounded! Purple Dragons, *attack!*"

A ragged shriek of rage and dismay rose like a wall of wailing in his face. The King of Cormyr flung himself forward to the highest perch within reach—atop a moss-cloaked boulder—and planted his feet, staring intently into the furious tumult below. Surprise lost and ambush ruined, most of the furious goblins charged at the king's warriors on one front, while others turned to attack the foe who'd shouted.

Azoun Obarskyr awaited those howling goblins calmly, standing alone and swaying with weakness, but wearing a wolfish smile. His eyes were looking for just one thing: ready crossbows in goblin hands. The moment he saw one, he triggered the first of the two blade barrier spells the plainest ring on his left hand held and sprang back down from the rock.

No quarrels sped at him out of the grisly whirlwind of shredded leaves, wet goblin screams, and thudding bodies that followed. He calmly unleashed the second and last blade barrier off to the right of the first, where he could see more racing goblin bodies.

He took the ring from his finger and hurled it into the

heart of the butchery of conjured blades, watching where squalling goblins fell and where amid the moss and dead leaves their weapons landed.

When he saw what he wanted, Azoun was down from behind his rock like a striking snake. He had a cocked goblin crossbow in his hands and was darting sideways to scoop up a quarrel before any goblin nearby even knew it.

"Never," he murmured aloud as he settled himself under a thorn bush with the bow ready to fire, "was a ring of spell storing quite so valuable to the Crown of Cormyr. Have my thanks, Vangey—wherever you are."

Both the main body of goblins and almost all the leaves in the area where the spell-born blades whirled were shredded now—a dark, wet mass of huddled ruin beneath whirling emptiness. He suspected he'd not have much longer to wait before—

Like a dark thunderbolt, a ghazneth plunged down. Flashing blades melted away like mist before a gale as it drank in the magic of Azoun's unleashed spells, paying them almost no attention as it sought the ring.

Azoun calmly put his quarrel into the thickest part of its body as it stalked forward, then threw himself down, not pausing to try to recognize it. "Men of Cormyr," he bellowed up at the shredded branches above, "empty every bolt and arrow you have into this beast! Stint not! Fire at the king's will!"

He rolled upright and peered over the edge of the rock. He'd not taken the time to try to recognize the ghazneth before, and he doubted he could be sure of it now. It was almost entirely obscured by the thudding rain of arrow after arrow as the Purple Dragons enthusiastically feathered it with iron arrowheads by the dozens.

Azoun watched in satisfaction as the ghazneth staggered, took two or three frantic running steps through the trees, then beat wings that shook and trembled until it was aloft, crashing through dozens of branches in its heavy, faltering flight away.

"Purple Dragons, to me!" Azoun roared, sitting down behind the rock again. Now would not be a heroic time to take an arrow from his own men, either mistaken or deliberate. There must be some in Cormyr who blamed this war on the Obarskyrs. There always were.

In but a few moments the king was surrounded by familiar, grinning faces above breastplates emblazoned with the Purple Dragon. "Well met, Your Majesty!" a dragoneer bellowed, extending a hand to his king.

Azoun took it and was hauled to his feet. "Well met, indeed!" he boomed, looking around as armored men clustered around him. "What news?"

"More losses, my liege," one of the swordlords growled. "The war wizards, too, have deserted us."

"Deserted?"

"Easy, there," a lancelord reproved the first officer, and turned to face the frowning king. "They said they'd learned by magic that neither you, Your Majesty, nor Arkenfrost, had been seen at court. They told old Hestellen they feared treachery on the part of certain nobles—they named no names—and said they could trace you, if you stood nearby, through your clothes that they'd but lately handled. And with that they went."

"To Suzail?"

"Aye."

"Stormshoulder, Gaundolonn, and . . . ?"

"And Starlaggar," the lancelord said unhappily.

The king nodded grimly, seeing again a bloody, booted foot tumble to earth. "I fear their journey ended in the dragon's jaws," he told the swordlord. "Speak no ill of them. I'll be needing to use the healing vials of an officer or two, though, if they left no healing magic behind." He drew in a deep breath, and asked the question he must know the answer to. "How is our muster now?"

"Your Majesty," the swordlord began, his tones matching the general unhappiness, "I'm sorry to say th—"

He was astonished when the king flung up a hand in a soundless order to be silent, but obeyed, watching mutely as Azoun took two swift steps away and swung his arm to bid all of the men around him to keep silence and fall back.

Father.

Alusair's voice, in his mind, trembled on the sword's edge of helpless tears. "Yes, lass," he muttered, as gently and warmly as he knew how. "I'm here. Speak."

Utter slaughter. Dragon. Few of us left—goblinkin on all sides. I fear I can't get my men out.

Azoun threw back his head, looking up through bare, hacked branches at a sky that was thankfully free of dragons, and drew in a deep breath. He knew in that moment that he was going to Alusair's side.

Tanalasta was just going to have to deal with the problems at court on her own. The gods and all Cormyr knew she'd had long enough to get to know the nobles and their ways, and a trial by fire while a certain Azoun Obarskyr lay near death and a grasping young Bleth romanced her and sought to dupe his way onto the throne. Moreover, the crown princess had come a long way since those dark days, and learned much. In these last few months, she'd continually surprised him with the sudden flowering of her confidence and ability.

The Steel Princess, on the other hand, was a known quantity. She was a warrior who could lead Cormyr and keep it strong even if all of her kin—especially one old, white-haired, wheezing warrior who happened to wear a crown on his head—were to fall. She was a blade no kingdom should throw away, even if she hadn't been his favorite daughter.

More than that, to stride into the palace now would be to rob Tanalasta of any chance for a victory at court, or increased confidence, or a reputation for anything in the eyes of anyone, or learning anything from what had befallen—all would be swept away as "the little girl mishandling the throne ere her father returned."

It hadn't been such a hard decision after all.

"Make ready, men," he called, making sure Alusair would hear his words through their rings. "We go north as swiftly as we can, to join the force under the Steel Princess. No battle cries, now, and no noise. The dragons seem to be bad this year."

He wasn't sure who groaned more grimly at that, the men around him, or Alusair in her desperation, standing wearily on a hilltop leaning on a blade black with drying orc blood.

23

hey were sitting on the veranda of the grand
Crownsilver estate, three of them—Maniol Crownsilver himself, Duke Kastar Pursenose, and the
Lady of Pearls, Bridgette Alamber—drinking
merlot and staring out over the rolling grounds of the estate.
The lands looked as though a rare freeze had drifted in from
the north and overstayed the tolerance of its hosts. The pear
orchards had withered to neat rows of twisted black skeletons, the much-vaunted flock of Silvermarsh sheep lay
bloated and huffing in their brown pasture, and the vineyard
had vanished beneath a snowy blanket of white mold.

"A pity about the vineyard, Manny," said Lady Alamber,
draining the last red drops from her glass. "There simply is
no equal for the Silverhill merlot. I shall miss it, I'm afraid."

"We still have a barrel or a hundred in the cellar." Maniol
drained the last of the ewer's contents into Lady Alamber's
glass and set the empty container on the table edge, where
an anonymous hand in a white glove took it away to be
refilled. "I'll have a cask sent over for you."

"You're too kind."

"Not at all," said Maniol. "All I ask is that you keep it away from your magic."

"You may rest assured," said Lady Alamber. "It would be a pity to have such a fine vintage spoiled by one of these ghazneth things. Perhaps I'll even accept the princess's offer and send my magic to the castle for safekeeping."

The mockery in her voice drew a sardonic chuckle from both men, and the anonymous hand returned the ewer to the table. Duke Pursenose offered his glass to Maniol to be refilled.

"Tell me, what are we going to do about this Goldsword business?" he asked.

"*Do*?" Maniol poured for the duke. "The same thing we always do, of course—wait until the matter sorts itself out."

"Really, I don't know what the princess could have been thinking," said Lady Alamber. "It's bad enough to sleep with a petty noble, but to *marry* him?"

"And a Cormaeril at that," agreed Maniol. "Was she *trying* to make allies for Goldsword?"

"Still, there are those who feel she showed nerve, and who admire her candor," said Pursenose. "With the setbacks in the north, they say she has been showing leadership."

Maniol nodded and poured for himself. "The Hardcastles and Rallyhorns—and the Wyvernspurs, as well . . . Now that they have the old Cormaeril estates, they've become a family to be dealt with."

"Precisely the point." Lady Alamber drained her glass again. "On the one hand, she's produced an heir." She held one hand out and lowered it dramatically. "On the other hand—it's a Cormaeril." She held out the other hand and lowered it. "There's no telling who's going to win this thing."

"That is hardly important, my dear," Maniol said, refilling her glass. "What is important is that we don't lose in it."

"In normal times, yes," said Pursenose, "but with these dreadful ghazneths running about tearing the place up and orcs and goblins loose to the north . . . it's bad for the ledgers, and it could get worse. It might be less expensive if we simply choose a side."

Maniol shook his head vigorously. "And what if we were to choose the wrong side? You saw what Azoun did to the Bleths and Cormaerils after the Abraxus Affair. I doubt the Sembians would be any more gracious if we were to side with Tanalasta against them." He took a long pull from his glass, then made a sour face. "I say, the mold must have gotten to this cask."

Pursenose had already noticed the same thing, but had not wanted to insult his host by complaining. "There does seem to be a touch of vinegar to it," he said politely. "But it seems to me we're overlooking the ghazneths in all this. Aren't they the real enemy? If we let things go on like this, we'll all lose our crops this year."

"Which will only drive the price of our stores that much higher." Maniol's sly smile was tainted by a sudden flushing of the brow. "Nobody ever said it was easy to be a noble." He grimaced at a sudden burning down in his belly, but managed to keep a polite smile as he turned to draw Lady Alamber back into the conversation. "Wouldn't you agree, Bridgette?"

But Lady Alamber was not saying anything. She sat slumped in her chair, mouth agape and red-rimmed eyes staring into the sky. Bloody drool ran from the corner of her mouth and an acidic stench rose from the chair beneath her.

Duke Pursenose hissed in pain and the glass slipped from his hand to shatter against the stone patio. "I say, Maniol," he gasped, slumping down in his own chair. "This wine does seem a bit . . . foul."

Lord Crownsilver was past caring. His head hit the table with a hard thump, and a long, wet rasp gurgled from his mouth. Still gloved in white, the anonymous hand reached over and removed the ewer from the table.

* * * * *

From the King's Balcony, the Royal Gardens resembled the camp of some vast army settling in for a long siege. It was filled with smoky pillars rising from small campfires, and old sails, waxed tarps, and anything else that could serve as a tent were strung between delicate fruit trees and carefully shaped topiaries. There were people everywhere, gathered together in small, miserable groups, sleeping alone under trees, milling about listlessly looking for lost children and familiar faces. The smell of food, squalor, and aromatic flowerbeds all merged into one, creating a greasy, too-sweet aroma. The cloying smell reminded Tanalasta of an old noblewoman whose nose had grown too accustomed to her own perfume.

"They started arriving last night," Korvarr explained. "We told them the park was not for sleeping, but they refused to leave. With the royal palace so close, they said it was the only safe place in Cormyr to sleep."

"I'd be willing to argue the point with them," Tanalasta said dryly. "Let me think on the matter for a time. At the moment, I'm more concerned about these assassinations."

She turned to Sarmon the Spectacular, who sat behind her in a wheeled chair that Alaphondar had designed for him. Though she knew the wizard to be no more than fifty, he looked close to twice that age, with baggy eyes, wrinkled alabaster skin, and hair so thin she could see the liver spots on his scalp.

"You have been looking into this. What are your thoughts?"

"Lord Crownsilver and his guests bring the total number of assassinations this tenday alone to fifteen," said Sarmon. "You really must have Lord Goldsword arrested before there are more."

Tanalasta did not turn from the garden. "And we know he is responsible how?"

"By the fact that *we* aren't," said Sarmon. "He's cutting your support from beneath you."

"*Her* support?" asked Owden, standing as always at Tanalasta's side. "I thought what made these killings strange is that all the victims are neutral."

"Lord Goldsword is discovering how the nobles are leaning," said Sarmon. "Clearly."

177

"It is not so clear to me." Tanalasta turned and looked down at the old mage. "How does he find out before *we* do?"

Sarmon's wrinkled fingers tightened on the arms of his chair. "The war wizards cannot eavesdrop without drawing the attention of a ghazneth, Highness."

"Of course. I didn't mean to imply you weren't doing everything possible." Though frustrated by the situation, Tanalasta refused to be short with a man who had lost fifty years of his life defending her. She turned to her mother. "But what of our other spies?"

The queen looked away uncomfortably and said, "I am afraid the loyalty of many is only to your father. There has been little to report."

"What's wrong with these people?" Tanalasta shook her head and looked out over the refugee camp. Not for the first time, she wished Vangerdahast were there to guide here— or at least to activate his own formidable network of spies. "Can't they see how much danger Cormyr is in?"

"The only danger they see is their own," said Alaphondar. "With the setbacks in the north, I fear Goldsword's call to accept help from the Sembians is falling upon more receptive ears."

Tanalasta slapped the balustrade. "We would not need Sembia's help if our own nobles would pick up their swords and fight!" She paused a moment to collect herself, then looked to Owden and said, "I am beginning to think I should have married Dauneth. At least the nobles could not use my husband's name to flout my authority."

"They would find another excuse," said Owden. "Do you really think they would become brave only because you lacked the courage to trust your own heart?"

The priest's question allayed some of Tanalasta's anger. "I suppose not." She turned from the balustrade to her mother. "Speaking of cowards and traitors, have you had any luck locating the spy in our midst?"

Filfaeril met Tanalasta's eyes evenly. "Of course," she said. "I have known his identity for some time now."

Tanalasta began to have a bad feeling about her mother's conclusion. "And you didn't tell me?"

"It would have accomplished nothing, except to alert the spy."

Tanalasta bristled at her mother's tone. "If you know who he is, then why don't I have him in our dungeon?"

Filfaeril smiled. "Because spies can be very useful—especially the enemy's spies."

Tanalasta raised her brow and asked, "Would you care to elaborate?"

"Not at this time." Filfaeril held Tanalasta's eyes and did not look away.

"As you wish," Tanalasta said, realizing she would just have to be patient. "I suppose we're done here."

"What about Lord Goldsword?" asked Sarmon. "You *are* going to arrest him?"

Tanalasta shook her head. "If I do that, it will look like I'm frightened of him. That's no way to inspire confidence among our wavering nobles."

Sarmon's knuckles whitened on the arms of his chair, but he did not argue.

"A wise choice, but we must do *something*," said Alaphondar. "With matters as bad as they are, the people are losing confidence. They need to see you act."

Tanalasta glanced over the balustrade and cringed at the sight of all the people she was failing.

"What those people need, Alaphondar," the princess said, "is food."

The old sage frowned. "Of course they do, Highness, but what does that have to do with the matter at hand?"

"Nothing," Tanalasta admitted. She continued to stare into the Royal Garden and suddenly knew what she had to do. "Nothing and everything. Clearly, I can do nothing to stop the ghazneths, and it may even be that I can do nothing to stop Goldsword, but there is one thing I can do."

Alaphondar looked thoughtful. "And that would be?"

Tanalasta turned away from the balustrade. "I can feed my people." She motioned Korvarr forward. "Lionar, send a man to fetch the cooks, and have the bailey set with tables. I'll be down in an hour, and I expect a ladle to be ready for me."

Troy Denning and Ed Greenwood

* * * * *

They met in a place in Suzail where such meetings took place, in the dimly lit store room of a shady tavern in a seedy quarter where no decent lord would be caught dead. That was why the six nobles had donned elaborately conceived costumes and disguised their faces with false beards, why they had dyed their hair and taken such care to be certain no one had followed them. The chamber stank of stale mead, mildewed wood, and unbathed sailors. It was surrounded on all sides by rooms kept vacant at the steep price of five gold crowns each, a price which had drawn even more attention to the group than the perfumed handkerchiefs they held over their noses as they approached their hidden refuge.

Frayault Illance was speaking, his dandy's face ridiculously disguised by a purple eye patch and a trio of wax scars. "It's the princess. Natig Longflail told me himself that he had it from Patik Corr that the princess's own dressmaker told his wife that she had sewn no wedding dress for Tanalasta, and he said he would support no bastard on the Dragon Throne, be it the child of Rowen Cormaeril or Alaphondar Emmarask or Malik el Sami yn Nasser—then he was dead! Her spies found him out, I tell you, and it was *her* assassins who killed him."

"And you are not blaming the princess just because she would have none of your soft talk, Frayault?" asked Tarr Burnig. A broad and burly man who normally wore a bushy red beard, he had cut off all his whiskers and disguised himself as the guard of a merchant caravel not long from the sea wars, and he was one of the few men there who looked the part he had assumed. "Natig told me that as long as the princess was married when she made the child, he'd stand with her, and to the Nine Hells with Emlar Goldsword and his Sembians."

"And why couldn't the Sembians be the ones behind these murders?" asked Lord Jurr Greenmantle. "It wouldn't matter to them which way we were leaning at all. They could just keep killing us until there aren't enough of us left to stand with Tanalasta, even if we wanted to. She'd have no choice but to ask for their help."

The room erupted into a spirited debate, until a tall, dark-haired figure with a long beard rose and began banging his dagger on the table. "Enough! Enough!" The voice belonged to Elbert Redbow, who was neither tall nor dark, but wealthy enough to make himself appear that way for one night. "We could argue this all night, with every one of us coming to a different conclusion. I have even heard it said it could be the ghazneths—though I don't know why they'd bother. Against them, the princess has proven ineffective enough as it is."

"Hear, hear!" It was the first thing all six had agreed about all night.

"So have you a plan, Lord Redbow?"

"I do." His voice grew even deeper, and he braced his knuckles on the table. "We must stop *re*acting and start *acting*."

Again, there was agreement. "Hear, hear!"

"We'll send a man to all the suspect parties," explained Elbert. "He'll pretend to be a craven coward in fear for his own life and claim I've called a secret meeting to divulge evidence about the identity of the assassin."

"And we'll know the identity of the cur by who shows up to kill us!" cried Tarr. "A grand plan, just grand!"

"As far as it goes," said Frayault, "but what do we do after we find out?"

"You really are as slow as you look, aren't you?" asked Lord Greenmantle. "We join them, of course!"

It was at this point that someone knocked on the door. The eyes of all six lords darted toward it, and Elbert Redbow had the presence of mind to snarl, "We said not to disturb us!"

"Yes, but you have not ordered a single mug of ale," replied the tavern keeper. "How am I to pay for the room's use? You must all buy at least one drink."

Elbert snorted in disgust, then looked to the others. "What say you? I'm thirsty anyway."

Lord Greenmantle nodded and stepped to the door.

Troy Denning and Ed Greenwood

"A little refreshment never hurt anyone."

Greenmantle had barely slipped the chair from under the latch when the door crashed open and an anonymous hand tossed something tiny into the room. Elbert Redbow cursed and hurled himself across the table to make a diving catch. Something crackled, and suddenly the room stank of oil and brimstone.

Lord Redbow cursed again, and the air went scarlet.

24

eep well apart!" the swordlords shouted, turning as they strode to look at the Purple Dragons trudging along behind them and to gesture with their swords at dragoneers they judged to be gathered too closely. King Azoun almost smiled. It had been well over half a century ago when he'd first noticed that officers seemed to love pointing and gesturing with their blades. Perhaps many of them kept those swords unused and shiny in a diligent search for the greatest effect, so the steel would gleam and flash back the sun impressively when employed in such sweeping gestures.

The scouts were well ahead, their horns lofting from time to time to warn the advancing army of orc and goblin patrols or battle forays. The horn calls most often persuaded goblins to try to sprawl on the ground and await a chance to gut the unwary with knives before springing to their feet and racing away, but usually they made orcs retreat, trading muttered oaths and wary warnings. These retreats inevitably led to larger and larger whelmings in the hills ahead, until in the

183

end, the king's forces would face a tusker army.

Azoun wasn't worried about that occurring as any sort of surprise. A massed orc attack would be heralded, he was sure, by the appearance—probably involving diving out of the sky to tear men apart or incinerate them with fire—of the dragon. It seemed odd, really, that the sky had been empty of the vengeful wyrm for so long now.

If only outpourings of magic didn't bring ghazneths swooping down to the attack. If only he could use the war wizards as they should be used, so he'd know where the dragon was and what she was doing at all times. She might have torn apart Suzail by now, roof by roof and wall by wall, or sunk half the ships tied up to the docks in Marsember, or . . .

It was beginning to gnaw at him, this not knowing, and Azoun was past the age where nothing much made him fret, and even farther past the years when he'd welcomed fresh challenges atop ongoing adversities. He was beginning to be a lion of shorter temper and earlier bedtimes, who ached all too often, and who welcomed the familiar.

He was beginning to feel truly old.

Azoun answered the next swordlord's shout with a wordless snarl that made the man blink and blanch and mutter some sort of confused apology. Azoun waved it away and dismissed the matter without even looking at him. The King of Cormyr was going to die out here, sword in hand and far from Filfaeril. His body would fall cold in the rolling backlands of the realm without ever warming his throne again or seeing younglings in bright finery take their first awkward strides at court after kneeling to their king. He was—in a shining moment of firmly clasping his sword hilt and lifting his head to stare away over the endless trees and the marching purple mountains beyond—quite content with it all. If he could but snatch magic enough so that he and Faery could look into each other's eyes one last time, and say proper good-byes that both could hear . . . it would be all right. Truly. He would not mind dying out here, if die he must. After all, 'twas the lion's way . . . and like it or not, he was the old lion.

A different horn call suddenly floated up from the ridge ahead, and Azoun forgot all about the death and doom to come. It was the signal that friendly forces had been sighted. That could only be Alusair and whatever she'd managed to salvage of her noble blades.

Another, more distant horn replied, ringing out bright and clear. This was Alusair herself, telling all that she was coming in haste, with foes on her tail. All around the king, men drew weapons or checked on the readiness of daggers with a sort of satisfaction. The Steel Princess always brought either battle or revelry with her, and these men were at home with either.

The pursuing enemy would be orcs, no doubt, perhaps accompanied by the dragon. It was time to save Cormyr again.

"You'd think that after all these years I'd be good at it," Azoun remarked to the empty air, causing more than one nearby helmed head to turn in curiosity then carefully look away again. Madness in one's king is neither to be admitted nor encouraged, unless desperation descends. "I wonder if I am. While, we shall see. Aye, we shall see. . . ."

In the next moment he saw her, cresting the ridge. Alusair's armor was glinting in the sunlight and her hair streamed around her shoulders in the usual tangled mess, with her helm—also as usual—off or lost. The Steel Princess was waving her sword just as Azoun's swordlords were wont to, commanding, directing, and cajoling like any growling swordcaptain.

Prudence counseled a forewarned army to take up a strong position and await the foe, but all around Azoun men were running forward and shouting, excitement lifting their voices. The Steel Princess had that effect on the men of Cormyr who went to war. It was as if the gods touched her into flame, a beacon for men to look to and take comfort in—a beacon that was running up to him now, arms spread wide to embrace him, and with a brightness in her eyes that could only be tears. Azoun thought he'd never to be alive to see those tears again.

"Father!" she cried as she came. "Gods, but it's good to see you."

"Old bones and all, eh?" Azoun replied, sweeping her into his arms in a clamor of clashing breastplates.

Her arms were strong, and they rocked back and forth like two bears locked in some sort of shuffling dance for a moment before a laughing Alusair broke away, crying, "Enough! You can still break my ribs. I'll grant you that without requiring hard proof."

"While you, lass," Azoun murmured, sweeping her face close to his with one long and insistent arm, "can still lift the hearts of an entire army. This one of mine will follow you in an instant!"

"That's good to know," she said with sudden, quiet seriousness, "because I seem to have lost most of mine."

"That weight never goes away," Azoun replied just as quietly. "You just have to know you always spent lives in pursuit of good purpose, and cling to that. Lives used to guard Cormyr are never wasted . . . though I can't say the same for those who fall because of royal folly."

"Am I guilty of that now?" Alusair asked, looking at her father sidelong through the worst tangle in her hair. The words might have been uttered with a defiant toss of her head, but the Steel Princess was listening very intently for his answer.

Azoun did not pause to weigh his words, knowing that to have done so would have been to hand Alusair a silence more damning than any words could undo. "The only royal folly either of us has been guilty of since the present peril fell upon the realm," he said firmly, "is trying to raise armies to meet our foes in bright and ordered array—when those foes either swoop from the sky to tear bloody havoc from our ordered ranks, or swarm all over the countryside with us in chase, burning farms at will."

Alusair nodded as sagely as any of the old retired battlemasters Azoun had ever studied under, and said, "I hope that means we won't try to chase a hundred goblins along a hundred trails at once—or try to lure any goblinkin into an ordered battle up here in these wilderlands."

"I only wish that were possible," the king replied. "Try though we might, we can never get all the orcs and goblins to stand on one field and face us—so I can never strike the blow that humbles them."

"Well," his daughter replied flatly, "even if that opportunity seems to yawn open right in front of you, you *must* ignore it."

"Oh? How so?" Azoun asked, cocking his head to one side. This lass of his was sounding more like a veteran battle-master all the time. What she said next might tell him if she was already fit to be a trusted leader.

"It'll be a trap, set to lure you to your doom," Alusair assured him. "To hold the gathered might of Cormyr out here to be butchered by orcs and goblins beyond counting."

Azoun raised both eyebrows. "Is our situation so dire?" he asked, still playing a part to draw his daughter out.

"Father, it *is* that and more," the Steel Princess told him. She took two quick steps back to a high rock and sprang up on it. Azoun hid a proud smile.

"There!" Alusair snarled, pointing with her sword. "And there!"

Her father looked, knowing full well what he'd see. Scattered bands of goblins, and orcs beyond number were streaming down at the embattled Cormyreans from all sides. The tuskers were pouring over knolls and rock out-crops like rivulets of water poured over dry soil, seem-ingly endless dark fingers reaching greedily for human lives—reaching on three sides, and soon the fourth. If the Cormyreans didn't flee like the wind from this place, they'd be surrounded and butchered in vain, leaving all the realm undefended against the dragon and her raven-ing creatures.

"Sound the horns," Azoun said almost bitterly. "It's Arabel for us, though I begin to doubt if even its strong walls will be shield enough. *Gods*, look at them!"

"The ballistae and catapults on the walls should thin a few hundred out of those," Alusair mused, "though I'd be happier if we had a blade to use on them that could slay thousands at a stroke. They *are* numerous, aren't they?" She gnawed thoughtfully on her lip. "No time to dig fire trenches . . ."

"That water ditch, though," the king said slowly, "is not finished yet, if I recall Dauneth's last report. It should be dry."

"Yes . . . it should run about a mile west from the walls by now," Alusair murmured. Their eyes met, not needing words for agreement.

If the orcs could be trapped between the ditch and a hasty line of piled lamp oil jugs and brush, the ditch filled with more oil, and both set alight with fire arrows, ballistae and catapults ranged on the space between could slaughter thousands of tuskers.

"You listen too much to battle boasts, father," Alusair sighed, knowing it wouldn't—couldn't—be half so neat and easy as the king's leaping thoughts might have it.

"And I've been doing so for far more summers with a sword in my hand than you've been alive," Azoun reminded her with a grin, swatting her armored shoulders playfully with the flat of his sword.

Alusair rolled her eyes and barked in a mockery of aged gruffness, "Aye, but have ye learned which end of it to keep hold of, yet?"

The royal response was a mock thrust with the blade in question. Their eyes met over it, they chuckled in unison, and the king turned to his frowning, looming bannerguard and said, "We march on Arabel as swiftly as we can. Pass the order."

The war captains had evidently been watching. Before the hulking armored man could more than turn, trumpets blared. Men rose, lifting packs and weapons—save for those who'd served with the Steel Princess before. They looked to her, seeing just what they'd expected. Her hand was raised in the "to me" rallying signal, as she strode to where the marchers' rear guard should be.

Quietly, without any fuss, those men started to move to her. Alusair drew in a deep breath and wondered how much longer they would.

25

angerdahast was the proverbial fly on the wall in the goblin war room, save that he was actually a mouse-eared bat and, in deference to the diverse menu of his subjects, an invisible one at that. With Nalavara gone, he felt free to use all the magic he wished, so he had made use of a live spider from the kitchen's garnish box and a pinch of coal dust from the cooking ovens to cast a spider climb spell on himself as well. He was hanging quite comfortably in a high quiet corner, looking down on a sand-covered situation table surrounded by bronze-armored goblin generals. At the near end sat the high general's chair, with a back so tall Vangerdahast could not see the occupant. At the far end rested an even larger chair with a skunk fur seat, vacant save for the iron crown Nalavara had tried to press on him. Rowen was not in the room. He was outside, hiding in a small hollow near the top of the Grodd Palace, drizzling rain on twenty legions of puzzled goblins assembled in the great plaza below.

Troy Denning and Ed Greenwood

A smallish goblin in an iron breastplate rose from the high general's chair and clambered onto the situation table. The goblin—Vangerdahast still could not tell the males from the females—crawled to the middle of the table, where a thin leather strap enclosed a pebble gridwork that bore an uncanny resemblance to Arabel's street plan. Intersecting the model at right angles were four strings, each representing one of the highways that met at the Caravan City. In the quadrant between the High Road and Calantar's Way, there was even a small stand of crow feathers to represent the King's Forest southwest of the city.

A second goblin followed the leader to the middle of the table, then fished two handfuls of dead beetles from its belt pouch and tossed these onto the sand, one in the quadrant northwest of the city and one coming out of the forest to the southwest. With the others looking on, the leader carefully arranged both groups of creatures into the triple-wide ranks of a Cormyrean Heavy Company with a war wizard complement. The lead beetles of both groups converged on the High Road just west of Arabel and seemed to be heading into the city.

The goblin pointed to the company coming from the north. "The Legion of the Steel Princess is this." Having made good use of the ingredients in the palace kitchens, Vangerdahast had also cast a comprehend languages spell and recognized the leader's voice as that of Otka, the High Consul of the Grodd. "She has given our tusked allies much trouble."

Otka pointed to the company from the south. "The Legion of the Purple King is this." She held her hand out behind her. Her adjutant passed her a handful of dead ants, which she carefully arranged in two squares flanking the rear of Azoun's army. "The legions of Pepin and Rord have turned him back, and still the Naked Ones control the south."

An angry rush filled Vangerdahast's round ears. That he should be trapped here helpless while a bunch of goblins passed freely back and forth into his home plane outraged him to no end.

Again, Otka passed her hand back. The adjutant gave her a handful of cave roaches, which she arranged in an amorphous mass behind Alusair's army. When one of the creatures turned out to be not quite dead, she angrily snatched it up with a handful of sand and swallowed both down, then carefully rearranged the other roaches and smoothed the resulting divot.

As soon as she was finished, her adjutant turned to another adjutant, who produced a beautiful red dragonfly mounted on a long thin wire. Almost reverently, the assistant presented the thing to Otka, who took it in both hands and carefully sank the wire into the sand next to the High Road, so that the dragonfly hovered over the convergence of the two Cormyrean armies.

"The Giver has joined the tusked ones, and now must the Steel Princess flee into the great fortress at Four Roads." Otka jammed a finger into the great palace complex in Arabel, then said, "Here we stop the human things before they do to Grodd what was done to Cormanthor. Here we repay the Giver for all she has taught us."

Vangerdahast expected Otka to continue on, but instead she simply accepted a pouch full of dried ants from her adjutant and began to arrange them in Arabel's streets. "This way the Legion of Makr goes, to fill the east streets with fire and death. This way the Legions of Himil and Yoso and Pake go, to take the western gate and to the tusked ones throw it open. This way the Legion of Jaaf goes. . . ."

Vangerdahast listened in growing horror as Otka outlined a plan to eradicate not only the Cormyrean army but the entire city of Arabel as well. The goblin did not need to describe what would come next. Her legions would sweep over Cormyr, driving all humans from the land and reducing their grand cities to smoking midden heaps. Shadowdale and Sembia and the other neighboring realms would send troops either to aid Cormyr or to bite off what they could, but the efforts would come too late and be too small. By the time they mobilized, the Grodd would control all the crucial points—Gnoll Pass, Thunder Gap, High Horn, the port cities, Wheloon and its crucial bridge. Their numbers and

191

organization would astonish all comers, and with Nalavara to back them up, the kingdom would be theirs.

Vangerdahast listened intently as Otka rattled off assignments, trying to discern some hint from the goblin's instructions of how she communicated with the legions she had already sent to Cormyr. Thinking that perhaps Nalavara's disappearance had lifted whatever magic kept him captive in the caverns, the wizard had already tried to teleport and plane walk home, but the only result had been that he and Rowen spent the next several hours searching each other out. His luck with communication spells had been no better. Save when he tried to contact Rowen, all he ever heard back was the mad rushing of empty space.

And yet Nalavara had gone to Cormyr when he wished her out of existence, and the goblins were as free to pass back and forth as Xanthon had been. Even now, they were standing along the rim of the black void where the dragon had raised herself from the plaza, arrayed in neat ranks and ready to step through the darkness into the very heart of Arabel. Vangerdahast cursed himself for not understanding how Nalavara had imprisoned him and for being foolish enough to free her on Cormyr. The truth of the matter was he had expected everything that had happened. Had he held his tongue, Nalavara would have destroyed Rowen and perhaps him and the Scepter of Lords as well, then departed in her own time. All the wish had done was preserve his hope, and that was really all he had expected to gain.

As Vangerdahast watched Otka lay out her legions of ants—he had deduced her scale now, one ant per cohort—he thought about using the wish again. If Nalavara had been moved to Cormyr by being wished out of existence, perhaps Vangerdahast could do the same thing by wishing himself out of existence. He could tell by the way Rowen's pearly eyes were constantly drawn to the ring that it still had plenty of magic in it, and it seemed reasonable to hope that if a thing worked once, it would work again.

The trouble was that wishes *were* reasonable things. They were entirely reasonable, and it was that which made them entirely unpredictable. For the multiverse to stay in balance, there had to be a certain equilibrium to wishes, so that even as the thing the wisher asked was granted, something he did not wish also came to be. If people could simply go around wishing things without consequences, the multiverse would quickly grow unstable and spin out of control. By wishing Nalavara out of existence, he had merely taken her out of his immediate existence and placed her in another where he wanted her even less, and the multiverse had stayed in balance.

To wish himself back to Cormyr, he would have to wish for what he did not desire and hope that what he actually desired came about in reaction. He would have to wish himself out of existence but choose his words carefully enough to be certain that he came back into existence in Cormyr. That would, of course, trigger another reaction, since what he really desired could not possibly be as important as what he truly desired but did not wish. . . . Vangerdahast felt as though he were standing between two mirrors trying to find the last reflection when there simply was not one. No matter how carefully he worded the wish, he would be playing knucklebones with his own life. Even if he did find a way to cheat the spell, he would be gambling with the multiverse itself. That he could not do, even to save Cormyr.

Otka made her final assignments and turned to address her generals, reminding them of how much they owed Nalavara for bringing them the gift of iron and civilization, and that all the Giver had ever asked of them was that one day they would go stop the depredations of the human things.

As she spoke, Vangerdahast found himself staring across the room to where the iron crown sat in the empty throne. Twice Nalavara had offered him the crown, and twice he had refused it. Even if he did want to rule a nation of goblins—which he did not—he had seen no reason to trust the dragon. The offer had seemed a mere trick to bind him to her service or more likely an empty taunt meant to mock the dark ambitions everyone save the wizard himself seemed to sense lurking in his soul. He had dismissed the crown as a thing of no value to him or anyone else—and yet there it was, sitting empty in a seat of honor.

It had value to the goblins.

Still invisible, Vangerdahast dropped out of his corner and spread his wings, swooping so low over the Otka's head that she ducked and cried out as he sifted past. The other goblins looked at her as though she were mad, and she gazed around the room with wide, suspicious eyes.

Vangerdahast landed in the center of the chair and slipped his wingtips under the rim of the crown, then changed back into a man. If the goblins noticed his transition from an invisible bat to an invisible wizard, they showed no sign. The wizard found himself sitting in the throne, holding the iron crown over his head with both hands. The Scepter of Lords, which had been absorbed into his body when he changed into a bat, re-emerged in the crook of his elbow—then slipped free and clattered to the floor.

The goblins looked instantly in his direction. Vangerdahast lowered the crown onto his head, then canceled his invisibility spell and pointed at Otka. "No!"

Even Otka shrank from the thunder in his voice. Vangerdahast took the opportunity to pull a piece of twisted horsehair—goblin thread—and two tiny goblin thimbles from his pocket. He pictured Rowen's dark face in his mind and uttered a quick incantation. As soon as the ranger's pearly eyes shifted, the wizard thought-spoke to him.

Come quick. In war room, down in—

That was as much as Vangerdahast could think before he felt the spell's magic dissipating out into the iron crown. Trying not to let his alarm—or his confusion—show, he stood and pulled from his sleeve a pellet of red glass he had taken from one of the iron trees in the goblin graveyard.

In his most commanding royal magician voice, he spoke again in Grodd. "This shall not be!"

Vangerdahast pointed at the center of the situation table, simultaneously tossing the glass pellet at the model of Arabel and hissing the words of a lightning spell. Again, he felt a strange, disk-shaped surge of energy from the center of his head into the crown. A meager flash of red lightning fizzled from his fingertip and razed the tiny city. Though hardly the awe-inspiring demonstration he had planned, the spell was sufficient to cause the goblin generals to back away and press themselves to the walls.

Otka was not so easily impressed. She narrowed her eyes at Vangerdahast and said, "Where you came from?"

Drawing himself up to his full height, Vangerdahast leaned on the edge of the table and said, "Otka does not know the Iron One?"

This drew an incredulous murmur from the generals. Some pressed their palms together before their faces and inclined their heads. Others let their claws drop toward their swords and looked to Otka. She narrowed her eyes and started forward, motioning her generals to follow.

As the Royal Magician of Cormyr, Vangerdahast was as accomplished in the art of politics as any man alive, which was to say that he had no doubt forgotten more about it than even the high consul of the Grodd had ever known. He was also well versed in the worth of a symbol, so when he decided that the time had come to eliminate his rival, he did not have to think twice about how to do it. He merely pulled a pinch of iron dust from his pocket and tossed it toward the ceiling above Otka's head, at the same time speaking the words of his iron wall spell.

Instead of the strange draining he had experienced earlier, Vangerdahast's head nearly burst as the crown released its store of magic. The energy shot through him in a searing flash and left his hand. A huge sheet of iron appeared beneath the ceiling, blasting the walls apart and filling the room with billowing clouds of dust.

Otka had barely enough time to look up before the slab dropped. It flattened not only her but the generals who had been moving forward alongside her.

Vangerdahast barely noticed, for it felt as though his skull had been chopped off from the iron crown up. Dizzy, blind, and sick, he collapsed screaming into the throne and tried to tear the burning circlet off his head.

It was too tight. He could not slip his fingers under the band, nor push it up, nor even twist it around beneath his pressed palms. The thing had melded itself to his skull, and nothing he did would loosen it.

Eventually, a gentle drizzle cooled his brow to a temperature less than feverish, and the pain subsided to the point that Vangerdahast could think of something beside his aching head.

"Vangerdahast?"

He looked up to see Rowen's dark face peering down at him from atop a four-foot slab of iron. Flanking the ghazneth were a dozen goblin generals, their greenish faces paled to sickish saffron. Their iron swords remained sheathed, and they took care to keep a reasonable distance between themselves and the Naked One.

"Not Vangerdahast, you fool!" Vangerdahast hissed, glaring up from beneath his new crown. "The Iron One." He reached down and picked the Scepter of Lords up from the foot of his throne, then used it to push himself to his feet. "King of the Goblins."

26

t really doesn't matter what any of us want, Dauneth," Alusair snarled, bringing her fist down on the map-strewn table with a resounding crash. "This city is going to fall!"

The High Warden cast an anxious glance over his shoulder at the closed doors, knowing two local born men-at-arms were standing guard on the other side of them. He cleared his throat, imploring her silence with his eyes.

The Steel Princess jerked her head at a tapestry on the other side of the room. "Myrmeen's spy's over there," she said in a dry voice. "Her ears are the ones you have to worry about."

Dauneth Marliir grimaced in frustration. "Your Highness," he hissed, "I'm trying to stop any more panic!"

"Our healing kept Myrmeen alive," Alusair snarled, "averting the worst cause for panic I can think of—except for the one we lack men enough to deal with: the orcs raging through the streets! Gods, Dauneth, how can you be so dense? And to think that my moth—"

"Daughter," Azoun said warningly, "*enough*."

The King of Cormyr laid a hand on Alusair's arm and added, "Dauneth is being as loyal and as helpful as he can. Whatever schemes the queen may have had regarding weddings and your sister are neither here nor there. For the record, I think he's worked wonders, with Myrmeen lying near death and half the old families of Arabel trying to flee with the best of our horses and wagons and mounted guardsmen, while the others snarl at him for not defending them well enough and at the same time try to wring concessions and funding from him as if this crisis was intended purely for their benefit and no officer of the crown could possibly have anything better to do than offer them his ear and fawning attention. He's not beheaded a single Arabellan yet, nor thrown anyone in chains—not even bellowing princesses. Stand back and let the man do his work."

Alusair turned a gaze on her father that had raging fire in it. Dauneth Marliir quickly turned away and became intensely interested in the nearest tapestry, trying to stop the trembling that seemed to have suddenly afflicted his hands. The last three days had been a waking nightmare. The sight of orcs raging through the streets was almost as bad as seeing Myrmeen Lhal, the Lady Lord of Arabel, lying white-faced and near death on a litter made of shields that were swimming with her spilled blood. She'd held off dozens of snortsnouts before falling under three black, hacking blades. Those blades had done cruel work before the nearest Purple Dragons could fight their way near enough to protect her . . . or what was left of her.

"Father," Alusair said at last, her voice quavering in anger, "let me say jus—"

"No," the king said flatly. "Words said cannot be unsaid. We lack the time right now for Alusair's temper, just as we can't spare it for many other things. Flay my ears later, lass, but for now, be as sensible, prudent, and calm as I hear you always are in battle."

Alusair's gasp of rage was almost a sob.

"Give me your wisdom," the king continued. "You alone

know which of your men we can best put to defending this lane here or that section of the ramparts there. I need to know who the hotheaded heroes are so I can throw their lives away fighting in the streets, and who knows how to tend the sick, or remember fire buckets, or how to anticipate where orcs'll try to sneak to. Do you understand, girl?"

Dauneth clenched his fists until the knuckles went white, wishing he was anywhere but there. The silence stretched, and it seemed a very long time—until it ended, he didn't realize he was holding his breath—before Alusair said calmly, almost meekly, "Very well. You're right, Father. Turn around, Dauneth, and help us with these maps."

The High Warden of the Eastern Marches plucked an old mace and an even older shield down off the wall— almost every one of these older rooms in the Citadel boasted a dozen such relics, or more—as he turned around. He put on the shield, presented the mace to the princess, and said gently, "If you'll feel better after hitting someone . . ."

Alusair's eyes widened, something like savage glee leaping in her eyes. She hefted the mace and, to Dauneth's surprise, the Steel Princess threw back her head and laughed—as loud and as hearty a guffaw as any man's. Dauneth stood in confusion for a moment, noting the smile that rose to touch Azoun's lips, before Alusair returned the mace gently into his waiting hands.

"Well done, Warden," she said wryly. "Dense you're certainly not." She sighed and added, "But Arabel is still doomed."

"Your Highness," Dauneth murmured with a courtier's smooth half bow, "your eloquence has quite convinced me."

It was Azoun who snorted in involuntary mirth this time. "Enough sport," he growled a moment later. "Purple Dragons are dying out there." He strode to the barred doors that opened onto a balcony, and threw aside the bar.

"The maps?" Alusair ventured, raising an eyebrow.

"I'm through with maps for the moment," the king said shortly, laying his hands on the great wrought-iron door latch.

"Your Majesty," Dauneth cried warningly, "if there're ghazneths waiting out—"

"I believe I'd welcome a ghazneth about now," Azoun snarled over his shoulder, flinging the doors wide.

Nothing dark and powerful flapped at him, or reached out with claws for any of them, as the King of Cormyr strode out onto the old stone balcony to gaze out grimly over the Caravan City.

The balcony was high on the frowning west wall of the citadel. From the citadel to the western end of the city Arabel was either a battlefield or already in orc hands.

Orcish hoots and howls rose above the dirgelike drumbeats that seemed to accompany tuskers everywhere into war. The steady thudding could be heard even above the roaring of flames from the worst fires, and the clash and clang of steel as Purple Dragons waged a valiant house-by-house defense—or, to be a trifle more accurate, a fighting retreat.

Smoke hung heavy over the city. Perhaps it was keeping the dragon away. At least for this they owed some thanks to the stupidity of the orcs, who always seemed to feel the need to burn immediately after the joy of destruction and looting was spent. The orcs were coming on in waves.

"Gods," Dauneth groaned, coming up beside the king, "is there no end to them?"

"That's always the problem with goblinkin," Azoun said with dark irony. "Your scribes are always too busy fighting—and dying—to get accurate counts. Afterward, of course, it no longer matters."

"I find this inspiring," Alusair said bitterly, gripping the stone balcony rail as if it was a squalling orc's throat. "It makes me want to get down there and kill!" She flung her head around to regard her father so sharply that her hair cascaded down over the rail, making her look momentarily like a young lass trying to be seductive, and asked, "So why exactly are we standing up here when we could be of more use down there?"

"Steady," Azoun said reprovingly, then threw back his head and drew in a deep breath. "Dauneth," he said to the dark, dripping ceiling formed by the balcony above, "do you concede that Arabel is lost?"

The High Warden of the Eastern Marches cast a regretful look down over the rail, then said firmly, "Majesty, I do."

"Then we must think on how to get our people out as safely as we can. That means south, one way or another, and I hate the thought of long columns of trudging folk going down the Way. Even if we could spare the men to guide, feed, shelter, and guard them, all my mind shows me is the dragon swooping down at will to pounce and rend and roll and . . . *play*, forcing us to fare forth and fight her in ones and twos . . . and *die* in ones and twos."

Dauneth nodded grimly. "And so?" he almost whispered.

"I've some measure now of just who we're defending," the king said, waving his hand at the floor to indicate the families who'd been gathered into the citadel all the day before and this morning, "and I think we can house them in the Citadel of the Purple Dragons in Suzail, and in the palace, if need be. The women and children, at least, each with a carry-chest of family valuables and our oldest warriors to guard them. The men and boys hungry for blood and glory can stay here and fight alongside the rest of us."

"You're thinking of some sort of magic, to whisk folk from here to there," Alusair murmured. "Might I remind you that any sorcery will swiftly bring down these magic-drinking ghazneths?"

Azoun's jaw set in a line like the blade of a drawn sword. "I'm thinking of the war wizards of the realm working their mightiest magic ever, because the realm has great need of it," he said curtly. "Standing in the face of charging foes like any warrior without a hope of ever casting a spell does . . . leaping in to keep the magic working when a fellow mage falls on his face in exhaustion . . . there is no difference. A portal like the mages of old spun, a door in one citadel that opens into a door in the other, so that all of Arabel can step through it, is what we need. A single step that takes them from here to Suzail, spanning all the miles between, is all that might save them."

Dauneth's eyes widened, but the king's gaze never left the carnage below and his hand never unclenched from its ready grip on the hilt of his sword. "And if the ghazneths come," he added grimly, "we'll just have to deal with them. We'll crush them under iron ingots, dice them with iron blades . . . whatever it takes."

Dauneth's heart leaped at the king's resolve and stirring words, but he felt moved to ask, albeit tentatively, "What if we can't stop them?"

"Then," Azoun said softly, looking at him with something like fire leaping in his eyes, "the strongest Purple Dragons will stand in a human shield around the gate to keep ghazneths away while we get the women out. They are the future of the realm. Our war wizards will scatter, heading to Waterdeep and Shadowdale and Silverymoon and Berdusk—and, by the gods, Halruaa!—and wherever else we can find powerful mages who'll agree to help in return for a good share of our treasury. After all, if the ghazneths aren't stopped, no wizard will be safe, anywhere in Faerûn."

Dauneth shivered. "You would really do that?"

Azoun spread his hands. "You can see another choice?"

He let the silence stretch—a silence in which the warden opened his mouth thrice to speak, then frowned and shut it again. A silence broken by a long, despairing scream from the streets below, and a horrific crashing sound as flames ate away support beams, and three floors above a shop collapsed and fell into the street in front of it with a roar.

All three of the people on the balcony turned their heads and watched the first of the flames lick up from the tall, arched windows of the nearby palace, creeping like dark tongues up the ornately carved stone.

Azoun watched the first of its painted glass windows explode into the street in molten tears before he added bleakly, "This is what it is to be a king, Dauneth. You might tell your more rebellious kin that."

A thin smile crossed the king's face, and he added almost playfully, "Someday, that is, when we all have time for such things."

* * * * *

"Now!" a bristle-mustached lancelord shouted, his eyes on the dark form of the dragon gliding through the smoke.

The catapults let go with deep thumps, their rocking making the rampart shudder underfoot as they let go their stony loads. Most sailed short to plummet down into the ruined western city, but a few thudded home. Nalavara the Red wheeled away in anger and vanished behind the smoke.

"*Work* those wheels!" the lancelord bawled. "She'll be back, and we'll look pretty silly if she can just glide down here and tear us to dog meat. Leap to it, lads!"

The sweating crews swarmed over the catapults, sweat-drenched muscles rippling in their bared arms and backs, but Alusair turned away. "Those won't touch the ghazneths," she snarled. "Too slow—and probably no harm to them if they do take a load right in the face."

"We're ready for them, Highness," a stern-faced war wizard assured her. "All of us are ready."

"Oh?" the Steel Princess said, whirling around to face him with one gauntleted hand on her hip and the other holding a warsword it appeared she was itching to use. "And just how do you intend to deal with them, sir wizard? They'll eat your spells like a wolf biting down a rabbit."

"If Your Highness pleases to see," an older wizard said calmly, "the gate is opening right about now. The ghazneths'll be here soon enough."

Alusair looked at him, lifting an eyebrow at his confident tone ... then her eyes fell to the end of his graying beard. His fingers were locked in it, twisting nervously, already so badly tangled in the locks that most of them would have to be cut out of it.

"I'll stay," she said softly, "and be of what use I can."

An unearthly shriek rose up the nearest vent shaft, from somewhere in the citadel below, and the Steel Princess whirled around to face it. "What by all the waiting hells was *that?*"

"That," said the older war wizard, with something that might almost have been satisfaction in his voice, "would be the lady mage's pain as she opens the spell gate."

Troy Denning and Ed Greenwood

*   *   *   *   *

"They're starting," the swordcaptain muttered unnecessarily, licking his lips.

"Just stay back against the wall," the old swordlord growled, "where she told us to stand—no matter what you see. Watch, and be still. Pass the word."

That was a clear order, so the word was passed, redundant though it was. If the wizards could be believed, a magical door was to open here in Suzail—in the open space right in front of them—and the folk of Arabel would flee from that beleaguered city, flooding into this hall. The warriors waiting here would then step through the gate to Arabel and ply their blades as needed to get every last citizen out.

Every man's eyes were fixed on the two women standing alone in the center of the cavernous main hall, as they had been since the Lady Laspeera and the sorceress Valantha Shimmerstar had first calmly begun removing their clothing.

Bare and slender, now, they stood on either side of a glowing, pulsing oval of spell light, a blue-white radiance that seemed to throb around their calves as they each raised an open hand. With the small silver daggers they held, they calmly slit open their own palms.

Both sorceresses threw the knives away as violently as a man in fury hurls a goblet, and turned to face each other. From the falling blood, white fire roared into life.

The fire burst forth from their mouths as they moaned, sobbed, then began wailing. A slowly rising ululation became shrieks of pain as the fire leaped across the space between them, becoming blue-white lightning.

"Gods," the swordcaptain gasped roughly, as snarling bolts of lightning played from fingertips to thighs and breasts, and the two curvaceous sorceresses trembled, their flesh seeming suddenly to waver and flap, as if torn out of shape by gales no one else could feel. As warriors of Cormyr watched with narrowing eyes, the spell light between the two struggling sorceresses became almost blinding.

Lightning suddenly stabbed out from the forming star at the center of the chamber, reaching to the ring of naked war wizards sitting on the floor close enough to the walls for the cowering soldiers to reach out and touch—had any of them dared. The wizards whose nakedness, born of the need to preserve enchanted clothing and adornments from the ravening fire of the mighty magic being attempted here, had attracted rather fewer gazes than the two women standing in the center of the hall. Around the ring, fat, hairy men and sunken-chested bearded younglings alike gasped and wavered as the magic plucked at their vitality, calling forth the fire of their lives to build what was needed.

Their cries of pain joined the rising shriek and were echoed by the gasps of the warriors around the chamber walls, as the light suddenly became a ring. The ring raced somewhere else to become the end of a tunnel, and Laspeera Inthré suddenly threw back her head and sobbed, "Durndurve—*anchor me!* I can't take the pain!"

They saw her image rise up over the glowing ring, a large and ghostly projection of the magic. Rings of lightning raced up and down her shuddering arms. Her once bound and coiled hair was wild and free, licking around her shoulders like dark flames, as she threw her head back and wept. Flames spurted from her very eyeballs as Valantha's ghostly face, also set in pain, snarled through set teeth, "Hold on, Lady! *Hold!*"

Suddenly Laspeera's body shuddered and seemed to topple—only to rise slowly and smoothly upright again like a falling sapling righted by a forester's hand.

"Lady," a man's voice spoke, seemingly out of her forehead, "I am here. You have reached me in Arabel. You do us all great honor."

A slow and crooked smile spread across Laspeera's face as the pain fell away. She sighed, and the lightning suddenly fell from its wild whirling to coil around her breasts.

"We're through," she gasped. "Now the true test begins."

The warriors grasped their weapons firmly and peered through the still eddying starry splendor of magic at the ring, in case what came through it was a foe.

Troy Denning and Ed Greenwood

They saw a grim-faced man-at-arms, the Purple Dragon blazing on his breastplate, looking back at them over his own drawn sword. Behind him was the wide-eyed face of a woman with a babe held against her breast and behind them other helmed heads and staring women. They stood in a room some of the warriors recognized as a chamber in Arabel.

"By the gods," the swordcaptain said, his voice quavering on the edge of tears, "they've done it!"

"For Cormyr!" the first man-at-arms called, raising his sword heedless of the lightning that sprang from the gate to snarl up and down it.

"For Cormyr!" a hundred throats roared from all around the walls. Men surged forward as if a revel had begun.

For in a way, one had. . . .

* * * * *

"Now!" the war wizard commanded, and mages all along the wall clutched their foreheads and shouted in pain. There was suddenly a boulder just above the streaking ghazneth—and a moment later, another below.

As a dark head twisted upward in puzzlement at the sudden lack of sunlight, a war wizard roared in pain, falling heavily to his knees. The two rocks seemed to leap to meet each other.

There was a wet sound from between them, and war wizards all along the battlements reeled and fell. The boulders promptly tumbled from view, to strike the orc-flooded square below with a mighty crash.

"Impressive," Alusair murmured, picking herself up from where the impact had hurled her, "but look! Another comes."

The old war wizard didn't bother to rise from his hands and knees beside her. He merely bent his head, growled something, and the air suddenly held what had to be most of a toppled city house. It smashed into the second ghazneth and hurled it helplessly sideways in the air, crumpled and broken, into the nearest building that was still standing.

As the crash shook the very citadel, the battering stone broke apart into its smaller blocks and rubble and fell away, leaving a bloody smear of ghazneth down the cracked and teetering walls. The building groaned as if it was an old man, then slowly sighed into ruin, spilling down into dust.

"We can't kill the ghazneths like this," the war wizard gasped, "but we can certainly slow them."

Alusair looked down at the dust rising from the square, and half-crushed orcs screaming under scattered stones, and could see no hint of dark wings. "You're restoring my regard for wizards, I'm afraid," she said slowly.

The old mage chuckled. "Think of us as big swords who talk back to officers," he said, his voice still raw with pain, "and you may yet learn to work with us quite easily."

Alusair shook her head in amusement, then asked the smoke-filled sky in mock despair, "I had to lose a city to learn this?"

"Well," the wizard gasped, his eyes scouring the sky for more ghazneths, "you could listen to Vangerdahast a little more closely."

Alusair looked at him sweetly, then uttered a stream of oaths so colorful that the old mage winced and turned his head away—which was when another ghazneth burst out of the smoke.

* * * * *

Guldrin Hardcastle screamed as the curved orc blade burst through his fancy armor, under his right armpit, and thrust up and out of his throat—then he was gurgling forth his own blood too swiftly to scream any more.

Choking, he struggled to cry out to his brother, knowing already he was doomed and furious beyond all imagining that he was going to die here, unpraised, never to claim Hardcastle House as his own and stride into court as the head of—

"Rathtar!" at last he managed to find breath to cry. "*Rathtarrrr!*"

He'd never felt such pain—a sickening, wrenching burning that threatened to overmatch even the fire of his fury. It was tearing at his guts, it was—

He hacked and kicked, and screamed in pain at what that did to him, even louder than the orc he'd just hewn down . . . his slayer, dying now as surely as he was. Red-eyed, raging . . . and fading, fading into a deep purple dimness . . .

"*Die*, tuskers!" the Steel Princess roared, her voice as raw and deep as any man's, her sword and dagger dripping black with orc blood.

She was everywhere along the line, her blade leaping like a fang over the shoulder of this cursing, reeling Purple Dragon, and that blood-drenched, exhausted man of Arabel. Where she went, her hair streaming out behind her, men shouted their exultation and hacked and slashed with renewed vigor. It had been hard, brutal work, cutting their way out of Arabel step by bloody step with the orcs roaring all around them and the dragon swooping down time and again to spew flame or just rake away heads with its claws, as it swept past so low overhead that the wind of its passage made men stagger or crash face first onto the heels of those staggering just ahead.

The king strode into their midst, and his warden led the men and women of Arabel. Many of them were content to carry wounded fellows or the exhausted war wizards who'd worked to hold open the magical gate that had taken so many Arabellans to distant safety. Many of the marchers trembled in fear, kept from utter shrieking collapse only by the spells of the grim-faced, fearful priests who walked with them, as the dragon wheeled and glided over the Cormyreans again and again.

Alusair snarled as she saw a black orc blade burst through the mail of the Purple Dragon ahead of her. As the man sobbed and started to fall, she ran right up his back, binding the blade that had slain him in his ribs, and with the toe of her boot secure on his belt, rose on high to stab down over him, driving her blade down with both hands into the throat of the orc who'd slain the man.

The orc squealed, and the sound he was making became deeper and wetter. He stopped trying to wrench his sword free and sat back onto the trampled ground to die. The orcs all around were roaring at Alusair and straining to reach her with their curved black blades. She roared "Death to you all!" right back at them as her perch fell dead to the ground under her. The dragon's talons stabbed ineffectually at the air where she had been moments before, raking a bloody toll on the orcs instead of the fighting princess of Cormyr.

The shout came raggedly to her ears in an instant's lull in the almost deafening clash of arms: *"Rathtarrrr!"*

She spun around as she rose, slashing blindly out behind her in case any overbold orc was springing at her back and looked to where she'd thought that shout had come from.

She was in time to see Guldrin Hardcastle go down.

"Rathtar!" she cried, pitching her voice high and shrill to cut through the grunts and roars of orcs and the curses and groans of men rushing together all around her.

A head turned—darkly handsome, as sullen as ever. Rathtar Hardcastle was killing his share of orcs with his resentment borne before him like a shield. He was just one of scores of young, handsome noble wastrels baffled as to what they must do to get the respect they felt Faerûn—or at least the court of Cormyr—owed them.

A sort of hope kindled in his eyes as Alusair beckoned him with a jerk of her head, already a stride past him as she cut down an orc with brutal efficiency.

"Come!" she snapped, pointing with her blade as the gape-jawed orc fell away from it.

Rathtar sprang to follow, almost stumbling in his eagerness. When he regained his footing, he found seven orcs or more lumbering into Alusair's path. The Steel Princess never slowed, her blade singing back and forth as if it weighed nothing and the snarling, stinking orc bodies it cleaved were made of feathers or mere shadows.

The man who did not yet know he was mere breaths away from becoming the Hardcastle heir swung his own blade with enthusiasm. This was something he could do, some way he could prove himself as every bit as much a bright hero of

Troy Denning and Ed Greenwood

Cormyr as those old and grizzled men in medal-bedecked uniforms who limped sagely around the court, staring disapprovingly at anyone younger than themselves. Why, when he . . .

The last orc fell away under Alusair's savage charge—gods, what a woman! Rathtar was more than a little afraid of her, even with her shapely behind waggling inches in front of his nose and the sleek line of her flank rippling as she turned to dart her sword tip under a struggling Purple Dragon and into the snarling face of an orc the dragoneer was grappling with.

She was leading somewhere, for some glorious task, no doubt. Rathtar Hardcastle was going to be recognized at last, was going to be—

Alusair spun suddenly, almost casually striking aside Rathtar's lowered blade as he almost ran it through her, and clapped him on the shoulder just as he'd seen her do to a hundred weeping or pain-wracked Purple Dragon veterans.

"Yours," she murmured into his ear, and her lips brushed his cheek for just a moment as she spun away, murmuring, "I'll stand guard."

It felt like his cheek was burning, where her lips had been. Rathtar reached up almost wonderingly to touch it as he stared down and suddenly, chillingly, knew what this was all about.

His older brother Guldrin, as large and slow-witted as ever, was staring up at him with eyes that were going dull, blood oozing like a dark red flood from his slack mouth.

"Y-you heard me," Guldrin mumbled, as Rathtar crashed to his knees on dead orcs and reached out for him. His lips twisted. "For once."

"Are you—?" Rathtar snapped, trying to lift him.

Guldrin nodded almost wearily. "Dying? Aye. You're . . . heir now. You with your looks and giggling lasses every night, and . . . and . . . oh, gods, have my blessings and make Father proud."

Much blood fountained from his mouth, and he groaned weakly before gasping, "T-tell him . . . tell him I died well."

"I will! Oh, gods keep you, Guld, I *will!*" Rathtar shouted, finding himself on the verge of tears. Somewhere inches but a world away, steel rang on steel and Alusair snarled at the orc she'd just slain and hurled aside, and at the one behind it who was fast losing enthusiasm for facing this warrior woman with the eyes of flame.

They stared into each other's eyes for a moment, the older brother and the younger, then . . . then Guldrin was simply gone from behind those staring eyes.

Rathtar let his head fall slowly among the dead, blinking back hot tears, and spat, "Death! *Death!* Death to all orcs!"

He thrust aside Alusair as if she was an inconvenient hanging tapestry and plunged into the orcs beyond her, stabbing and slashing like a madman. The Steel Princess raced after him, calling his name vainly and trying to guard his flanks, though she could only reach one.

It was only a few breaths before a black orc blade burst through the flank she was guarding, driven in from the other side, and Rathtar Hardcastle went down on his face without a sound. Alusair cut open the grinning face of his orc slayer as she spun around to race back to safety, reminding herself to stay alive to get to Suzail and personally tell Ildamoar Hardcastle how bravely both of his sons had fallen in battle. Cormyr owed the loyal old nobleman that and more.

Someone stumbled over backward, arms windmilling in almost comical futility, two orc blades standing out of his back. Ilmreth Illance, another of the men that unpopular family had already lost in these last few years, and probably not the last. Alusair sighed. She didn't want men to die bravely—she wanted them to live on to ripe old ages and die in bed, happy and safe and prosperous in a Cormyr free of Obarskyr sins and armies marching because of them.

"Arabel may be burning," she heard a Purple Dragon grunt behind her, "but it's one big orc oven. I saw one street chest-deep in tusker bodies, their blood running in a river down into the sewers."

"You've caught up to us, Paraedro!" someone else called happily. "You must have run like the very wind."

211

"No," the dragoneer replied sourly, "I walked—butchering orcs every step of the way. Slow work, but if you lot were any slower at slaying orcs, I'd have passed you and been halfway to Immersea by now."

"Be our guest!" another voice bellowed, over the ringing clang of his sword shattering an orc blade. "We've saved plenty of tuskers for you!"

"Aye," Paraedro replied in dry tones. "I'd noticed."

27

he huge refectory doors swung open, and the first nobles filed into the sparse room looking confused and uneasy. Each was accompanied by two dragoneers, one to carry his scabbards, jewelry, purse, and anything else that might conceal a weapon, the other to stand guard over him with a bared sword. When they saw the four dining tables placed together in the center of the room and the unadorned benches upon which they were being asked to sit, their expressions changed from apprehension to irritation.

Tanalasta, seated opposite her mother at the center of the table, stood as the first lords drew near. Her purpose today was not to assert her authority but to win the hearts and minds of Cormyr's nobles, just as her efforts to care for the refugees had won the love of the common people. Queen Filfaeril remained seated in her throne, which was the only trapping of royal privilege in the room. The queen would be representing the crown, not to direct the proceeding but to bestow the royal blessing on whatever occurred there that day.

Troy Denning and Ed Greenwood

Young Orvendel Rallyhorn, wide-eyed and pale, was shown to a seat a little down from the queen. Because Urthrin Rallyhorn was already in the north fighting at King Azoun's side and Korvarr was needed to oversee the guards, Queen Filfaeril had insisted that the awkward youth speak on behalf of his family today. That he did not yet know of her command accounted, perhaps, for his queasy aspect and trembling hands.

Tanalasta gave the boy a reassuring smile, then forced herself to nod politely as Emlar Goldsword came to stand next to the youth. The arrangement was no accident. The princess had intentionally arranged the seating to break up cliques and power blocs. Emlar returned Tanalasta's nod with a spiteful glare, showing no curiosity about the manner of his summons nor the unusual site of the meeting. She wondered just how extensive his spy network was.

When the last noble had been shown to his seat—or hers, for there were more than a few matriarchs in the gathering—it was one of the neutral lords, Melot Silversword, who turned to glower at Tanalasta.

"Your assassins were not fast enough?" he demanded. "Or have you decided it will be more expedient to arrest and exile us?"

"No one is under arrest, Lord Melot. You are entirely free to leave." Tanalasta glanced down the huge table in both directions, then let her gaze linger a moment on Emlar Goldsword. "You all are."

A few brows rose, but there were too few friends seated next to each other for the resulting murmur to be more than gentle. Tanalasta allowed a moment for any noble who wished to leave to do so, but it was a mere ploy to make them feel they were attending of their own will. No one would leave before hearing the reason for her unusual summons. Of that she felt certain.

When none of the lords surprised her, Tanalasta nodded. "Good. I apologize for bringing you here under guard, but I wanted to be certain you arrived alive."

She motioned them to sit, not bothering to elaborate.

The rash of assassinations had continued unabated for well over a tenday now, and the ghazneths, starved for magic by Tanalasta's ban, had begun to attack nobles in search of hidden magic items. That the creatures had an uncanny knack for assailing only lords who insisted on safeguarding their own magic suggested to Tanalasta that their spy was well-placed indeed. She had heard that Emlar Goldsword had another, more mercenary explanation.

After the nobles took their seats, Tanalasta continued to stand. "I summoned you because, as nobles of the realm, I thought you should be the first to hear some devastating news received by the palace just this hour. Arabel has fallen to the orcs."

A few of the nobles cringed and closed their eyes, suggesting that Tanalasta's words were mere confirmation of the rumors they had already heard through other sources. Most, including Emlar Goldsword, simply let their jaws drop and stared at the princess in shock. Only Orvendel Rallyhorn, staring around the table with an expression that could best be described as smug, did not seem shocked.

"What . . . what of the king?" asked Lady Calantar.

Still puzzled by Orvendel's reaction, Tanalasta tore her eyes from the youth and turned to the noblewoman, whose winsome face had gone as gray as ash. The question was, of course, foremost on the mind of every lord and lady in the room. With Emlar Goldsword and his followers standing in more or less open opposition to the crown princess, the king's death would bring Cormyr to the brink of civil war and all but assure a "stabilizing" invasion by Sembian mercenaries.

Tanalasta was about to answer when Emlar Goldsword cut her off. "The king is alive." He stared directly at the princess as he spoke. "If the king were dead, do you think I would not have joined him already? The princess's assassins have proved themselves most capable."

Tanalasta was careful not to nod. "The king is well, as is the Steel Princess. If they were not, Lord Goldsword would be in Prisoner's Tower, not a grave." She resisted the urge to accuse the coward of trying to put the blame for his tactics

215

on her. If this meeting degenerated into a shouting match between her faction and Goldsword's, Cormyr was lost. "I have called this council to inform you of the crown's decision to send its remaining troops north to reinforce the survivors from Arabel."

The room broke into an immediate uproar, and several of the guards stationed behind each noble stepped forward to push a protesting lord back to his seat. Only Emlar and his supporters remained quiet, some studying Tanalasta and clearly waiting for the other shoe to drop, others observing her with an air of self-righteous satisfaction—convinced, apparently, that Arabel's fall would force her to accept Sembia's offer.

The princess watched Orvendel watch the others, his eyes wide and the corners of his mouth curled up almost unnoticeably. The youth was enjoying this. Why? Because it made him feel important? Tanalasta gestured for quiet. Under the gentle prodding of the dragoneer guards, the chamber slowly fell silent.

As soon as the tumult had died, Lord Longbrooke said, "This is outrageous!" He was so angry that even his heavy jowls were red. "You'll leave the south undefended."

"*That* is for this council to decide," said Tanalasta. "A small garrison will remain to defend the royal palace and keep order in Suzail, but the rest is up to the nobles."

"This—this—this is coercion!" sputtered Longbrooke. "We'll not stand for it."

"The crown's troops are the crown's to do with as it pleases," said Tanalasta. "The first companies are marching north even as we speak. The decision before this body is a simple one. Will the nobles stand and fight, surrender to the ghazneths, or invite an invasion from Sembia?"

Finally, Goldsword smirked. "You would condone their help?"

"*I* would not," said Tanalasta.

"Nor would the crown," said Queen Filfaeril. She leaned forward to look down the table toward Goldsword. "At the moment, however, the crown has no more say over that than this council has over the disposition of the Purple Dragons and war wizards. You will do what you will do, and we'll all live with the consequences. There are, however, some things you should know."

Filfaeril leaned back in her throne and nodded to Tanalasta.

"Giogi Wyvernspur remains poised on the border and will invade Sembia the instant their mercenaries cross into Cormyr," the princess said, "under any circumstances. He lacks a large enough force to win a victory, of course, but we all know how tenacious Lord Wyvernspur can be when he gets to bulling around. I shouldn't be surprised if he managed to destroy every bridge in the realm and set half the cities ablaze before the Sembians finally tracked him down."

"Then call him off," said Goldsword.

Filfaeril's answer was simple and plain. "No."

Goldsword's face began to redden, and Tanalasta continued, "There are also the Letters of Marque to consider."

"Letters of Marque?" It was Longbrooke who asked this.

Tanalasta turned to Hector Dauntinghorn, Commodore of the Imperial Flotilla based in Marsember. He was attending both in his capacity as a naval officer and as a representative of the Dauntinghorn family, his uncle being in the north with half the family retainers and King Azoun.

"After Ambassador Hovanay's visit, the crown issued Letters of Marque to every ship loyal to Cormyr," Hector explained. "In the event of a Sembian invasion, they are to consider any vessel flying a Sembian flag or entering or leaving a Sembian port as an enemy. In the event of said invasion, they are authorized to capture or sink every such vessel they encounter and keep all booty recovered."

Goldsword's eyes narrowed. "You would plunge Cormyr into a second war rather than accept aid in winning this one?"

"The crown would fight a second war rather than let its nobles sell the kingdom cheap," Queen Filfaeril corrected. "But the choice is yours. As I said, we can't stop the nobles from doing what they will do."

"But you don't have to!" burst Orvendel Rallyhorn. "You know how to stop the ghazneths!"

217

Tanalasta tried to warn the boy off with a quick shake of her head, but he was too busy looking around in surprise as everyone turned to face him.

"What did you say, *Lord* Rallyhorn?" asked Emlar.

The flattery was all that was needed to make the youth continue. "Princess Tanalasta knows how to rob the ghazneths of their power. She and Alaphondar have been working on it for more than a month. All they need is some help from us to catch them."

"Is that so?" asked Lady Calantar.

Trying to ignore the angry look her mother flashed her, Tanalasta sighed and half-nodded. "After a fashion. We know how to weaken the ghazneths temporarily, but with the spy on the loose we have not been able to get close enough to the monsters to put our knowledge to use." The princess did not need to explain which spy she meant. The entire royal court was abuzz with speculations about the identity of the ghazneth's informant. Tanalasta furrowed her brow at Orvendel. "The ghazneths know every trap before we set it. Orvendel knows this."

Orvendel was too caught up in his moment of fame to heed her warning. He turned to Emlar Goldsword. "What I know is that if you weren't such a coward, Princess Tanalasta would have troops to put everywhere, then it wouldn't matter if the ghazneths had a spy."

Emlar gave him a cobra's smile. "We can see that *you* need never fear the princess's assassins."

"Actually, neither do you," said Queen Filfaeril. "These assassins belong to Princess Tanalasta no more than they belong to you. I can assure you of that personally."

A stunned silence fell over the room as the nobles worked through the implications of Queen Filfaeril's words. Even Tanalasta found her head reeling at what she thought she heard her mother saying. For the queen to know who did *not* control the assassins suggested she knew who *did*. If that were so, Tanalasta could only guess at the reason her mother had kept the knowledge secret.

Emlar seemed to reach his conclusion before everyone

else. "You are to be commended for defending your daughter's reputation, Majesty," he said.

Filfaeril's pale eyes grew icy. "Do you call me a liar, Goldsword? Or perhaps you think me irresolute enough to let such behavior go unpunished." The queen leaned back and looked past Ildamoar Hardcastle to Korvarr Rallyhorn, who had been assigned to stand guard over Emlar personally. "Lord Goldsword has impugned the dignity of the queen. Execute him."

"What?" Goldsword's face grew stormy and indignant, and he braced his hands on the table so he could stand and look toward the queen. "You can't—"

Korvarr cut the objection short by catching Emlar by the hair and pulling him off-balance to the rear to prevent him from defending himself. For a moment, Tanalasta thought the lionar would stop there, but then he jerked his captive's head back and pressed his dagger under Lord Goldsword's quivering jaw.

"Wait!" Tanalasta cried.

Korvarr cast an inquiring glance at Filfaeril, who raised one finger to delay the execution. "You have something to say before we proceed, Princess?"

Tanalasta started to say that her mother could not simply have a man executed, but of course she *could*. The princess swallowed, then said, "If Lord Goldsword were to apologize, perhaps he might be excused for challenging your claim, Majesty. I myself doubted I understood you correctly until I considered *The Rule of Law*—particularly the passages relating to Time of War."

The icy hint of a smile crossed Filfaeril's lips, and Tanalasta knew with a sudden hollowness that she had guessed right. While Iltharl the Abdicator's treatise *The Rule of Law* was not *exactly* the law of the land, it had been quoted as precedent for more than a thousand years and was certainly the foundation of Cormyrean common law. The particular passage Tanalasta referred to stated that during Time of War, any royal representative of the crown had complete authority to punish crimes against the crown. While it might be argued that execution was a rather severe

219

penalty for affronting the queen, the treatise stated explicitly that during Time of War, the punishment was at the representative's sole discretion and could not be appealed. In other words, Queen Filfaeril could execute not only Emlar Goldsword, she could execute any noble who committed even the smallest breach against the crown—and questioning Tanalasta's right to call for troops could well be construed as a crime against the crown.

Queen Filfaeril remained silent, apparently considering her daughter's appeal. A soft murmur rose around the table as the few nobles familiar enough with *The Rule of Law* to know the passage she cited explained it to those who did not. A lot of faces paled, and the unarmed lords began to cast uneasy glances at the dragoneers standing behind their benches. The loyal lords—Ildamoar Hardcastle, Hector Dauntinghorn, Roland Emmarask, and a handful of others—appeared more astonished than frightened. Only Orvendel Rallyhorn's reaction did not make sense. Though he was practically touching Lord Goldsword, who remained off-balance with Korvarr's dagger to his throat, Orvendel did not look astonished or frightened or even alarmed. He looked frustrated—frustrated and worried.

After giving the lords a few moments to appreciate their dilemma, Queen Filfaeril turned from Tanalasta. Her gaze lingered on Orvendel an instant and flashed icy hatred before continuing on to Lord Goldsword, and the princess knew that her mother's surprises for the day were far from done. The queen had insisted on young Rallyhorn's presence for a reason. Tanalasta had the sinking feeling she knew what it was—and this time, she would not be able to beg the crown's mercy.

The queen let her gaze rest on Emlar until the room grew quiet again, then asked, "What say you, Lord Goldsword? Do you apologize?"

Emlar nodded. "Aye, I apologize for doubting you but not for speaking against the princess. I hold the Sembians to be Cormyr's best hope now more than ever, and I'll not apologize for that."

"And I would not ask you to," said the queen. "Obviously, the crown finds your opinion mistaken, but at least it is honest and takes into account Cormyr's interests as much as your own. We are not in the habit of executing people for bad opinions and honest mistakes."

Filfaeril motioned to Korvarr, who pulled his dagger away from Emlar's throat and gently lowered him to his seat. The color returned to the lord's face and to the faces of his supporters. Tanalasta knew that in a few moments of terror, her mother had won the cooperation she had been struggling to earn for months.

Emlar knew it as well. "Her majesty is most forbearing." He inclined his head to the queen, then tried to salvage at least the appearance of compromise by adding, "The Goldsword house shall abide by the decision of this council."

Filfaeril ignored him and turned to glare at Melot Silversword. "What the crown cannot abide are self-serving intriguers who straddle the wall until they see on which side the most profit will lie for their house. Such nothingarians cause harm enough when the realm is at peace, but during Time of War, they are tantamount to spies."

Melot straightened himself in his chair. "Majesty, I hardly think such a comparison warranted. It is no fairer to blame a man for his caution than—"

"I would not press the matter, Lord Silversword," said Tanalasta. "You are still alive—and may even have a reasonable chance of staying that way."

"Provided he abides by the decrees of this council," agreed Filfaeril. "Now, there is one other matter I wish to dispose of."

"If it pleases the queen, I would rather handle that myself." The princess caught her mother's eye and glanced quickly in Orvendel's direction, then grimaced inwardly when the queen gave an icy nod. The chain of betrayal flashed before Tanalasta's eyes. Orvendel drawing the information out of his older brother, then passing it to the ghazneths—but why? That was a question the boy would answer before he died. Trying to ignore the sick feeling in her stomach, she turned to Orvendel and said, "Young Lord Rallyhorn, you and I will speak after the council."

A nervous expression came over Orvendel, but it was nothing compared to the shock on Korvarr's face. The lionar's jaw fell, his shoulders sagged, and the princess was certain that only duty kept him from closing his eyes and starting to weep. Clearly, the queen had warned him that the traitor would be named today, but had not said who it was.

Not wishing to draw undue attention to the dragoneer's internal struggle, Tanalasta looked away and ran her gaze down both sides of the table, taking care to linger on the faces of those nobles who had sided with Goldsword instead of her. When only loyal nobles dared meet her gaze, she decided the time had come to follow her mother's approach and exert her authority.

"On the morrow, the crown will greet half the retainers of each noble house outside the Horngate," she said. "They will come prepared for a long march, as they will be journeying north to join King Azoun. At noon, the crown will accept the magic items of each noble house into the Royal Palace for safekeeping and will welcome an additional quarter of each house's retainers into the king's service for the purpose of garrisoning various fortresses across the south. The last quarter of each house's retainers will remain at their home estate for the purpose of securing the lives and property of the manor occupants. Is there any discussion?"

"Discussion?" scoffed Lady Calantar. "Do you really expect us to pretend we are agreeing to this willingly?"

Tanalasta turned toward Lady Calantar but looked past her to the dragoneer standing guard behind her. "Lady Calantar is fostering treason. Take her outside and behead her."

Lady Calantar's eyes grew wide. "You can't—"

Her protest was cut off as the dragoneer behind her clasped a mailed palm over her mouth and dragged her from her seat. He looked to Tanalasta and raised a querying eyebrow. When the princess nodded, he clenched his teeth and pulled the noblewoman off the bench.

As the soldier dragged her out the door, Roland Emmarask turned to Tanalasta, "If a loyal lord may be so bold as to ask—you truly can't intend to behead Lady Calantar."

"Of course I can," Tanalasta replied evenly. "How would you expect King Azoun to deal with a traitor?"

Faces around the table began to go white. Emmarask, who had once spent a few pleasant months courting Lady Calantar before his parents decided the match would not be a good one for the family, continued to press the matter.

"Certainly, no one can argue that execution is an unjust punishment for a traitor, but Lady Calantar can hardly be considered that." Emmarask cast a meaningful glance in Goldsword's direction. "Not when those who have said far worse go unpunished."

"Perhaps you did not hear Queen Filfaeril," Tanalasta said, regarding the lord coldly. "The crown has no interest in punishing those who have spoken against us out of love for Cormyr. We respect their courage, if not their wisdom." She cast her gaze in Melot Silversword's direction. "The true traitors are those who would risk nothing in the matter, the self-serving ones who remain silent until it grows clear who will win and how best to turn that victory to their own advantage."

Silversword's heavy jowls began to quiver. "I assure you, the Silverswords are interested in Cormyr's advantage only."

"Good." Tanalasta searched the faces of other lords for any further hint of defiance. Finding none, she decided the time had come to reaffirm her victory. She glared directly at Emlar Goldsword, then asked, "Is there any more discussion?"

Goldsword shook his head. "My retainers will be there as decreed. May the gods bless the crown."

"I will be happy if they only favor Cormyr, though we thank you for the thought." Tanalasta glanced around the table once more. When everyone looked away, she smiled and said, "The crown is most grateful for your support. To show its appreciation, you are all invited to guest at the Royal Palace until such times as your retainers arrive and are dispatched to their new assignments. Your escorts will show you to your rooms and provide messengers for your orders. We will see you for the evening meal."

If any of the lords found the invitation less than gracious, they were wise enough not to say so. They simply stood and thanked the princess for her hospitality, then turned to follow their escorts out the refectory door.

Orvendel expressed his thanks without meeting Tanalasta's eyes, then turned to follow the others . . . and found himself staring at his brother's broad chest.

"Princess Tanalasta asked you to stay behind." Korvarr pushed the boy back to his bench. "Or did you forget?"

"No, no . . . I . . ." Unable to meet his brother's eyes, Orvendel spun toward Tanalasta. "I don't know what I'm doing here."

"I think you do," said Tanalasta. "And please stop lying. There is nothing I hate more than a man who makes a fool of me."

28

grow tired of running," the King of Cormyr growled as the familiar howling began again, down a hillside to their right. Alusair waved a wordless hand-signal to the nearest bowmen to stand and fire.

It was goblins this time, streaming down the slope in a torrent, waving their blades and yammering for blood. Human blood.

"Is it time to turn and fight?" Alusair replied, turning in her saddle to give her father a dangerous look that added the words "I would" to her words as loudly as if she'd shouted it.

"*You* would, aye," Azoun returned, spurring his horse forward, "thinking only of yourself. If I turn and take a stand I risk all our lives, the crown, and the stability of the kingdom. With all these nobles foaming for the throne like stallions given a chance at a ready mare, and all our farmers and commoners between here and the sea, if we fall who's to stop these vermin from pillaging all Cormyr?"

"Gods, with all those cares it's a wonder that horse can carry you!" Alusair snapped back. "You're right. I did mean to risk only myself and the blades who ride with me. The rabble of nobles you so dismiss as eager traitors, remember? What loss to the realm if they fall?"

Azoun leaned over in his saddle until their faces almost met, and muttered, "If I lose my Alusair, I lose my hope for Cormyr's future—and the best general in the realm. And yes, I am measuring you against Ilnbright, Taroaster, and me. You're the best of us, and more than that you're the one commoners and Purple Dragons alike look up to, with love."

Alusair went white, and almost snarled, "They love you, too, father!"

Azoun nodded, but replied, "A different love. I am the 'now,' with all the feuds and disputes and annoyances they know. You are the future that shines ahead. You they'll follow to death with hearts full of hope. Me, they'll go down with grimly, doing their duty."

Alusair bent her head over her saddle for a moment, then looked up and met her father's eyes squarely.

"I never thought I'd hear a man be so honest," she almost whispered. "I am honored beyond belief that the man is my father and that he gives such honesty to me." Then her eyes caught a movement to the south, her head snapped in that direction, her face changed, and she added, "Rider—messenger, come to meet us."

She raised her hand to make another signal, but Swordlord Glammerhand was already sending two kadrathen of Purple Dragons through the ranks of the bowmen to cut down the last of the goblins and sounding the horn that would bring the bowmen back to a steady march.

The envoy proved to be no excited young soldier or war wizard cloaked in his own importance, but one of the veteran King's Messengers from the palace. He was a sleek man, Bayruce by name, known well to both king and princess.

He bowed his head formally as he brought his horse to a weary walk, and said, "From Queen Filfaeril, glad greeting and good news. The crown princess prevails at court, and our loyal nobles whelm many swords in good array, north to meet with you and fight for you. Such is the whole of my message."

Azoun inclined his head in formal thanks and asked, "So, Bayruce, if we were but two carters in a tavern over tankards and I asked you, 'Pray, how many of our nobles be loyal to the crown enough to whelm swords for war?' how would you answer?"

The messenger did not bother to hide his smile. "Majesty, I cannot say." His smile fled again before he added, "If you faced no dragon nor these dark flying things that eat magic, the men I saw in my ride would be more than enough . . . but then, you do face those foes, and these goblins would not have reached beyond Arabel without them, no?"

Alusair and Azoun nodded in grim unison. "No," they agreed. The king did not pause, but added, "Sir Messenger, rest your horse. We shall tarry here for a time, while the Princess Alusair essays an attack, planned yestereve, on those who harry us."

The Steel Princess turned her head, jaw dropping in astonishment. As her eyes met those of the king, her father winked and said simply, "Do it."

Alusair clapped her hand to her shoulder in a smart salute, spurred her horse away, and shouted back, "Redhorn's riders carry the best wine, Bayruce. Mind you get to it before His Majesty, if you want any!"

* * * * *

"This dragondew *is* good," Azoun agreed, wiping his mouth. "How did I sire such a daughter?"

"Do you desire me to say innocently, 'In the usual way, Your Majesty'?" Bayruce asked the sky smoothly.

Azoun gave him a chuckle and turned his head back to the battle. Alusair had done just as he would have. Two arms of men were flung out like the arms of a crab, behind hills, bills and spears to the front and archers behind, to fire when their fellows were forced to retreat. Alusair had placed herself with the largest, strongest men in the center, to take a stand against the main company of goblins while the two hidden arms reached around to strike.

A brief struggle, then horns would sound the retreat and they'd flee south again, probably to the Starwater, and make a stand there. Giogi would just have to lose a year's grapes and the good wine that came from them.

The goblins came over a rise and roared with excited fury when they saw their foes standing ready for them. They lumbered into a charge without a one of them looking up or to either side. Yes, goblins loved to fight. "*Glath!*" they called. "*Glaaath!*"

"Blood!" that was, in Common. Azoun smiled thinly. Let it be goblin blood. The goblins struck the line where his daughter was standing with a crash that made him wince, and he and the messenger watched intently as the charge drove Purple Dragons helplessly back. Those long hacking swords were busy now.

Alusair's hair was streaming about her shoulders. "Gods above, girl, they don't care how beautiful you look!" Azoun roared, standing up in his stirrups. "Put your damned helm back on!"

Alusair never turned her head, but both men thought that her long warsword thrust up at them in a rather rude gesture. Archers were lying on their bellies behind the fray, firing arrows point-blank up at any goblin they could get a clear shot at. At such close range, the shafts were tearing clear through screaming goblin bodies or plucking their victims up into the air and hurling them well back among their fellows.

They saw Alusair step forward to face a goblin who stood half a head taller than all the rest and saw her shudder and stagger under the shock of their blades meeting. Sparks flew around her as the Steel Princess struck back, their blades meeting again. She threw herself onto her back, hauling hard on their locked swords and driving a boot into the goblin's belly. He hurtled over her to crash helplessly on his face and die under the daggers of half a dozen enthusiastic archers.

"Well, now," Bayruce said in soft admiration. "Well, now . . ."

Alusair was up again, hand dipping to her belt. A moment later, the clear horn call went up, and the Cormyreans fell back. Both of the pincer-arms came into view over the rise as they rushed to take the last few goblins from behind, their bills dipping in deadly unison.

"Well hammered," Azoun agreed in satisfaction. "We can't afford to lose many men, so she's nursing them like a mother. A born battlemaster!"

With one accord, the king and his messenger reached for more dragondew. The wineskin was almost empty.

* * * * *

"There are more orcs than you can count two or three hills back, but that's most of the goblins," Alusair said in satisfaction, as she reined in her mount. She was spattered from head to boots with black goblin blood.

Azoun leaned over in his saddle to embrace her and growled, "Have you forgotten what helms are for, young lady?"

His wayward daughter's eyes danced as she laughingly replied, "Ah, but it's good to fight alongside you, Father!"

"Sure you don't prefer scores of ardent young noblemen?" Azoun asked teasingly.

"Well, their pratfalls to impress me *do* provide more unintentional entertainment than you do," the Steel Princess told him, "but as steady feast-fare, even pratfalls can bring on yawns."

Azoun chuckled, then a sound caught his ear. He looked to the south and his face changed.

"More messengers," Bayruce said for him. "Riding hard."

"Trouble, Father?" Alusair asked quietly, reaching for her sword.

Azoun shrugged. "I know not—but I do know that this would not be a good time to have to fight any traitors among the nobles."

Alusair lifted an incredulous eyebrow. "They'd be fools enough to stab at our backsides with dragon-led

229

goblinkin sweeping down the realm to their very gates?"

"Larger, grander pratfalls," Azoun replied in dry tones.

* * * * *

The messengers proved to bear good news. Well-armed forces had indeed been whelmed by many nobles and now awaited the king's pleasure near Jester's Green under the command of Battlemaster Haliver Ilnbright, an old, grizzled Purple Dragon respected by many nobles who'd fought alongside him down the years.

"We'll make a stand at Calantar's Bridge," Azoun decided, turning in his saddle, "then fall back into the hill farms when we must."

Everyone fell silent and grim then as the dark form of the great red dragon rose into the sky, silhouetted against the setting sun, and flew leisurely back and forth over the Heartlands of Cormyr.

After a few breaths, the tiny silhouettes of six ghazneths could be seen rising to meet it. Alusair shivered, and Azoun reached over wordlessly to hold her hand.

"Sorry," she murmured.

"Don't be," he muttered back. His hand tightened, warm and reassuring.

"Seven scourges," she murmured. "So who and where is the last one?"

"Don't ask me," her father growled. "I'm just a king."

Suddenly, Alusair found herself shrieking with laughter.

29

ike everything else about the betrayal, Tanalasta found the summoning signal complicated, juvenile, and utterly disheartening. She was atop Rallyhorn Tower, watching from the darkness as Orvendel ran the crudely sewn standard of a ghazneth up the family flagpole. The banner depicted a broad-shouldered male with upraised wings and huge crimson eyes. It clutched the Royal Tricrown of Cormyr in one hand and a bolt of lightning in the other. One foot rested on the chest of dying man, the other on the blocky ruins of a noble tower.

"The sick little bastard," hissed Korvarr. "I had no idea."

"Obviously," Tanalasta replied.

After hearing Orvendel describe almost proudly how he had played on Korvarr's emotions to learn Tanalasta's plans, the lionar had resigned his commission and asked to share Orvendel's punishment. Tanalasta had accepted the resignation but declared Korvarr's contrition punishment enough. According to the elder Rallyhorn, Orvendel's poor eyesight and studious habits had made him something of a laughingstock growing up. In the wild days of his youth, Korvarr and his friends had delighted in playing practical jokes on the gullible boy. Early in the ghazneth invasion, however, the lionar had momentarily fallen under the sway of Mad King Boldovar's delusions and came to appreciate how damaging those hoaxes could be. Vowing to change his cruel ways, he immediately sent his brother several apologies.

All of the messages were rebuffed, for Orvendel's resentment had already blossomed into a festering rage—and not only for his brother. Lord Rallyhorn had also earned the hatred of his youngest son by not bothering to conceal his disappointment in the boy's physical awkwardness and lack of strength. So did the rest of Cormyrean society, which followed the lead of the brother and father in treating the boy either as an unfortunate sibling or the family buffoon. It was no wonder, then, that when Orvendel began to hear reports of the damage being done to the realm by the Scourges of Alaundo's prophecy, he was secretly delighted.

Orvendel became obsessed with the ghazneths and learned everything he could about them, finally coming to see the dark creatures as tools of his personal vengeance. It was an easy matter to raid the family magic vault and sneak off to attract their attention, and by the time Korvarr did a sending to say he would be teleporting home soon with the princess, Orvendel had already established a relationship with Luthax. Under the ghazneth's tutelage, the young Rallyhorn had finally accepted his brother's overtures of friendship and become a spy, exacting his vengeance by helping the monsters devastate southern Cormyr.

Once the spiteful banner reached the top of the pole, Orvendel lit a storm lantern and shone it on the banner. "You'd b-better go downstairs now." The youth did not look at Tanalasta or his brother, and he was so frightened that the lantern beam wavered as he spoke. "You don't want him to see you."

"Steady your lamp, Orvendel," said Tanalasta. "We don't want him to think anything's wrong."

Orvendel looked down at his trembling hands and

exhaled a couple of times, then gave up and braced the back of the lantern against his stomach. "It's all right. I . . . I've been nervous before."

"And you're sure he'll see it?" asked Korvarr.

"He'll be watching," answered Orvendel. "He'll be starved for magic, and he won't wait long. Hurry."

"Go ahead, Highness," said Korvarr. "I'll stay by the door with my crossbow in case he tries to escape."

Orvendel glanced at his brother and said, "Do you think you're faster than a ghazneth?" Even frightened as he was, the boy's lip was raised in a slight sneer. "If you stay here, dear brother, Luthax will kill you. It makes no difference to me, but it would certainly give away the princess's plan."

Tanalasta took Korvarr's arm. "Orvendel won't betray us this time. Luthax would kill him anyway, and I'm sure he'd rather be remembered as the hero who saved Cormyr than the child who betrayed it."

Orvendel's entire body started to shake, and he turned to stare over the dark city. After his defiant confession—which had come even before Queen Filfaeril finished laying out her evidence—Tanalasta had spoken the hardest words of her life and sentenced the boy to death. After leaving him to consider his fate for a few days, she had begun to play him, describing all the horrible executions of past traitors, then pleading for his cooperation so she could name something quicker and more painless. Orvendel had endured this part of the interrogation surprisingly well, remaining defiant and proud until Korvarr began to talk about how his peers would ridicule him after his death.

These descriptions had upset Orvendel far more than the tortures Tanalasta described, and the boy had finally agreed to help them lure Luthax into a trap. Given his fear of mockery, the princess felt sure he would do as he promised. As a girl in her teens, she herself had suffered anxieties similar to Orvendel's, and she knew better than most how powerful such feelings could be.

Tanalasta took Korvarr's arm and pulled him down the stairs after her, wondering how she would live with herself when the "Time of War" ended. A mere tenday earlier, at what had already become known as the "Council of Iron," she had had Lady Calantar executed for the mere crime of protesting a royal order. Now she was using a frightened boy—a young man by law and custom, but still a boy in his heart and hers—to lure a ghazneth into her trap. If the lad did well, his reward was to be a painless death.

Tanalasta could not help shuddering at what she was becoming. She was a ruler who needed to see the south safely through this war, perhaps, but what about after? When she saw Rowen again, would she be able to look him in the eyes and describe all the terrible things she had done?

As Tanalasta stepped out of the stairwell, Owden Foley took her arm and guided her into Urthrin Rallyhorn's spacious study.

"Highness, you're shaking!" he said. "Are you cold?"

"I fear I am growing so." Tanalasta glanced around the chamber and asked, "Is everything ready here?"

Though the room looked empty enough, the princess knew that more than a dozen dragoneers stood concealed behind a wall of false bookshelves along the near wall. A pair of war wizards sat inside a curtained arrow loop, and two more were crouching behind the duke's heavy desk. The rest of the company—a hundred handpicked warriors and another dozen war wizards—waited in the stairwell below, ready to charge into the room the instant the trap was sprung.

"We are as ready as we can be," said Owden.

He led Tanalasta across the room to a broad oaken wardrobe and opened the door. Inside, the cabinet looked less like a closet than a coffin built for two. It was actually an iron box disguised as a wardrobe, with a thick lining of padded leather and a steel lock bar that could only be opened from the inside. The princess knew better than to think it would prevent a ghazneth from getting at her, but it would certainly buy a few moments to use her weathercloak and escape.

Tanalasta stepped inside and took hold of the weapon she would use to destroy Luthax—an ancient gem-encrusted crown that had once belonged to King Draxius Obarskyr.

She glanced down at her stomach, now so swollen she could no longer see her toes, then said, "I hope the door will close."

"I'm quite sure it will, Highness," Owden said. He stepped in beside the princess and, despite his confident assurance, pulled the door shut to make sure. "You see?"

"Quite," Tanalasta said. The leather padding pushed her belly up toward her breasts, but she heard the locking bar clack as it fell into place. "But let's not close it until we must, if you don't mind."

Owden let out a growl of disapproval, but opened the door again. Almost at once, Tanalasta smelled the acrid odor of brimstone and noticed a yellow haze hanging in the room. Her first thought was that Luthax had smelled a trap and was trying smoke them out, but then something heavy landed on the roof and the whole tower began to tremble. A gravelly voice reverberated down through the ceiling planks, as powerful and as deep as an earthquake.

"Where have you been, child? I have needs."

"I . . . I know." Orvendel's reply was barely audible as it drifted down the stairs. "The princess has forced all nobles to bring their magic to the royal palace. You must have—"

"So I noticed," rumbled Luthax. "You should have warned us. Had there been time, we could have ambushed them. With all that magic . . . you know it would not have been long before we made you one of us."

Tanalasta's heart skipped a beat, and she heard Owden hissing through his teeth next to her. This was not something Orvendel had told them—that he was trying to become a ghazneth—but it made perfect sense. In her mind's eye, she could see him pointing down through the ceiling and mouthing the word "trap." She felt like a fool for thinking she understood how the boy thought—but not too big a fool. Even as they spoke, there were a hundred dragoneers approaching on hippogriffs, ready to meet the ghazneth in the air and drive him back down to the roof. In the end, the only difference would be how Cormyr remembered Orvendel Rallyhorn and how Tanalasta thought of herself.

But Orvendel was not as naive as he had once been. There was a long pause, then he said, "I've helped you find twice that much magic. If you were going to make me one of you, you'd have d-done it by now."

The next sound Tanalasta heard was a body tumbling across the roof. She thought for a moment Luthax had killed the boy, then the ghazneth addressed him again.

"I have a thirst, child. It is not a good time to toy with me."

"I'm not." Orvendel's voice was so soft that Tanalasta barely heard what followed. "I have something special for you."

"Where?" demanded Luthax. "I feel no magic."

"Not magic—something better," said Orvendel. In the box next to Tanalasta, Owden cursed under his breath, apparently convinced that the boy meant to betray them yet. Orvendel continued, "Come downstairs."

"Downstairs?" Luthax's voice was suspicious. "Bring it up."

"Uh, I can't."

"Are you playing at something, child?" A muffled slap sounded from above, followed by the thump of Orvendel hitting the roof again. "Do what I tell—"

"Orvendel?" Tanalasta called. She passed Draxius's crown to Owden and pushed out of her hiding place. "Orvendel, I heard voices. Is someone up there with you?"

The roof went silent, and Owden caught hold of her arm. "What are you doing?"

"Quiet!" Tanalasta hissed. She pulled free and went to the base of the stairs. "Orvendel! Answer me!"

Something rustled across the roof, and the brimstone cloud grew thicker and harsher. Korvarr emerged from the stairs below and took Tanalasta by the arm.

"Orvendel!" Tanalasta yelled. "I won't wait much longer for this surprise of yours. A princess's time is—"

"Orvendel?" Korvarr called sternly, now following Tanalasta's lead. He stepped in front of the princess and began to back away from the stairwell, pushing her toward her coffin. "If this is another of your childish games...."

"Hardly!" rumbled Luthax's deep voice.

A tongue of crimson flame licked out of the stairwell, striking Korvarr square in the chest and blasting him into Tanalasta. She stumbled backward and fell, her nostrils filled with the sickening stench of charred flesh. Korvarr landed square atop her, howling and screaming as his burning limbs pounded the floor beside her.

A wizard's head poked out from behind the curtain over the arrow loop, then the bookshelf began to sway as the dragoneers hiding behind started to slide the case aside.

"Stop!" she yelled, putting a tone of royal command into her voice. The wizard's head vanished behind the screen at once, and the bookcase stopped moving. She sighed in relief, then repeated herself in a more panicked voice, "Stop moving, Korvarr!"

Though the order had not really been meant for him, somehow through his pain and fear, Korvarr found the strength to hold still. Tanalasta rolled him off her and tried desperately to think of what she would do next, were she not aware of Luthax lurking on the roof above, listening to her every move and trying to smell out a trap.

"Help!" Even as she screamed the word, she motioned Owden to close the "wardrobe" and waved the rest of her companions to remain where they were. Korvarr, she left burning on the floor beside her. "Guards, help!"

That was all Luthax needed. A tremendous crash rumbled down the stairwell into the room, followed by a choking fog of ash and smoke. In the center of the cloud stood a manlike silhouette with a sizable wizard's paunch and crooked, stick-thin legs. His fiery eyes swung in Tanalasta's direction, then he took one step forward.

A tempest of coughing erupted behind the false book shelf, and the ghazneth's eyes grew as wide as saucers. He spun toward the sound raising a finger.

"Now!" Tanalasta screamed. "Do it now!"

The bookcase toppled forward, slamming Luthax to the floor. A circle of crimson flame erupted beneath it, shooting out to lick at Tanalasta's feet and set the carpets ablaze, then a dozen dragoneers scrambled forward and pulled the iron backing off the shelves.

A pillar of flame shot up through the opening, blasting a horse-sized hole in the room's oaken ceiling. Two dragoneers fell back screaming, hands pressed to their melting faces. The others began to hack and stab through the hole with their iron swords.

Now that the ghazneth was trapped, Tanalasta turned her thoughts to Korvarr, whipping her weathercloak off and spreading it over the lionar's still burning body. He screamed and rolled away, entangling himself in the cloth and smothering the flames.

A tremendous crack shot through the room, then the floor on the far side gave way and dropped into the story below. Choking and coughing on sulfurous fumes, Tanalasta rushed forward and peered over a knee-high curtain of flame into the smoky room below.

The false bookshelf lay square in the center of a larger section of burning floor, beneath which lay dozens of groaning, screaming dragoneers. Luthax was just rising to his knees, poking his head up through the back of the case. The ghazneth was surrounded by perhaps thirty dragoneers, their iron weapons clanging off each other as they struck at him madly. Though many of the wounds seemed to close as fast as they opened, some did not, and Tanalasta knew they were prevailing by sheer numbers.

"Owden, the crown!" She thrust her hand out behind her, then pointed at the wizards who had been hiding behind the huge desk. "And get your box down there!"

The wizards flipped the top off the desk, exposing the large iron box that had been concealed beneath the walnut veneer, and shoved the heavy crate toward the hole. In the room below, Luthax finally seemed to realize even he could not regenerate his wounds as fast as his attackers were inflicting them. He stop struggling and closed his eyes in concentration. A low rumble shook the tower. The wall tapestries began to undulate rhythmically, and tiny bits of mortar started to drop from the seams between the stones.

"Move!" Tanalasta ordered, waving the wizards and their box toward the hole.

Owden slapped the crown into her hand, then hurled his shoulder into the iron box. The heavy crate slid forward, then tumbled over the edge and crashed onto the top of Luthax's skull. The ghazneth went limp and fell to his back, the box resting atop his chest, the crown of his head smashed flat.

The shaking ceased and the smoke started to clear, then the dent in Luthax's skull began to pop back to normal. Tanalasta pulled her weathercloak off Korvarr's charred form and used it to dampen the flames at the edge of the hole. She swung her legs over the side and raised an arm to Owden.

"Lower me down."

Owden's eyes grew wide. "That must be fifteen feet."

"Which is too far to jump," she said, "but I will if I must."

"Not necessary." Owden clasped her wrist and dropped to his belly, then lowered her over the edge. "A little help below!"

Several pairs of hands reached up and caught hold of Tanalasta's legs, then gently set her on the floor below. Though the whole process took no more than thirty seconds, by the time she stepped around the iron box to kneel at Luthax's side, his smashed skull had returned to normal.

Tanalasta held the ancient crown over his black, bald pate. "Luthax the Mighty, High Castellan of the War Wizards, as a true Obarskyr and heir to the Dragon Throne, I grant you the thing you most desire, the desire that made you betray what you loved most." As the princess spoke, Luthax's eyes shot open. She slapped the crown on his head, then finished the speech Alaphondar had written for her. "The Crown of Draxius Obarskyr is yours."

"No!" Luthax's hand shot up and caught the princess on the side of the head.

Her ear exploded with pain and everything went black. For a moment she thought Alaphondar must have been wrong, then her vision cleared and she saw the fire leave Luthax's eyes. The shadow lifted from his face, and Tanalasta found herself looking into the bitter eyes of a hateful, power-mad old wizard.

Luthax's arm came up again, but this time a dragoneer blocked it in mid swing. The wizard's eyes widened in shock. He jerked his hand free and began to scratch at the crown, trying in vain to slip a finger beneath the circlet and fling it away. He succeeded only in tearing four bloody furrows down the side of his head.

Tanalasta sighed in relief. "It's no use, Luthax." She raised a hand and let out a weary groan as someone pulled her to feet. "You wanted that crown, and now it's yours."

"Yes, so I did." His voice sound brittle and petty. "But what do you want? I have it, I think."

Luthax's gaze dropped to his flabby chest, where Tanalasta was surprised to see a silver chain supporting a silver belt buckle shaped like a budding sunflower.

The buckle was as familiar to her as the holy symbol she wore around her own neck. It was the same buckle Rowen Cormaeril had worn on his leather scout's belt, the same buckle that she had caught herself watching a hundred times on her journey through the Stonelands with the quiet ranger, the same buckle she had worked so hard to unfasten on her wedding night.

Tanalasta jerked it off Luthax's neck. "Where did you get this?"

The old man smiled. "So you are interested," he said. "Funny, I can't seem to recall with this crown on my head . . ."

"Never." Wondering what sort of wife would refuse the bargain Luthax offered, Tanalasta kicked the old man in the ribs and stepped away. "Lock this monster in his box."

Owden stuck his head down through the ceiling. "And be certain that he can cast no spells!"

"Yes," said Tanalasta. "We must be certain of that. See to it that his hands and jaw are broken—and broken well."

30

oose!" The arrowmaster's voice was level and calm, his eyes on the river below. The third volley of shafts he'd ordered hissed into the air, briefly sought the sun, then fell in a deadly rain on the orcs struggling below.

Tuskers staggered and fell in water that was already dark with their blood. The heaped bodies of those who'd fallen earlier rose out of the river like a dozen grotesque islets, so choking the Starwater that it was threatening to spill beyond its banks into the mud the orcs were advancing through.

They'd not even reached the front rank of Purple Dragons yet—a bristling line of lowered pikes and bills halfway up the hill that fell away to the river, fangs ready to greet their foe—so the archers of Cormyr could fire freely, raining their shafts on anything in or near the river. Hundreds of tuskers were already down, and still they came on, more afraid of the dragon behind them than the humans before them.

Even the arrowmaster winced at the sight of blinded, maddened orcs striking out at their fellows around them, snorting and squealing like gigantic hogs, with arrows that hadn't yet slain them jutting out of their eyes. Those who hadn't been hit lumbered ahead tirelessly, a few of them having wits enough to pluck up the dead and hold them over their heads and shoulders as meat shields against the hungrily hissing shafts.

"How fare you?" a self-important swordlord coming along the line shouted into the whistling din of arrows.

The arrowmaster did not—quite—smile as he replied, "Still standing, sir. No losses yet, and we've plenty of shafts still."

"Why're those men doing nothing?" the officer snapped, pointing with his drawn sword.

"They're not doing nothing, sir. They're waiting, shafts at the ready, you see?"

The swordlord blinked at the silence that followed the question, not realizing an answer was expected, and after a moment asked flatly, "Why?"

"They're waiting to defend the bridge."

The swordlord frowned like a lost thundercloud. "But we're holding the bridge untouched! The tuskers haven't even reached it yet, thanks to our bowmen down there—bowmen who, I might add, are fighting hard whilst these stand idle."

The arrowmaster nodded. "Indeed, sir. My eyes have actually revealed that to me, too, sir."

The swordlord drew back as if he'd been slapped, then thrust his face up against that of the archer, nose to nose. "Are you *mocking* me, soldier?" he snarled. "Explain why they're waiting, this instant."

Without bothering to turn his head, the arrowmaster bellowed, "Loose!"

As the swordlord flinched back with a snarl, another hissing volley of death leaped into the sky.

The arrowmaster gestured after it, to where dozens of orcs were falling, clutching at the shafts that had transfixed them. "This slaughter can't go on, sir, without something more from the foe."

" 'Something more'? *What*, man?"

"The dragon, sir. If we keep this up much longer, she'll come, sir. She'll strike at the bridge first, where men are crowded in and can't run from her. When it's clear, the tuskers'll be across it and up here for us, sir."

The swordlord swallowed and stared at the arrow-master's calm face, then he looked back down at the bridge, and back again at the arrowmaster. Along the way, his face went slowly white.

"Ah, carry on," he choked out, and stumbled away down the line. The arrowmaster did not bother to watch him go. His eyes were on the unfolding attack he'd been expecting—and fearing.

The beast the soldiers were calling the "Devil Dragon" was every bit as huge as the talk over the fires had painted it. It was a red dragon larger than any living wyrm the arrowmaster had ever seen, yet as menacingly graceful in the air as a falcon.

It soared into view around the flank of a hill, banked over the killing ground where the archers of Cormyr were working butchery on the orcs, and swooped down on the bridge. The arrowmaster could see the men there cowering as the dragon's jaws opened.

"At the jaws—loose!" he shouted, but the order was hardly necessary. He'd made his own walk along the line earlier, explaining to each man and maid that the battle could well depend on their bows—at the moment the dragon opened its mouth.

"I want all your shafts down its throat," he repeated his order grimly, as bows twanged all around him. The hand that could no longer hold a bow itched and ached at his side the way it always did when there was a crucial shot to be made. "Tempus, be with us," he breathed, clenching his fist around the sharp flint in his palm, to make the blood flow and take his prayer to the war god.

His mouth fell open in astonishment.

The dragon was flying into a hail of arrows, aye, shuddering as many shafts went home in its tender maw, but it was committed. Its wings were folded back to let it glide, its claws out, gushing a flood of flame before it that even now was splashing on and around tall shields that would not be able to stand against dragonfire and were beginning to waver.

Behind those shields, however, men were heaving and shoving as if demented, hurling aside what the arrow-master had thought were full crates of arrows and shoving other crates in and under what had been hidden under those crates. It was a battering ram that had lain in an armory vault for as long as the arrowmaster could remember. Its rear end had been sharpened, the axe blows so recent that the wood was still bright. The sharp end was now rearing up, as the grunting warriors thrust crates filled with rocks under it as wedges.

Lost in the lust to rend, the dragon saw its peril only at the last instant. It flung itself aside, roaring. The old ram, tipped with ancient, gem-edged dwarven axe blades from the Royal Armory, failed to pierce its breast, but merely gouged open the dragon's belly. Scales flew away in the dragon's wake like clay jugs crashing down from a merchant's bouncing cart.

Screaming, the dragon twisted away, so low that had the Starwater not been there, it would have crashed into the ground. Smoking dragon blood showered down on the Purple Dragons waiting there, open-mouthed in awe, as the dragon turned almost over on its back and fled back north over the forest. The beast trailed a long cry that might almost have been a scream. It crashed through several treetops before it disappeared from view.

Moans and cries arose from the orcs and goblins north of the river, and there was much milling about, snarling, and cracking of whips.

From a little above the arrowmaster, King Azoun looked down on the confusion with satisfaction.

"This is our chance," he said to the Steel Princess as he turned, eyes flashing. "I'll lead a foray across the bridge, offering ourself to the goblinkin as if overbold. You take your bladesmen across the river down there—beyond that fire, where its smoke will cloak you—and advance inside the forest. I'll charge the main orc camp like an idiot swordswinger, and they'll have to abandon it or stand up and fight me."

Alusair nodded. "They're orcs," she said simply, "They'll fight."

Her father nodded. "At the horn call, you bring your blades out to take the orcs from behind. We should be able to slaughter them. If they flee east, our archers can feather them for a good two miles ere they can find cover enough to escape. We can be rid of the orcs by nightfall—and win this war yet."

Alusair knew her face was wearing a broadening grin to match his. As he took her by the shoulders and shook her exultantly, one warrior to another, she shook her head warningly and reminded him, "We're gambling on the dragon not returning."

Azoun nodded, more soberly, then his eyes flashed again and he barked, "Well? Isn't it a gamble we have to take?"

The Steel Princess nodded. "Of course," she said, then acquired the ghost of a smile and added in a voice of mock doom, "but your majesty forgets the goblins."

Azoun grabbed her shoulders again and drew her close. He kissed her fiercely on the forehead, dealt her shoulders a roundhouse slap, and growled, "Get gone with you, and win this thing!"

Alusair knelt, murmuring in flawless mimicry of a courtier's most fluting and insincere singsong voice, "By your command, O Lion Among Kings."

She bounded to her feet, whirled, and was gone before the king could cuff her again. His laughter rolled out after her like a warm benediction.

31

oncentrate."

The silver bud began to swing back and forth, and Tanalasta's eyes followed it.

"Picture his face."

Tanalasta tried to recall her husband's face and found it anguishingly difficult. She had been with him barely a month, and now it had been fully seven times that long since she last saw him. She still possessed an almost tangible sense of him, but his face had become a nebulous thing with a cleft chin and dark eyes, surrounded by an even darker mane of unruly hair. How could she lose his face? A good wife knew what her husband looked like, but so much had happened in the last seven months. Their marriage seemed a lifetime ago, and she had good reason for wondering if she were even the same person.

Tanalasta had signed the execution order for Orvendel Rallyhorn just that morning. As she had promised, the boy's death would be both quick and honorable. He was to be smothered in his sleep, then mourned across the land as the brave soul who had shown the Purple Dragons how to capture ghazneths. As badly as she had wanted to commute the sentence, she could not—not in Time of War. The boy's treason had cost too many people their lives and had very nearly cost her father Cormyr itself. Some acts simply could not be forgiven.

"Can you see him?" Owden asked.

Tanalasta raised a finger. "One moment." She glanced around the spacious dining room of the Crownsilver country manor, which the family matriarch had graciously consented to lend the crown for the expected battle. "Is everyone ready?"

As during the capture of Luthax, an entire company of Purple Dragons stood in ambush, with a dozen war wizards and several priests of Tempus in ready reserve. Her "coffin" stood open nearby, as did an iron prison box for each ghazneth. The princess did not expect all five phantoms to arrive at once—at least she hoped they would not—but only the gods knew what would happen when Owden cast his spell. Her magic ban had driven the ghazneths into such a frenzy they had begun to attack noble patrols in the hope of causing a panicked war wizard to fling a spell at them. The tactic worked just often enough to make the phantoms continue, which was as Tanalasta wished. Better to keep them in southern Cormyr and control the magic they received than to let them fly off and seek it elsewhere.

"Do you want to find Rowen or not, Princess?" asked Owden. "I didn't spend half a tenday meditating on this new spell as a leisuretime activity."

Tanalasta returned her attention to the harvestmaster. "I know." She leaned closer and lowered her voice. "I'm having trouble remembering his face."

Owden's scowl softened. "Perhaps you're afraid to know."

"No." Tanalasta shook her head harshly. "If he's dead, I want to know. It's better that than to think of him in some orc slave camp—or worse."

Owden nodded, then reached across the small distance between them and tapped her brow. "You're trying too hard. He's still in there. Remember something you did together. Relax, and let his face come to you."

Tanalasta thought of their first kiss. They had been in the shadow of Anauroch's great dunes, about to distract a ghazneth that had Alusair's company trapped in the ruins of an old goblin keep. Tanalasta started to step through the gate to attract the phantom's attention but was seized by a sudden urge to kiss the handsome scout. She grabbed him by the lapels and pressed her lips to his, and he pressed back and wrapped her in his arms. Such a godsent hunger ran through her that she had nearly forgotten about her imperiled sister.

Owden began to swing Rowen's holy symbol back and forth, and Tanalasta's eyes followed it. She had begun to run her hands over Rowen's body, and he had done the same to her, sliding his palm up to cup the softness of her breast. . . .

His face returned her, handsome and swarthy and chiseled, with a gentle smile and brown eyes as deep as the forest. A rush of relief rose up inside her, and Tanalasta said, "I have him."

"Good. Now keep watching his holy symbol. It is the trail that will lead you to him. Keep watching . . ."

Owden broke into the deep chant of his spell, calling upon Chauntea's godly power to reforge the mystical link between Rowen and what Luthax had taken from him. Tanalasta continued to watch the swinging symbol, holding her husband's face in mind and praying to the goddess to answer Owden's plea. Rowen's image melded into the silver bud and became one with it, and there was just her husband's head, sweeping back and forth in front of her. The room vanished around Tanalasta. She had the sense of plunging down a dark tunnel into a blackness as vast as the Abyss itself.

An inky shadow fell across the face before her, and its features became gaunt and harsh. The brow grew heavy and sinister, hanging over a pair of luminous white eyes as round and lustrous as pearls, and the nose swelled into a brutish, hooked thing as sharp as a hawk's beak. Only the chin remained the same, square, strong, and cleft.

"Rowen?" Tanalasta gasped.

The white eyes brightened and looked away, vanishing into a misty gray cloud. For a moment, Tanalasta did not understand what she was seeing, then a fork of lightning danced across her view and she realized it was rain.

"Rowen?" she called again.

A different face appeared, just as gaunt but bushy-browed and cob-nosed, with sunken gray eyes and a bushy black beard that covered it from the hollow cheeks down. An iron circlet ringed the figure's filthy mop of hair, with bare patches of scalp and red scratches along the temples where the wearer had tried to tear off his crude crown. There was something vaguely familiar in the impatient furrow of his brow and the harshness in his eyes, but Tanalasta could not think of how she might know the haggard old man.

"Who are you?" she demanded. "What happened to Rowen?"

What happened to Rowen? mocked an all-too-familiar voice, the sound of it echoing in her mind. *Is that all you want to know? No "how are you, Old Snoop?" "Where have you been?" Not even "Are you dead or alive?"*

"Vangerdahast?" Tanalasta gasped. "*Are* you dead?"

The wizard looked insulted. *No!*

"Then where are you?" Tanalasta grew faintly aware of warm bodies pressing close around in the Crownsilver dining room. She ignored them and kept her concentration focused on the swinging face before her eyes. "What happened to Rowen?"

The City of the Grodd, in answer to your first question, replied the wizard. *And in reply to the one that will surely follow my answer, I have no idea. Suffice it to say I've been trying to get out for . . . well, a very long time.*

"But you're younger," Tanalasta observed.

Vangerdahast cringed and touched the crown on his head. *The benefits of rank, I suppose. How long will this spell last?*

"Longer than we have. A ghazneth will be arriving any moment," said Tanalasta. "I was looking for Rowen—"

Yes, so you've said, but that'll have to wait. A giant red dragon appeared in Cormyr.

249

It was a statement, not a question, but Tanalasta confirmed it anyway.

"Yes—a dragon, and whole armies of orcs, and goblins, too," she said. "The nobles and I are fighting the ghazneths in the south."

The nobles? Vangerdahast raised an astonished brow.

"It's too long a story to tell," said Tanalasta. "I've figured out how to render the ghazneths powerless, but I can't seem to kill them."

Forgive them, Vangerdahast said.

"What?"

Call them by their proper names and forgive them, the wizard repeated. *They've all betrayed Cormyr, and it's that festering core of guilt that binds their power together. Absolve them of their crime, and the core crumbles.*

"It's that simple?" Tanalasta gasped.

You will have to survive long enough to say the words, Vangerdahast reminded her. *And I suspect it must be you or the king himself who'll have to do it. Only the absolution of a direct heir to the crown would have meaning to them.*

Tanalasta furrowed her brow. "How do you know all this?"

There isn't time to explain. Vangerdahast's eyes shifted away. *Now, what of the dragon? She is their master and your real trouble.*

"Father and Alusair are in the north fighting . . . *her*, is it?—and her orcs and goblins as well." A shout from upstairs announced the appearance of a ghazneth on the horizon. Tanalasta fought down a sudden panic and forced herself to concentrate on Vangerdahast. "We have only a few moments more, I fear."

The wizard nodded his understanding. *There should be no more goblins to trouble you.*

"Nor the dragon for much longer, with a little luck," Tanalasta replied. "The king seems to have her on the run."

The wizard's eyes grew wide. *Stop him! That dragon is Lorelei Alavara.*

"Lorelei Alavara?"

Vangerdahast's voice grew dark. *Your father will know who she is.* He looked away for a moment, then lifted the top

250

of a golden scepter into view. It was fashioned in the figure of a sapling oak, with an amethyst pommel carved into the shape of giant acorn. *He needs this to kill her. The Scepter of Lords. Tell him.*

Tanalasta nodded. She knew of the Scepter of Lords and was dying to learn how Vangerdahast had come into possession of it, but she had only a moment longer. The sentries were calling down a running account of the ghazneth's approach, and the thing had already grown from a mere sky speck to a winged figure with two arms and two legs.

"How will you get it to him?" Tanalasta asked.

Vangerdahast closed his eyes and said, *I can't.* He tried to slip a finger under his iron crown and succeeded only in scratching a new furrow into his skin. *You found me . . .*

The sentries yelled the final alarm, then a huge hand covered Vangerdahast's face and Tanalasta suddenly found herself sitting in the Crownsilver dining room across from Owden Foley.

The harvestmaster slipped Rowen's holy symbol around her neck and said, "It's Melineth Turcasson." He uttered a quick prayer, then touched his hand to the silver sunflower now hanging on her chest. "This will protect you and the child from disease."

Tanalasta nodded, then allowed Owden to guide her into her iron hiding place.

They were still pulling the door closed when the oak window shutters exploded into splinters and Melineth Turcasson streaked into the room. He landed atop the great banquet table, his scabrous black wings smashing into the delicate chandeliers as they brought his flight to a halt. At once, the room filled with the clatter of firing crossbows, and the astonished ghazneth sprouted a coat of iron quarrels. He roared in anger, spewing his rancid black breath across the room, and tried to spin away from the barrage.

Another tempest of clacking filled the air, and Melineth began to resemble a porcupine with wings. He dropped to his knees and began to pluck the quarrels from his body, his wounds closing as fast as he emptied them. A dozen dragoneers leaped onto the table and started to flail at the ghazneth with iron swords. Roaring, he gave up on the quarrels and whirled to defend himself.

Two men died before they could scream, their heads merely swatted from their shoulders. Another pair perished when his powerful wings sent them flying across the room and their helmets split against the stone wall. One soldier fell when Melineth snapped his neck and hurled his limp body into three of his fellows, knocking them all from the table. The last four all managed to land blows before the ghazneth killed them in a flurry of smashing elbows and snapping jaws.

Melineth turned toward Tanalasta's hiding place. He was a powerful-looking figure with hulking shoulders, gangling arms, and a blocky, almost handsome face.

"Too clever, my dear," he said, spewing more of his rancid breath into the air. Dragoneers began to cough and retch, filling the chamber with a vortex of loathsome sounds and smells. Melineth kicked a body off the table, then started toward Tanalasta. "Too clever by far."

A handful of dragoneers raised their crossbows and fired, but they were coughing too violently to fire accurately. The bolts ricocheted off the walls, thumped into the shutters, and tinkled through the remains of the chandelier. Three trembling soldiers moved to block Melineth's path. They were sweating profusely and so weak they could barely lift their halberds, much less use them.

"Time to go!" Owden hissed, starting to pull the coffin door shut.

Tanalasta stopped him. "No—we can do this." She pointed to the three soldiers who had moved to defend her. "Give them strength."

The ghazneth grabbed two of the men by their arms and, staring in Tanalasta's direction, squeezed. The pair screamed in agony, and their arms withered into black, rotten sticks.

The third soldier drove the tip of his halberd through the bottom of the phantom's jaw, pinning it closed.

Tanalasta did not even see Melineth's leg move. The man simply flew across the room, a foot-shaped dent in the center

252

of his breastplate and blood pouring from his mouth. The ghazneth released his other two victims and stumbled back to the edge of the banquet table, struggling to pull the halberd from his jaw.

"Now!" Tanalasta shoved the coffin open and pushed Owden into the room. "Use your magic."

The priest raised his arms and stepped forward, calling upon Chauntea to dispel the ghazneth's evil and strengthen Cormyr's brave soldiers. Tanalasta followed him and snatched a halberd from the hands of a retching soldier. She was doing something she had promised her mother she would not do—risking her own life and that of her child—but the time had come to win the war or lose it. If she fled now, every soldier in southern Cormyr would doubt her ability to stop the ghazneths. If she destroyed Melineth, no one in the kingdom would question her eventual victory.

Giving up on the halberd in his jaw, Melineth snapped the weapon off below the head and launched himself at Owden. Tanalasta stepped past the priest and tipped her weapon forward to catch the ghazneth's charge. She did not get the butt braced before the phantom's powerful chest struck the blade.

The impact drove her back toward her coffin, but the iron blade opened the ghazneth's chest and sank deep into the yellow bone of his sternum. She wrapped her arms around the shaft and braced her feet on the floor. Roaring in anger, Melineth leaned forward and lashed out with his gangling arms. The princess ducked and was driven another step backward. The butt of the weapon struck her coffin and stopped.

Melineth tried to strike again, still driving forward in his fury. Tanalasta's face erupted into stinging pain as two long claws slashed across her cheek. A tremendous crack reverberated through the dining room. The ghazneth's chest opened before her eyes, spilling all manner of black, stinking offal onto the floor.

Melineth's eyes widened. He tried to open his mouth to scream, but found it still pinned shut and could not. He stumbled back, dragging Tanalasta's halberd from her

253

hands and snorting black fume from his nostrils. He tried to pull the weapon from his chest, failed, and dropped to his knees.

The dragoneers were on him, hacking and slashing with their iron blades until the ghazneth was little more than a bloody pulp. Exhausted and trembling, Tanalasta fell back against the wall. She felt feverish and achy and queasy from her wound, but she managed to remain conscious.

A dozen war wizards rushed up with the ghazneth's iron box, and Owden yelled, "Get him in! Bring the coins!"

Half a dozen dragoneers grabbed the ghazneth and instantly began to cough and retch. Still, they managed to pitch the ghazneth into the box before collapsing to the floor. They were quickly dragged away, and six more men stepped forward to take their place. They hacked the shaft off the halberd Tanalasta had planted into creature's breast, then began to pour golden coins over him.

Owden took Tanalasta by the arm. "I know you feel ill. . . ."

"I can do it." She allowed Owden to help her to the prison box, then grabbed a handful of coins and dumped them onto Melineth's forehead. "Melineth Turcasson, father of Queen Daverna and Lord Mayor of Suzail and the Southern Shore, as a true Obarskyr and heir to the Dragon Throne, I grant you the thing you most desire, the thing for which you betrayed your daughter and the sacred trust of your king. I grant you gold."

The strength left Melineth all at once, and the foul blackness bubbling up from his chest became frothy red blood. The shadow lifted from his body, then his face screwed into a mask of horrid pain. He began to scream and flail about in his gold-filled coffin, flinging coins in every direction.

Then, recalling what Vangerdahast had told her only a few moments earlier, Tanalasta touched her hand to the ghazneth's brow and spoke again. "As heir to the crown and a direct descendant of King Duar, I forgive your betrayal of Cormyr, Melineth Turcasson. I absolve you of all crimes against the crown."

Death of the Dragon

Tanalasta had hardly spoken the last word before Melineth's flailing arms fell motionless. His eyes rolled up to meet hers. She thought for a moment that he would speak, but his eyes merely filled with black fume and dissolved into nothingness.

32

uietly," Alusair growled in a half whisper, for perhaps the fortieth time. "There'll be plenty of time, if we stay unseen."

She shook the shield she was crouching beneath, reminding the excited nobles behind her to keep their own cloak-shrouded shields raised, and crept forward a few cautious paces more.

It wasn't easy trying to simultaneously find safe, quiet footing in the tangle of wet moss, mud, and old fallen branches, and to peer ahead for lurking goblins or forest menaces—owlbears, for instance—that might have been drawn near by the bloody smell of the battle. The cloak-wrapped shields were to keep any sun-flash from blades or armor from alerting orcs. This had to be a hammerstroke no tusker expected.

If the dragon only stayed away to nurse its wounds long enough, she could outflank the orcs, Cormyr could strike at the snortsnouts from both sides, and with the very slimmest shard of Tymora's luck they'd shatter the goblinkin army.

The realm could at last turn to do battle with the ghazneths then—and the Devil Dragon—and perhaps end this madness once and for all.

Her father deserved that much. He deserved a few last years of peace—or what passed for peace in intrigue-ridden Cormyr, with every third noble ready to serve the king with either a dagger or a flagon of poison—before his old bones failed him and he was laid to rest in the land he'd served so long.

Gods, but she'd miss Azoun the Great when he was gone—not just as a father, but as the strength so alert and sure upon the throne that Sembia and Zhentil Keep and Hillsfar and half a hundred treacherous nobles could spend years plotting the downfall of the Dragon Throne, and so rarely dare to do anything to bring their dark dreams even a step nearer reality.

There wasn't another man on a throne anywhere on the face of Toril to equal him, not a man to stand up against him who didn't have spells spilling from his fingertips or scores of wizards to stand at his back, hurling lightning upon command. Or a woman, for that matter. They were all spell-hurlers or anointed-of-gods or ruled hard and cruel with spells and swords aplenty. No land but Cormyr could afford so many contrary and plotting nobles. No realm had a king strong enough to let them behave so.

Azoun IV was a hero among kings. A man, yes, she was proud to serve.

But she'd miss more than that. Yes, Alusair the Steel Princess, scourge of a thousand brigands and beasts, the hardest warrior among armies of hardened warriors, the wild lass who bedded and fought and hurled aside courtesies and graces at will, wanted her father and would miss him when he was gone.

She wanted to see more of him. Not the stern and disapproving Azoun, or the Lion of Cormyr raging in one of their many fights, but just the old man, watching her with admiration in his eyes—with love in his gaze. She wanted to hear him laugh and trade clever words with a courtier, and see him dance with her mother and make Filfaeril smile that smile she kept only for him, that made her whole face light up. Gods, Alusair Nacacia might even shock the court by turning up in a gown, painted nails, perfume, and with her hair tamed. Not to see their jaws drop, but to see the look on her father's face . . .

She hadn't realized she was smiling or that tears had come into her eyes, until one of the men behind her—Kortyl Rowanmantle, who was still drooling at her heels every day, somehow oblivious to the fact that there was at least one woman in the kingdom that he fancied, princess or not, who wasn't smitten with his easy good looks and artless, swaggering charm the moment she laid eyes on him—asked, "Is something . . . ah, wrong, Lady?"

"Nothing that matters now, Kortyl," she murmured. "Nothing that matters now."

"Oh," he said, then added in a rush, "That's good. As I've mentioned a time or two before, if there's anything I can—"

"My thanks, Kortyl."

"After all, Highness, my prowess . . . with a *blade* . . . is not unknown across our fair kingdom, and the lands and coins and castles I command are not inconsiderable, if—"

"They are, aren't they? I must bear that in mind, Kortyl," the Steel Princess murmured, "when you aren't stirring me so."

There was a little silence before Kortyl Rowanmantle almost yelped, "Stirring you, my Lady? I'm stirring you?"

"Indeed," Alusair replied, turning to give him a sweet, tight, and yet fierce smile. She leaned close to him—so close that he parted his lips invitingly, for her to kiss at last—and added in a whispered snarl, "Stirring me to fury, dolt, with the noise you're making when I've commanded *quiet!* Keep this up, and the next casualty of this war will be one Kortyl Rowanmantle, executed by a blade through the throat because he disobeyed a royal order on the battlefield."

Two fingers closed ever so gently on Kortyl's windpipe. Swallowing was suddenly painful—and that was unfortunate, because he felt a sudden, urgent need to swallow.

"But-but—yes, of course, Highness," he husked, then fell silent as if the threatened blade had slid home when the princess laid a finger across his lips, then drew the other slowly across his throat.

Without warning, she kissed him.

Kortyl Rowanmantle was still grinning in startled amazement when something suddenly fell across the dappled sunlight ahead.

Alusair looked up and screamed.

"The *dragon!*" she howled, in a voice so loud and harsh it was scarcely her own. "Scatter!"

The words had barely left her throat when the tops of two duskwood trees ahead of her exploded like kindling snapped across a forester's knee.

Nalavarauthatoryl the Red burst through them like an eager fox plunging over a wall into a henhouse pen, diving down heedless of branches and another possible impalement.

Dark drippings were still coming from the dragon's belly, but it looked not nearly as wounded as the Cormyreans had hoped. Its talons were spread wide to clutch and rake, and its jaws were agape—the jaws from whence the flames would come.

As she hurled herself desperately aside, away from much shouting, Alusair could have sworn the dragon was grinning.

All Faerûn exploded into flames around her.

33

he rain fell in sheets, pounding down on the iron canopy with such a roar Vangerdahast could hardly hear himself think. Peals of thunder rolled sporadically across the low ceiling, loosening tiny flakes of ancient Grodd fresco and sending them fluttering to the watery floor. Another lightning bolt lanced across the room and shattered a stubby little pillar. Chips of marble sprayed out like shrapnel, shredding the faces of half a dozen goblin courtiers and compelling them to run for the door, lest they insult their king by bleeding in his presence.

Vangerdahast sat at the edge of the Iron Throne, peering up at Rowen from the shelter of its small canopy. "You are making me reluctant to give you any more magic."

"You know I can't stop it," Rowen said. He seemed a mere silhouette of man-shaped darkness against a torrent of gray rain. "And I am upset. Tanalasta saw me."

"But only for an instant." Vangerdahast had to shout to make himself heard above the storm. "And she didn't know it was you."

"How can you be sure?"

"Had she thought you were standing here beside me, do you think I could have changed the subject?"

The thunder did not rumble quite so loudly. "Good. How did she seem?"

"Surprised." Vangerdahast kept his answer short and tried to sound irritated. He had actually come to like Rowen—perhaps even admire him—and the last thing the wizard wanted was to discuss the telltale shadow on the princess's lip. Queen Filfaeril's lip had grown similarly dark during all three of her pregnancies. "She was expecting to reach you."

"And she did, but how?"

Vangerdahast barely heard the question, for it had just occurred to him he finally had at least a vague time reference. Tanalasta's face had seemed weary and tired, but also much rounder than he remembered, with a certain heaviness below the jawline that bespoke a considerable weight gain. She had to be near the end of her pregnancy. For her to have met an eligible young noble, been properly courted, wed, and now be close to childbirth . . . it had to have been at least a year—and that only if she had given up the silly notion of marrying for love.

"What's wrong?" asked Rowen. "Why do you look so pale?"

The wizard waved the questions off, pretending to be preoccupied until he could think of a plausible answer, but his preoccupation was no act. His thoughts returned to Tanalasta at once. She had seemed very firm in her decision to marry for love (Vangerdahast recalled something about a vision from Chauntea), so the time had to be closer to *two* years—at a minimum. She would have needed time to forget Rowen, then there were the mere odds of meeting and falling in love with someone else. The process had taken twenty years the first time.

Then Vangerdahast understood. Had the princess fallen in love with somebody else, she would not have been looking for Rowen several years later. He glared up the ghazneth.

"Did you sleep with the princess?"

Rowen's pearly eyes brightened, then he looked away. "That is hardly any business of yours."

"Of course it is!" Vangerdahast snapped. "Do you not think it the business of the Royal Magician of Cormyr when a low-born, scurrilous dog takes advantage of the crown princess?"

"Takes advantage?" Rowen echoed. The room erupted into a tempest of crackling lightning, compelling the goblin courtiers to withdraw to the corners of the room. "If the princess must tell you everything, I am sure she also told you she was as eager as I was—though I still fail to see how what a wife does with her husband is any business of the royal magician's."

"Husband?" Vangerdahast's head began to feel like it was filled with wool. "I thought you two never left the Stonelands. When did you have time for a wedding? How did you get the king's approval?"

"A marriage is between two people," Rowen said. The lightning ceased. "We had Chauntea's blessing, and that was enough. Tanalasta did not tell you?"

"No." Vangerdahast sank back in his throne and shook his head, trying to work through the ramifications and guess how the news had been received in Cormyr. "Actually, she didn't need to tell me anything. I saw it for myself."

"Saw it? How could you . . ." Rowen let the question trail off, then his jaw dropped and the throne room grew very still. "I'm going to be a father?"

* * * * *

Even after the dead and wounded had been removed to the kitchen, the Crownsilver dining room looked more like a charnel house than the banquet hall of a great manor. Spattered crescents of crimson arced across the silken draperies and masterful wall murals. Claw marks and blade gouges furrowed the rosewood table. Glittering shards of crystal chandelier lay strewn across the floor, and the stench of blood and sickness hung in the air like smoke over a fire.

A fresh company of warriors, this one composed of the finest knights from the loyal noble houses, stood between the high windows along the exterior wall. They held their weapons high and ready but seemed unable to take their eyes off the chair where Tanalasta sat, still oozing blood from the gashes in her face. The tale of how she had grabbed a halberd and split open Melineth Turcasson's chest had spread across the estate like wildfire, growing in the telling as it passed from one building to the next. By the time the account reached the stables where the knights were waiting as a mounted reserve, the story had her destroying the ghazneth single-handedly, hacking him apart piecemeal as she chased him across the chamber. It was not an account any sensible man would believe when he saw how hugely pregnant she was, but the princess let the tale stand without comment. Having won fame for her ruthlessness, she thought it wise to earn a reputation for bravery as well.

Seeing that all was ready, Tanalasta nodded to Owden.

The harvestmaster removed Chauntea's sacred amulet from around his neck, then asked, "Are you sure you're ready to do this again so soon?"

Tanalasta nodded. "The king must hear what Vangerdahast said. I am ready." She looked across the room to the company of knights she would be relying upon. "Are you?"

"We are," answered Korvarr Rallyhorn.

It had taken seven priests of three different faiths nearly four days to put Korvarr together again after the battle with Luthax. As soon as he could stand again he rejoined his family retainers and promptly found himself elected captain of a company mustered from several loyal households. Few of those who had chosen him knew of his loose tongue with Orvendel, but Tanalasta doubted he would make such an error again and had gladly asked to have him assigned to her in reserve.

Owden gave the knights a few moments to prepare themselves, then kissed Chauntea's amulet and stooped down to touch it to the inflamed gashes Melineth had opened across Tanalasta's cheek. He spoke a prayer asking the goddess's blessing, then intoned the words of his spell. Chauntea's healing magic flowed into Tanalasta's face, and she felt the inflammation and poison leaving her.

The lookout's voice echoed down the stairs. "Ghazneth on the horizon!"

Owden uttered another spell, and Tanalasta felt the edges of the wound close.

"Shape now visible," called the lookout.

Another voice echoed down the stairs after the first. "We've got one to the east, too! Still a fleck."

Continuing to hold his holy symbol to her face, Owden paled. "Given what we've been through—"

"We'll take them both!" Tanalasta commanded, speaking over Owden. "Send the reserves upstairs. Have their war wizard cast a false aura as the second one approaches, then hold until we finish the first."

Owden finished his spell and removed his hand from Tanalasta's face, then muttered under his breath, "And pray there are no more."

"And that neither of these is Boldovar," Tanalasta added under her own breath. They had prepared enfeebling artifacts for every ghazneth except the Mad King. As of yet, no one had thought of a way to betoken what he desired. She leaned her head back over her chair and called, "Status!"

"To the west, wings and feet clearly visible. No hint of identity."

"To the east, cross shape just visible. It's hazy."

"Xanthon," Tanalasta said to Owden. "I'm going to enjoy this."

"Remember, you must forgive him."

"I must *absolve* him," Tanalasta corrected. "Besides, that's one ghazneth I'd *like* keeping locked in an iron box in the dungeon."

"That would be a big risk," Owden said warily.

"I know." Tanalasta had hardly been able to sleep since locking Luthax in the dungeon, and she had assigned fifty men to stand a constant guard over him. "But even princesses have dreams."

"They also have the power to make their dreams come

true." Owden stepped back and motioned to her weather-cloak's throat clasp. "So they must be careful."

Tanalasta sighed, then closed her throat clasp and pictured her father's stately face. When the piercing brown eyes began to look sunken and the dignified bearing seemed to grow weary, she spoke to him in her thoughts.

Vangerdahast trapped somewhere strange. He has Scepter of Lords. You need to destroy dragon, which is Lorelei Alavara. Who's that?

The look of guilty fear that flashed across the king's face made Tanalasta wish she had not asked.

You wouldn't know, came the king's reply. *Lorelei not in history books, and no time to explain. Thanks, and all luck with the ghazneths.*

The king's face vanished as the throat clasp's magic faded, and Tanalasta found herself looking at a room full of nervous knights.

"The king is well and sends his wishes for a successful battle." Tanalasta raised a hand and allowed Owden to pull her weary bulk out of the chair. "What of the ghazneths?"

"The first is almost here, Highness," said Owden. "The lookout thinks it is Lady Merendil. It has a narrow waist and waspish wings."

"It is," Tanalasta confirmed. She glanced over at the nervous looking knights. "I have faced Lady Merendil before. She's the Scourge of War, and you will find yourselves consumed by a mad bloodlust. You mustn't yield to it. Pray to your gods and keep your head about you. Remember who the enemy is, and we will do well."

The voice of experience seemed to comfort the knights. The doubt vanished from their faces, and they began to finger their holy symbols and utter prayers for strength. Tanalasta allowed Owden to help her toward her hiding box, at the same time summoning a pale-looking dragoneer who had been assigned to stand in the doorway as a messenger.

"Is the second ghazneth still trailing a hazy tail?"

"He is."

"Good. That will be Xanthon Cormaeril." She gestured through the door toward a hallway on the far side of the sweeping staircase. "Tell your war wizards to hide in there. On my command, one after the other, they are to blast him with their quickest, most powerful magic."

"Magic, Highness?" gasped the dragoneer. "On a ghazneth?"

"He is the youngest," Tanalasta explained. "I've seen him stunned by powerful spells."

"True," said Owden, "but if you don't get to him—"

"I think it is time for us to go to our place," Tanalasta said, cutting off the protest. "It cannot be long before Lady Merendil arrives."

The princess's words were truer than she would have liked. They had barely reached her hiding box before Lady Merendil's waspish form streaked through the window Melineth Turcasson had smashed open earlier. A tempest of clacking echoed off the walls as the knights fired their crossbows. Merendil shrieked in pain and fell from the air, bouncing off the banquet table and still somehow managing to angle toward Tanalasta.

Realizing that the thing was coming for her, Tanalasta was seized by a terrible blind fury. She found herself pushing the door of her hiding box open and pulling her iron dagger. Owden caught her by the hair and jerked her back inside.

"Have you gone mad?" He slammed the locking bar down, sealing them inside the dark box, then grasped Rowen's holy symbol and thrust it into her hands. "Calm down. Take your own advice and pray to the goddess."

The ghazneth hit the door with a deafening clang, then tried to rip it open and toppled the box over instead. Tanalasta landed on her stomach with a painful *whumpf*. The dark interior erupted into a cacophony of thunderous booms as Lady Merendil tried to tear the iron box open, then the crate suddenly rose on end and toppled over backward. Tanalasta's head sank through the leather padding and struck the iron beneath.

She thought for a moment that the muffled ringing in her ears was from a cracked skull, then she heard the dull thud of iron biting bone and the sharp crack of snapping limbs and the anguished howls of dying men, and she knew the knights were carrying the battle to the ghazneth. Tanalasta reached across Owden and felt for the locking bar.

The harvestmaster caught her by the wrist. "What are you doing?"

"I've got to get out there!" she said. "They need my leadership."

"They need you alive, or all is for naught." Owden shoved her arm back. "Say your prayers—now!"

Though she was fuming inwardly, Tanalasta clasped Rowen's amulet and did as the priest instructed. A sense of calm came over her almost at once, and she realized Owden was right. She had fallen victim to the very bloodlust she had warned Korvarr's knights against. Continuing to hold the silver holy symbol in her hands, she listened to the muted battle sounds and waited for the proper moment to show herself again. If her own experience was anything to go by, the men outside hardly needed inspiration, and getting herself killed for no reason would do nothing to destroy the ghazneths.

The box began to vibrate with a muffled drone, and tiny insect wings began to brush past Tanalasta's face. "By the plow! Xanthon's here already."

Owden laid a hand on Tanalasta's wrist—whether to comfort her or restrain her, she did not know. "Patience. We have heard no sign that he is downstairs."

Something stung Tanalasta behind the ear, then something else bit her below the eye. She cursed and tried to swat the insects away, but in the dark tight quarters, it was difficult work. The princess managed to keep the things more or less off her face, but they crawled up beneath her hairline and down her collar and into her sleeves, stinging and biting and driving her mad. She killed the ones she could and tried to tolerate the rest, and finally the battle outside seemed to drift away.

Tanalasta was in no hurry to release the locking bar, for she knew the insect cloud would only grow thicker when they opened the box.

A sharp rap sounded on the door. "Princess, we're ready." It was Korvarr. "Open up!"

Troy Denning and Ed Greenwood

"Now?" Tanalasta asked.

"It would seem so." Owden released the locking bar.

The lid flew open, and a gauze-like fog of buzzing wasps descended into the box. Owden began a prayer to disperse the insects. Squinting and gritting her teeth against the stinging cloud, Tanalasta raised an arm toward Korvarr.

"Help me up."

"With pleasure, Princess."

A hard hand grasped her by the wrist and jerked her to her feet, and she found herself looking into the bloodied, deranged face of Korvarr Rallyhorn.

"Korvarr?"

"Killer!" Korvarr released Tanalasta's arm and back-handed her across the mouth, then reached awkwardly across his body for his dagger. "This is for Orvendel!"

For a moment, Tanalasta thought Korvarr had actually betrayed her. She stepped forward, pinning his arm against his chest and brought her knee up between his legs. He let out a horrid groan and doubled over, and it was then the princess noticed the finger bruises on his forearm and the impossible bend of the bone and realized what had happened. She lashed out with one hand and caught him by the ear, then brought her opposite elbow around and smashed it into the opposite side of the head, throwing her entire pregnant weight into the attack.

Her self-defense instructors had taught her well. Had she struck four inches higher, the blow would have shattered Korvarr's temple and killed him instantly. As it was, the strike merely dislocated his jaw and left him unconscious at her feet.

Owden finished his spell, filling the room with pale, cedar-sharp smoke that sent the insects droning for the exits.

Astonished, Tanalasta turned and cocked her brow. "I am being attacked, and you are worried about wasps?"

"It was only Korvarr," Owden replied. "If you can't handle one man, what business have you trafficking in ghazneths?"

A ringing clamor echoed through the door behind them, and they turned to see a dozen dragoneers tumbling into the foyer beyond.

"That would be Xanthon now. Stall him."

Tanalasta pushed Owden toward the steel tangle, then turned back to the dining room. A whirling knot of darkness and iron was slowly drifting away from her, moving toward an ancient throne at the far end of the room. Though the churning mass contained at least fifty knights, it almost looked as though they were loosing the battle. Plate-armored bodies came flying out at regular intervals, helmets staved in or breastplates cleaved open or truncated limbs flinging crimson arcs through the air. Had the ghazneth not been weak and slow with magic starvation, Tanalasta could not imagine what the battle would have been like.

A steel clamor sounded from the main stairwell, and Owden called, "Tanalasta, he's coming!"

"When he reaches the bottom of the stairs—tell the wizards then!" Without waiting to see whether the harvestmaster understood, Tanalasta rushed into the steel tangle before her. "Stand aside! Let me at her!"

The knights, consumed as they were by bloodlust, paid her no attention. She barreled into the tangle from behind, forcing it toward the throne and tearing battle-crazed warriors out of her way. Several times, the princess was forced to duck the wild swing of a mailed hand or parry a low dagger, but she had practiced such drills often enough to understand the principle of redirection and always managed to steer these attacks toward others blocking her way. Furious knights began to spin off in groups of four and five, battering one another with their iron weapons and doing far more damage to each other than Lady Merendil had caused.

A fiery roar rumbled through the doorway as the war wizards unleashed their spells. Realizing she had no more than a minute before Xanthon recovered and began to convert the magic into a catastrophe for her, she grabbed a knight by the back of the helmet and shoved forward, using him like a battering ram to clear her path.

"Out of the way!" she screamed. "By royal command, stand aside!"

The tangle never parted, but she pushed into a region of hacking iron and flying black gore. The whole snarl seemed to lunge forward, and she found herself peering over an armored shoulder at a shadowy, mangled figure that could only be what remained of Lady Merendil. Tanalasta grabbed hold of the shoulder in front of her and raised her leg, thrusting her heel into the thing's chest.

"Lady Ryndala Merendil, as a true Obarskyr and heir to the Dragon Throne, I grant you the thing you most desire, the thing for which you betrayed your liege duty and your loyalty to Cormyr, the throne of Azoun the First!" Tanalasta kicked outward, knocking Lady Merendil's butchered form back into the burnished walnut throne behind her. "And as heir to the crown and a direct descendant of Azoun the First, I forgive your betrayal and absolve you of all crimes against Cormyr."

Lady Merendil's mouth opened in a black, silent shriek, but Tanalasta was already backing out of the crowd and rushing toward the door.

"Again!" she cried. "Hit him again!"

Tanalasta left the dining room to find the entire foyer filled with slashing iron blades. The blood-smeared floor was littered with naked rat tails, long-whiskered mouse snouts, and scaly-headed snake pieces. Coughing, stumbling dragoneers ran in every direction, hacking at anything that moved on the floor. The ceiling was alive with spiders and the walls were crawling with scorpions. Men lay everywhere clutching twisted black hands and arms swollen to the size of thighs.

Tanalasta smacked a dragoneer in the side of the helmet. "Where's the ghazneth?"

"There." The warrior pointed to a mass of mangled flesh surrounded by chopping blades, then grabbed Tanalasta's hand and shouldered his way forward. "Make way for the princess!"

The disciplined dragoneers immediately opened a path. By the time Tanalasta had pulled the signet off her finger, she was standing over Xanthon's butchered figure, watching in horror as the wounds on his dark body closed faster than they could be opened.

Tanalasta kneeled at his side and grasped the flayed remains of a hand. There were only two fingers left, and she chose the largest.

"Xanthon Cormaeril, first cousin to my husband Rowen and second cousin to the next heir of the Dragon Throne, I give you the thing you desire most, the prestige and honor of the Obarskyr name."

Before she could slip the ring onto his finger, Xanthon jerked free of her grasp. "Trollop!" he hissed. "You would sleep with any traitor among us. Rowen is one of—"

An iron halberd came down across his mouth, cleaving his jaw off and pinning his head to the floor. An armored foot secured his arm alongside it, then the tip of an iron sword unfurled the remaining two fingers.

"Perhaps the princess should try again," said a gruff voice.

"In a moment," Tanalasta said. "What is this about Rowen?"

Xanthon's jaw drew back toward the rest of his head, healing before the princess's eyes. He smiled and said, "He's a Cormaeril. Do you really need to ask?"

Again, the halberd came down across Xanthon's mouth, and the gruff voice said, "Pay him no attention, Princess. He's only trying to buy time to save himself."

Tanalasta nodded. "Of course." Though she did not quite believe the dragoneer, she knew better than to think Rowen would ever have betrayed Cormyr—or her. She grabbed Xanthon's black hand and shoved the signet ring onto his finger. "Xanthon Cormaeril, I name you royal cousin."

The shadow did not fade from Xanthon's body so much as simply vanish. In the next instant there was a man, horribly mutilated and screaming in agony, lying on the ground with Tanalasta's signet ring on his finger. Content to have him thrown in an iron box and left that way, she rose and turned away—only to find herself looking at Owden Foley.

"I believe you have forgotten something," the priest said. "The ghazneth cannot be destroyed until you forgive it."

"*Absolve* it," Tanalasta corrected. She turned and looked down at the screaming thing on the floor. Now that she had placed her ring on its finger, its wounds were no longer healing and it looked like no more than it was—a tormented traitor screaming for mercy. "He doesn't deserve it. You heard what he said about Rowen."

"What he said about Rowen does not matter." Owden tapped her over the heart, pushing his finger into the soft swell of her upper breast. "How you react does."

Tanalasta considered the priest's words, then kneeled at Xanthon's side. "I will give one more chance to clear your conscience, cousin. Tell me what became of Rowen."

"I . . . told . . . you," Xanthon gasped. "He's one of . . . us."

"Liar!" Tanalasta took a deep breath, then reluctantly clasped the ghazneth's wrist. "As an heir to the Obarskyr throne and daughter to King Azoun IV, I . . . absolve you of your crime."

"And forgive your betrayal," added Owden.

Tanalasta waited to see if Xanthon would perish. When he did not, she added, "And forgive your betrayal."

The pain seemed to leave Xanthon's face. "Now it is you who are lying." He closed his eyes and smiled. "Cousin."

34

he last of the snortsnouts are down, my liege," the battlemaster growled through the protesting squeal of his visor being pushed up and open. "We've lost some good men, but fewer than I'd feared."

King Azoun nodded grimly, his eyes still fixed on the line of trees where the forest began, not far to the west. His mouth was set in a tight line, and a lone muscle twitched beside his mouth. It was a sign that few men there had ever had the misfortune to see before.

Battlemaster Ilnbright, however, was one of them, and knew well that it meant fear warred with anger in Azoun's thoughts. He did not need to follow the dark fire of the king's gaze to know the source of the royal fury. Every man gathered on the hill, and the many now cleaning their blades and finding places to rest weary backsides on the slopes below, knew the same dark truth. As Purple Dragons and growling orc warriors had met and the ringing din of blades had risen, Azoun had given the signal that should have brought the

Troy Denning and Ed Greenwood

Steel Princess and her noblemen charging out of the trees to strike the orcs from the rear, long swords flashing. The blare of the signal horns had been as loud as any Haliver Ilnbright had heard, in tens of summers of riding under the Purple Dragon banner . . . but no one had come out of the forest.

Not a single blade. Outnumbered and exposed to the foe on three flanks, Azoun's warriors had fought hard and well, and hacked every last tusker into the dirt. Without Alusair's forces, the choice had been simple: win victory, or welcome death.

The king had long since sent scouts to find Princess Alusair and order her to rally her men back to the royal standard. Three veteran rangers—each alone so one at least should escape ill—Randaeron, Pauldimun, and Yarvel, good men all, had gone out. Either they had found ill or not found the princess. How long must it take to travel a mile or two? Less long than they'd already taken, surely.

"Back to the river, or make camp here?" the battlemaster asked gently, mindful of the royal mood.

"Here," Azoun said, the word clear and cold. A long breath of silence passed before he added, "I'd not welcome fighting my way back across the bridge next morn, just to reach this height again."

Ilnbright turned and gestured. Men who'd been watching for it reached with swift, practiced speed for the first poles that would soon become the royal tent.

The guards standing close around the king were weather-beaten, eagle-eyed veterans. Gaerymm and Telthluddree had the better sight, still able to outshoot many of the arrowmasters, but the hulking bannerguard, Kolmin Stagblade (no one ever seemed to use just one of his names, perhaps because of his mountainous, inexorable bulk) stood a good two heads taller than either, so it was he who said suddenly, "Randaeron Farlokkeir returns. Alone, but laden."

In silence the other men stepped aside to allow Azoun to stride forward and peer along the bannerguard's pointing arm.

After a moment, Azoun turned away. His voice was almost gentle as he said to the nearest messenger, "Wine. Flamekiss. Just the flask."

That flask was empty by the time the scout trotted around the men driving home the last lines of the royal tent. He went to his knees before Azoun, stretching his arms forth in silence to place a scorched helm and a half-melted, twisted shield on the trampled turf. A sharp burnt smell came to the hilltop with him—the smell of cooked flesh.

The helm might have belonged to any Purple Dragon but for the battered cheek guard. All of the men standing on the hill knew a certain scar and bend in it. The shield, too, might have belonged to a hundred hundred soldiers of Cormyr— but its unblemished upper corner bore a device that was Alusair's alone, a steel-gray falcon leaping up from the palm of a war gauntlet.

"Majesty," Randaeron murmured, "these were all I could find that I could be sure were the princess's, in a place of many bones and bodies." He spread his hands helplessly, and added, "The dragon . . ."

"Everyone slain?" Azoun asked, in apparent calm. "Torn apart or . . . cooked?"

"There were signs of many men in boots fleeing into the forest, each by his own path rather than together or along a trail. I searched the remains a long time, while Paulder and Yar followed the signs into the forest, but I cannot say that I found her highness . . . or know that I did not. So many were . . . bones."

The ranger's voice broke, then, and it seemed for a moment that the hands of the king trembled. When he reached down to put a hand on the scout's shoulder and to take up the ashen helm, however, they seemed steady enough.

"My thanks, Randaeron," Azoun said quietly. "Tarry here in camp, at least until your fellow scouts return. I am sure no man could find more among the dead than you did."

Without another word to anyone the king walked away. Down the hillside he went, his steps slow and aimless, looking at the helm in his hands as if it held his daughter's face.

Not a man moved to follow, though all of his bodyguards shifted to where they could clearly see where Azoun went, and the hillside below him. They saw the Old Blade of the

Obarskyrs walk ever more slowly, until he entered a little hollow where he sat down as wearily as any overweight pike-dragoneer.

"Is she dead, d'you think?" a lancelord standing by the tent muttered to his superior. Keldyn Raddlesar was too young to know when to keep quiet.

"Lad," Ethin Glammerhand growled back, "how could she not be? I doubt w—"

A shadow fell across the lowering sun, and both men fell silent, staring up into the sky in mounting terror as the Devil Dragon plunged down upon them.

Nalavarauthatoryl the Red was huge, as large across as the main turrets of High Horn, with jaws broad enough to swallow half a dozen horses—and their riders—at a single bite. They were gaping wide now, revealing the dark, vibrating throat from whence the flames would come. Eager fire burned in the dragon's eyes, and its cruelly curved talons were spread wide to strike. In places the wyrm's body was a deep, angry purple, almost black, and men were screaming as its racing shadow fell across them—screams echoed in the raw, mounting roar of fear and defiance that burst from the throats of the warriors on the hilltop, as they scrambled to stand apart from one another and raise their tiny weapons.

The dragon's talons were aimed for the royal tent, but it must have noticed that no one rushed into that pavilion to warn anyone, or hastened forth—and that no bodyguards stood watchfully by its entrance. It veered aside at the last moment to pounce on one man whose raised and ready blade seemed to glow as if alive with magic.

Randaeron Farlokkeir screamed as he died, torn open from belly to chin by a talon an instant before his hands were bitten off, his enchanted sword vanishing with them into a mouth as large as his cottage.

"As large—as—" he managed to gasp, before a sudden tide from within him choked his words—and the world— away.

As the mutilated scout reeled and collapsed in a rain of his own blood, the dragon landed heavily beyond him, its tail sweeping aside a trio of sprinting dragoneers, and a sudden silence fell.

In that strange calm, the dragon looked around with an almost feminine, menacing smile.

"Well," it said, its breath acrid and stinking, "where *is* the human king?" The voice, too, was female. The loudest reply to it came from the mouths of the Cormyrean officers slowly advancing on it. That response was an eerie chorus of teeth chattering in fear.

"*Die*, dragon!" one of them shouted suddenly, charging forward with his blade thrown back over his shoulder, ready to chop down.

"Die!" another echoed, starting to run in turn.

Both had seen what the dragon must not have. A lone, bareheaded figure sprinted up behind the dragon, drawn blade flashing as it raced along Nalavara's flank. The Devil Dragon was about to find the man she was seeking.

As Nalavara almost casually smashed her attackers with a wave of one talon, the King of Cormyr bounded into the air and thrust his blade behind the corner of her jaw. His steel slid home easily, gliding with oily ease into the spot where no scales waited. Black blood spurted forth, smoking.

"Here, dragon!" Azoun snarled, his eyes blazing. "Murderer! Despoiler of my realm! *Here I am!*"

He jerked his blade free, and as the dragon turned her head with snakelike speed and a fearsome snarl, Azoun struck again, thrusting his steel deep into her tongue then plucking it out to leap away, rolling desperately in under the dragon's chin.

Fire roared forth, setting grass afire and crisping an unfortunate dragoneer who was caught in its full fury and sent tumbling away through the air like a burning leaf. The king was gone.

Gone, that is, until the royal blade stabbed upward between the small, soft scales behind the dragon's chin. The sword rose like a bloody fountain through Nalavara's mouth and tongue.

"For Alusair!" the king cried. "For my *daughter*, wyrm!"

His words were lost in the squall of pain that burst forth

277

from the dragon's throat. She thrust her head up, baring her throat to the furious monarch, but he couldn't drag his sword free in time, wallowing in blood-drenched dimness, to strike before Nalavara twisted away.

A talon longer than the king stood tall stabbed out for him. It missed his shoulder by a foot, no more, as the dragon gathered herself to spring into the air—doubtless for a short flight that would end in another swoop at the hilltop, and more fire, and the death of Azoun.

But Nalavara trembled, faltering, and above Azoun's head there were ragged shouts of, "For Azoun! For Alusair! For *Cormyr!*"

Above his head?

Azoun rolled, keeping hold of his sword only with difficulty, and came out into the sunlight to see warriors running up the hill with fear white on their faces, but swords and spears and axes in their hands.

A rope was stretched tight up and over the dragon, one end trembling under the frantic sledge-blows of a sweating knot of warriors, and the other—

The other was driven deep into the muscles of one of the dragon's wings, held there with a savage smile by Swordlord Ethin Glammerhand. Lancelord Raddlesar was bounding up slippery scales to meet him, slashing at whatever parts of the wing he could reach as he hastened. A gruff sword-captain wasn't far behind, his axe rising and falling as if dragon meat was wanted on his cookfire forthwith.

Nalavara roared deafeningly and bucked, hurling the lancelord off his feet. The dragon rolled over, one slash of her jaws severing the rope, then scrambled upright as swiftly as any cat. The swordlord bounced helplessly against her scales, clinging to his sword's hilt. Nalavara raked her talons across the Lancelord Raddlesar, cutting him to ribbons as he lay twitching on the ground, and bit down on the warrior in front of her.

Swordcaptain Theldyn Thorn was suddenly gone above the waist—blade, breastplate, and all.

His hips trembled, swaying, then crashed to the ground under the impact of the tumbling swordlord, spilled from the dragon's wing high above. Spears bounced harmlessly off dark red scales, and King Azoun charged in once more to hack at all he could reach—the blood-drenched talon that had slain his lancelord and so narrowly missed him.

The dragon turned her head, spitting out torn gobbets of flesh, and drew back to either spew fire on the raging king or thrust her head down and bite him.

A priest of Tempus stammered out a spell that made the air around Nalavara's head erupt in a sudden, dancing storm of blades, but the snarling dragon flapped her wings in the very heart of the whirling steel, as if their flashing points weren't there at all, then bounded into the air. A flick of her tail smashed Swordlord Glammerhand into the heart of the steel storm. Two men leaped onto the king as he bounced helplessly, keeping him just beneath the whirling blades. They could do nothing to stop the dragon as she bent down, eyes closed against the flashing steel fangs, and bit blindly at Azoun.

The King of Cormyr rose to meet her, throwing off the lords trying to shield him as if they were lap dogs, and thrust his sword mightily through welling dragonfire and into Nalavara's lip. Black blood gushed forth once more. The dragon roared and shook her head, one fang hurling the king away in a tangle of torn armor and royal blood. The two lords rushed desperately forward again.

Rings on their fingers flashed as the dragon bit down once more. This time cruel teeth closed on something unseen and skittered vainly across air, well above the struggling men.

The Devil Dragon roared her rage in the heart of the steel storm, then flapped her wings, rending the air with a sound like a clap of thunder, and ascended, ignoring the few arrows that reached for her, and all the shouting below. She trailed a few smoking wisps of blood as she flew in a wide, climbing arc west over the forest, not looking back at the hilltop, and disappeared north.

In the wake of the dragon, the hillside was slick with blood and littered with moaning men or the torn fragments of what had been men. In their midst, two of those whom the

nobles of Cormyr liked to contemptuously call "little lords"—
men recently ennobled by the crown for service, and lacking
long years of proud family power—lay panting, face to face,
atop their groaning king.

"Best end the shielding," Lord Edryn Braerwinter
gasped, "lest one of those ghazneths comes."

"Is it . . . gone?" his fellow lord gasped, not daring to look.
Braerwinter nodded, lacking the breath to speak again, and
rolled slowly off the King of Cormyr.

Azoun Obarskyr lay with his eyes closed and his mouth
twisted in pain, his limbs moving restlessly. Tendrils of
smoke from the black blood of the dragon rose from him, and
his armor was crumpled into ruin above one hip, and
entirely bitten away above the other, all along his flank,
which was dark and wet with blood. Wherever his breast
was dry of blood, it was dark with the ash left by dragonfire.

Men were hastening up on all sides, now.

"He needs healing," Lord Steelmar Tolon gasped, finding
his feet, "but we must get him into the tent before half a hundred archers start spreading word that they've seen him
lying dead. Take his other arm . . . under the shoulders . . ."

"What're you *doing?*" Battlemaster Ilnbright roared, as
the two lords staggered upright, Azoun hanging limply
between them.

"To the tent!" Lord Braerwinter snarled. "Get him some
healing—*now!*"

"You can't just—"

"Well, we *are*," Lord Tolon roared, in a voice even louder
than the battlemaster's bellow. "Get out of the way or die!"

He held up the hand in a menacing fist and his ring
winked. Ilnbright, not knowing for certain what that ring
did, fell back, face black with rage, then turned and shouted
for priests.

"Bring me healers!" he roared. "Every holy man on this
field, whatever his rank or protests. *Haste!*"

The ring on Tolon's finger winked again, and the battlemaster fell silent, blinking in surprise. The ring's magic had
carried his shout miles distant, in a great and terrible roar.
All over the field Purple Dragons were on the move,

snatching up robed men by the elbows and collars.

"Bring the king's sword," Lord Braerwinter said to the astonished officer. "A warrior feels better if he can hold his blade."

Still blinking, Battlemaster Ilnbright bent over and meekly scooped up Azoun's mighty warsword.

* * * * *

A little later, two weary lords staggered through the grim ring of archers, ignoring the hard eyes that watched them go down the hill. The dragon had not come again, but if it did, the army of Cormyr would be ready. A splayed forest of shafts rose from the ground in front of each bowman, and the archers were standing almost elbow to elbow, all around the height where the royal tent rose.

"There," Braerwinter murmured, pointing at the little hollow where the king had sat.

Alusair's blackened helm still lay there. Tolon bent and picked it up as the two men sat down together, back to back so as to be able to see anyone approach, and in unison thrust their fingers under their gorgets to pluck forth pendants.

Hidden on the backs of those pendants were clasps akin to the weathercloak clasps that war wizards bore. Etched beside each was a tiny symbol, the badge of Filfaeril, the Dragon Queen, whom Braerwinter and Tolon had served now for many years. Laspeera had laid longspeaking enchantments on them that even Vangerdahast—or so it was said—knew nothing about.

"Lady Queen," Braerwinter murmured, picturing the cold beauty of the lady they both served—and loved, "there is no gentle way to say this. His majesty has fought the dragon, and lies sorely wounded. The wyrm is fled, the orcs lie slain, and we hold the field against hosts of goblins still. They advance again, as we speak. More, the dragon came down on the Princess Alusair, and she is feared lost, with all who served under her. We gave the king all the healing magic we carried, ghazneths or no, for many healers have died already this day, but, your Highness, our potions seemed to do nothing to help him. I know not how much longer he has to live. He lies in his tent, atop the first hill north of Calantar's Bridge, just east of the Way. More priests are coming, but if you could send hence the mightiest clergy . . ."

They both heard the gasp that came from Filfaeril's distant lips before she replied, her voice very steady, *You've done well, I doubt not, and my thanks for this news, dark though it be. Guard my lord, both of you, and yourselves. Cormyr will have more need of you, soon.*

"We hear and obey," the two lords chanted in unison, not failing to hear the sob that escaped the queen's lips before the magical connection faded.

Lord Edryn Braerwinter looked at his friend and said, "Well, I guess we'd best—"

That was as far as he got, through a vain shout from nearby, before a dark form swooped down out of the sky, cruel talons spread, and tore off both their heads.

Cold laughter trailed the ghazneth as it soared into the sky again, pendants clutched in fingers that trailed blood, as the torn husks that had been Lords Braerwinter and Tolon toppled to the ground in bloody ruin. Arrows stabbed into the sky after the laughing scourge, but as usual they were too few, too feeble in flight, and too late.

35

t might have been the brisk way the door opened or the odd heaviness in Alaphondar's step, but Tanalasta knew at once something terrible had happened. She stepped away from the great map table and waved the others in the room silent.

"What's wrong?"

Alaphondar stopped inside the door, scanned the gathering of weary faces, and opened his mouth without speaking. His eyes were red-rimmed and glassy, his expression numb and vacant. Tanalasta tossed her pointer onto the map, not really caring as it scattered the company emblems she and her war council had just spent the last hour arranging, then went to the sage.

"Alaphondar, what's happened?"

She gave him a little shake, and he emerged from his daze.

"The queen . . ." He glanced around the room again, this time seeming to see the faces before him, and looked at Tanalasta. "The queen received a sending. The dragon has destroyed Princess Alusair's army."

Tanalasta tried not to think the worst. The loss of the army hurt, but Alusair had faced any number of such calamities and always returned. "And the princess?"

Alaphondar looked away. "They found her helmet and shield in a heap of scorched bones."

Tanalasta felt a sudden stillness in her chest. "But not the rest of her armor?"

Alaphondar shook his head. "It was something of a mess."

"We'll pray for the best, then." Tanalasta turned back to her war council, putting on a brave face, but also placing a hand on the map table to take a little weight off her shaking knees. "Our thoughts go to the dead and wounded, but Alusair has a way of surviving these things."

"Highness, I'm sorry, but there is more."

Tanalasta stopped and tried to pretend she did not notice every eye in the room watching her. The act must have been unconvincing, for Owden Foley came to her side and took hold of her elbow.

"Yes?" Not wanting to appear distressed in front of her war council, she motioned the priest aside and faced Alaphondar again. "Go on."

This time, the sage could not prevent tears from welling out of his eyes. "Your father's army is under attack, and the king has fallen."

"Fallen?" Tanalasta's legs lost their strength. She forgot all the eyes watching her and stumbled over to a wall, barely pivoting into a chair before her knees buckled. "Is he dead?"

"Not dead," Alaphondar said. "They say he was burned badly and also opened from collar to groin."

"But is he with his healers?" Tanalasta demanded.

"I fear his healers were killed in the battle. Lords Tolon and Braerwinter were trying to carry him to safety when they informed the queen. They promised another sending the moment it is safe."

"Then the battle continues?" asked Korvarr Rallyhorn, now recovered from the murderlust Lady Merendil had roused in him when she broke his arm.

Alaphondar nodded and said, "The queen has ordered a

troop of war wizards to ready themselves to teleport there."

Korvarr turned to Tanalasta. "If I may, Princess, my company is standing inspection at the moment and could leave on the instant."

Still too shocked to speak, Tanalasta simply nodded and waved him out the door.

"Are you sure that's wise, Princess?" asked Lord Longbrooke. "We are already stretched thin in the south."

"And hunting only two ghazneths," countered Hector Dauntinghorn.

"Only two ghazneths, but Sembia's ten thousand already equal us man for man," noted Melot Silversword. "We must not forget they are fresh. . . ."

Tanalasta barely heard the debate. She was too stunned. Her successes against the ghazneths had blinded her to just how uncertain victory remained. The dragon and her orcs already controlled everything from Dhedluk north. If the royal army collapsed—and Tanalasta was not fool enough to believe it could stand long with Alusair missing and her father fallen—the rest of Cormyr would soon follow.

Even that realization left her more numb than panicked. She felt dizzy and hollow, perhaps because the anguish of losing a sister, father, and kingdom all at once was simply more than she could bear. The sensation was similar to her longing for Rowen, a cold deep ache that never went away, that was always there ready to pull her down into a swirling black void of despair. It was a feeling to which she could never surrender, not even for a moment. Too much depended on her—and she was thinking not only of Cormyr. Her child would be coming soon, and she wanted to have a kingdom for it to be born into.

When Tanalasta grew aware of her environment again, she found herself surrounded by a host of disheartened faces. Melot Silversword and Barrimore Longbrooke were huddled together, looking terrified and whispering something about Sembia. Even Ildamoar Hardcastle and Roland Emmarask looked pale and dismayed. Clearly, everyone in the room thought the war lost, and it soon would be if Tanalasta did not do something to restore their confidence.

The princess thought first of going north to assume command of the royal army "until her father recovered," but—thankfully—the thought flashed from her mind as quickly as it appeared. Even were she as clever a tactician as Alusair (and she knew she was not), and even were her presence as inspiring as that of King Azoun (and she knew it was not), an immensely pregnant woman who could barely waddle—much less lead a charge into battle—would not inspire the royal army to stand firm against Nalavarauthatoryl and her orcs.

But she knew who could.

Tanalasta braced her hands on the arms of the chair. "Lord Longbrooke, I am sure that you and Lord Silversword would not be discussing calling for the aid of Sembian troops." When the two men shook their heads, she pushed herself up. "Good. I doubt Vangerdahast would approve."

"Vangerdahast?" gasped Roland Emmarask. "Then you know where he is?"

"Better than that. I think Harvestmaster Foley has determined a way to free him." Tanalasta turned to the priest. "Isn't that so, Owden?"

Owden smiled and inclined his head, a sure sign of his displeasure. "When was the princess suggesting? Given tonight to complete my studies, I could possibly be ready by dawn."

"I was thinking sooner." Tanalasta removed Rowen's holy symbol from around her neck and passed it to the priest. "Perhaps *now* would be good."

Owden was too subtle and loyal to let anyone but Tanalasta see the annoyance in his eyes. He had first proposed opening a gate into Vangerdahast's prison with the understanding that he would trace the route by himself, so the princess would not be endangered by such an unpredictable spell. When it had grown apparent that Owden did not have a strong enough emotional connection to find Vangerdahast through Rowen's holy symbol, however, Tanalasta had begun to press for her own involvement. So far, the priest had steadfastly refused, claiming she was as likely to be sucked into Vangerdahast's dimension as the reverse. Until now, Tanalasta had acquiesced.

When Owden did not readily agree, Tanalasta turned to the door guard. "Send for Battlelord Steelhand."

"That won't be necessary," Owden said. He motioned Tanalasta back to her chair. "The princess is right. The time has come to open the door and see what spills out."

Owden dangled the holy symbol in front of Tanalasta's eyes and began to swing it back and forth. "Concentrate. Picture Vangerdahast's face."

Tanalasta followed the silver amulet with her eyes and pictured Vangerdahast as she had last seen him, strangely young and haunted, with a bushy black beard and a crown of iron ringing his ragged mane of hair. The image melded with the symbol and began to swing back and forth, then the map room and the men in it vanished from sight, leaving only the face of the royal magician sweeping back and forth in front of her.

She had the sense of plunging down a long tunnel into a huge black vastness. An inky darkness fell across the amulet. Vangerdahast's face vanished, replaced by the gaunt visage she had first glimpsed when she had tried to contact her husband. The stranger's brow was heavy and sinister, the eyes white as pearls, the chin square and strong with a hint of cleft. This time, Tanalasta did not call out, and the pearly eyes stared at her for a moment, brimming with joy and sorrow and some unspeakable craving a thousand times more powerful than even the longing she felt for Rowen.

The air grew gray with rain, and the face vanished. An instant later Vangerdahast was there, scowling and impatient as ever.

It's about time.

"I have him," Tanalasta reported to Owden. To Vangerdahast, she said, "Do you have the scepter, Old Snoop?"

Vangerdahast frowned in confusion, but nodded and brought the amethyst pommel into view. *I do.*

"Good," Tanalasta said. "Owden, we're ready."

The harvestmaster rattled off a long string of mystic syllables. The distance between Tanalasta and Vangerdahast seemed to vanish. The wizard's eyes grew round. He let out a startled cry and seemed to fall toward the princess, arms windmilling and legs kicking. Behind him, she glimpsed an iron throne and a crescent of little green goblins, the flashing bolts of a thunderstorm and a dark figure scrambling back from the portal.

Then Vangerdahast was there on top of her, sprawled across her and hugging her like a mother, laughing, weeping, and screaming all at once, cold and clammy and wet, stinking like he had not bathed in months.

He kissed her full on the lips, then scrambled off her and stooped down to kiss her swollen belly, then planted the tip of the golden Scepter of Lords beside her chair and leaned down to kiss her on the mouth again.

Tanalasta pushed him off. "Vangerdahast!"

The wizard gave her a waggish grin. "Don't tell me you're not happy to see me!"

"I am." Tanalasta wiped her face, less to rub off the dampness left by the wizard's rain-soaked beard than to freshen her nostrils with the perfume on her cuff. "But we have work—"

Tanalasta was interrupted by the knelling of an alarm bell, and the map room broke into a tumult of voices and clattering boots. Vangerdahast turned slowly on his heel, watching in amazement as the nobles rushed off to join their companies.

"Are they running *toward* battle?"

"You might say that, old friend," said Owden. He clapped a hand on Vangerdahast's shoulder. "Or you might say they are fleeing what Tanalasta would do to them if they hesitated."

"Is that so?" Vangerdahast cocked his brow at the princess. "I'll be interested to hear how you did that."

"And I have a few questions for you as well," Tanalasta said. "But they will have to wait. We have a ghazneth coming."

Vangerdahast's brow rose in shock, then he looked around the map room as though confirming he was where he thought he was. "Coming *here*? To the Royal Castle?"

"So it seems." Tanalasta struggled out of her chair and started for the door. "And let us pray it is not King Boldovar."

36

s this all that's left of us?" Kortyl Rowanmantle almost squeaked, looking around at the grim gaggle of men crowded among the trees. "Two hundred men, maybe less?"

At their center rose a great, gnarl-rooted stump, taller in its ruin than the tallest man there—and atop it stood the Steel Princess, her hands on her dragonfire-blackened hips, and most of her once-magnificent, unruly mane of hair now a scorched ruin.

"Evidently so, Kortyl," she replied almost cheerfully. "All the more goblins for the rest of us."

An uneasy silence greeted her words. Squalling earfangs were neither glamorous nor all that easy to slay, when they came rushing in their swarms—and come in swarms they did, endless streaming tides that overwhelmed weary sword arms and butchered all too well . . . leaving too few survivors here, panting, in the forest.

On the other hand, goblins weren't nearly as glamorous—or as deadly—as the Devil Dragon. More than a few of the Cormyreans glanced up through the green gloom at the branches overhead, seeking a gap large enough for a huge red dragon—gliding along just above the treetops, as she'd met with them not so long ago—to see them through.

The wyrm had burst upon the nobles with such sudden fury that many had been scorched to ash before they'd had time to do more than see their doom, and scream. The trees around them had burned like torches, and not a few had toppled, crushing those beneath them and showering everyone else with sparks. The forest had been their cloak and salvation, though, the crackling topfires hiding the terrified men in their smoke. The deeper, unburnt green depths gave them a vast lair to scatter in and hide.

It had taken a grim Steel Princess, sword drawn and so much soot caking her that more than one man thought her some sort of black-hided monster at first glance, to find and gather them. Sword drawn and only her eyes and teeth bright, she looked like something out of a horror-tale whispered to scare children. Her doffed helm had been lost in that first burst of dragonfire, its hiphook-straps burnt away as she twisted and rolled, and her shield was gone too—hurled down in half-melted, red-hot ruin after it had saved her from the direct stream of dragonfire that had been the wyrm's attempt to cook a princess.

A frown crept back onto Alusair's face as she came back to that thought, for perhaps the tenth time. The dragon had seemed to be looking for her. . . .

Enough reflection. "This is the harshest test Cormyr has faced in centuries," Alusair said abruptly, looking around to meet the eyes of man after man, "and the lives of those you hold dear, whether they be within the walls of Suzail or in manors all over this realm, now depend on your swords. We are the realm's best . . . and now it's time to prove it. I'm going back to find that dragon, and hack it down. If I die, I'll go down knowing I did what I could for Cormyr and did not cower and hide, waiting for goblin blades to find me in the night. Whatever happens, I stood forth to defend the people of Cormyr."

She looked around, in a silence as sharp as a sword point. They were listening hard, their burning eyes on her, seeking hope. She gave it to them.

The Steel Princess calmly unbuckled her breastplate and swung it open. Her bodice beneath was a sweat-soaked mess of fresh bloodstains and shredded quilting, and fresh blood was glistening among the older, darker gore. More than one man murmured as he guessed at the wounds that must lie beneath, but Alusair unconcernedly thumped her breasts with a fist and announced matter-of-factly, "This still beats. As long as it does, I shall be hunting that dragon. So much is my duty."

She turned slowly, pointing at man after man with her drawn sword, and added softly, "As nobles of the realm, only you can determine your own duty. Your families have always been the backbone of the realm—because your mothers and fathers and grandsires knew their duty, and did it. You know your duty too. When I leave this place, I'll not look back to see who skulks away into the trees, and who strides with me. I won't have to, because I know who— and what—you are. You are the very best and the bright hope of Cormyr's future."

She smiled, slid her sword into the crook of her arm, and buckled up her breastplate again. "We just have a little task before us, that's all. We must ensure that Cormyr *has* a future."

There were some grim chuckles at that.

The Steel Princess looked up from her buckles with that wry, lopsided, come-hither grin that her men knew so well, and asked softly, "Are you with me, men of Cormyr?"

"Aye!" Kortyl Rowanmantle shouted. "Aye!"

"Aye!" three men said together, raising their swords. "For the Steel Princess!"

"For Alusair, and *Cormyr!*"

Alusair sprang down from the stump and raised her own blade. "Then follow me—but save your shouts for when our blades cut deep into the dragon. No war cries!"

She turned and sprang away, to begin her usual swift

lope—only to stagger, wince, and almost fall as one leg failed her. Swift hands shot out for her to grasp, and she leaned on them gratefully for a moment, stamped her injured leg down hard, winced again, then set off at a limping run, her men following.

It seemed only a short time before the trees thinned, and Alusair spun around and held up her hands for a halt. As panting noblemen gathered around her, she said, "The hills beyond are alive with goblins and their scouts, and the dragon has been landing on the hilltops beyond. We can't avoid being seen, but magic will only bring our foes and darkness confuses our eyes, but not theirs. Moreover, the lives of many Cormyreans may be lost if we delay. So it's time to be fools, I'm afraid, and just rush out to be slain. Let's see if we can't draw the dragon down to us in the process."

She turned, blade flashing, ducked between two trees, and was gone.

After a startled moment, the noble sons of Cormyr—the expectation of looming death now clear upon their faces—charged after her.

Where the woods ended, farm fields began. It was rolling pastureland for the most part, with rubble-and-stump boundary fences, and goblins. The humanoids were camped in little clumps here and there, gathering on distant hills and sure to see the rushing human band, unless . . .

A curious wall or hump of mist filled a low spot not far off on their right. It was a bank of fog that by rights should not have been there, unless the little creek that meandered along beneath it had suddenly spouted hot springs.

Alusair peered at it, as suspicious as any warrior who knows the countryside well and sees something strange in it, then shrugged, pointed at the mist with her drawn sword, and veered toward it. The men trotting behind her followed her into the whirlwind of mist, peering and keeping their blades ready in case this fog should prove to hold the dragon or another deadly beast.

They found no such hidden peril before Kortyl gasped to the princess, "How far do you think this extends, then, Highness?"

Alusair turned to answer, her face making it clear that "I don't know" was going to feature in her utterance to come—then the world changed.

Everything was suddenly a deep, bubbling blue, and the ground was gone from beneath their feet. They were upright, and yet falling endlessly, or perhaps Faerûn was falling away from them . . . then there was suddenly bare rock under their boots, without any sense of landing or jarring, and the deep blue radiance was fading, into deeper darkness.

"Torches!" Alusair commanded, stripping off one of her boots and plucking up the inner sole to shake a tiny glow-pebble out of a hollow heel. "Use this to light them by."

Those without torches or lanterns waited tensely in the darkness, listening with blades drawn until the torches flared up. Nothing rushed at them.

The flickering flames showed them a large, dank cavern on all sides—a *very* large cavern, with tunnel mouths opening like dark eyes in every wall.

"Where," Kortyl Rowanmantle cursed, looking around in astonished dismay, "by all the dark pits of the Underdark and the fiends that dance in them, *are* we?"

His commander came up behind him and put a reassuring arm around his shoulders, bringing with her a smell of scorched hair and leather and smooth, muscled curves that awakened a sudden stirring in the noble knight as they pressed against him.

"Wherever we are," Alusair told him calmly, "our work is clear. We slay the foes of Cormyr wherever we find them, until we see that dragon dead and the realm saved."

"And where in all this murk are the hills of goblins and the dragon?"

Princess Alusair Obarskyr gave him a wolfish smile and replied sweetly, "And how by all the dark pits of the Underdark and the fiends that dance in them should *I* know?"

* * * * *

Azoun groaned, and his body spasmed, seeming to bound off the bed as it arched, and dragging astonished underpriests with it. They clung to the royal limbs and turned pale, frightened faces up to their superiors.

Aldeth Ironsar, Faithful Hammer of Tyr, rose from his knees with a face as grim as it was puzzled. "So it is with my healing, too. What do you make of it, my holy lords? I cannot believe this valiant king is cursed of *all* our gods!"

"Perhaps," the Loremaster of Deneir said slowly, "the wounds given him by the dragon are no ordinary hurts but something different than what the healing prayers we've employed are intended to treat."

"We've done this before, all of us," snapped the high huntmaster of Vaunted Malar, gesturing down at the unconscious king. "Azoun Obarskyr has hazarded much, and received much healing, down the long years. Perhaps a body—any body—can only receive so much healing ere it has tasted enough, and the magic must fail."

Several faces turned sharply to regard the Malarite, wearing fresh frowns of their own. If there was any truth to that thought, many more folk than the king of Cormyr stood in imminent peril . . . not a few high priests among them.

"I have heard," the Lord High Priest of Tymora said heavily, "of persons who desired death—husbands who'd held their slain wives in their arms, and wives who'd beheld their dead husbands—taking no benefit from even the strongest healing spells. As if they willed the magic to pass away from them, and do them no good."

He strode a few slow paces away, then told the nearest tent pole, "The lantern of the king's mirth, so far as I could see, went out in his face when he heard of the death of the Steel Princess."

"Whatever the reason," Battlemaster Ilnbright said from the entrance to the tent, "we dare not try more healing now. A ghazneth is come upon us."

The priests looked up at him, only too ready to sneer at a mere warrior—even if he was a nobleman, and regardless of the sense of his words—but their denunciations died in their throats at the sounds that came from behind Haliver Ilnbright then.

Outside the tent—*just* outside the tent—they heard a startled shout, thudding footfalls, the clang of a sword ringing off a shield, and the heavy fall of a body. Then they heard a wet, grisly sound. It was a sound of rending flesh, accompanied by a rising, choked-off, disbelieving shriek.

It was the sound of a man being torn apart, and it was followed, after a sudden soft rain that could only be the spraying of much blood, with cold laughter. It was mad laughter, high and shrill, that faded into the distance as the throat it was issuing from ascended into the air, and flew away.

The laugh was followed by the groan of a disbelieving veteran Purple Dragon starting to be sick.

After a moment, several of the priests in the tent echoed that last sound with an enthusiasm none of them wanted to feel.

37

eeping the ghazneth centered in Alaphondar's new spyglass was not easy, especially not when it was circling directly overhead and kept vanishing behind the palace roof for two seconds at a time. Vangerdahast had developed a painful crick in his neck, and his arms ached from holding the heavy brass tube over his eye. His vision had grown spotty and painful from continually swinging the lens across the midday sun. Still, the device worked well enough for him to glimpse a pair of leathery black wings, two thin arms, and two crooked legs. The thing was definitely a ghazneth.

Vangerdahast lowered the spyglass and returned it to Alaphondar. "It works better than the last one. I saw what I was looking at."

The sage beamed at the compliment. "Not as clear as one of your spells, but it has its uses."

"Could you tell which one it was?" asked Tanalasta.

Vangerdahast shook his head. "Alaphondar hasn't improved it that much."

"The priests have stopped trying to heal Azoun," said Filfaeril, speaking from the balcony door. It was the first time in decades Vangerdahast had seen her looking less than radiant. Her eyes were swollen and rimmed in red, her face puffy and pale, her expression haggard and mad with worry. "They say the spells don't work. They say the magic only gives them away to the dragon and draws ghazneths."

Vangerdahast went to the door and clasped Filfaeril's arm. "I'll get there," he promised.

He saw Tanalasta exchange a nervous glance with Owden.

"I have no doubt," said the princess, "but we must decide how. When you leave the palace, that scepter will draw the ghazneth to you like a vulture to a dead man." She nodded into the drawing room, where the Scepter of Lords rested in the grasp of a wide-eyed palace guard. "Even an escort of two full companies wouldn't guarantee your arrival."

"There are safer ways to travel—and faster," said Vangerdahast.

"Not if you mean teleporting," Tanalasta replied. "Not with Nalavara so near."

"She takes teleporters out of the air the way hawks take sparrows," explained Owden. "The realm has lost too many men to her already."

"The last just this morning, I fear," said Alaphondar. He was seated in the corner, leaning back against the balustrade with the spyglass to his eye. "No one has heard from Korvarr and his company since they left."

Vangerdahast saw the guilty look that flashed across Tanalasta's face and realized she was beginning to second-guess her decisions. He gave Filfaeril's arm a last squeeze, then returned to the balcony to stand beside the princess.

"When this is over, we must remember to commend Korvarr for his sacrifice," Vangerdahast said. "No doubt, it was his distraction that allowed Lords Tolon and Braerwinter to carry the king to safety."

Tanalasta smiled and took his hand. "What did you do with our royal magician? The Vangey I recall would not have been so kind." She looked past Vangerdahast, her attention

297

returned to the distant ghazneth. "Alaphondar, any guess as to who that is?"

"I don't think it's Boldovar," answered the sage. "The body appears too lanky, and there seems to be long hair blowing over its back."

"Suzara, then." The relief in Tanalasta's voice was clear. "Do you think we have any chance of luring her down here?"

"She's being very cautious," said the sage, "but she must be desperate or she wouldn't be circling the palace."

"Then we must appear desperate ourselves and offer her something tempting," said Tanalasta. She stepped past Vangerdahast and addressed the guards in the drawing room. "Send a messenger. The Queen's Cavalry is to prepare at once for a hard ride, and have the royal magician's coward of a horse readied to go with them."

"Cadimus?" Vangerdahast gasped. At least there was some good news. "He's here? How?"

"It is a long story," said Tanalasta. "But were I you, I would stay close to that horse. He has a talent for survival."

As Tanalasta explained her plan and issued the necessary orders, Vangerdahast could not help swelling with pride. The princess had become as natural a leader as her father and sister, though with a harder edge than Azoun and a keener sense of human frailty than Alusair. Even Filfaeril, as distraught and frightened as she was over Alusair's loss and the terrible wounds Azoun had suffered, seemed to take comfort in Tanalasta's sure orders. The crown princess was going to make a fine queen someday—though preferably not too soon and preferably of something more than Cormyr's ruins.

When Tanalasta finished her commands, Vangerdahast nodded sagely. "A sound plan, Princess, but I do have one suggestion."

"You may *suggest* anything, Vangerdahast," said Tanalasta, "but do recall that I have destroyed four of these things by now."

"I could hardly forget, Highness," he said, smiling. She had given him a complete account of each ghazneth's destruction, including that of spiteful Luthax, who had mumbled curses and threats from inside his iron box even as she absolved him of his betrayal. Vangerdahast touched his iron crown, which even Owden had not been able to dislodge with his prayers. "All I ask is that you let me handle the iron. Iron I can do, and since your plan depends on impressing Suzara with the palace's luxury, it might be wisest not to tear the place up before she sees it."

Tanalasta nodded, then issued orders for her dragoneers to wait outside the door in case something went wrong and asked Alaphondar to the escort her mother to a safe place. Vangerdahast was surprised when Filfaeril did not protest. Matters had changed a great deal over the past eight months—a very great deal.

Once the queen was gone, the princess guided Vangerdahast into a quiet corner where they would not be overheard as dragoneers bustled about making final preparations.

"While we're waiting, there was something I wanted to ask you about."

Vangerdahast's stomach filled with butterflies. He had a good idea what she intended to ask, and his promise to Rowen prevented him from giving an honest answer. Ordinarily, he would not have been troubled by the prospect of a little prevarication, but this was a different Tanalasta than the one he had left behind. She would not be easily deceived.

He folded his hands behind his back. "Of course, Highness," he said. "Ask me anything."

Tanalasta hesitated, then said, "When I contacted you, I was trying to reach Rowen."

"So I gathered."

She fingered the silver amulet that hung from her neck. "We were using Rowen's holy symbol as a focus."

Vangerdahast raised his brow. "How very unusual that you contacted me, then."

"Yes, isn't it? And both times before I saw you, there was a shadowy face first—a shadowy face that resembled Rowen, but with white eyes."

Vangerdahast put on a concerned frown. "And what did Owden say about this face?"

"That he didn't know what to make of it," said Tanalasta. "Any more than why Rowen's symbol should have led me to you."

"And so you are asking *me*?" Vangerdahast shook his head sagely. "Souls are Owden's concern, not mine."

Tanalasta sighed. "Of course they are, but I was wondering if you might not have been there alone."

"I was hardly alone, Highness." Vangerdahast tapped his iron crown. "There were plenty of Grodd. They made me their king, if you'll recall."

"I'm not talking about goblins."

"Then I guess I don't know what you're talking about." Vangerdahast shrugged. "I can assure you, I was the only man there. My, er, *subjects* would certainly have brought it to my attention if there were others."

"The thing is, if Rowen was there, he might not have looked like a man." Tanalasta looked at the corner, then continued with a catch in her throat. "Before I destroyed Xanthon, he said something cruel."

"That's hardly surprising. I hope you made him suffer for it."

"Nothing I could have done would have been enough," she said. "He claimed that Rowen had betrayed Cormyr."

"Rowen?" Vangerdahast tried to sound surprised.

Tanalasta raised a hand. "He said that Rowen was one of them."

"What? A *ghazneth*?" Vangerdahast shook his head in mock disappointment. "Princess, I'm surprised at you. I'd have thought you understood by now how evil feeds on doubt."

"I know," said Tanalasta, "but there was that face. It looked so much like Ro—"

"Because that is what you wanted to see," Vangerdahast interrupted. He took the princess by the shoulders and turned her to face him. "Rowen would never betray Cormyr, or you. I know that, even if you do not."

Tanalasta's face softened. "Thank you, Vangerdahast." She wiped the tears from her eyes, then said, "You're right. I do know it."

"Good." The sigh under Vangerdahast's breath was not quite one of relief. The princess had given up a little too easily, perhaps because she really did not want to know the truth. He took her hand and started toward the center of the room. "We should see to our ghazneth."

Tanalasta looped her arm through Vangerdahast's elbow. "By all means. And, Vangerdahast, why did you never ask me who fathered my child?"

"I didn't?"

Tanalasta shook her head. "You didn't seem curious at all."

Vangerdahast assumed a gruff voice. "I assumed it to be Rowen. It would be too much to hope you had married somebody appropriate."

"Really. And who said I was married?"

Vangerdahast cursed under his breath. The girl was too smart for her own good. "You'd better be," he said. "The last thing Cormyr needs now is a succession war."

He stopped in the center of the room and took the Scepter of Lords from the nervous guard, then pointed the man to the balcony. "Young man, in a handful of moments I'm going to come streaking through that window like a flaming star. You and two men of your choosing are to slam and bar the doors behind me—and do it quickly, for all our lives will depend on it."

Tanalasta looked nervous. "Vangerdahast, if there is any risk to this plan . . ."

"Risk? There's no risk if this boy does as he's told—and is quick about it." Vangerdahast motioned the guard off, then started to the balcony doors. "The royal magician has returned."

With Tanalasta following along behind, Vangerdahast went to the balcony entrance. He pulled a pinch of powdered iron from the pouch he was using to carry spell ingredients and rubbed it over the doors, at the same time uttering one of the spells he had fashioned to make the best use of his burdensome crown. His head erupted into white pain as it always did when he made iron, but he was prepared for the shock and managed to endure it with no more than a long grunt. A gray-black darkness spread over the doors, then a long series of creaks and pops echoed through the room as the wood and glass changed to thick, heavy iron.

The ghazneth bell clanged to life, filling the bailey with a deep, insistent knelling.

"Your magic seems to have caught our visitor's interest," said Tanalasta.

"It's not Boldovar come to join us?"

"That would be a different bell," answered the princess, "and I would be much paler."

"Well then, let's have at her and be done with it."

Vangerdahast stepped out onto the balcony and saw that Suzara had circled down to within a hundred yards of the palace roof. She was close enough to see what was happening, yet high enough to make her a difficult target for the archers' iron-tipped arrows. He could just make out the red flush of her oblong eyes glaring down at him, and for the first time he wondered if his boasts about how easily he would subdue her had been somewhat overstated. From such a low height, she would be on him almost the moment he was in the air.

"Is something wrong?" Tanalasta asked.

Vangerdahast glanced back and saw not only the princess studying him, but Owden and the guards as well. If he changed plans now, their confidence would go the way of Korvarr and his company.

"Just planning my route." He shooed Tanalasta back into the room. "To your hiding place."

"Be careful, Old Snoop."

"I will be quick." Vangerdahast drew a crow's feather from his spell pouch. "That is better."

As he started his flying spell, the ghazneth dipped a wing and began to circle lower. Vangerdahast brushed the feather over his arms and finished the incantation in a flurry, then took the Scepter of Lords in both hands and sprang into the air. Even as he banked toward Lake Azoun, he felt the iron crown drawing his spell's magic into itself, robbing him of precious speed and flight time. It might have been wise to warn the princess about this particular handicap, but then again maybe not. She would probably have insisted on doing things her own way.

The ghazneth bell began to clang madly, and Vangerdahast knew Suzara was coming after him. He dropped down below the crest of the outer curtain and banked hard toward Etharr Hall. A sharp thump sounded behind him as his pursuer hit the wall and dropped to the ground. The erratic clatter of firing crossbows echoed across the bailey, and Vangerdahast glanced back to see a cloud of iron quarrels descending on the ghazneth from the ramparts above.

Though more than a few bolts found their mark, Suzara spread her wings and launched herself, dodging and weaving, after Vangerdahast. Even as she flew, her wounds began to close. The quarrels dropped from her body and clanged to the cobblestones below, and only a handful of new ones took their place. Vangerdahast soared over the roof of Etharr Hall, then dropped low and skimmed the ground, circling around the building back toward Palace Hall.

The ghazneth shot over the roof of Etharr Hall in the opposite direction but saw Vangerdahast and dipped a wing to wheel around. Praying he had the speed to outrun her for just fifty more paces, he soared back toward Tanalasta's balcony. A flurry of bowstrings throbbed from the windows along both sides of the bailey. Dark streams of arrows zipped through the air behind, tracing the ghazneth's progress as she closed the distance to him.

Finally, the balustrade loomed before Vangerdahast. He scraped over it screaming in terror—it was only an act to distract the ghazneth, of course—then shot through the open doors and across the entire drawing room before a deafening clang sounded behind him.

His flying spell expired an instant later, a dozen steps into the long hallway outside the drawing room. Though only traveling at a quarter speed, he hit hard and tumbled headlong down the floor. A pair of dragoneers managed to grab hold and prevented him from plunging down a sweeping staircase.

"Lord wizard, are you all right?"

"What do you think?" Vangerdahast allowed the guards

303

to pull him to his feet, then shook them off and stumbled back into the drawing room.

By the time he arrived, the battered balcony doors were already open. The ghazneth was surrounded by a handful of dragoneers, all hacking and chopping at her while Tanalasta knelt at her side, struggling to pull a glittering necklace of diamonds over her broken skull.

"Suzara Obarskyr, wife to Ondeth the Founder and mother to Faerlthann the First King, as a true Obarskyr and heir to the Dragon Throne, I grant you the thing you most desire, the thing for which you abandoned your husband and son—I grant you the luxury and wealth of the Suzail Palace."

Vangerdahast arrived to see the darkness drain from Suzara's face, leaving behind the careworn visage of a brown-haired woman who did not look so different from Tanalasta herself. The woman's eyes rolled back in their sockets, and she began to groan and froth at the mouth and jerk about spasmodically, as the victims of head wounds were sometimes prone to do.

Tanalasta touched her hand to Suzara's trembling brow. "And as a direct descendent of your line and heir to the crown, I forgive your betrayal and absolve you, Suzara Obarskyr, of all crimes against Cormyr."

When the princess removed her hand, Suzara simply continued to thrash about and foam at the mouth. Tanalasta frowned and looked to Owden, who could only scowl and shake his head in bewilderment. Vangerdahast knelt beside Tanalasta and pressed her hand back to Suzara's shattered skull.

"And in the name of Cormyr and its royal line through thirteen centuries, and its strong and loyal people, we thank you," the royal magician said. "We thank you for the sacrifices you *did* make, and we pledge to honor your memory even as we honor Ondeth's."

Tanalasta nodded. "So it will be," she said. "As Crown Princess Tanalasta Obarskyr and a daughter of your line, I pledge it so."

Suzara's eyes opened again, then she fell still and silent and sank, at last, into a peaceful rest.

38

A fellowship of gloom crowded together in the dim depths of the royal tent, close around the silent king.

At the head of the bed where Azoun lay wounded, two bodyguards stood in stolid, watchful silence, their large and callused hands never far from the hilts of their swords.

The men they faced, down at the foot of the bed—half a dozen priests and a war wizard—brooded in a more restless silence, born of futility and mounting fear. Their most modest healing spells had failed, and they dared not try more powerful magics. Not with the ghazneth circling the hilltop like a vengeful hawk, casually diving down from time to time to rake and rend Purple Dragons at will.

At each shout and skirl of blades outside the tent, the men sitting around the bed tensed and threw up their heads, peering vainly at the tapestry-hung tent walls as if some helpful, lurking enchantment might pluck the canvas aside to reveal the fray without, but the unhelpful canvas never moved.

Always, after a few moments, a scream of pain would rise close outside—sometimes brief, more often a long howl of agony that sank into the wet gurgling of a bloody death—and cold laughter would begin, fading as the eerie slayer took wing again into the sky.

The king never dozed through these brief battles. His eyes would snap open, anger sharpening his features, and his fingers would close like claws on the linen. Twice he made as if to rise, but each time pain too fierce to conceal flashed across his face, and he fell back to lie listening with fury in his eyes. Azoun was a king as impotent as the men he shared his tent with.

"This can't go on forever," the war wizard muttered, after a seeming eternity measured by twenty-seven separate death screams. "The battle could sweep right up to us, and find us no more ready than so many helpless children."

As if his words had been a cue, the door hangings suddenly swirled and parted, held aside by the spears of two guards, who stepped into the tent and moved apart to allow someone to pass between them. The slightly stooped, stout figure in robes, who wore an iron crown on his head none of them had seen before, was otherwise familiar to all as Vangerdahast, the Royal Magician of Cormyr.

Azoun struggled to thrust himself up on his elbows and failed. The faintest of groans escaped from between set royal teeth.

The court wizard frowned and hastened forward. The sweat-streaked, working face before him opened pain-misted eyes for a moment, blinked, then stared. The king's mouth twisted into a crooked grin.

"Vangey!"

The court wizard winced—his love for that nickname had never been great—but replied with a smooth bow, "My liege. I live to serve you still, and am come with words you must hear without delay."

"Of course," Azoun replied airily, for all the world as if he was gesturing with a wine goblet at a revel and not lying on his back bleeding his life away. "I expected no less. How came you by yon crown?"

"That reply must wait," Vangerdahast said with a smile. He looked at the gathered priests, then gestured at the entrance.

No one moved, so he repeated the slow sweep of his pointing hand, clearing his throat and lowering his brows. The war wizard rose hastily, and the royal magician gave him an appreciative nod—which brought Eregar Abanther, Ready Hand of Tempus, a man known for neither slow wits nor pomposity, to his feet. Eregar made a low bow to the king, and departed.

Slowly the other clergy followed, their glacial responses tempered by their various desires to demonstrate the exaltitude of their rank or their lack of any need to obey a mere mage. When all others had risen, the war wizard almost had to thrust the high priest of Tymora out of his seat, but he settled for looming so close over him that Manarech Eskwuin clucked and sighed loudly—it was closer to a snarl—in disgust, before he shifted.

"Keep them ready, just outside," Vangerdahast commanded and barely waited for the mage to nod and leave before he leaned forward over the bed and murmured, "I've—"

The point of a sword swept in from beside the bed to hang, glittering-sharp, under the royal magician's nose. Vangerdahast straightened and favored the bodyguard holding it with a withering look, but the blade did not move.

"You may leave," he snapped, but the warrior's only move was to advance a step—as did his fellow Purple Dragon, on the other side of the royal bed, their weapons rising in unison to menace the royal magician.

Kings' Blades take orders only from their king. Not from a wizard wearing a crown they did not recognize, who might just be any mage using a spell to look like an old court wizard—*the* old court wizard they'd never liked much anyway—the wizard whose fingers, many said, had itched for years to take the crown of Cormyr onto his own head.

Their blades did not waver. Neither did Vangerdahast's glare.

Troy Denning and Ed Greenwood

Azoun tried to hide a smile, and failed. "Step outside, my loyal blades," he murmured, "but remain close and ready for my call."

The swords swept down. Their owners bowed to the king and shouldered past Vangerdahast—in the case of the Bannerguard to the King, Kolmin Stagblade, it was as if a moving mountain had brushed the wizard aside, sending him staggering helplessly back a pace or two. The ruler of all Cormyr and his old tutor were finally alone.

Vangerdahast cast a suspicious glance all around the tent, as if expecting to find another dozen or so defiant guards skulking in the shadows. Finding none, he drew something out of his robe and thrust it into Azoun's hands.

The king cradled it curiously on his palms, looking up and down its beauty. The thing looked elven, and old—and yet alive, almost glowing with power. It was a scepter of bright golden hue, longer than most, and fashioned into the likeness of a sapling oak with a small and delicate array of branches set seemingly at random. Its pommel was a giant amethyst cut into the shape of an acorn.

Azoun did not bother to utter his question but merely looked up at the old wizard.

"As far as I know," Vangerdahast told him gravely, "you hold in your hands the most powerful creation of the elf Iliphar, Lord of Scepters. You'll need it."

He straightened—only to feel something tugging at his robes, holding him half bent. It was one of Azoun's hands, clutching a fistful of material firmly, and its owner growled up at him, "To save the realm, no doubt. *How?*"

The Royal Magician sighed. "It has far more powers than either of us has years left to unravel or master, and it's the key to defeating the dragon and ending this war—*if* used correctly."

"And what, O most mighty of wizards, is 'correctly'?"

Vangerdahast's brows drew down. "I'm hardly as knowledgeable as you seem to think," he said reprovingly. "Misjudgements as to our own competence are a large part of this . . ."

". . . dark tangle that presently imperils the realm,"

Azoun finished the hanging sentence smoothly, then drew down his own brows and growled, "Wizard, get on with it."

Vangerdahast was silent for long moments before the tiniest trace of what might have been a smile crawled along his lips and was gone.

"My king," he said at last, "the touch of this Scepter of Lords, in your hands, can wound the dragon more than any spellbolt or blade—but you must first atone aloud for the murder of Lorelei Alavara's betrothed, then strike with this, in heartfelt compassion for what she and all elves have lost with the rise of the realm of Cormyr."

Azoun's smile faded. "The murder of Lorelei Alavara's betrothed?" he echoed, raising an eyebrow.

It was hard for Vangerdahast to avoid lecturing the man he'd taught for so many years. "The dragon, known among dragonkind as Nalavarauthatoryl the Red—though the goblins she commands more often use the shorter form she herself employs, 'Nalavara'—was once Lorelei Alavara, a young elf maiden. Red-haired, skilled at magic, and prouder than most, I gather. She was betrothed to Thatoryl Elian . . ."

"The first elf to be slain by a human in what is now Cormyr—Andar Obarskyr," Azoun murmured. "I've not forgotten."

"Vengeance has kept her alive these fourteen centuries and more," Vangerdahast murmured, something akin to awe in his voice. "Satisfying that hunger may cost the fourth ruling Azoun his very life. To break what drives her on may mean willingly surrendering to her and offering her your life—perhaps even letting her take it."

Azoun looked up, a fire in his eyes that Vangerdahast had not seen there since the birth of Foril, dead now these many years. "Can you promise me, Vangey, that such a sacrifice will destroy the dragon and deliver Cormyr from all this ruin?"

"In matters of magic, nothing is ever certain," his old friend and tutor said quietly. "To claim otherwise would be wildest falsehood. Yet I believe this to be so. I know something of how elven oaths and blood-magic work—a very little, actually, but enough to say this: the Obarskyr ruler or heir alone can end the power of the dragon by such an offer. Your doom is not certain, but very likely. Likewise, the deliverance of the realm is uncertain, but very likely."

"Certain enough," Azoun said firmly. "If one must go into the darkness that awaits us all, let my road there be the high one. Let it be in one last service to Cormyr."

His last words seemed to echo, as if they rolled out across vast distances beyond the dark corners of the tent, and for just an instant, Vangerdahast thought he heard the distant toll of a great bell—a god, marking a fateful decision? The ghazneth bell in Suzail, which after all lay not all that far off? Or could it be . . . but no matter. It was gone, and might have only been a trick of his mind supplying him with something he hoped to hear. Some reassurance that he wasn't urging one of Cormyr's greatest kings to throw his life away in a possibly mistaken, empty scheme.

"More than that," Azoun added, a few moments later, sounding more than ever like the young prince Vangerdahast had once despaired of, "let it be done now. I'm ready— as ready as I'll ever be!"

With that, the King of Cormyr flung back the bedcovers and stood up, brandishing the Scepter of Lords like a long sword.

The royal magician was old and feeling older by the hour, yet he wasn't quite so decrepit as to be unable to move in great haste when he had to. Moreover, his hands were deft— and proved quite capable of plucking reeling rulers of the realm out of the air as they started to topple, and lowering both them and ancient elven scepters gently to resting places on handy beds.

"If this is your idea of ready," he muttered, as he took the gasping king under the arms and heaved him back up onto his pillows, "I tremble for the future of the realm."

A weak sputter of amusement and mock indignation told him that Azoun retained, at least, his senses.

"So you have served the realm as capably as ever, and we have the grand plan," the king gasped when he was strong enough to speak again. "We also have this . . . small problem of my being unable to stand. Somewhat of a handicap in facing down . . . dragons, you'll agree . . ."

"Your wounds are this bad," Vangerdahast replied gravely, "because some of the dragon's blood is in you—gnawing at your innards, melting away all of Azoun it can reach. Nalavara exists to destroy all of Obarskyr blood and is doing so all too well. I can purge you of the blood just as I delivered you from the Abraxus venom, but it will take magic, *powerful* magic."

"Which my dark-winged ancestor out there is waiting to pounce upon and drink . . . leaving me unhealed," Azoun concluded grimly.

"Indeed," Vangerdahast said, and shut his mouth like a slamming portcullis as the word left his lips.

Azoun regarded him in silence for a moment, then almost whispered, "I know you too well, old friend. You do see a solution and don't want to offer it. I know enough not to command you to speak . . . so I'll just lie here and wait as, eventually, the battle sweeps over us."

The royal magician gave him a dark look, then said, "There's no chance of healing you with Boldovar circling, just waiting for magic to be awakened. He must be lured elsewhere, with other magic, and held or trapped for long enough to restore you. It won't take me long, but it *will* take me much too long to manage if he's just soaring after a spell hurled from atop another hill, or a war wizard firing a wand—even a dozen war wizards, one after another."

The old wizard drew in a deep breath, then let it out in an unhappy sigh. "And I know of only one person in Cormyr skilled and experienced in the baiting and destruction of ghazneths."

"My daughter, Tanalasta," Azoun said quietly. "To save the king, we imperil his heir and the hope of the kingdom to come."

Vangerdahast nodded, his face dark with apprehension. "She has faced them and prevailed," he murmured, "but Boldovar is the strongest of them all—and no prince or princess, whatever their resolve or prowess, can be confident of handling such a madman. We may well be dooming

311

her just as surely as we're thrusting you to the edge of your grave."

Azoun looked up at him, then lifted his shoulders in a shrug. "Cormyr has never been a carefree garden, ours by right and without striving. My daughters both know that now—and both are defenders of the realm every bit as worthy and as capable as their father. What service do we do to the next Obarskyrs, if we fight all their battles for them, and rob them of the chance—nay, the right, the privilege—of rescuing Cormyr for themselves?"

Vangerdahast nodded. "Yet, you're her father . . ." he murmured.

"And her king," Azoun said, staring into the darkness. "They take turns being harder roles, Vangey. They always have."

39

hundred forks of lightning lanced upward from the palace ramparts, brightening the sky even in broad daylight. A long string of noisy crackles echoed across the city roofs. The still waters of Lake Azoun turned the color of a flashing silver mirror, and the air filled with a smell like fresh rain. The display was followed by an endless chain of fireballs. They arced out from the walls one after the other, trailing stubby tails of black smoke and roaring like dragons, then plummeting into the water to a sizzling, hissing end.

"That will attract his attention, don't you think?" asked Tanalasta. She was standing beside Owden Foley, watching the display from Vangerdahast's private tower outside the palace. "Even the Mad King cannot be so distracted he fails to notice that."

"Or misses its purpose," Owden added darkly.

"I think the ghazneths have known what we're doing for some time now." Tanalasta winced as the baby kicked her kidney, then continued, "Suzara didn't come down until we made her think she could snatch Vangerdahast and run. We'll use a different gambit on Boldovar."

As Tanalasta spoke, a green aura of visible magic began to glow above the palace. Despite its appearance, it was actually a minor spell Sarmon the Spectacular had developed, designed to create a powerful ambience of magic with a minimum of mystic energy. Even if Boldovar absorbed the spell, he would find it about as satisfying as Vangerdahast would a glass of water, but of course Tanalasta did not expect the Mad King to fall for such an obvious ploy. Like every Cormyrean monarch since Embrus the Old, he had been a student of chess and would recognize a diversion when he saw it.

And when he saw the diversion, he would start looking for the thing they were trying to hide. Tanalasta stepped away from the window.

"Shall we get started, Harvestmaster?"

"If you insist," Owden said, "but I still think you should take Vangerdahast at his word."

"Only because you do not know him as well as I do." Tanalasta crossed to the far side of Vangerdahast's study, slipping through a dozen of Owden's Chauntean priests, and dropped into a comfortable reading chair. "He *knew* Rowen and I were married."

"Perhaps he knows you better than you think," Owden said. "After you met Rowen, one of his first concerns was that you would end up marrying 'a ground-splitting Cormaeril.'"

"Even if he were that perceptive, there is still the matter of Rowen's holy symbol and the dark face." Tanalasta propped her feet on a stool. Her legs ached almost constantly now, and she was looking forward to the day when there would be a little less weight for them to carry. "Instead of explaining, Vangerdahast shifted the onus to you. He's a master of such tactics."

"That doesn't mean he was hiding something," said Owden. "Perhaps he really thought I could explain."

"Can you?"

When Owden shook his head, Tanalasta removed Rowen's holy symbol from her neck and held it out. "Then let's bring my husband home."

314

Owden did not take the symbol. "And what if that wasn't Rowen you saw? Why would Vangerdahast lie about a thing like that?"

Tanalasta gave a scornful look. "Why do you think?"

Owden shook his head. "He wouldn't. Not even the old Vangerdahast would leave a man trapped alone back there."

"I love Vangerdahast dearly, but he's done far worse to 'protect' Cormyr," Tanalasta said. "What better way to handle Rowen? If a Cormaeril must be Royal Husband, then at least let him be kept out of sight—permanently."

Owden's gaze dropped. "You can't believe Vangerdahast would do such a thing, not after all he's been through."

"I find no other explanation of the facts before us," said Tanalasta. It occurred to her that she was sidestepping Owden's question as neatly as Vangerdahast had sidestepped hers, but it really did not matter. If the dark face was not Rowen's, she was determined to know that as well. "When there is only one way to interpret a set of facts, then it must be the explanation—no matter how unpleasant."

"And what if there is another explanation?" asked Rowen. "Xanthon may have been telling the truth."

"Rowen? A ghazneth?" Tanalasta rolled her eyes. "You never met Rowen. Even Vangerdahast said nothing could make him betray Cormyr."

Owden shook his head, clearly uncomfortable with her doubts about Vangerdahast.

Tanalasta swung her feet off the stool, then leaned forward and pressed Rowen's holy symbol into the harvestmaster's hand. "Please, Owden. I must know."

Owden closed his eyes and sighed, then reluctantly nodded. "You deserve at least that much." The harvestmaster took the symbol and lifted her legs onto the stool again, then motioned his subordinates over. "Clagl, keep watch for Boldovar. You others, stand by me. It may be that this dark man is Rowen, or it may be he is some other thing we would rather not bring into Cormyr."

The priests quickly arranged themselves as ordered. There were no dragoneers or war wizards within five hundred yards of the room, for Tanalasta's troops had learned through hard experience the power of Boldovar's delusional tricks. Only clerics seemed able to withstand the madness he induced, and even they had to gird themselves with prayers and holy symbols.

Once all was ready, Owden began to swing the symbol before Tanalasta's eyes. "Concentrate . . ."

Tanalasta followed the silver amulet with her eyes, picturing the same dark face she had glimpsed twice before—a heavy brow and pearly eyes, brutish hooked nose, the familiar cleft chin. The image melded with the symbol and began to swing back and forth, and she had the sensation of peering down a long black tunnel, then the inky face was there before her, gaunt and sinister-looking, half hidden by a gray curtain of rain.

"Rowen?" Tanalasta called.

The brow furrowed, and the eyes grew white and angry. The dark figure shook its head, then started to turn away as before.

"Rowen, no!" When the head did not stop, Tanalasta yelled, "Now, Owden! I have him."

The harvestmaster rattled off a long string of mystic syllables, and the distance seemed to vanish between Tanalasta and the dark figure. He pivoted back toward her, and the air behind his head began to flash with silver lightning.

"No!" he cried.

The voice was deeper and raspier than Tanalasta recalled, but its dry northern accent left no doubt in her mind that it belonged to her husband. The portal through which she was viewing him seemed to grow larger, and she saw that his body was as dark as his face and as naked as the night they had conceived their child—though she no longer found it irresistible. Far from it. Everything seemed strangely out of proportion and brutish, with hulking shoulders and bulging arms and an impossibly narrow waist. His thighs were as large and round as wine casks, his groin covered by a mosslike tangle of hair that hung nearly to his knees.

Rain and thunder began to spill through the portal, soaking Tanalasta and shaking the room. Owden cried out in alarm, and his priests pressed close, moving to interpose themselves in the narrow gap between the princess and whatever was coming out of the gate. The dark figure spun away, turning a small pair of leathery ghazneth wings toward the portal.

"No!" Tanalasta screamed.

Her eyes had to be deceiving her, or perhaps it been her ears, when she thought the creature sounded like Rowen . . . then she hit on the only possible explanation. Boldovar was there. Somehow, he had snuck into the chamber and begun to deceive them, and it was one of his mad illusions she was seeing.

"Rowen, don't go!" she yelled. "I know you're not—"

It was too late. The ghazneth's wings had already begun to absorb Owden's magic, and the portal was shrinking before her eyes. One of the priests screamed in terror and slipped over the edge, then two more went. Tanalasta felt it sucking at her feet.

"Close it!" she yelled.

Owden's only response was a pained yell. Tanalasta swung her feet off the stool and drew them up into the chair with her, curling into the seat as well as her swollen bulk would allow. The portal shrank to the size of a window, pulling the rest of the priests in after it and leaving the princess staring over the top at Owden's straining face.

"Owden, close it!"

"Ca—"

That was as much as the harvestmaster could say before he tumbled forward and pitched headlong into the portal. The hole closed with a sharp hiss, leaving Tanalasta alone on her side of the room and only Clagl standing on the other.

The palace's ghazneth bell started to ring through the window.

40

ods above watch over us," Lareth Gulur murmured, watching the huge red dragon settle on a hilltop four miles or so away. The farm fields between it and a wandering brook not far below where they stood were covered in a cloak of moving goblins. "Earfangs, the scourge of mens' knees. I never thought they'd get this far."

"If we don't stop them," his superior grunted, "they'll be at the gates of Suzail tomorrow—and yon Devil Dragon'll be coiled around the towers of the palace."

Gulur shuddered. He had a new and better-fitting breastplate because a valiant Purple Dragon had died fighting the dragon the night before, but his helm was the same old dented one that had cradled his brains for a decade. It's hard to salvage a helm when a dragon's swallowed the head wearing it whole, but gore can readily be washed off a breastplate if it's fresh enough. The thought made him glance down, involuntarily. When he looked up, Hathlan Talar was regarding him with a grim smile.

"Just try and stay out of its jaws until Vangerdahast does his work," Talar said. "Then you'll see what a red dragon looks like falling ready-cooked out of the sky."

Gulur looked up at the gathering gray clouds, and shuddered. "Like something to stay out from under?" he joked weakly.

Talar gave him a hollow laugh, clapped him on the shoulder, and strode off down the tense line of waiting men, all on foot. Goblins meant no horses. Their hooves might claim half a dozen or more, but the animals always fell, and fell hard, losing the lives of their riders to swarming goblin blades. Goblins ate horses and, for that matter, men. Fingers and toes, he'd heard, were delicacies. Along with . . . other things.

Goblins he could handle, given swords enough, though he'd never seen this many goblins before, and knew from the tales of the older soldiers that so many had never before swarmed into Cormyr to take the field against any army. It was the dragon, though, that none could stand against. With flame, claw, and spell it—no, *she*, they said—smote the most valiant knights and the shrewdest battlemasters, sniffing out war wizards whatever their disguise and rending them to pieces.

She seemed to know Cormyr better than the oldest veteran Purple Dragon scouts and know magic better than any war wizard. She was a very "devil among dragons," as one mage had choked, viewing the dismembered bodies of his three apprentices. The Devil Dragon it had been to the realm from that moment on, the name spreading across farms and barracks like sunlight in the morning. And there she was, only a few lazy wing beats away.

As Gulur squinted across the fields at her, the red dragon suddenly raised her head and looked, he thought, right back at him. He could see the glitter of one of her eyes.

"Gods defend me!" Gulur gasped, turning his head away with an effort. Even as he drew a sword that didn't need to be drawn and looked along its length in an entirely unneeded examination—a length that trembled more than he cared to admit—he could feel the fell, cold weight of the dragon's gaze upon him.

Troy Denning and Ed Greenwood

A trumpet blared, calling each man to arms. Gulur lowered his visor and saw to his lacing. Hathlan came down the line again offering murmured courage and warnings. A small gap in the lowering clouds fell across the field, and the sun shone warm and bright upon the hill where they stood. Gulur looked around at this small corner of fair Cormyr for what might be his last time, and drew in a deep breath. The goblins were across the brook and toiling up the hill. It wouldn't be long before the call to charge came.

* * * * *

"Is this wise, my liege? We're so few!" Durmeth Eldroon called, spurring his black stallion over to the king. Even from the height of his saddle, he found himself staring up into the stolid face of a mountain of a man in plate armor. This was Kolmin Stagblade, Bannerguard to the King. Stagblade held a fearsome battle-axe in his hands, its blade turned out to keep even excitable Marsembian nobles at bay.

"You see another choice?" Azoun asked calmly in return. "If we retreat to Suzail or Marsember, we abandon our farmers—and their crops—to the goblins. We'd be left to fight the dragon on our own rooftops, with all the war-ruin on the heads of our wives and children. If we retreat beyond our cities, Cormyr is lost. If we cannot stand against these foes here, let us fall as dearly as we can, so those who come to the gates of Suzail and Marsember are as few and as wounded as we can leave them."

"That's all that's left to us?"

Azoun shrugged. "A ruler does what he can and tries to find or make new roads, new chances . . . but my time for that is past. Now I must bar and guard the gate on the road I've built. It's the task left to me."

Eldroon's reply was a wordless snarl as he spurred his stallion back along the ridge to where his troops stood in a knot, still not fallen into formation.

"There's trouble waiting to happen," Battlemaster Ilnbright growled, glaring after the dwindling noble.

Death of the Dragon

The veteran Purple Dragon commander looked like the hewn and hardened warrior he was—a chopping block as wide as he was tall, as massive as a cask in his deliberately dulled armor.

Azoun shrugged. "No time to right it now. If any man here sees aught amiss with our friend Eldroon's deeds on this field, and lives to see the end of it, take word to either of these two men."

Men looked where he pointed. The king's gauntlet was extended at a grim-looking Dauneth Marliir, High Warden of the Eastern Marches, and a nervous-looking Lord Giogi Wyvernspur. They sat on horses—swift errand-mounts, not war-horses—behind the crest of the hill.

"'*Take* word'?" Haliver Ilnbright growled. "Where're they going, then?"

"To Jester's Green, to command the last hope of the realm," the king said, loudly enough for all of the war captains gathered around him to hear. "If we fall, and our foe goes on to threaten Suzail, these two lords have the duty to lead our eldest veterans and youngest reserves in the field. Their task will be to guard the walls of Suzail as long as possible, and get as many Cormyreans—your wives and children—away safe from our shores if need be. There are already coins from our vaults, hidden away safe, in certain cities elsewhere. If Cormyr falls, its royal treasury goes to its citizens, a hundred gold each, and thrice that for heads of families."

A lone voice cut through the general murmur that followed. "Gods bless you, my liege," one of the older war captains growled, bowing his head. "That's one care gone from me, right there. If I fall, I'd not want my king to go unthanked for such service to me and mine."

"Aye! Well said," and the like came from a dozen throats. Amid their thunder, Azoun gestured to Dauneth and Giogi. They saluted and turned their mounts away, down the slope that led to the next hill closer to Suzail—a height where the king's tent had been erected, and a few hostlers stood holding nobles' war-horses.

"What about Marsember?" a lone voice asked softly, as the war captains turned grimly to face the foe again.

"We've not swords enough to spare to guard both," Azoun said bleakly. "The navy holds Marsember with the aid of some hired adventurers. If a thousand thousand goblins appear at its gates, there're boats enough."

"But . . ." the voice began, then fell silent.

Battlemaster Ilnbright's broad and hairy hand fell on the Marsembian's shoulder. "That's the hard part of being king, lad," he growled in a whisper that was audible half the hill away. "There's never enough to do anything proper, or please all the folk. Ye do what ye can, and yer subjects hope ye've a heart and honor to be their shields. This one does—be thankful ye live in Cormyr and not someplace a lot more cruel."

"Haliver," the king said quietly from close by, "sound the trumpet. It's time."

Battlemaster Ilnbright nodded, squared his shoulders, and took the horn from his broad belt. He did not hesitate as he blew the call that would send almost every man on that hill down to his death.

* * * * *

Ilberd Crownsilver had never been in a battle before. He was here now only because he was a Crownsilver, young and expendable enough to ride into possible death so as to serve the king and bring glory to the family. He'd been young enough to be excited and even nonchalant about the clash of arms. After all, how much harm could one take, riding with King Azoun and Royal Magician Vangerdahast? He was even looking forward to swaggering into eveningfeast to grimly tell his kin of his bravery and tell them of how the king had personally praised his cool manner and valor. At least, he'd been young enough for all that about an hour ago.

Now he was cowering behind a rampart of fly-swarming goblin bodies, the stink of death and his own vomit strong around him, hoping to somehow see the end of the day alive. His ears were ringing from the constant din of screaming, blades crashing upon blades and armor—some of these knights used their swords like clubs or threshing flails, battering their foes into the dirt by simply hammering on armor and shield until the limbs beneath broke or were wearied and beaten down—and he'd yet to see a valiant death. Or even a clean one.

Their first charge had slaughtered goblins by the thousands. The brook was running black with goblin blood and flooding the field, its channel so choked with little humanoid bodies it created a wide marsh of blood-hued mud. Their second charge fared as well, but the earfangs were endless. On they came, in an endless howling flood, and more and more men were beginning to fall. Perhaps four hundred were left—no more—and still the goblins came on, waving their spears.

And the Devil Dragon had not yet taken wing. Almost lazily she lay sprawled on that hilltop, gloating, as her forces surged on in their hundreds and thousands, overwhelming the Purple Dragons by the sheer weight of their numbers. The army of Cormyr had retreated back up the hill to force their foes to climb to meet them. The hillside was heaped with dead goblins, slaughtered almost at will until the arrows and quarrels ran out, sword arms grew tired, and the patient sun beat down.

Still the goblins came. Each wave forced its way a little higher up the slope. Each left behind a red wash of fallen, but there were armored men aplenty among all the goblins now, and though he'd swung his sword all of twice, Ilberd was reeling with weariness.

He didn't know how the battlemaster and the other older, larger knights could even stand up, yet they spent the time between each wave drinking water from troughs, mustaches dripping, and pointing out particular goblins to strike at when the next wave came. The time during waves they spent hacking like merry madmen, bellowing war cries and bounding around like boys at play. Gods above, if he *ever* lived to see the sunset, this would be the last battlefield he'd ever—

"Guard yourself, lad!" Haliver Ilnbright bellowed, clapping Ilberd between the shoulders with enough force to

Troy Denning and Ed Greenwood

make him stagger, and striding on without breaking stride. "They're coming again!"

"Slow to learn, aren't they?" a white-haired old knight who'd lost his helm in the last fray drawled. "This is getting to be like a proper romp in the Dragonjaws, it is! I'll have to get my minstrel to write a ballad about this. . . ."

"I hope he sings swiftly," a Purple Dragon armsman growled. "Here they are!"

The howling spilled over the bodies in another rushing tide of flapping leather, slashing swords, and beady goblin eyes. Men planted themselves—no running and leaping now—to hew steadily, like harvesters with scythes and many fields in front of them, in a rhythm of death.

Ilberd dodged a yelling goblin, slipped, found himself nose to nose with another—and was promptly blinded by its blood as a foot took it in the face and a blade bit deep into its neck.

" 'Ware, lad," Lareth Gulur shouted through the din of steel all around them. "Hold your place . . . 'tis hard to fell goblins when you're wallowing about on the . . ."

His next words, whatever they may have been, were lost in a little scream as one goblin ran right onto his blade, a second thrust a blade deep into his crotch, and a third bounded up to slash his face.

The Purple Dragon spun around, clawing at the air for support, and crashed down on his face. Ilberd didn't even have time to gape. It was all so *sudden*. Sudden, and final.

And the realm said the Steel Princess did this every day—*had* done this every day, for years. Gods, but she must have been frightening to stand near!

"*Back*, boy, if you don't know how to use that!" Hathlan Talar roared, shouldering him aside and slaying a trio of goblins with a deft fore-and-back cut. He tripped over Gulur's arm, saw who it was, and cursed like a fiend, then he snatched up his fallen friend's blade, shook the dead goblin off it, and charged down the hill with both blades flashing in his hands like bolts of lightning. Goblins fell in droves around Talar, as he stood alone in their midst roaring like a walrus. Tears were streaming down his face and he was shouting curses so fast the words were tripping over each other to get out of his mouth.

Ilberd Crownsilver gaped at him in utter astonishment—and was still staring like a statue when hurled goblin maces battered Talar down, and a snarling swarm of goblins surged over him, hacking and stabbing.

The young Crownsilver flung down his sword and fled blindly up the hill, weeping. He had to get away from this, had to get anywhere. He had to be where men weren't shrieking and dying, their lives spent in an—

Fingers of iron caught hold of his shoulder and shook him until his teeth rattled. The hands spun him around, setting him so firmly on the ground that both Crownsilver heels were bruised right through his boots.

"We don't need the rear guarded *quite* yet, lad," Battlemaster Ilnbright growled. "We're in rather more pressing need of our line on this end of the ridge not collapsing completely. Just stand in this gap here and kill goblins, hey? It's not that hard, you just need a bit of practice!"

A sword was slapped into Ilberd's hands with numbing force, then the mountainous commander was off down the line again, racing in to stand beside a faltering, bleeding lionar to hack down half a dozen goblins before the wave fell back down the hill, shrieking their rage as they went.

Ilberd swallowed, then his stomach heaved, and he tried to be sick again, though he'd nothing left to empty from it. When he could stand upright once more, he looked up at the crest of the hill and his jaw dropped.

King Azoun had lost his helm in the fray and was bleeding from one ear. A second slash across his cheek was already drying into a dark line. He was holding up a staggering giant of a man—the bannerguard, Kolmin Stagblade.

Kolmin took two faltering steps, looked up at the darkening sky, then crashed over onto his side with a landing that shook the dirt under Ilberd's boots. The man lay still. Azoun bent to him, then straightened, looking grim. The flies were already swarming.

A sudden coldness settled over Ilberd Crownsilver's chest. It was at that moment that he abandoned all thought of a triumphant entry into the family halls and decided that he'd never see them again. He wasn't going to leave this field alive.

The clouds were covering the sky now, blotting the sun from view, and in the sudden gloom Ilberd saw Battlemaster Ilnbright striding up to the king. Wisps of white hair blew in the breeze on both their heads, and Ilberd suddenly realized how *old* these men were. They'd stood on fields like this one forty years ago, and more.

And they were still alive.

He was grinning at that, heart suddenly lighter, when his thoughts fell upon a new idea. Just how many other eager young men had stood with them then who weren't alive to stand there now?

* * * * *

It was three grim, weary hours later when Battlemaster Ilnbright fell, roaring to his last breath, under a cloak of struggling, scrambling goblins. Ilberd himself hewed down the last of them, tears of rage and grief temporarily blinding him.

When he looked up, it was to see perhaps sixty men still standing around him or sitting wearily on the ground, some groaning from their wounds.

The field below the hill was knee deep in dead goblins. They were heaped head-high in some places. Still, a fresh wave, a thousand strong or more, was trotting out from behind the hill where the dragon lay sprawled at ease.

"That's it," someone said quietly. "We're doomed."

"What?" someone else growled. "And not have a chance to take some of these home to Malaeve so she can try her recipe for goblin stew?"

No one bothered to laugh, but there were a few silent smiles as men took up blades and worked aching arms in slow swings, waiting for death to come up the hill and snatch them down.

"For Cormyr," someone whispered, almost as if it were a prayer.

"For Cormyr," a dozen throats muttered in response. With something like wonder, Ilberd discovered that his own voice had been one of them.

* * * * *

Somehow they'd withstood that wave, the exhausted and blood-drenched few on the hilltop, though one lionar lay twisting and sobbing, his guts on the grass around him, pleading to someone—anyone—to cut his throat and end the pain.

King Azoun took a flask from his belt and put it to the man's lips. The healing potion did not close the grisly wound, but the pain faded from the warrior's face, and the king put one arm around his shoulders to help him stand. They were standing together grimly, knowing how little time they had left to live, when the thunder began.

Men looked up at the scudding gray clouds, racing across the sky as if in haste to be elsewhere but as endless as the swarming goblins. No lightning split that sky, and no rain fell. Could the dragon be working a spell? Or was this the work of the royal magician?

Ilberd glanced along the hill at Vangerdahast, who'd lain on his stomach murmuring spells and reading scrolls aloud for most of the day. He'd been wreaking great havoc among distant goblins but took no part in the hewing on the hilltop. If the strength of Cormyr on this hilltop shrank to any less, the young swordlord thought grimly, the wizard might not have any choice about fighting with blade and boots when the next wave came.

The thunder deepened, becoming a steady sound, and louder. The Devil Dragon was on her feet now, twisting around to look behind her. She sprang into the air with a ripple of powerful shoulders, great batlike wings beating once before she plunged down in a pounce on something out of sight, behind the hill.

Someone near Ilberd muttered, "The elves, come again? That can't be...."

The thunder swept around the hill, driving a red foam of shrieking, spitted goblins before it before they were trampled and ridden down. Purple Dragon banners flapped above the riders. They raised their swords in a shouted salute to the king, then they crashed into the goblins between the hills.

"Gwennath," Azoun said quietly. "Thank all the watching gods—Tymora most of all—that I've a marshal who knows when to disobey orders."

"She's emptied High Horn!" a war captain bellowed joyously. "See the banners—they're all here!" He burst into unashamed tears, not caring if half the world saw his mustache dripping.

A figure in black armor rode at the head of that thundering mass of knights—a figure that raised one slender arm to Azoun as the riders swept past up the valley, driving the helpless goblins before them.

Azoun returned the salute, and laughed in delight.

He was still laughing when the gigantic red dragon swirled into view around the hill, clawing and biting as she roared past mere feet above the heads of the High Horn cavalry, and plunged down on the front ranks of the galloping Cormyreans, biting and clawing.

When she rose from the confusion of rolling, screaming horses and shouting men, jaws dripping with gore, the dark-armored figure could not be seen. When the wyrm turned in the air and breathed fire along that line of death, nothing but dark-armored figures could be seen, toppling amid the smoke.

"So passes Gwennath, Lady-Lord High Marshal of Cormyr," a knight beside Ilberd murmured. "Who rode all the way from High Horn to win this battle for us—and lose her own life."

"Win it?" someone else growled. "Forgive me if my eyes fail, but I seem to see a dragon . . ."

The Devil Dragon turned in the air with indolent grace and plunged down upon the cavalry, taking them in the rear just as they had done to the goblins. She skidded along, shaking the ground in fresh thunder with the force of her passage, and snapping her jaws like a dog ridding itself of stinging flies. A bloody cloud trailed from her as she swept her foes in a terrible tangle down the battlefield, leaving a long, bloody smear.

When their heaped, shattered corpses brought her to a halt at last, she bounded aloft again, scattering those who tried to hurl lances at her with a sweep of a mighty tail. She circled, looking down at those she was going to slay at her next pass. Or the next one.

* * * * *

Gwennath may have been dead, but she'd left one last trick for her slayer. The great red dragon had barely begun her dive down at the cavalry when there was a flash from within its close-packed ranks, then another.

"That's magic!" someone on the hilltop shouted.

"Lord Wizard?" someone else barked. Vangerdahast peered, and kept peering, and said simply, "Aye. Magic."

They stood and watched as the dragon came down, large and terrible in the sky—unmoving, claws outstretched and mouth agape as the ground rushed up, her eyes rolling wildly at the last.

"It's spellbound!" someone cried excitedly, as horsemen scattered in the valley below.

The dragon crashed headfirst into the valley.

The ground shook, and many of the men on the hill fell as the ground quivered under them. Those who kept their footing saw men and their mounts cartwheeling helplessly through the air in the vale below, twisting in agony and despair, and vain attempts to catch hold of something in the roaring chaos that engulfed them.

The ground shook for a long, groaning time. The stiff-winged wyrm slid along like a giant plough, choking out a cry that sounded very like a human woman sobbing, as it helplessly hurled a great cloud of dust and dirt at the sky in its wake.

Clods of earth rained down on the hillside, and men swore in awe and threw up their hands—too late—to shield their eyes. The earth itself seemed to groan and echo its complaint back from the hills around, as at last the Devil Dragon came to a halt.

A horn sounded even before the great wyrm stopped moving, and lancers in the valley below spurred their mounts forward in a charge that ended at those curving scales as they milled around, thrusting and hurling for all their might.

The dragon surged as her assailants raged around her, heaving herself up once, twice, then twisting and rolling over on her side among screaming horses and sprinting men. She thrashed, flailed, then shook herself all over, hurling bodies like broken dolls in all directions, and righted herself.

Ilberd could have sworn the Devil Dragon was wearing a grim look as she flapped her wings, bowling over men and horses like so many toys and clearing a wide area around herself. She reared up and beat her wings in earnest, then, faltering only once. When she took to the air, she was not quite free of the magic, and her wavering flight was straight to her hilltop, to a crashing, heavy landing.

The beast lay motionless, but for her heaving sides, for some moments. The men on the hill saw many spears moving up and down with her scales.

"Blood to us," a war captain growled in satisfaction. "Now let's get over there and finish the task."

They were already moving forward when a lancelord pointed and snapped, "Gods above! *More* of them!"

Up into view from the far side of the dragon's hill were coming more goblins—a steady stream of fresh faces, shields, and waving blades.

The men on the hill came to an uneasy halt—all except for the king and the wizard, who trudged steadily on amid the goblin bodies, heading down the hill into the blood-drenched valley. The cavalry swept past the way they'd come, seeking more goblins to slay or perhaps a place to take shelter from red dragons on the wing.

Lancelord looked to lionar, then down at the dwindling figures of the king and the wizard, then at each other again.

Helpless shrugs followed and the grim, bloody survivors began to descend the hill once more.

"King Azoun?" one of them called uncertainly.

"On! Our work's not done yet!" the king called back, rather grimly.

"What price glory?" Ilberd Crownsilver grunted wearily, as his slippery descent brought him down beside his ruler. "Haven't we slain goblins enough?"

"We're not here to win glory, lad," Azoun growled. "We're here because Cormyr needs us. Or at least that's why *I'm* here."

The young swordlord stared at him for a moment, face going pale, then suddenly ducked his head and went on down the hill.

As they came to the blood-choked stream, the king drew his sword again.

41

he knelling of the ghazneth bell barely registered in Tanalasta's mind. She sat crouched on the comfortable reading chair in Vangerdahast's study, staring at the empty space into which Owden and his priests had just vanished. Her head was whirling and her stomach churning, and she felt numb with shock. What had happened seemed unthinkable. It seemed unimaginable that her husband had become a ghazneth. It seemed impossible that Owden and the others had been drawn through the gate into Rowen's dark world.

Clagl turned from the window where he was standing watch and said, "Your plan worked, Princess. Boldovar ignored the palace and came here. He's circling the tower now."

The young priest paused for a response. When there was none, he asked, "Princess? What are we to do?"

Tanalasta felt hollow and sick inside. Had she listened to Owden, he and the others would be there now. Instead, she had chosen to ignore his warning, to trust her own selfish emotions and Vangerdahast's gentle lies and declare that Rowen could never become a ghazneth. What a fool she had been. Vangerdahast might be harsh and manipulative, but he did what was right for Cormyr. In second-guessing him, she had condemned Owden and his priests to some wet hell she could only imagine. Worse, she had lost a dozen loyal men and women when Cormyr needed them most.

"He's circling lower," Clagl reported diligently. He stepped back from the window and came to take Tanalasta's arm. "We must get you out of here."

Tanalasta jerked away. "No, I'm going to destroy that ghazneth." She pulled an iron short sword from its scabbard inside her hiding box, then snatched a pair of silver manacles from Vangerdahast's study table. "I won't run—not after what I did."

"This isn't about you, Highness." Clagl's tone was stern. Like most of Owden's priests, he spoke even to Tanalasta with no fear of recrimination. He pointed at her huge belly. "It's about your baby. You mustn't risk it so foolishly."

"This baby is hardly the most important thing in the realm," Tanalasta shot back, growing more furious by the moment. "No traitor's child will ever sit . . ."

Tanalasta let the sentence trail off when she saw the shock in Clagl's face and realized what she was saying. Her anger was at Rowen and herself, not the baby. It was not the child's doing that its father had betrayed her and Cormyr, and even if it never would sit on the Dragon Throne (Vangerdahast would see to that), she was still its mother. She still loved it. She still had to keep it safe and healthy.

The chamber grew dark. Tanalasta looked over to see Boldovar's black silhouette sweeping past the window, his fiery eyes shining crimson in a wild halo of black hair. A gaping crescent opened in the center of his unkempt beard, and a long red tongue shot past a pair of yellow fangs to wag at Tanalasta.

Clagl pulled the lapels of her weathercloak closed. "Use your escape pocket. I'll hold him."

The chamber brightened again as Boldovar cleared the

window. He dipped a wing and banked out over Lake Azoun, wheeling around for a direct approach to the window. Clagl turned to go and block the window, but Tanalasta caught him by the sleeve.

"No." She pulled him toward her iron hiding box, which was standing open in the corner. "The child must be protected—but so must Cormyr."

The priest looked confused. "But we are only two. How can we—"

"By stalling," Tanalasta interrupted. She stepped into the box, pulling the priest in after her and returning her short sword to its place. "Until we know what is happening in the battle against Nalavara, we must hold Boldovar here."

Clagl swallowed. "Very well."

He slipped the iron locking bar into place, plunging them into darkness, then a loud puffing sounded outside the box as Boldovar streaked into the room and spread his wings to halt.

Tanalasta closed the throat clasp of her weathercloak and pictured the hard-bitten face of Battlelord Steelhand in her mind. She felt a surge of warm magic rushing into her head, then the battlelord's thin eyebrows rose in surprise.

Bring a dozen warpriests to Vangerdahast's tower—no one else! Tanalasta commanded, speaking to him in her thoughts. *We are alone and Boldovar is upon us.*

Two minutes, came the reply.

The princess would have liked to know how the battlelord intended to reach Vangerdahast's tower in only two minutes, since it was at least a ten minute run out the gate and over the nearest bridge. Probably, he intended to have a band of war wizards teleport his party into a nearby street, then run the rest of the way. That meant Tanalasta would have to work hard to keep Boldovar's attention focused on the magic *inside* the room.

Outside her hiding place, Boldovar's clawed feet began to tick across the floor. Tanalasta removed her commander's ring from her pocket and slipped it on, then whispered, "King's light."

An eerie, blue-white light filled the box, illuminating Clagl's frightened face beside her. The young priest was holding one hand on the iron locking mechanism, as though his grasp would keep the door secure where a full inch of iron could not. With the other hand, he clutched his iron mace close to his chest. The ticking of Boldovar's feet grew louder, and loud snuffling sounds began to hiss through the seams of the iron box.

"Magic!" he rasped. "Magic I smell . . . and magic I'll have!"

He ran his claws down the face of the iron door, and a deafening screech reverberated inside the box. Tanalasta heard Clagl hissing through his teeth, then felt him grasp her arm in reassurance, and she realized she was the one making the sound. Boldovar let out an angry grunt and tried to rip the door open. The box tipped forward, then teetered on the edge of falling and rocked back to clang into the wall behind it. Tanalasta's head slammed into the leather padding and began to ache.

She felt a sudden tightness low in her abdomen, then noticed something warm and fluid inside her legs.

"No." It couldn't be happening now.

Boldovar tried again to rip the door open, then grew frustrated and simply slammed the iron box down on its face. Tanalasta took the impact entirely on her belly and felt her womb cramp in reaction. The spasm did not subside. A heavy thump sounded above their backs as Boldovar jumped on top of the box. He began to scratch his claws down the seams, looking for a weak point.

"You can hide, but you can't hide," chuckled Boldovar, making no sense at all. "I smell your magic . . . I smell you, and I'll have both I will!"

The screeching sharpened to an abrupt ping and ceased, only to be replaced by a childish tempest of striking hands and feet. So thunderous was the pounding that Tanalasta thought the thick iron might split beneath the ghazneth's blows. The cramping in her womb sharpened, growing so acute she wailed in shock.

"Princess? What's . . . ?"

The rest of Clagl's question was lost beneath the roar of

Boldovar's hammering fists, for the sound of Tanalasta's pain seemed to have driven him into a frenzy. The pounding moved down toward their feet, then the box began to tip up on its head. The princess had just enough time to work her hands up above her shoulders before the box tumbled across the room, clanging and crashing.

They came to a rest against the opposite wall, resting upside down and at an angle, so that they were lying head-down on their backs. The pain in the princess's womb had grown crushing, and she had to scream or burst. Something was wrong. Her water had barely broken, and labor was not supposed to come until hours later.

"Princess?" Clagl shook her arm. "What's wrong?"

Tanalasta managed to wrest a scream into a word, "Baby!"

Clagl's response was lost in the boom of Boldovar's foot striking iron up near their feet. The box spun off the wall and crashed to the floor, then twirled across the room and smashed the legs from under a table. An eerie stillness followed, and Tanalasta felt as if someone had dropped a door on her stomach. There were no contractions, none of the rhythmic tightening her midwife had told her to expect. There was only steady, horrid pain growing worse each passing moment and a strange feeling of slackening everywhere below her waist.

Clagl laid a hand over her womb and began to gently feel around the underside of her belly. Tanalasta's scream faded to a grunt, not because her pain had dwindled, but because she had run out of air. She heard her breath coming fast and shallow and knew she was starting to panic, and that knowledge only made her breathe faster.

A distant cacophony of muffled voices grew audible over Tanalasta's low groans, and she knew Battlelord Steelhand's men were in the street below the tower. Boldovar remained ominously silent, perhaps because he had gone to the window to investigate the noise. The princess certainly hoped that was what he was doing, and not thinking up some way to pry up the lid off her hiding place. Now, when she most needed to be strong for Cormyr and herself, she felt more vulnerable and helpless than she had at any time since the start of the crisis.

Finally, Clagl pulled his hand away. "I know it hurts, but there's no need to be frightened. You're only giving birth. Everything will be fine."

"Don't lie to me!" Tanalasta screamed the words, more to express her fear than her disbelief. "This isn't labor. My midwife told me what to expect!"

"I'm sure she also told you every birth is different." Clagl laid a reassuring hand on her arm. "The ghazneth seems to have hurried yours along a bit."

"Then stop it!" How could her body do this to her? How could it pick this moment to betray her? "The baby can't come now."

"I'm afraid we have no choice in the matter," whispered Clagl, "I'll stay here and decoy the ghazneth. Perhaps you should use your escape pocket—"

The priest's suggestion was interrupted by an anguished scream. This time it was not Tanalasta's.

"Tanalasta . . . don't lift the door." The voice was husky and familiar, with a dry northern accent that the princess would recognize anywhere. "Whatever you do, stay—"

The muffled snap of a breaking bone brought the sentence to a screeching end.

"What say you, girl?" Boldovar cackled above them. "A husband for a couple of rings and a weathercloak?"

Another crack sounded above the box, and shot through Tanalasta's heart.

Boldovar spoke again. "Decide quickly. You know how easily I grow bored."

Tanalasta's thoughts whirled in pain-addled confusion. Boldovar's prisoner certainly sounded like Rowen, but that could not be. Rowen was a ghazneth, imprisoned in the same wet hell where Vangerdahast had been trapped—or was he? Owden had told her how Xanthon had impersonated her at the Battle of the Farsea Marsh. Perhaps the ghazneth in the cavern had not been Rowen after all. Perhaps Vangerdahast had been telling the truth all along.

Terrified at how events were slipping out of her control,

Tanalasta unclasped her weathercloak and slipped off her commander's ring. "You have . . . a bargain." She forced the words out between clenched teeth. "Let him go."

"Tanalasta, n—"

Rowen's cry was cut short by the sharp clap of a hand striking flesh. A heavy body slammed into a set of bookshelves and thudded to the floor, then lay groaning on the floor behind them.

"He's free," said Boldovar. "Now throw out the magic, or I'll finish what I started."

Tanalasta reached over Clagl to undo the locking bar, but he caught her hand. "What are you doing?"

"I need Rowen!" she answered. If she had Rowen, she would be strong again, in control. "I can't let him . . . kill Rowen."

"You won't." Clagl pushed her hand toward the holy symbol hanging around her neck. "Say a prayer."

"But he'll—"

"Don't let Boldovar trick you," whispered Clagl. "Say a prayer, and you will see—or open the door and see your child killed."

The priest released Tanalasta's hand, and her hand hovered below the locking bar for a long moment.

"What is this?" called Boldovar. There was a loud thump and a pained groan, then he asked, "Am I growing bored?"

Tanalasta touched the holy symbol and whispered, "Chauntea, watch over me."

And she instantly recognized the next thud as something more like a wing slapping the wall than a man being hurled into it. "*Aaagggh!*" The voice was mocking and snide and did not resemble Rowen's at all. "Tanalasta, don't! Stay in where you are safe!"

"I will!" Tanalasta called. She was still terrified, but she felt as though she had regained some measure of command over the situation . . . if only her body would cooperate. The belt of agony tightened around her middle, and she could feel the baby slipping out toward the world. Fighting to maintain control of her own emotions—if nothing else—she yelled, "I know who you are . . . you . . . sick . . . *worm!*"

There was a moment of stunned silence, then Boldovar broke into a mad cackle. "Ah, well I see that Rowen loved you more than you did him. He would rather have died himself than listen to you beg for death."

"*What?*" Though her thoughts remained addled by pain and fear, the little control Tanalasta now had over the situation gave her the strength to grasp the ghazneth's implication. "What did you do to him?"

"Oh, *now* you're interested," sneered Boldovar. "Throw me the rings, and I'll tell."

There was no need, for even without knowing the details, Tanalasta understood all too well how Boldovar had baited her husband into becoming a ghazneth—and why the ranger had been too ashamed to come through the gate. Only one thing that could cause Rowen to betray his duty to Cormyr: the fear of betraying Tanalasta.

The muffled drumming of boots began to rumble up the stairway, and the princess heard Boldovar's claws clacking across the floor toward the window. She summoned to mind the incantation of her magic bolt spell and pointed her finger toward the seam of the door. She was not going to let the ghazneth escape, not after what he had done to Rowen.

"Clagl, give me a crack to fire through." Knowing the priest would argue, she quickly added, "Now!"

Clagl gulped down a deep breath but pulled the locking bar back and pushed the door up. Boldovar stood across the room gathering himself up to spring out the window, his drink-bloated face pivoting around at the sound of the iron door being unbarred.

"Where you going, lady killer?" Tanalasta's voice was as snide as she could make it. She uttered her spell and sent a single bolt of golden magic streaking high between his legs. It struck the window sill in front of his groin, and the casing erupted into a spray of stone shards. "Afraid the little pregnant princess will make a eunuch of you?"

Boldovar glanced at the fading magic in the shattered window sill, then raised his lip in a yellow-fanged sneer and spun toward the box. Clagl let the door drop and had it barred before Tanalasta could give the order, but even so he was very nearly not fast enough. A loud squeal rang through the box as the ghazneth's claws raked at the seam, then the princess's stomach sank as the iron box rose into the air.

Tanalasta began to feel helpless and panicked again. This was not something she had expected. The box clanged and spun as it banged out the window casement, then the princess lost contact with the padding behind her shoulders as they plummeted groundward. Boldovar's wings pounded the air like a bellows, and still they sank. Tanalasta grabbed Clagl's arm and reached for her escape pocket, then pitched sideways and cracked heads with the priest as they splashed into Lake Azoun.

She blacked out, but awoke a few moments later coughing and choking. Lake Azoun's muddy water was already filling her mouth and lapping at her nostrils. Clagl lay completely submerged beneath her, facing the side of the box and not moving.

Thanking the goddess she had returned to consciousness before drowning, Tanalasta gulped down a last breath. She pushed her hand down into her weathercloak, fighting through a floating morass of heavy wool. By the time her fingers located the escape pocket's leather-lined mouth, the box was completely filled with water. Clagl had begun to convulse and did not respond to any of Tanalasta's prodding and poking. Even if the princess managed to turn herself so the dimension door did not appear between them, he would be incapable of following her through on his own. She would have to pull him, which meant she would have to squeeze her swollen, aching stomach back around toward the front of the box. There was no time for that. She slipped her free arm around Clagl's neck, then removed her other hand from her escape pocket, reached past him, and pulled the locking bar back.

The door flew open. The light and the air came flooding in, and Tanalasta found herself staring up into Boldovar's mad red eyes, gasping for breath and struggling to understand how the ghazneth could be standing upright in the depths of Lake Azoun, shaking his fat belly at her and cackling in laughter.

Before the answer came to her, he stepped into the iron box, grinding his heel down on Clagl's neck and crushing it with an audible crunch.

"For me? How kind." As Boldovar spoke, his dark hand flashed down and grabbed the collar of Tanalasta's weather-cloak. "Thank you very much."

The ghazneth ripped the heavy cloak off over her head, taking with it the simple smock underneath and leaving the princess in nothing but her breast bindings and loins girdle. He hardly seemed to notice. Boldovar simply buried his face in the black cloth and let out a long, satisfied groan as he began to absorb its magic.

The watery depths changed to Vangerdahast's study, and grotesque and lascivious carvings began to appear on the walls. Finally coming to understand how she had been tricked, Tanalasta screamed in anger.

"No!"

Boldovar looked up and smiled, the remains of her shredded smock draped over his head. "Oh, yes."

Battlelord Steelhand's voice boomed up the stairs. "We're coming, Princess! A few moments more . . ."

But they did not have a few moments more. The depth of color was already fading from Tanalasta's weathercloak, and the chamber now looked more like a ghastly festhall devoted to unnatural cravings and monstrous delights than Vangerdahast's study. If she allowed the ghazneth to absorb any more of her magic, Steelhand and his men would have no chance at all of destroying the thing.

Gritting her teeth against the crushing pain in her abdomen, Tanalasta propped herself up and drew the iron sword secreted in the door of her hiding box. Every day, her self-defense instructors drilled one simple lesson into her: strike to cripple, then strike to kill. But how to cripple a ghazneth?

To stop Boldovar, she knew she had to do more than crush a knee or slash a hamstring. She had to assault him in the very heart of his sick existence. The answer came to the princess easily. She pushed herself to her knees and brought the short blade across Boldovar's loins in a vicious backhand slash.

"Coward!" she cried.

Boldovar's crimson eyes grew as wide as coins, then he let out a surprised little whimper and allowed the weather-cloak to slip from his grasp. Tanalasta brought the sword back in the opposite direction, opening another dark gash in the underside of his belly. Her own pain seemed to vanish—or rather, her fear seemed to vanish. She was still aware of her labor, of the crushing feeling around her waist and the baby moving steadily closer to the world, but now she was in control. She brought the blade around for an overhand hack at the center of his big belly.

"Enough!"

Boldovar's arm flashed out to block. The blow caught him across the wrist and nearly lopped it off, but the ghazneth hardly seemed to notice. He circled his forearm around as though it were a blade, forcing Tanalasta's sword back against her thumb and stripping it from her grasp. The weapon fell free and clanged off the rim of the box.

Tanalasta turned toward the stairwell door, where the sound of pounding boots had grown so loud the princess swore the warpriests had to be in the room with her. They very nearly were. The battlelord and his first three men stood at the top of the stairwell, panting for breath and running in place, apparently convinced they were still ascending the spiraling staircase into Vangerdahast's study.

"Steelhand!" Tanalasta called. "Run forward!"

"What are you calling him for?" Boldovar demanded. "You asked *me* to play."

The ghazneth's hand slammed into Tanalasta's head so hard that she heard half a dozen teeth clatter off the wall. Her vision narrowed and her hearing grew distant, then she felt herself being jerked out of the iron box and hurled against the stone wall. The impact moved the baby lower, and she felt its head beginning to crown.

When her eyesight returned, Boldovar was standing in front of her, holding her against the wall with his mutilated forearm and glaring at her with an insane, maniacal grin. "Good. You're back."

Something sharp and hot pierced Tanalasta's abdomen just below the navel, then her belly exploded into agonizing pain. She looked down and saw the ghazneth's arm pressed against her stomach. At first, she could not quite fathom what she was seeing—then she noticed the collar of red blood around his forearm, and felt a huge hand feeling around inside her.

"Let me see . . . where is that baby?" He grabbed something up near her rib cage and pulled.

Tanalasta's world became a red fiery scream. She brought her knee up more by instinct than intention and felt it connect hard. Boldovar did not groan, but the impact was enough to send him two steps back. He was holding something brownish and bloody in his hand. It wasn't a baby, and that was enough for Tanalasta.

Boldovar smiled and raised the bloody mass to his mouth—then pitched over forward as Battlelord Steelhand and his men barreled into him from behind. Their swords rose and fell in a tempest, hacking the ghazneth into a mangled black mass. It hardly mattered. The wounds closed almost as fast as they could inflict them. The Mad King pushed the bloody mass he was holding into his mouth and broke into a maniacal laugh, then began to chew and swallow.

Tanalasta felt the strength leave her legs and slumped to the floor. The pain was all gone now. There was a cold numbness up under her ribs, where Boldovar had ripped her life out, and a warmer, happier emptiness down in her womb, where she felt her baby sliding out into the world even as she faded. She reached down and felt its head, waxy and warm and tiny. It was all she would ever know of the child. The ghazneth had sealed her doom when he ate whatever it was he had eaten, for even the finest healers in the kingdom could not save her without all of her organs.

But the child would survive, and through the child, Cormyr. Tanalasta bore down with what little strength remained to her and felt the child slip completely free. It snuffled and began to cry. She tried to raise it to her breast, but could not.

"Boldovar . . ." she gasped. "King Boldovar the Mad. I grant you . . . the thing you desire most."

Boldovar threw off one of Steelhand's warpriests, then raised his head to glare, crimson-eyed, at Tanalasta. "Quiet, trollop!"

"King Boldovar the Mad, I grant you my pain."

The darkness drained from Boldovar's face. He did not stop struggling, but his efforts grew ineffectual, and little pieces of his body began to fly off beneath the impact of the warpriests' blades.

Tanalasta raised her fingers—as much as she could do to signal a stop—then said, "Enough. Just hold him."

The blows stopped, and the warpriests stamped their hobnailed boots down on his arms and legs to hold him in place.

When Tanalasta did not speak again, Battlelord Steelhand looked over and seemed to realize there remained one thing he could do for his princess. Leaving Boldovar to his subordinates, he kneeled at Tanalasta's side, then took the infant from between her legs and laid it on her breast.

"Thank you," Tanalasta said. She looked back to Boldovar and, to her surprise, found that the next words were not difficult to say at all. "King Boldovar, as an heir to the Obarskyr crown and a direct descendant of your sister's line, I forgive your betrayal and absolve you of all crime against Cormyr."

Boldovar's eyes flashed their old crimson. He opened his mouth as though to speak, then simply crumbled into black dust.

Steelhand looked back to Tanalasta. "You've done well, Princess."

Tanalasta tried to nod, but made it only as far as lowering her eyes before the last of her strength left.

Steelhand smiled, for as a High Priest of the War God Tempus, he had seen a thousand warriors die and knew a good death when he saw it. He placed a mailed hand under the infant's naked bottom and boosted it higher on the princess's chest and guided her nipple into its mouth.

"Well met, little one," he said. "And long live the prince."

lusair had only two hundred men left, and half those were wounded. The rest of her company had already fallen to the teeming hordes in . . . wherever they were. She had no idea where that might be, except that it was dark and full of little green goblins. The company was down to one iron-tipped arrow per man, and they were holding those in reserve. After an all-night chase—except that nobody really had any idea what "all night" meant in this city of darkness—she had finally come to some high ground and decided to make a stand.

They had built a low stone breastwork and lit the perimeter with magic lights, but the little buggers just kept charging up the stony slope, wave after wave of them armed with little iron spears and little iron swords. Alusair's dragoneers were well-trained, proficient with their weapons, and in good condition, so they cut down most of the creatures at the breastwork. Still, even her men weren't perfect, and every three minutes or so one of the tiny bastards slipped through to drive a spear through the belly of one of her soldiers. Soon enough, she would lack the manpower to defend the barricade, then the hordes would come pouring in and finish them off.

Alusair had been in worse situations—much worse. "Ready the fall back!" she called.

The Steel Princess raised her sword to signal the retreat—then cowered in shock as the cavern erupted into a deafening roar of thunder. Blinding sheets of lightning crackled up the slope, clear-cutting whole swaths of goblins and turning the ground into a slick black mess of gore. The enemy charge simply vanished, and in the flashing light that remained, Alusair saw a circle of ramshackle stone walls, broken at odd intervals by the crooked windows and tilted doorways of the vast goblin city.

Rushing out of the tunnels were the next wave of goblins, brandishing their little iron swords and clambering up the slope over the entrails and blood of their predecessors. Alusair ignored the mad charge and continued to scrutinize the passages, looking for the source of the strange lightning storm. There were only a handful of magicians in Faerûn capable of such a flurry of magic—and only one who had good reason to help her.

Instead of Vangerdahast, she found a dozen men in rusty chain mail rushing out of a tunnel far to her right. They were all soaking wet and carrying iron maces, screaming supplications to Chauntea even as they raised barriers of thorns and bubbling mud between themselves and the goblins.

Alusair sighed in disappointment but decided that if she could not have Vangerdahast, a dozen Chauntean priests would have to do. She waved her sword toward the small party and commanded, "Prepare to support with bow fire by number."

Half of her dragoneers exchanged their swords for long bows and nocked arrows. When the first goblin broke through the priests' barriers and raised his sword to hamstring the group's wiry leader, a single iron-tipped arrow sizzled down from the barricade. It took the little warrior square in the ribs, knocking him from his feet and sending him tumbling down the slope backward. The priest raised his mace in salute, then—of all things—it began to rain.

At first, Alusair did not know quite what to make of the storm. The rain came in driving sheets, with forks of lightning dancing every which way and peals of thunder rolling across the cavern roof. Rivulets of water poured down the slope along courses that had never held a trickle before, and Alusair began to wonder if she had somehow come under the influence of Mad King Boldovar.

A dark figure burst from the tunnel behind the priests and she finally understood. So far, they had only identified six of the Scourges mentioned in Alaundo's prophecy, but here was the seventh—floods and storms—chasing a group of Chauntea's priests up the slope in front of her. She could not understand how either of them had come to be in that cavern any more than she understood how she had, but her course of action remained clear: help her allies and attack her enemies.

"There's a ghazneth!" Alusair yelled. "Every man, ready iron arrows. Fire on my command only!"

A soft clamor echoed through the cavern as every man along the line prepared his bow. Amazingly, the goblins fell back at the sight of the ghazneth—perhaps feeling he could handle a mere two hundred humans alone.

Alusair was determined to prove the error of their ways. If she accomplished nothing else in this dark place, she was going to teach these little green-skinned discipline mongers to respect the human way of doing things. She waited until the priests had closed to within a dozen steps of their breastwork, then lowered her sword.

"On the ghazneth—fire!"

The cavern reverberated with throbbing bow strings, and a wall of iron points sailed down the slope to plant itself in the ghazneth's body. The impact of so many arrows actually lifted the monster off its feet and hurled it a dozen paces down the slope.

A howling wind tore through the cavern instantly. The rain began to fall from the ceiling in buckets, and the lightning came so fast Alusair thought her head would burst from so much light. She raised her sword and began to clamber over the breastwork.

Before she could order the charge, the eldest Chauntean priest, a short wiry man with a hawkish nose, blocked her way. He reached up and plucked the sword from her hand as though she were a child.

"No!"

Alusair scowled, then yelled, "This is my command—"

"And you have no idea where you are, or who that is!" the priest shouted back. His subordinates began to clamber over the breastwork and set to work healing Alusair's wounded soldiers. "We have been trying to catch you for days."

The ghazneth sat up and began to pluck the arrows from its body, though the holes did not close as Alusair had seen the wounds of the other monsters do.

Alusair narrowed her eyes, offended by the man's angry tone, yet intrigued by what he was saying. "And you are?"

"Owden Foley," he replied. Owden waved two of his priests down the slope toward the ghazneth. "And if you are through skulking about down here, we have some real work to do. The goblins are on the march."

Alusair frowned. Though she recognized Owden's name as that of her sister's favorite priest, she was still having trouble understanding . . . well, pretty much everything.

"On the march?" she said. "To where?"

"To reinforce Nalavara, of course," Owden waved a hand at all the priests he had brought with him into the darkness, then continued, "But I seem to have discovered the secret to traveling between the two realms. If you have done with your sightseeing down here, it is time we return to Cormyr and turn your blades where they will do some good."

'm beginning to wish the goblins had driven us back to Jester's Green," a war captain panted, as they toiled up a slope wet and slippery with goblin gore. "At least it's flat."

Azoun chuckled. "If you think I'm sparing breath to sound a horn right now . . ."

"I'd have to be crazed enough to be King of Cormyr, hey?" Lanjack Blackwagon grunted.

The king laughed aloud and clapped the oversword on the back—or tried to. In the attempt he slipped on a tangle of goblin bodies and almost fell instead. Three arms shot out to steady him.

Perhaps twenty men in once-magnificent armor, now scarred and hacked, spattered with mud and blood, and creaking and clanking where it was torn or twisted, still stood around the king and the puffing, red-faced highest-ranking wizard in the land. War captains all, officers of senior rank through noble birth or battle prowess, they were all that was left, it seemed, of the once-mighty army that had

349

fared forth to leisurely rout one more goblin rising before eveningfeast.

Well, the wrong side might have done the routing, but goblins now lay dead in their thousands on this rolling field—yet there still seemed to be many around, stooping among the slain to pluck up swords and knives and coins. They kept well away from the small, purposeful band of their human foes, but cast many baleful, hissing glances at the passing men.

Ahead, atop the hill the battered-armored Cormyreans were climbing, the Devil Dragon was rallying more goblins, her huge batlike wings arching up into the air like restless, menacing sails as she skulked to and fro. This battle was far from done yet.

"Aye, if we were on the Green, the ladies could almost watch us from the walls of Suzail," Kaert Belstable joked, striking a valiant pose.

"And adjust their bets," the lancelord next to him added dryly, touching off a chorus of mirthful grunts and chuckles.

Azoun glanced around and met the startled eyes of Ilberd Crownsilver for an instant. He gave the lad a wink and a smile as they crested the hill—and found themselves facing a lot of goblins.

Goblins who looked fresh and eager for battle, drawn up in three neat ranks, their shields gleaming and maces hanging ready in their hands, flanked by wedges of spear carriers who were even now trotting forward to encircle the small and weary band of humans. Above and behind them hung the heavy-lidded, leering head of the Devil Dragon, regarding her last handful of foes in open triumph.

Harsh, high voices barked commands, and there was a rattle of chain as hundreds of goblin arms moved in unison, laying maces back on their shoulders for that first blow before they charged. Ilberd Crownsilver licked his lips and glanced swiftly to his left and right. He seemed to be the only fearful man present. On the older faces around him he saw only fierce determination and grim resolve.

Ilberd swallowed, shaking like a leaf in a freshening wind, then heard a disturbance behind him. He turned almost wearily, fearing silent goblins had risen up in their rear to transfix the last few men of Cormyr on their spears, like boar spitted for the fire.

No goblins, nor even alarm. Someone was pushing forward through the ranks, someone old and stout and armorless, his breath ragged. It was Vangerdahast, wearing that strange iron crown. War captains slid smoothly aside to give him room.

Ilberd Crownsilver relaxed. A spell from the court wizard or a blast from his wands, and the battle would be done.

Vangerdahast reached the forefront of the Cormyrean band and threw up his hands. The crown on his brow seemed to sparkle for a moment, dazzling the eyes. His voice, when it came, thundered across the battlefield as if he were an angry god or colossus. The words that boomed and rolled forth were harsh and unfamiliar to Ilberd's ears. They sounded akin to the shrill cries of the goblins. When they ended, there was a little silence but for the last rolling echoes, as the humans and the goblins regarded each other.

Then, in eerie silence, the goblins went to their knees, laying their weapons gently down on the much-trampled ground, and touched their faces to the dirt.

The dragon's head snaked back and forth in obvious astonishment as she saw her force disarm itself. She reared back and bounded into the air. All around Ilberd, armor rattled as warriors tensed, trying to raise shields they did not have.

Vast she was, yet sleek and terrible in her power. The young Crownsilver gaped at her magnificence, standing transfixed as she soared into the sky then turned, wings rippling, and plunged down upon them. He'd never seen such catlike grace, or sheer size—the beast was as large as some castles of the realm. He'd never seen such—

—swift and casual death. The dragon raced into the Cormyreans, spewing fire when she was perhaps twenty paces from the royal magician and following it like a giant torch thrust through cobwebs. Men were hurled in all directions. Ilberd saw Elber Lionstone tumbling along the dragon's scaled back, his face a mask of pain and his frantically stabbing dagger rebounding from its scales in futility. He fell sideways from view, to crash somewhere back down the hillside whence they'd come. Red fire streamed along the dragon's path, blazing in the grass around their boots. Men groaned or cursed weakly as they staggered or struggled to rise. Many a gauntlet dipped to a belt flask to quaff enchanted healing and banish searing pain.

For a moment it seemed the royal magician had vanished—burned to ashes by the dragon's fire or devoured by it, perhaps—then, as the Devil Dragon passed overhead, returning to her chosen spot, Ilberd saw King Azoun staggering along with a body in his arms that seemed more ash than flesh. Ilberd stumbled forward to help. Azoun gave him both a fierce grin and the limp, senseless, and gods-be-damned-heavy Vangerdahast to hold.

"Time for swords, it seems," the king said cheerfully, watching the goblins who'd surrendered stream down and away from the hilltop.

They left their weapons behind, shields and gleaming steel covering the hilltop between the dragon and the Cormyreans like a cloak of war metal. At the base of the hill, cleaving up through them, were other goblins, answering a hissed call from the dragon. These new earfangs held their weapons ready, and showed no sign of imminent surrender.

"I must get to the dragon!" the king shouted suddenly. "To me, men of Cormyr!"

A breath later, they were pounding across the hilltop, slipping and sliding on the discarded weapons underfoot, and the dragon was turning her head in their direction, looking as startled as any boy surprised in a pantry in mid-theft.

She gathered her mighty wings to spring aloft, and Azoun roared, "Don't let her fly away!"

"Ahead of you, my king," a lancelord with the arms of Tapstorn on his shoulder shouted back. "Behold!"

Ilberd saw a ring on his finger—a prized heirloom of the Tapstorns, no doubt—gleam with sudden fire. Magical fire blazed only for an instant as the ring blackened and crumbled away, leaving Murkoon Tapstorn wincing and shaking scorched fingers. The flames streaked across the hilltop to pounce on the dragon's head, raining down blows of something unseen like a crashing, ringing chorus of forge hammers. The great wyrm shrank back, ducking her head and retreating. The striking spell seemed to move with her, its battering ceaseless.

They reached the first hissing, snarling goblins, mere steps from the great bulk of the dragon. Ilberd was gasping under the weight of the royal magician, who rode upon his shoulders like a dead man—who, by the gods, might well *be* a dead man.

The clang of steel began, quickening swiftly to a constant skirling song as the weary men hacked and hewed in a mad frenzy, cutting their way through an ever-increasing flood of goblins with cruel hooked blades in their hands and hatred in their eyes. Ilberd saw Skormer Griffongard fall, the bannermaster's helm torn away to reveal his long, tawny mane of hair and his eyes two blazing flames of fury as he hacked and stabbed his way through wine-purple goblin blood. They literally ran up his body, cutting and stabbing, and he sank from view under their howling tide.

Murkoon Tapstorn staggered, spun around with blood streaming from one sightless eye socket and a snarl of pain on his lips, and fell over a goblin corpse. A dozen or more earfangs pounced on him, and the gauntleted hand that was punching and tearing at them soon went limp and fell from view.

Ilberd swung Vangerdahast's body around like a ram, its limp boots smiting aside squalling goblins, and kicked out with all his might. He felt ribs break under his boot and that goblin sailed away, trailing a thin scream. Ilberd charged forward into the space where it had stood, stepping high and not caring what he trampled. A sharp, burning pain just above his left knee marked a successful stab into his leg. He roared out his pain and punched that goblin assailant in the face, wheeling to stab down with his sword. The movement made the wizard fall from his shoulders, crashing down atop half a dozen squeaking goblins. Freed of the weight, Ilberd spun and lunged and danced like a madman, butchering goblins until they fell back around him and he could scoop up Vangerdahast once more.

As he turned and straightened, he saw six goblin spears pierce Kaert Belstable, sliding bloodily out of the oversword's back. Belstable staggered, dark blood gushing from his mouth and nose, and with a snarl threw himself forward onto one of his attackers, clawing at the earfang's eyes with bloody, failing fingers. They went down together, and goblins swarmed over the warrior, stabbing enthusiastically.

Lanjack Blackwagon—or rather, the twisting top half of him—crashed down bloodily onto goblins streaming forward beyond that fray, his legs and guts spilling from the jaws of the Devil Dragon as she laughed aloud.

Ildred watched in horror as that head—as long as a cottage, and lined with yellowed, hooked teeth as tall as a man—reared. Murkoon's battering spell was gone, and the beast opened steaming jaws to savage the man who stood beneath it, sword raised.

The king!

Flame gushed forth in a white-hot torrent, setting the grass alight and driving goblins into shrieking flight in all directions. It was too hot to see through, but when it died away and Ildred blinked the afterglow from his eyes, Azoun of Cormyr was standing where he had been before, his great warsword raised, enchanted runes glowing blue up and down its blade. He was unscathed.

Even as Ildred gaped at what he was seeing, Azoun sprang forward like a much younger man—and the dragon followed her gout of flame with a lunge of her own, her many-toothed jaws snatching at the running man, to bite his torso from his legs as she'd served Lanjack.

Azoun gasped something, his armor flashed, and his breastplate suddenly became a bar of steel, a double-ended piercing javelin as long and as thick as a man. The dragon's jaws closed on it, black blood spurted, and the Devil Dragon screamed in pain. The cry sounded female, and somehow . . . graceful.

Death of the Dragon

The dragon was still shaking her head to dislodge the steel fang that had so wounded her when Azoun tore something free from a sheath or wrappings beneath his breastplate, and struck the nearest flailing piece of dragon—its right wing. There was a flash of golden light so bright that the clouds overhead momentarily lit up, and the dragon screamed again.

For just a moment, Ilberd Crownsilver thought it dwindled from a huge, scaled wyrm into a nude, winged elf maiden, dancing in pain with her long red hair swirling around her and her broken, many-feathered wings dangling. She threw back her head sobbing, and her eyes were two diamonds of fury and fire. Then she reared back with a roar that made Ilberd's ears ring and was a dragon again. He blinked, scarcely believing he'd seen that other form.

"Man," the dragon roared, "what did you strike me with?"

"The Scepter of Lords," Azoun replied calmly. "The greatest of Lord Iliphar's craftings."

"You're unworthy to even utter his name, *human!*" the dragon spat. Tiny tongues of fire spilled out of her jaws, but seemed to curl away from what the king held. In the hand that wasn't full of a notched, darkening warsword there was a golden scepter carved into the likeness of an oak sapling sprouting delicate branches seemingly at random, its pommel a giant amethyst carved into the likeness of an acorn.

"No, Nalavara," the King of Cormyr told her, almost conversationally. "Lord Iliphar bargained with my ancestor, and gave him the power to rule, and rule well. That bargain has come down to me. In some ways, he's the guardian and father of my house."

The Devil Dragon shrieked in utter fury and tried to pounce on the man before her, but her broken wing failed her, and she fell sideways to the earth, crashing down atop many goblins and rolling upright again heedless of how many she crushed.

The thunder of her fall was loud in Ilberd Crownsilver's ears as a goblin sprang up onto his shoulder and tried to slit

355

his throat. The goblin died when Ilberd, surprising himself as much as the goblin, reversed the blade into the little humanoid's own throat. Ilberd let the goblin fall onto a pile of its comrades and knew that even if that goblin had succeeded in killing him, he'd seen the Devil Dragon die, and Cormyr saved.

In truth, though, the dragon was far from dead.

Azoun struck once at the dragon's head, reaching as far as he dared, knowing he might never have so fine a target in this fray again. Hot blood gushed from between the scales a little forward of her right eye, but Nalavarauthatoryl the Red tore herself free and away from him, crushing more goblins heedlessly, and snarling, "Elves do not hold to bargains with murderers of their kin! Iliphar bargained with you, but no soft words will bring back my betrothed. Nigh on fifteen centuries the one I was to marry has been dust, fifteen centuries have I been alone—never to know his arms again, never to have the happiness together that should have been ours. I spit upon your bargain, human—spit *fire* upon it!"

Flames roared forth again from the dragon's throat, but this time they were dark red, fitful, and came with a spray of much smoking black blood. The dragon shook her head in pain and frustration, even as the flames she'd snarled forth began to blaze in a spreading ring on the hilltop, driving back chittering goblins and leaving the king alone with his foe—and the fallen, including one ash-cloaked royal magician.

Azoun circled slowly sideways, forcing the dragon to turn and follow, until he stood over Vangerdahast. Perhaps he'd able to snatch some bauble of magic or other from his old tutor's body, or . . .

"I, too, have known loss in this war," the King of Cormyr told the dragon, raising both his sword and the scepter, his blade outermost to protect Iliphar's precious crafting from the swipe of a claw or wing or tail. Unlike a true dragon, Nalavarauthatoryl never seemed to use her tail in a real battle, but forgot it save as something to keep her balance. "Hundreds of my subjects lie dead, fallen before you and the creatures you have whelmed."

"*Pah!* What are their deaths to me? They're vermin—vermin who must be destroyed or driven out to cleanse these forests for the elves. I will see their fields, stone towers, and all torn up that the trees may once again grow over all."

Nalavara bit down, but winced away as that sharp blade laid open her lip, just at the edge of her scales. Shaking her head with a savage roar, she batted at the lone human with one clawed forefoot. The warsword struck again, and with it—with another burst of golden light, and more searing, numbing pain—the Scepter of Lords.

The Devil Dragon hissed and drew back. Her eyes glittered with hatred as they met Azoun's, but the king looked back at her calmly.

"I, too, have lost a beloved to you," Azoun said. "My daughter Alusair was burned to bones in the fire you gout."

"So what is that to me, human? In what way does a human life equal that of an elf?"

"Both are ended," the king said bleakly. "Both are gone, never to tread this fair land again."

The dragon bit down again but this time wheeled away from the ready blade before being cut—and before actually biting anything.

"And even if they were measured equal, human, why should I care—when humans have raped and despoiled the land itself? What is this Cormyr but the Wolf Woods all thinned and cut back and choked with your refuse and your stone buildings and even your graves, earth wasted to lay out bones that could feed new trees and flower forth?" Nalavara turned restlessly, seeking to use her greater size to outpace the king's sword and reach around to strike at him from behind.

"This Cormyr," Azoun told her almost gently, "that you burn and tear apart and visit plagues and goblin infestations and insect swarms and the like on, Lorelei Alavara, is the fair land you care so much about."

"How *dare* you?" The dragon almost sobbed, rearing up above him in a tall and terrible way. She threw herself down upon him, broken wings spread, snarling, "Have my life too, then, human! Strike me down. Or is it you that shall go down first, eh?"

They rolled, the human frantically, to avoid being crushed, and the dragon after him, seeking to grind him into bloody pulp with her great weight. She clawed at him as she went, gouging great furrows in the earth. Goblins fled down the slopes of the hill crying in terror.

* * * * *

After a dazed and drifting time, Ilberd Crownsilver remembered his name. He remembered his fall, and the terrible lunge of the dragon before it, and the battle before that. He was lying sprawled on his back with the same gray, tattered-smoke clouds above him that had hung over him then . . . and he was lying on cold, still, and unpleasantly sharp goblins. He was seized with the sudden desire get up and stand again and know his fate—even if it was to die under the blades of scores of cruel earfangs.

The young nobleman struggled to his feet, the world heaving and rocking through his swimming eyes. Something red—his own sticky blood, he discovered, looking at his fingertips calmly—was streaming into his right eye, and he'd hurt something low on the left side of his belly that involved torn armor and more blood beneath.

"Well, you did want to taste glory," he growled to himself. "Tastes a lot like blood to me, but there it is, hey?" He coughed weakly, spat out a lot of blood, and looked around. There were goblins in plenty, wandering the field dazedly or picking over bodies for blades and helms, but none near. Some of them even seemed to be fleeing from the hill he was standing on.

Ilberd looked back up the hill to where he'd stood with the king against the Devil Dragon—in time to see that great wyrm hurl herself down on Azoun and roll about trying to claw at him, for all Faerûn as if king and dragon were two children brawling in the dirt.

"Glory," he said in disgust and spat blood again. His helm

and dagger were gone in his fall, somewhere, but his sword was still in its scabbard. He drew it, deliberately, admired its weight and heft in his hand one last time, and started up the hill.

Cormyr needed him—and if that was good enough for his king, dying in the dirt up there under a dragon's jaws, well . . . it was good enough for him. Smiling, Ilberd Crownsilver went to find his doom.

* * * * *

"This is madness, Nalavara," Azoun gasped, as they rolled apart and clambered upright, each in their own way. "We both fight for Cormyr—to guard and keep unstained the land we love!"

The red dragon's eyes glittered. "Clever words," she hissed. "Humans are always spewing more snake-tongued cleverness. *Die*, human king!"

Her flame this time was but a few wisps that barely challenged the failing defensive magics of his blade, but her bite was as swift and savage as ever. Armor plate shrieked under a tooth as she crushed Azoun's left shoulder and sent him staggering back, despite his thrusts into her chin with both warsword and scepter.

"I strike in sorrow," he gasped, as the golden light flooded around him once more, "and apologize to you for the sin of Andar Obarskyr and for the sins of my father and grandsire and forefathers back to Andar in keeping secret the murder Andar did—and for my own part in doing so, too. Will offering you my life for that of your beloved end all this?"

The red dragon drew back and stared at him in amazement, dragging her broken wing.

"What did you say, human?"

Azoun spread wide his arms, allowing her a clear path to his breast, clad only in sweat-soaked leather where the transformed and sacrificed breastplate had gone. He looked old, his hair white and his face weathered and careworn, but he also seemed almost contented.

359

Troy Denning and Ed Greenwood

"Will my own life atone for what you have lost?" he asked again. "If so, I yield it gladly. Take it, so long as you restore peace to Cormyr and, by your honor, Lorelei Alavara, *all* who dwell in it."

For a moment the red dragon's scales wavered, and he was seeing the sleek bare body of an elf maiden, her red hair cascading around her in a long and glorious cloak, her large, dark eyes almost pleading, her mouth trembling on the edge of a smile.

Then it was gone, and he faced the dragon once more—a smaller wyrm, it seemed, but bright-eyed in its renewed fury.

"No!" Nalavara snarled, "Your trickery comes too late. Too long has my hatred carried me, human, until it is all I have left. Nothing you can say or do will bring back my Thatoryl. As he crumbled, so shall you all. The peace you seek will fall upon 'fair Cormyr' only when the rotting corpse of every last human feeds the forest that has been so defiled!"

"Time changes Faerûn, as the dragons gave way to the elves, and your kin to mine," Azoun said gravely. "I can't bring Thatoryl Elian back, but I can raise a stone—or plant a grove—in his memory. My huntmasters tend the land even now, and leave some stretches untouched. I can make Cormyr far more a forest again . . . but the paradise you hunted in is gone, I fear, forever. Can we not work together to plant its echo? Must this end in more blood?"

Nalavarauthatoryl the Red reared up again, beating her wings despite the pain her broken one caused her, and snarled, "Of course it must, human! How else, whatever our 'civilized' pretensions, do elves and humans and dragons settle their disputes? No better than the goblins are we— and I cannot be something I am not. *Die!*"

Her jaws swept squarely down on Azoun this time, heedless of his warsword cutting into them and the scepter striking home—even when its golden radiance burst inside her head and her eyes blew out in twin balls of flame.

Ribs broke and the organs within burst before those jaws parted, sagging open again in death. Torn, Azoun gasped aloud at the pain, barely noticing as the Scepter of Lords caught fire in his trembling hands.

Yet its fury revived him from sinking into oblivion. He stood his ground, holding it deep in the dragon's jaws, and snarled, "For Cormyr!"

Let those ladies on the walls of Suzail change their wagers, damn them. He had a realm to save, whatever the cost, and this self-damned dragon was taking far too long to die.

Hot black blood boiled out of Nalavara's gullet then, washing over his chest and arms, drenching his wounds and raging through him wherever it touched his own blood. Azoun growled in pain and staggered as his foe shivered once, from end to end, then slowly gurgled into eternal silence.

As the Devil Dragon fell away, smoke rising from her empty, staring eye sockets, Azoun went to his knees atop the familiar form of Vangerdahast. It was done, his strength was spent, and it was time. Time for even a king to leave his throne behind in favor of a calmer place.

44

he Steel Princess peered through fog that was streaming across heaped bodies like smoke in a hurry to be elsewhere. The dead were everywhere, piled and sprawled across the rolling fields like a grotesque crop. Vultures and crows were already circling and gliding, looming out of the mist like lazy black arrows as they descended. The goblins were like a gory, countless carpet, but among them too many a brave knight or dragoneer lay stiff and staring. Even if this was the realm's last battle for a season or more, there'd be few Purple Dragons to watch the borders and patrol the roads. The Stonelands would just have to go unwatched for a year or three—and if Sembia or another eager reaver decided to reach out into the Forest Kingdom, little valor and fewer swords would be left to stand against them.

Alusair's boots slipped on a tangle of interlocked blades, and she nearly fell onto the goblins frozen in desperate striving with the lancelord who lay beneath them, his face cut away into a ruin of blood and crawling flies. She recovered

herself grimly and peered again at the battlefield. Somewhere ahead in all of this death lay her father. He'd have
been fighting the dragon chin to tail, no doubt, and that
would probably mean on a hilltop, given where dragons
prefer to swoop.

That one on the right, Alusair decided, would be her first
destination. She could see goblins clambering up its slopes,
a handful of living among so many dead. Swallowing, she
hefted her blade and glanced to her right, where a dark
cloud hid the ghazneth that the priest had so grimly but
insistently assured her was a friend and vital ally. The
ghazneth had once been Rowen Cormaeril. Gods above,
Alusair thought, what cruel joke are you playing on fair
Cormyr now?

The cloud was trudging along with her as obediently as
any war captain, and Alusair had curtly ordered him to be
treated as such, ignoring the raised eyebrows and dark looks
she'd received in return.

"Giving orders might not be easy or popular, but by crown
and Tempus, they are *my* orders to give!" she'd snarled.

She could see a large, dark bulk on the hilltop ahead, now,
accompanied by the canted, barbed ruin of a dragon's wing.
The Devil Dragon was down.

"Haste!" she snapped, pointing with her sword. "The
crown lies in peril!"

She could see now that a smaller hill, off to her left and a
little behind her, was crowned with the royal standard and
what could only be a tent. They looked undamaged, and she
could see the glint of a few—a very few—helms and shields
there. Azoun's own crown banner, though, wasn't flapping on
high. The king had not returned to his tent.

"*Move*, you oxen!" she snarled at the men around her, as
they slipped and slid wearily in goblin gore. "I've seen
bloated barons scuttle faster when their creditors came calling—or their wives to the brothel doors!" She lifted her blade
like a scourge and smacked her own hip with it, as if flogging
herself to greater speed. "Get *up* there!"

Someone among the grimly hastening knights made an
insolent lowing sound, and someone else echoed it. There

were chuckles, and a few tight smiles, and Alusair's spirits suddenly rose. Gods, but she was proud to lead men such as these!

A goblin squirmed under her feet, among the dead, thrusting upward viciously at her crotch. Before she could do more than dance aside, three swords had met in its squalling body, her knights sprawling to reach it with no thought for their own safety.

"Loyal idiots," Alusair cursed them fondly. "Get *on!*"

They were most of the way up the hill now, climbing over goblins heaped so high that the untidy piles were rolling and sliding downslope when disturbed, often carrying a cursing Purple Dragon with them. Ahead, on the summit, the living goblins were taking no notice of their advance but seemed locked in some sort of vigorous dispute involving something on the ground in front of the dead dragon.

Alusair licked suddenly dry lips, and murmured, "My father—it must be."

Owden Foley, laboring up the hill to her right, gave her a sharp look, then glanced at the dark cloud moving beside him. Before he could speak, a sudden wind howled across the hilltop, bowling many goblins over and away, and forcing the rest to the ground. It was a gale that moaned as if it was alive, but it scoured only the summit. The climbing Cormyreans could barely feel a breeze on their faces.

The slope ended and they were atop the hill, with the ghastly bulk of the dragon rising like a wall across the crest, and goblins sprawled helplessly everywhere. There were no heaped dead here—only living goblins, now screaming out their rage and terror as they saw the armored humans looming up with bloody swords drawn—and something more.

Something dark, wet, and glistening lay in front of the dragon's jaws. The dying wyrm's ichor had spewed forth in a huge pool, drenching two sprawled men who lay there, one atop the other. Both of them wore crowns and looked more or less whole. One—the one feebly moving an arm—was King Azoun. The other was . . . Vangerdahast?

A secret king of Cormyr? Or had be crowned himself king of some new realm? Alusair thought. Had he been playing us all false after all and commanding the foes of Cormyr? Or was the circlet some ancient adornment passed on by Baerauble, with fell powers to be used only when the realm tottered?

No matter—or rather, no matter to be worried about now.

Alusair turned her head with difficulty. Where she stood was on the very edge of the storm, and its winds shoved against the movement like a solid stable door that had smacked her cheek long ago.

"Rowen!" she called, knowing the gale tore the name from her lips before anyone upwind could possibly hear it.

She could not see the ghazneth, shrouded in its cloud, but it must have been watching her. The wind died in an instant, and Alusair charged forward, running hard across squalling goblins, heading straight for the king. The thunder of booted feet and the mingled curses of men and goblins told her that her knights and dragoneers were right behind her.

A goblin swung a wickedly hooked bill at her. Alusair caught its blade with her own and kicked out, as hard as she could, skidding on trampled grass as she came down. Yelling, the goblin tumbled through the air and away. The Steel Princess found herself teetering on the edge of the dragon's spew. Sudden balls of flame rolled up from it, coalescing out of nowhere, and a brief crackle of blue-green lightning played over it.

"Wild magic!" one of the priests gasped. "Thank Chauntea!"

"*Chauntea?*" Alusair snapped, bewildered, even as they wheeled around in unison to form a defensive wall around the darkened area. Snarling goblins surged forward against them, hacking and stabbing.

"He has to thank someone," a dragoneer panted. "Being a priest, he calls on his god."

"Thank you, sir wit," Alusair said sarcastically between pants of effort, as she spitted a goblin who'd run in behind one of his fellows, then lunged forward to hack at the dragoneer's ankles. "That much I managed. What I want to know—" she growled as her blade burst through a chink in a rusty forest of salvaged plates worn by the tallest goblin she'd ever seen, and her blade sank hilt-deep into it, the point running into the goblin behind, "—is why wild magic is such cause for thanks."

She had to kick with all of her strength to get the bodies back off her blade, and out of habit swung them sideways as a ram against others trying to swarm past. Spitting, snarling goblins were all around her now.

The dragoneer swung his sword like a scythe, raking goblins aside. One of them fell into the dragon's blood with a shriek of terror, rolled, and raced back out of it, limbs pumping frantically, as fresh fires arose around them.

Alusair stabbed down viciously with her dagger, slashed open a goblin face on her backstroke, and danced aside from two lunging spears. She booted the goblin she'd blinded right into the faces of the two spear-wielders, and followed it with two quick sword thrusts. Was there no end to goblins? What did they all eat, anyway?

"Livestock and the fair farmers of Cormyr who tend them," the dragoneer told her sourly, and Alusair stared at him in bewilderment for a moment before she realized she'd asked those questions aloud.

Lightning cracked across the hilltop then—blinding, ravening bolts that raked through the goblins surging forward to strike at the Cormyrean shield ring. Lightning lashed shrieking goblins as if it was a giant whip wielded with deft skill by some unseen giant, striking down this squalling earfang then that. When the fury died away, leaving behind a seaside tang in the air and the unlovely stink of cooked goblin flesh, only a handful of living goblins were left, almost cowering against the blades of the humans they fought. Some died immediately, and others fled, squeaking and gibbering in utter terror. Alusair did not have to snap an order for her warriors to let them go. They knew all too well what they were here for.

Sardyn Wintersun, wearing more blood than she'd ever seen on him before, grimly gave the order to "Stand fast, blades out, and hold against all foes!"

She opened her mouth to snarl that she hadn't died and left him in charge just yet—then closed it again, the words unspoken, as he waved her into the dark area within the shield ring. Alusair looked at him for a moment, then nodded in curt and silent thanks, and turned into the dark, wet gore. It was a glistening black, sucking warmly at her boots, and ankle-deep. Strange singing sounds heralded the magic raging fitfully within it as she advanced. Flames surged up around her boots as she strode— strange yellow-green tongues that tickled her nose and throat like exotic spices—and Owden was moving along grimly at her side.

The dark, grotesque form of the ghazneth was with them, stepping to the fore, and the magics boiling up from the black, slimy blood seemed to stream into it and vanish.

Their journey was only a few paces, but it seemed as if they'd been walking for hours across a strange realm before they came to where the King of Cormyr lay twisting fitfully atop the scorched, motionless body of the Royal Magician. Alusair went to her knees heedless of what the blood-magic might do, and was almost hurled back by a tongue of flashing, tinkling radiance. A dark hand reached out to drink in the fell flood, and Alusair flashed Rowen a smile of thanks before she stretched out cautious fingers to trace along her father's jaw, took firm hold with her other hand of the blade he'd let fall, and asked hesitantly, "Father?"

For a moment it seemed as if the King of Cormyr had not heard. He turned his head slowly, almost idly, his eyes staring up unseeing at the low, streaming ceiling of gray clouds, and twisted his lips in a bitter—or was it rueful?—smile.

The princess was about to speak again when Azoun said slowly, "So they did get you, bravest of daughters. Twice the warrior most of my knights are. My little Alusair. My Steel Princess. I'd begun to permit myself the tiny, sneaking hope that you'd somehow escaped the dragon, and yet lived."

"Father," Alusair said, leaning close to kiss him, "I *am* alive . . . and so are you. You've slain the dragon."

"Such long sadness," the king murmured. "So deep, so fierce. Her love as strong as any Obarskyr, but for a different Cormyr . . ."

"Father? Are you hurt?" Alusair asked sharply, shaking him gently. It was a foolish question if she'd ever uttered one. Owden Foley was already deep in muttered incantations, laying his hairy-backed hands on Azoun's throat, brow, and palms with careful care.

The princess sat back to give him space to reach. Under his careful hands, the king murmured something unintelligible. A fleeting lacework of purple fire flashed into being across Azoun's body, then was gone. The king convulsed, gasping, and his eyes fell shut. Alusair's own eyes narrowed.

"What was that, Harvestmaster?" she snapped.

Owden Foley's face was grim as he met her angry gaze. "The best healing I'm capable of—or so it began as," he said. "What it became, I've no idea. We've got to get his majesty out of this dragon's blood. I don't know why, but it's twisting all magic awry—and worse."

"Worse how?"

Owden lowered his voice to a whisper and leaned close to the princess to murmur his next words, putting a hand to his mouth to shield his speech from the man lying beneath them. "It's eating away his flesh, Your Highness—right down to the bones, if we let it work long enough. We have to move him."

"His tent," Alusair snapped, inclining her head in the direction of the other hill. "There'll be water there to wash this ichor away." She lifted her hands, now tingling—no, burning slightly—under their coating of black slime. She regarded them thoughtfully for a moment before she turned her head the other way and called, "Sardyn!"

"My lady?"

"Are you finished felling goblins, or do some of the lads feel the need to add to their sword-totals yet?"

"The hill is clear and we've all had our fill and more," came the heartfelt reply.

Alusair's lips twisted in a wry smile and she turned to regard the shield ring. Sardyn had turned to address her, but the others, true to their training, were still facing the battlefield, leaning on their blades and resting now. Gods, what brave swords!

"I need the king and the royal magician carried—as gently and as safely as possible, in a ring of blades—to the royal tent. Tarry not."

Sardyn inclined his head, then bellowed, "Break ranks! Walking ring! Elstan, Murrigo, Julavvan and Perendrin—to me!"

All around her, men started to move. Alusair stood, motioning Owden and Rowen to keep their distance from her, and went a little distance away, to where she could wipe the dragon's blood from her boots, knees, and hands. Her fingers went to the clasp of the weathercloak she wore, bunched and sweat-drenched, around her shoulders beneath the high-fluted shoulders of her armor.

"He's alive, Tana," she murmured in relief, as she fixed her sister's face in her mind and concentrated on it. "He's . . ."

The contact did not come. Frowning, Alusair closed her eyes and shut out the battlefield, its calling crows and tramping men fading away, to see Tanalasta as vividly as she could.

That time she'd thrown back her head and laughed so heartily that she'd spilled her tallglass of flamekiss . . . or when she'd slapped Alusair, and had her wrist grabbed and held, and they'd stared into each other's eyes as slow fear over Alusair's strength mounted in Tanalasta's eyes. Or . . .

Nothing. Emptiness, darkness—not even the confused, dim dream images of someone sleeping. The clasp tingled as she drew on it. Abruptly Alusair turned her thoughts away, calling up the face of one of the few men who'd attracted her for more than a few nights—the turret-merchant Glarasteer Rhauligan. Twice her age, and iron calm, with hair going gray and wrists as strong as steel. She wondered if the court spies had ever informed Vangerdahast or her father of *those* acrobatic liaisons among the shadows of the armory, or what they'd thought.

The contact was almost instant. Rhauligan was in an alleyway somewhere—Suzail, by the look of it—holding a man none too gently against a wall.

The next time you think armsmen off to war means their wives are yours for the taking . . . Rhauligan was snarling, the words echoing in Alusair's distant mind.

Even as he felt her presence, she breathed the words, "We'll speak later, I promise," and broke the contact.

So the clasp's enchantment was working, all too well.

She bent all of her will to capturing and holding as vivid a collection of remembered Tanalastas as she could, but met only with darkness, an empty sensation, and ominous silence.

Alusair threw back her head, her mouth suddenly dry, gulped in a deep breath, and rose to her feet. Owden and Rowen were waiting on either side of her, well away but obviously standing guard, and the procession carrying Cormyr's king and court wizard was just disappearing from view down the hill.

The Steel Princess ignored their anxious glances and stared at the royal tent on the distant hilltop. From her lips, after a moment, came a long, shuddering sigh. She shivered as a sudden chill washed along her shoulders and arms.

There could be only one reason why Tanalasta did not answer.

45

he fire of surging, thudding pain—a roiling that only comes from being struck hard and deep by magic seeking to slay—lashed the royal magician back to wakefulness. There was an iron tang of blood in his mouth, and his fingers were tingling as if they held huge, rushing spell energies overdue to burst forth. The world was lurching.

Vangerdahast was being carried across uneven ground, the sky storm-riven smoke above him. He was still on the battlefield, with the dark peak of Azoun's tent looming above him. The blood-streaked faces of the knights who bore him were turned toward it, and he thought he knew why.

Long ago, Baerauble had said it was the curse of the magely protectors of Cormyr to be right, all too often. The weak, bubbling voice that came to the royal magician's ears now told him he'd been right again.

Vangerdahast found that he could turn his head, as they laid him down, and see the king.

Troy Denning and Ed Greenwood

Azoun lay on a broad, creaking bed of shields set over rolled blankets to raise them from the trampled ground. The cloaks and sleeping furs atop those shields had been dragged into wildness by the king's clawing hands, and the king of all fair Cormyr was still moving in the restlessness of ravaging pain, threads of smoke rising from his groaning mouth as knights bent as near to him as they dared.

More smoke was rising from the hacked and torn rents in Azoun's armor, the places where the once bright plates had been torn away in the dragon's fury, and the cloaks beneath the king were drenched with dark blood.

More blood was coming from the king's mouth as he turned his head, fixing eyes that were bright with pain on Vangerdahast's face. For a moment Azoun's gaze roved, as if he did not see what lay around him but beheld something else, then the king's eyes grew sharp again. His lips twisted in what might have been cynical amusement, or might have been just the pain.

"It seems I still live," he said.

"Great lord?" Lionstone led a general rush of Cormyr's war captains to their king.

Unhelmed now, they were so many anxious hulks in scarred and scorched armor, sweat-soaked hair plastered to their faces or matted with blood, gauntlets gone to reveal bloodied fingers that reached for their king with anxious haste, and even more frantic gentleness.

"Help me rise," Vangerdahast snarled, never taking his eyes from his king. He had to repeat himself thrice before someone plucked him from the ground like an old sack and swung him upright. His legs felt curiously weak as they steadied him by the shoulders, but the royal magician found that he could stand on his own and that his body obeyed him. Gods, it even seemed whole. He thrust one hand into the neck of his robe, through the white and gray hair that curled across his chest. The wizard drew out certain things on chains, only to find just what he'd expected.

The handful of chased and worked silver talismans had been old when Cormyr was young, healing things made on the floating cities of Netheril and other elder lands. Mighty was their magic, lasting down the centuries, or, well, it had been. He was holding crumbling ashes now, lumps on the ends of fine chains that had dragged him back from the ravages of the dragon as he lay senseless and broken.

They'd made him whole by becoming themselves broken things, their ages-old magic exhausted. As he regarded them, even the chains started to crumble. Vangerdahast tossed them to the ground and murmured, "Step not there. Let no one tread there."

Azoun's head turned abruptly. "Is that my wizard?" the king snapped, struggling to sit up. Knights leaned and reached to help him, then recoiled, stumbling in their weariness.

Azoun's movement had awakened to full fury the dragon's blood that was eating him. A small ball of flame snarled up from his limbs to burst in the air head-high above him. Even as it faded into rising, drifting smoke, fresh lightning raged up and down the king and across his bed of shields, spitting sparks.

Ravaged armor shrank before the watching eyes on the hilltop, curling and darkening like leaves in a fire, and fell away from Azoun's arms and thighs. The gleam of bared bone shone forth from at least one ashen tangle beneath the tortured metal.

Vangerdahast took one unsteady stride, then another. Cormyr reeled under his boots, but did not heave itself over to smite him, and after another step, he was all right. The Forest Kingdom would have its royal magician a little while longer, at least.

"My king," he said gravely to the twisting figure atop the shields, as fresh lightning washed over that bed of pain and faded away into dancing sparks, "I am here."

"Vangey!" Azoun shouted—or tried to. The voice was like a distant cry, but the pleasure in it was unmistakable.

As the king drew himself up onto one elbow, the pauldron fell away from that shoulder, trailing fresh smoke. Paying the crashes of collapsing armor no heed, Azoun thrust himself properly upright and fixed his pain-bright eyes on Vangerdahast.

"Despite," the king gasped through lips that dripped black, oily blood in a constant stream now, "much provocation to the contrary—" he coughed, shoulders shuddering in a spasm of agony that forced his head down for one choking moment before he shook off the pain and looked grimly up again, "—you have always been my friend. More than that, the greatest friend Cormyr has had. Better than us all." His voice faded, and he murmured faintly, head sinking again, "Better than us all . . ."

Vangerdahast stepped forward, a frown of concern preceding him, and drew something from beneath his beard— the last of his hidden magical somethings. With a sudden wrench, he broke the fine chain that had held it hidden there against his throat. The eyes of many of the watching knights narrowed. The dancing ends of chain were green with age.

The royal magician stretched forth his hand with whatever it was clutched and hidden in his grasp to touch the king, but Azoun threw back his head and squared his shoulders again, almost defiantly, black blood raining down around him.

"By that friendship," he growled, eyes like two sudden flames as he stared into the wizard's gaze, "I charge you— stretch forth your magic and touch my daughter Tanalasta. Tell her she is to take the crown and . . . rule now."

Someone among those crowded around gasped, and Azoun nodded as if answering a disbelieving question. "Oh, yes," he said almost gently, "I'm done. The king too old and stubborn to fall is fallen at last. Not all the magic in you, Vangey—not all the magic in fair Faerûn—can save me now. Tana must rule. Tell her."

The wizard nodded slowly, his hand stretching forth once more. Azoun glared up at him and snarled, *"Tell her!"*

Vangerdahast's fingers touched the king. Azoun shivered, huddling back as if he'd been drenched with icy water, his face twisting in silent pain.

One of the war captains—a young man who bore the name Crownsilver—started forward with an oath, plucking out his dagger, only to come to a frozen halt as Azoun flung up a forbidding hand. King and warrior spoke together, the one wearily and the other furiously, "What is it you hold, wizard?"

"My greatest treasure,"Vangerdahast said in a voice that sounded for a moment like that of a small, high-voiced woman on the verge of tears. "The only bone I was able to find that was once part of the mage Amedahast. A little of her power is left in it, I think."

Ilberd Crownsilver stepped back, tears streaming down his cheeks. Vangerdahast raised the yellowing lump from Azoun's breast, where it seemed to fleetingly leave tiny wisps of smoke behind, and touched it to the king's mouth. The king stiffened.

Men watched like so many silent statues.

The red, searing pain suddenly left Azoun's eyes, melting away like shadows fleeing a bright sun. Men gasped, and there were more muttered oaths on the hilltop.

Color came back into the king's face, and his cracked, bleeding lips grew whole. The watchers leaned forward to stare in wonder, the old wizard still standing before the king with his hand thrust forward, as if lunging with a blade, holding the bone firmly in the royal jaws.

There was wonder on Azoun Obarskyr's face too. He drew in a slow, deep, shuddering breath, and they saw the ashes fading from his skin, leaving smooth, unburnt flesh behind. Old muscles rippled—but even as Ilberd Crownsilver drew breath for an exultant shout, the talisman crumbled, yellowed bone fading to brown dust that fell away into the air and was gone . . . leaving just two old men staring into each other's eyes. The ashes and bloody ruin did not return to where they'd been banished from the king's flesh, but neither did they fade farther.

After a moment, Vangerdahast let his empty fingers fall away.

In their wake Azoun shook his head slowly, and managed a smile. "Not this time, I'm afraid," he said calmly.

Vangerdahast stood still and silent.

The king's smile faded and he said, "Are you going to obey me this once, old friend? For the realm?"

The wizard's voice, when it came, sounded like the rusting hinges of a very old gate. "Of course."

Vangerdahast turned like a weary mountain and strode a safe dozen paces away, lifting his left palm out in front of him to cup the shimmer of the spell to come. He paid no heed to the armored giants in his path, but they melted or stumbled away in front of him as if he was the striding god of war himself.

All but one.

A single dark and slender figure stepped to meet Vangerdahast, blocking his way. A hand shot out above the wizard's, breaking his concentration. The royal magician's head snapped up, his eyes darkening with anger.

"Save the spell," Alusair murmured. "I tried to reach Tanalasta earlier, and—" she dipped her head and managed to choke out the last word, as suspicious war captains drifted closer on all sides, eyes narrowing as they cocked their heads to listen for treachery "—silence."

Vangerdahast may have looked like an old, dirty hermit in plain rags, but as he turned very slowly to look at the approaching warriors with the magnificent Purple Dragons on their breasts, his eyes were cold. He met their gazes, and the knights fell back.

"Secrets of the realm," the wizard said shortly, and at his words they retreated two swift paces in unison like so many trained dogs, leaving Alusair and Vangerdahast standing alone again.

"I'll try your mother," the royal magician muttered, not looking at her, and as Alusair threw back her head and gasped for air, she discovered that the sky was bright with tears. She realized that she was weeping, her face streaming with so many tears that her chin was dripping.

The Steel Princess brushed an impatient forearm across her face, not caring if the armor tore away skin, and shook her head as a dog coming out of a pond shakes away water. Her watery vision cleared enough to show her the nearest war captains, their faces wet with tears, too. They knew what was about to befall here on this hill.

Silvery threads of whispering air were curling about

Vangerdahast's shoulders—the magic he used when he wanted to speak aloud to someone distant but to have their words and his face cloaked from those standing nearby. Suspicion was spreading across the faces of some war captains as they watched those dancing threads gather. Alusair caught their eyes and reached out deliberately and laid a hand on the wizard's neck to ensure she'd be privy to the far-spoken conversation. Vangerdahast's response was to move a little closer to her, to ease her reach.

"Filfaeril," the royal magician said gravely, without preamble, "your Azoun hangs near death, and I cannot comfort you with the expectation of a recovery. The magics on him keep him asleep and make it dangerous for us to approach, but in his last wakefulness Azoun spoke to me of how precious your love has been to him, and to give you his last salute. He also commanded me to learn, and tell him, of Tanalasta's fate, and that of the child she bears. What news?"

"Good Vangerdahast," came a clear, cold voice out of the empty air, for all the world as if the Dragon Queen stood in front of the wizard, "my eldest daughter is dead—she died true and fearless, destroying Boldovar to save us all here—but her babe lives. It is a boy, another Azoun for Cormyr. I pray you, if your wisdom makes these our words private, that you not burden the heart of my lord and love Azoun with word of Tanalasta's passing, in his own last moments. Just . . . just . . ." Filfaeril's voice wavered on the edge of a sob, just for a moment, then steadied again into cold resolve. "Tell him, Vangey, just how much I love him. Farewell, my Azoun. Our love will endure when our bodies cannot."

Her voice broke entirely, and was a pleading agony as she whispered, "If you love me, old wizard, can you not bring me to him?"

Alusair felt a tremor pass through Vangerdahast then that marked his own sob bursting forth—a tremor that was promptly and with iron determination mastered, head bowed, as the royal magician murmured, "Oh, Lady Queen, I dare not try, lest I doom us all, your other daughter most of all. If this magic goes wild . . ."

Troy Denning and Ed Greenwood

"I understand," Filfaeril whispered. "Oh, gods, Vangey, keep Alusair safe and . . . and ease my Azoun's passing. If you have any magic, later, to show me what you saw and thought of his dying, I command you *show me*. I must see."

"Lady, you shall," Vangerdahast said gently. "Fare you well." He ended the spell with a weary wave of his hand, and turned to Alusair. "For the safety of the crown, I dared not bring her here," he said, sounding ashamed. "I want you to kn—"

Alusair whirled away, tearing free of his grasp, but not with the snarl of anger he'd feared and not to spurn him. Instead, she was crouching with drawn steel, like all the other war captains on that hilltop, awaiting fresh menace. The wizard peered around her.

The Steel Princess was facing a whirling chaos of growing radiance in the air a little way down one slope of the hill—the glow of manifesting magic.

"Translocational arrivals," Vangerdahast said loudly, to identify the magic for any who might not yet have recognized it. "Launch no attack until I bid y—"

"Be still, wizard!" one of the war captains snapped, eyes intent on the brightening glows. His voice sank to a mutter, Vangerdahast forgotten as he studied the flaring magic, and he added, "For once . . ."

Several heads snapped around to see how Vangerdahast would react to that outburst, but the royal magician's face was expressionless as he took a step sideways to place himself squarely between this burgeoning magic and the fallen king. Vangerdahast squinted into the flares of brilliance as they reached their heights, then sighed and stepped back, a sour expression flickering across his face so swiftly that Alusair, watching him, could not be quite sure she'd seen it there.

Some of the veteran war captains of Cormyr were not so discreet. Disgust and disdain were written large on their faces as Cormyrean high priests of various faiths appeared out of the roiling sparks and glows of their collective teleport. Loremaster Thaun Khelbor of Deneir, his face set with fear, glanced this way and that at the wrack of battle,

378

and was promptly shouldered aside by the High Huntmaster of Vaunted Malar, who in turn found himself in the striding wake of Aldeth Ironsar, Faithful Hammer of Tyr. Evidently the war wizards who'd sent them hence had lacked magic enough to send the upperpriests of each church who customarily accompanied their superiors everywhere. Every arriving priest ruled the Cormyrean churches of his faith.

"Trust the vultures to come *now*," someone among the watching war captains said loudly, as many blades—but by no means all of the swords held ready on the hill—were sheathed.

"Aye," someone else said bitterly, "now that the bloody work's done."

The Lord High Priest Most Favored of the Luck Goddess turned his head and snapped, "Who said that?"

For a long, cold moment there came no reply, then the air grew more frosty still when more than a dozen of the blood-drenched men in armor said in flat, insolent unison, "I did."

Manarech Eskwuin blanched and quickly looked away, striding on, like all of his fellows, up the hill to where the king lay. As if the magic that had brought him was rolling along before him, fresh flames and radiance burst into being around Azoun's body, and he roared and twisted in pain, spasming on the bed of shields. The taint of the dragon's blood had returned.

"Make way!" commanded the high priest of Malar. "We are come in Cormyr's hour of need to heal the king."

"This is not a matter for straightforward healing," Vangerdahast said warningly, standing his ground. Behind him, something that hissed and coiled arose from Azoun's mouth, and small puffs of flame curled up from his drumming heels. Fell magic was raging and gnawing within him.

"I fear there is nothing you can do here, holy men," the royal magician said politely, "save to let King Azoun die with the dignity he has so valiantly earned."

Some of the war captains there drew in to stand beside the wizard, barring the high priests from reaching the king, but others cast suspicious glances at Vangerdahast, and murmurs were heard of, "Refuse the king healing? What treachery's this?"

Augrathar Buruin, High Huntmaster of Vaunted Malar, raised an imperious hand. It was swathed in a furry gauntlet whose fingers were tipped with the claws of great cats, and whose outer side was studded with the bone barbs of beasts. He pointed at the royal magician, then swept his arm to one side, still pointing. There was a sneer on his face, and his eyes glittered with contempt through his obvious excitement. "Back, Vangerdahast!" he snarled.

The old man in the torn and dirty robe neither moved nor spoke.

The huntmaster snapped, "In this, wizard, you're but an ignorant, meddling courtier. Stand back, and take your puny spells with you. The divine might of Malar shall prevail, as it always has—and always will."

A swelling of light occurred in the air behind the priests then, and several of them whirled around in swiftness born of fear, faces tightening. The light outlined a figure, then swiftly faded into streaming sparks. Out of their heart trudged a man in hacked and blood-drenched armor. He was bareheaded, his face wore the weathered calm of a veteran warrior, and the bare-bladed miniature sword floating upright a foot in front of his breastplate marked him for all eyes as a battlelord, a senior priest of Tempus, come late to the feast. On this battlefield, first rank should be his, yet the huntmaster of Malar gave no sign of noticing the warpriest's arrival, but merely gestured imperiously to Vangerdahast once more to stand back.

Something that might have been the faint echo of a smile passed across the old wizard's face, and without turning away, he retreated three slow steps.

The huntmaster drew himself up in triumph and cried, "Oh, Malar, Great Lord of Blood and master of all who hunt, as this brave king has done, look down upon thy true servant in this hour of a kingdom's need, and grant thy special favor upon this endeavor! Let the strength of the lion, the suppleness of the panther, and the stamina of the ice bear flow through me now, to touch this fair monarch in his time of need!"

The healing spell needed neither the invocation nor the grand gestures that followed, but no one moved or spoke as the huntmaster almost leisurely completed what must surely have been the most spectacular casting of his holy career, stretching forth both hands to Azoun with white purifying fire dancing between them.

The fire leaped forth to the bed of shields and plunged into the body of the king. Azoun convulsed, hands curling into claws as the surge of magic lifted him, back arched, amid sudden snarls of lightning and rolling, fist-sized balls of flame. Fire fell to the turf, and smoked, shields buckled with a shrill shriek, and out of the fading white fire a crackling arm of lightning reached, with an almost insolent lack of haste, to wash over the huntmaster.

Buruin staggered back with a strangled cry of his own, crashing into the watching priests behind him. Only the steadying arms of Owden Foley and Battlelord Steelhand kept him from falling. As they steadied him, the Malarite's face was gray, his eyes were dark, staring pits, and his teeth chattered.

Holy faces turned pale, holy hands—some of them trailing radiance that hung in the air, glowing, in the wake of where the hands had been—hastily sketched warding signs in the air, and holy boots as hastily moved back. Fearful glances had not failed to notice that more than one war captain of Cormyr had half drawn a blade and stepped forward in slow menace, faces as cold and set as stone.

"Your concern for and your devoted service to the king are both noted and appreciated," Vangerdahast told the priests gravely, the iron crown on his brows giving him the look of an old and mighty monarch. "Stand you back, now, and bear witness. Your gods would desire you to be present and to pray, but the time for healing, I fear, is past." He allowed a frown to cross his face as he lifted an imperious hand and added, "The king fades swiftly. Rob him not of his last moments."

The priests hesitated, several mouths opening to launch uncertain protests, and glanced at the angry warriors.

The royal magician looked at Owden Foley, then at

Battlelord Steelhand, giving them both a nod that mingled unspoken thanks and a request. The two priests returned the nod, turned, and began to shoo their fellow clerics away, raising and spreading their arms in unison to form a moving fence that swept all the holiness a little down the hill.

Vangerdahast nodded again, satisfaction in his face, and turned back to where Azoun lay. Alusair and her fellow war captains gathered around the king, eyes darting from the face of the wizard to that of their king, and back again at Vangerdahast.

"My liege," said the royal magician, in a voice that for a brief, fleeting moment held the hint of a sob, "I have obeyed and in so doing learned bright news. The Princess Tanalasta has been delivered of a son, whom I understand is to be known as Azoun the Fifth. Cormyr's new prince will bear a worthy name onto the throne, when the time is right."

"That—is good," the king gasped, and panted for a moment in the aftermath of a sudden spasm of pain. For a moment he sagged back, face going gray, and his war captains threw out cradling hands like so many bloody, sweat-drenched, armored nursemaids, to hold him nearly in a sitting position. Ilberd Crownsilver choked back what could only be a sob as the king struggled to clutch at his balance and find the strength to sit upright.

After a few terrible, convulsed breaths, Azoun found it, somewhere deep within, and looked up to give them all a savage smile—almost a sneer—of contempt for his own weakness. The smile softened into genuine, gentle warmth as he looked around from familiar face to familiar face. Alusair glided forward, eyes dark and face as white as polished bone. Her lips were parted as if to speak, but she said nothing, her sword forgotten in her hand.

Her father looked at her, then up at the sky, and offered his next words to it. "It's been a good ride," he remarked conversationally to the scudding gray clouds, "but if my striving counts for anything, let my son have a better one, O you watching gods."

The king threw off the gentle hands that held him, and surged to his feet, a lion once more. Swaying, as hands reached out to steady him then fell away in uncertainty, not wanting to insult Azoun in his last moments, he stared around at his realm for one last time, his eyes already going dull. His gaze wandered from one face to another, and his lips trembled on the edge of a smile. Azoun's hand slipped twice on the hilt of his sword before he drew it forth with the grace of long-won skill, and raised it. If he noticed that it shivered like a blade of grass in a high wind, he gave no sign of doing so.

"I will not say farewell," the fourth Azoun to rule the Forest Kingdom told those standing around him almost fiercely, "because I'll be here, in the night wind, watching over the land I love, with cold steel for her foes, and whispered comfort for her defenders."

The sword fell from his trembling fingers, but Alusair was as quick as a snake, plucking it from the air to hold it up, and raising it into his grasp again.

Azoun's body shook and shuddered as he put failing arms around her. "Take this to your mother," he said, as he turned to kiss her cheek.

His lips brushed her skin, then he gasped in ragged pain and sagged, his full weight on her. Alusair turned to hold him up, and their lips touched.

Azoun's breath was hot and sweet, and tasted like blood and flame. A last tiny lightning played about their joined lips, but Alusair never flinched, even as dragonfire shook her like a leaf in a storm.

Her father moaned in pain, whispered "Filfaeril" in the heart of it, sagged again, then pulled back his head with a lion's roar of exultation.

For a moment Azoun clutched his daughter fiercely, strength returning in a rush until his embrace was almost bruising, then he thrust himself free from her, whirled around on his heels to look at all of those watching him grimly, and cast his sword into the air.

It caught fire as it whirled up. Blue flames flashed, then faded to a deep, roiling purple as it spun. As it slowed at the height of its journey it became—just for an instant, but long enough that all men there on that hill swore the rest of their

Troy Denning and Ed Greenwood

days that they'd seen it look down at them, talons wrapped around the fading sword—the ghostly outline of a dragon.

Alusair saw Vangerdahast's fingers crook in two subtle gestures just as the sword swept up, and their eyes met for a moment, but she merely nodded, almost imperceptibly, and said no word, as men gasped in wonder all around them at the apparition.

Azoun regarded it with an almost sad smile, as if knowing it as one last mage's trick, as it flashed into a burst of bright purple and silver fire, and was gone. He turned away and strode—a walk that in two paces turned into a last, doomed stagger—into his tent. Alusair and Vangerdahast moved at his heels, but the others stood staring into the sky.

Men blinked at the emptiness that had held sword and dragon, a gulf of air that even the clouds were drawing back from to lay bare deep, clear blue, and let their long-held breaths out in a chorus of faint regret.

Into the silence that followed, Azoun said his last words as he sank to his knees, like a tired tree deciding to slowly meet the earth.

"For fair Cormyr," he gasped, his voice almost a whisper now. "*Forever!*"

"Forever, father," Alusair said, her voice trembling on the edge of tears. "Be remembered—forever!"

The king of all Cormyr was smiling as his face struck the turf, and the long silence descended. When his war captains and his daughter and even the priests began to weep, Azoun did not hear them. His ears were full of echoing trumpets, a sound he'd almost forgotten, down all the years, the triumphant horns that had sounded over the castle to mark his birth, so long ago. High, bright, and clear. Gods, but it was good to hear them again.

46

angerdahast knelt at Azoun's side a long time after the breath stopped coming, rubbing the ring of wishes he still wore on his finger and wondering if he dared. A simple gesture, a few little words, and Thatoryl Elian would not have been in those woods when Andar Obarskyr passed by. Lorelei Alavara would have lived and died a happy elven wife, Nalavarauthatoryl the Red would never have risen, and Alaundo the Seer would never have uttered his dire prophecy.

What then? Had Thatoryl Elian not been in those woods when Andar wandered by, Andar would never have had reason to flee the Wolf Woods and tell Ondeth about them, and there would never have been a Cormyr—at least not the Cormyr he served and loved. Vangerdahast had wished Nalavarauthatoryl out of existence once before, and it had cost him Azoun and Tanalasta and very nearly the realm itself. That was the temptation of magic. Like any power, sooner or later those who commanded it always abused it.

Troy Denning and Ed Greenwood

Vangerdahast took Azoun's hands and folded them across the king's chest. As he did so, he quickly slipped the ring of wishes off his own finger and onto his friend's. Kings died and so did their daughters, but the realm lived on. It was better to leave it that way.

He uttered a quiet spell to hide the ring from sight, then said, "Guard it well, my friend."

Only then did the tears start to come, pouring down Vangerdahast's cheeks in long runnels. He slipped the golden tricrown off Azoun's head, then stood and faced the others.

"The king is dead," he said.

That was all he could think of, for Tanalasta was dead as well. The new king was an infant, not yet a tenday old, but the others did not yet know that, of course. He had kept Tanalasta's death from them just as he had kept it from Azoun, and so they stood there watching, waiting for him to say what should have followed, their eyes frightened and sad and curious—but also hard and suspicious and calculating.

There would be scheming nobles who seized on the child's paternity to challenge his throne, and there would be Sembia and the Darkhold Zhentarim and others who hoped to seize on Cormyr's troubles to nibble off little pieces for themselves. There would be a long, cold winter ahead with few crops to feed the people, and no roofs to shelter them from the snow and rain, and there were sure to be the ordinary hordes of orcs and bugbears and even a few garden variety dragons sweeping south out of the wilderness in search of easy plunder. Cormyr would need a strong monarch in the days to come, and Vangerdahast knew Alusair well enough to know she would not want to be sitting in Suzail while her generals were fighting battles in every corner of the realm.

"Vangerdahast, what is it?" asked Owden Foley.

"There is something . . ."

The words caught in Vangerdahast's throat, and all he managed was a rasping sob. He closed his eyes, then raised his hand to request time to compose himself and find the words he needed.

They did not come easily, and for a moment all he could do was stand and weep. Alusair and a few of the others also began to cry, and he realized he was not setting a very strong example. He reached up to the iron goblin crown on his own head, discovering much to his relief that he could finally slip a finger under it now that Nalavara was dead. He slipped it off and stood in the center of the crowded pavilion, holding one crown in each hand, and a gentle murmur began to rustle through the tent.

Vangerdahast stepped forward and was just about to ask for silence when a hard rain began to fall inside the tent. A cold hand clamped onto the arm holding Azoun's crown.

"What are you doing, old man?"

Vangerdahast looked down and saw Rowen Cormaeril's strong hand wrapped around his wrist. The ghazneth's flesh was black and cold against his own white, wrinkled skin, a stark reminder of the price for betraying Cormyr.

The wizard met Rowen's burning white eyes, then slowly raised Cormyr's golden crown. "I was taking this to Alusair."

"To me?" Alusair's face paled, and she shook her head. "Oh no, Vangerdahast, I'm not—"

"It is your burden to bear, Alusair Obarskyr, not mine." Vangerdahast pulled his arm free of Rowen's grasp, then pressed the crown into Alusair's hands. "I am afraid you must be regent until Azoun the Fifth is old enough to assume the throne."

"What?" It was Rowen who gasped this question. "But Tanalasta—"

"Destroyed Boldovar," he said sadly, "and died valiantly in the process."

Rowen stumbled back, his face withering into a mask of grief. "No! Why would you . . . you must be lying!"

Vangerdahast closed Alusair's fingers around the crown, then reached out to clasp Rowen's arm. "I fear not. I hadn't the heart to tell the king, but it is so. Tanalasta has gone to stand with her father."

A terrible sob escaped the ghazneth's lips, then there was no sound in the tent but pounding rain. Vangerdahast spread his arms and reached out to comfort Rowen.

"My friend, I . . ."

Vangerdahast could not finish, for the ghazneth pushed him away and retreated deep into the shadows. A beam of fading sunlight spilled across the floor as the door flap opened, then the rain stopped and Rowen was gone.

Epilogue

hough her new dress plate had been made by the same smith to the same specifications as her old battered field armor, Alusair felt clumsy, vain, and somehow naked in it. Made of the finest dwarven steel, it was fluted, etched, and trimmed in gold damascening. The Royal Dragon of Cormyr was embossed in purple relief on its abdomen, and it had been perfectly cast and joined by the royal armorers. The royal artists had decorated it beautifully, the royal pages had polished it to a mirror sheen, and the royal squires had hung it on her glove tight—and Alusair would rather have ridden nude into battle than in such elaborate harness. Not for the first time, the Steel Regent cursed Vangerdahast for foisting the crown off on her instead of having the courage to set it on his own head.

Alusair was standing between her mother and Vangerdahast on the Review Balcony, holding her ridiculous dragon's head helm in one arm and King Azoun Obarskyr V of Cormyr in the other, nodding numbly and smiling stupidly as noble after noble paraded past her with his company of knights. Half the lords were so fat that even a full-sized shire could not have charged more than a hundred paces with so much blubber and steel, while the other half did not seem to know which side of the sword to hold outward as they raised it in salute. It was all she could do not to go down and start barking weapon drills.

Young Baron Ebonhawk led his lancers through the Presentation Arch and nearly put an eye out when he snapped the wrong side of his curved falchion against his face. The bronze bill of his garish helm caught the worst of the blow, but did not prevent the keen edge—no doubt honed razor-sharp by some beleaguered squire—from opening a bloody line down his cheek. The whimper that followed drew a chortle even from baby Azoun, but the young lord managed to avoid further embarrassment by riding on without stopping to call for a healer.

Alusair smiled and nodded as though she had not noticed, then muttered under her breath, "If this is the best that remains, the realm is lost already."

"They're only border garrisons." Vangerdahast smiled and waved enthusiastically to the young baron. "And each company will have a lionar and a war wizard along to advise it—and to take command at the first sign of an engagement."

"And the lords agreed to that?"

"Not exactly," said Filfaeril. The queen looked strong and supple and somehow younger than she had seemed in years, though also much harder and infinitely sadder. "But what they don't know will kill them, should it prove necessary."

Alusair cocked her brow. "That should inspire loyalty."

Filfaeril gave her a patronizing smile and said, "My dear Alusair, you have much to learn." She patted the arm cradling young Azoun. "On this battlefield, all that matters is power—who has it and who doesn't. At the moment, you are holding it in your arms, and we must all do everything we can to make certain it stays that way."

Alusair glanced down at the chubby-cheeked baby and wondered if she were truly up to the job Tanalasta had left her. To be a queen and a mother and who knew what else in Cormyr's darkest hour. . . .

At least she would not be alone. Filfaeril would be there beside her, pointing out which nobles to trust, which to watch, and which to execute at the first sign of disobedience. There would also be Owden Foley, who had agreed at her insistence to stay as the child's spiritual educator and do what he could to help Tanalasta's legacy live in her son.

And, of course, there would be Vangerdahast, who was even now nudging her with his elbow and murmuring quiet guidance.

"Give Earl Silverhorn a big smile. The poor fellow has spent his entire fortune outfitting his cavalry, and we wouldn't want him to think you unappreciative."

Alusair did as Vangerdahast suggested, even going so far as to raise her nephew and wave one of his tiny hands at the passing company. This drew a roaring cheer from the spectators, which immediately caused the young king to break into a round of gurgling.

"Now you've done it," growled Vangerdahast. "Now every lord will want a wave from the king."

"I suppose I'll have the strength to manage that," Alusair growled back. "I *am* holding him in my sword arm."

"Sword arm?" harrumphed Vangerdahast. "It's about time you put that limb to a proper use."

"What?" Alusair thundered.

She turned to blast the wizard with one of her vilest cavalryman's curses and found him grinning at her. It was one of his old, kindly, sardonic smiles telling her that save for whatever annoyances she happened to be causing him at the moment, soon all would be well again in Cormyr—but Alusair had never seen the old wizard looking quite so dark, or thin, or tired.

FORGOTTEN REALMS

ELMINSTER IN HELL

Ed Greenwood

Wizards
OF THE COAST

Beginnings

emories are wonderful things.

Yet they can burn like the hottest fire, raging and consuming their bearers, or cut like cruel blades. I can trap one in a gem and hold it in my hand to give to another, and yet keep it also in my mind, fading slowly over time, like paths to favorite places that have become overgrown and lost.

What is a human, but a bundle of memories?

What better treasure can the aged keep, to warm and delight them whenever they rummage through the sack of their own stored remembrances?

And what more hideous crime can there be, than to snatch away memories from a man?

Only my kisses should be able to do that to him—and then only when Mystra deems it needful. Yet a *thing* called Nergal dared to do this to my man. I, Alassra, made Nergal pay a fitting price, and was damned in that doing—and care not, and would do it again.

I dare anything, and will die doing so. Fools of Thay and

other places know me for my slaying spells and my fury. Often it masters me, and men call me "mad," when they should use the words "reckless" or "lost in bloodlust." I *do* enjoy destruction, I admit—and yet I also nurture and defend and treat with kindness.

Here I've done both, showing all who read of the kindnesses I so love, the reason I'd lay down my life as freely as I do my body before this man called Elminster, even if he had no more magic than a village idiot. Some will say I've set down secrets that common eyes should never have seen, and to them I say two things: "Have I truly?" and "I care not!" Some have said holy Mystra and others of the divine will smite me for this doing—and yet here I still stand, unrepentant.

So come, and read secrets. Heed this tale I have gathered, and learn—or care not, and turn away, to walk defenseless the rest of your undoubtedly short days. Choose freely.

I am the Storm Queen, and I never threaten. I merely promise.

Chapter 1:
Rocks and a Warm Place

here is no greater blasphemy than this.

This is the thing forbidden, for all gods and men, for every living being of this or any world—to shred asunder the stuff of which we are all made, leaving rents of crawling nothingness in Toril. Roiling, weeping wounds for all the Realms to spill out through, and all the cold and gnawing void to rush in . . .

With all the selfish and headstrong and uncaring fools who'd hurled magic about for all these centuries, it was a wonder this didn't happen more often. This thought offered little comfort.

The worlds roared. White-hot and all-devouring, the torrents of force spilling from the Weave snarled all around the tumbling man, tugging at his robes and old limbs and beard alike as he spun along in a roaring rush of air. What might have been the green trees of Shadowdale turned crazily above his head. Beneath—or was it above?—his booted feet stretched a blood-red, sunless sky. He'd seen it a time or two before before and had no desire ever to see again.

Streamers of noxious gas streaked that crimson dome like dirty clouds. They whirled to form what looked like giant eyes staring down, eyes that were swept away before they could focus, only to form anew, again and again. Beneath the ruby glow lay a dark nightmare land of bare rock and flumes of sparks and gouting flame, where things slithered and scrambled half-seen in the shadows. Mountains clawed the ruby sky. The Land of Teeth, Azuth had once aptly called it, surveying the endless jagged rocks. This was the Greeting Ground, the realm of horror that had claimed the lives of countless mortals. He was whirling along above Avernus, uppermost of the Nine Hells.

"Mystra," the tumbling man groaned. He called to life all the magics on his body, bringing them to tingling readiness in his fingertips.

Whether the Lady of the Weave heard and assisted him or not, life ahead was not going to be pleasant for Elminster Aumar. He was going to have to spend all of his magic healing this rift, for the love of Toril that so seldom loved him, be burned and blasted in the doing, perhaps fail and be torn apart—and if he succeeded, plunge at the last down into Avernus, bereft of spells and defenseless.

Yet his duty was clear.

Dark, bat-winged shapes were already soaring aloft, beating their menacing way toward him, seeking to plunge through the rift or tear it open farther, ere he could close it. The rift could be closed only from this side, not from the more pleasant skies of Toril—and if he were to do it at all, he would spend his magic so swiftly that he could not help making himself a bright beacon to all infernal eyes.

Those eyes were watching. Oh, yes.

Elminster saw something huge and dark and dragon-winged rise from a distant mountain, spreading leathery wings and trailing a long, long scaly tail as it rose ponderously into the sky of blood. Rose, and turned his way . . .

Nearer at hand, lightnings cracked and stabbed out of the edges of the rift. Glistening black devils struggled to pluck it farther open . . . struggling, no doubt, under orders from unseen devils below.

Ed Greenwood

The hurtling wizard saw the blue sky of Toril one last time. A mighty crash of lightning thrust blinding-bright talons through devils. Sleek obsidian and crimson bodies twisted in pain as they burned, their blood blazing up in red flames even as their scorched ashes fell to the uncaring rocks below.

"To hell with ye all," Elminster murmured sardonically. He closed his hands into fists and drew forth the silver fire within him, as small and precise an unleashing of it as he could manage. When the rift closed, he'd almost certainly lose touch with the Weave and Mystra and be unable to regain magical power. Silver fire consumed the rings and bracers and even the vestments he wore.

Strange singings and snarlings filled his ears as enchantments dissolved, flowing through him to spin in glowing blue-white flames around his hands. The racing fires of his magics hummed with comforting power as they crackled, spat, and grew stronger. The Old Mage's clothes became tatters. Ancient metal bands around his fingers fell away in dust and were gone. His hat burst into a blue flame that sank down into his long tresses. He called in its power. A dagger in one boot crumbled, and then the boot itself. He said a fond mental farewell to his favorite pipe ere it fell into ash. In its last tumbling moments El spent tiny bolts of his precious magic to guide his fall, turning in the air to swoop back to the rift.

The scar was growing, spitting vicious lightnings in all directions across the dark sky of Avernus. Bolts arced across the bloody vault like so many angry stars streaking to fading falls. Far below, many red, glistening eyes looked aloft at the deadly splendor.

Lightning clawed the air nearby, and the gaunt old wizard sent forth blue fire from his fingertips to snare it, or some part of it, to turn that raging energy to his task.

The bolt plucked him from the sky like a gnat caught in a gale, whirling him away. His teeth chattered, his hair quivered on end, and the hoarse beginnings of a scream froze in his throat. Caught in its grip, Elminster of Shadowdale could not have moved even a finger. Fires charred him black. Surging, searing force flung his arms and legs rigid into a

398

scorched star, and then threw him across the sky.

When he could see again, tiny lightnings streamed from his nose. The rift was a bright, distant fire in the red sky. Its flames were suddenly blotted out by a black and grinning form, horn-headed and bright-eyed, racing through the air with claws outstretched to rend stricken wizards.

"Tharguth," Elminster murmured, recalling an old grimoire's name for such devils—abishai, these were, for he saw a second and third swooping along in the wake of the first.

And then there was no more time to think; the abishai rushed at him like a striking hammer.

It tore at the air eagerly with its claws as it came, its poisonous tail curled up beneath it to stab if need be. Elminster looked into the devil's exulting eyes. He felt a rush of warmth and the vinegar-like tang of its hide as its jaws gaped wide. Its head turned on an angle to bite out his throat. He fed it fire, searing claws and head alike to nothingness in an instant and letting it tumble away into the rocky darkness below.

The second abishai was coming too fast to veer; El twisted away from one sky-raking claw and sent a tiny blue-white bolt of his magic into the howling mouth of the third winged devil. Its head exploded. Its racing body arched back and clawed the air in silent, spasmodic agony as it rushed past.

A flight spell was one of the few left to the Old Mage; fearful the magic roiling within him might twist and shatter it, he cast it with infinite care. Another tiny tithe of power gave him greater speed than the spell alone could furnish. He needed to get back to the rift, swiftly.

He did not need to look back or hear the snarls of rage to know that the second abishai had turned to come after him. The sky was full of tharguth, now—black and green and even the larger, more cruel red abishai. Their eyes blazed like pairs of ruby flame as they rose to hunt him. Their cries of rage and glee rose into a roar that overtop the thunder of the rent. It grew larger . . . and larger. . . .

Elminster Aumar was not the least of Mystra's Chosen, but neither was he a great and vigorous creature of battle.

Ed Greenwood

Like a tiny blue-white star, he raced across the sky of Avernus.

Dark red dragons glided now among the devils, biting and pouncing like great cats, preying hungrily on this flock of flying food. Little spike-studded gargoyle-devils, spinagons, were in the sky, too, darting and ducking aside from the tharguth. Looking back, El saw the abishai that pursued him get gutted from belly to throat by something winged and hungry. It flew away almost faster than he could turn his head.

His gaze fell for a moment to the land below and its twisting ribbon of red that could only be a river of blood. His attention flicked up again to the swift beat of those elusive wings. The flying slayer was slowing to a halt, standing on air to watch him. Their eyes met.

El found himself looking into the eyes of a lone devil beating feathered wings in the sky. She was sleek and graceful and deadly, dusky-hued and more beautiful than any mortal woman: an erinyes, doubtless a spy for a greater devil dwelling deeper in the Nine Hells.

My, but he was popular. Avernus must furnish poor entertainment, for a lone human wizard to attract such interest.

Well, no. He set aside proud thoughts. It was undoubtedly the rift that was drawing the devils aloft.

El saw more bat-wings tumbling helplessly across the sky, caught by more lightning bolts from the torrents of force where world met world and clawed at each other.

Another bolt rushed at him, and Elminster was ready. Spreading his hands, with magics crawling between them in a blue-white chain, he plunged into its raging heart. With a wordless shout, he drank in power until it rose hot and choking within him. He was forced to rear up out of its flow and into the ruby sky again, gasping and trembling.

He'd been driven back only a little way this time, and his limbs were blazing bright with energies. In the distance, winged devils try to drink in the power of the bolt as he had done but plunged to their dooms as the bolts consumed them in brief gouts of red flame.

A dragon saw him and wheeled from its sport of tearing

apart tharguth and devouring them. It came thundering down at him like a great wall of scaled flesh. It spat fire, the ravening flames that did so little to devils but could cook and doom a mortal man.

Elminster swooped and drank in that dragonfire, setting his teeth and grimly riding out the fierce but brief pain of quelling its heat with his own gathered magic.

Gasping, he prevailed. The Old Mage was full almost to bursting now. His body trembled with the effort of holding such force. He was no longer its vessel, but its heart, wrestling with its surges and flows merely to move as he desired to and not be torn apart by its ragings.

Or by draconic jaws. The great red dragon, thrice the size of any he'd seen on Toril—even old Larauthtor, who'd filled the sky like a moving mountain—swooped, fangs gaping.

Elminster threw his hands behind him and let tiny jets of flame spurt from his fingers, hurling him up, forward, and away—beyond the reach of even a frantically twisting wyrm.

It clawed wildly at the air in its haste to turn. Snapping its jaws vainly at him, the dragon flapped its great wings so hard that the air cracked like thunder. Caught in a trio of rift bolts, the wyrm stiffened, scales melting into smoke. It was too wracked with pain even to scream as it died. Its eyes burst into flame and smoke that trailed from dark sockets and loosely flapping jaws. The wyrm fell away into the jagged darkness below.

None of this was getting Elminster back to the task of healing the widening rift, looming like a weeping eye in the sky of Avernus. Elminster called up a half-remembered snatch of a bawdy song as he banked on wings of his own spell-flames. He raced, singing merrily but badly, to meet his doom.

Bolts stabbed to meet him. He spun chains of snarling magic around them and dragged them around in roaring, sky-shaking arcs. They plunged back toward their source—a racing flood in which he joined. Falling headlong into the blinding brightness, he thrust his hands out before him.

Ed Greenwood

All sound died away in the echoing roar. Elminster became a racing dart among mighty flows of force. They rolled ponderously past him, a great chaos of surges that battered and tore at him, threatening to whirl him away into bone-shattered, bloody pulp.

When searing force burnt away his fingertips, he sent forth spellfire to cleave it and master it, plunging on to the roiling edge where Toril began. He plucked and swooped and wove, surfing surging torrents of force to knit the blue sky together again.

Devils screamed as they were torn apart or blasted to shreds somewhere behind him. Elminster scarcely heard them. He gazed hungrily at the world he must wall himself away from to save. He looked longingly down at Shadowdale, a little green gem far below, ere he flung himself across the sky, stitching its ragged edge in his wake with teeth-jarring, surging force.

"The bards could never find words for this," he gasped. Red sky and blue slipped and slid and battled for supremacy overhead. He raced along the raging line. Sickening force slammed through him like the sword that had once plunged down his throat and out his backside in one icy moment. . . .

Long ago, that had been, and with rather less hanging in the balance. A memory among far too many, always beckoning him for a wander among their shadows. The offers were more enticing as Elminster grew ever more tired—and weariness rode his shoulders like a heavy, clinging cloak these days. . . .

Suddenly he was done. Energies veered away to complete what he'd begun, reshaping what had been shattered and cloaking bright Toril from his view. The roar of the sky died, and he was falling, a dwindling star, into the deep ruby gloom of Avernus.

He'd done it. Dazed and exhausted, he knew that much. Toril was saved, and his own doom sealed.

"Have my thanks, Great Elminster," he told himself with dark humor, toasting himself with an imaginary goblet as black fangs of rock rushed up to meet him. "Fair Faerûn has seen thy greatest victory—though none know it, or care.

Welcome to the waiting dunghill."

With the last of his weary will, Elminster made himself into a lump of stone and hurled to one side, so that his fall would become a plunge deep into what was probably the Lake of Blood. Let its warm and fetid waters take his fall. The rotting flesh that cloaked its bed would hide him. Perhaps he could lie unnoticed there, until he had strength enough again to—

After such a fall, even a stone hits water as hard as a smith's hammer. His brutal shattering of the surface would have made Elminster gasp—if he'd had anything to gasp with. Warmth bubbled past as he sank, tumbling in the warm, wet depths, slowing now as . . .

Something dark and snakelike coiled out of the red depths and snatched him. The tentacle lashed around him with the searing bite of a drover's whip . . . and then he was being dragged back up again.

Well, in the hells it was hardly to be expected that there'd be any rest for the wicked. So—let the torment begin. Mystra preserve and forfend. Please.

He was up out of the blood-water now, dripping. Unfamiliar magic raged around him, darting into him in little numbing jabs. He was changing, forced under its goads, flowing and unfolding and becoming . . . himself again, a human with arms and legs and—eyes.

Eyes that swam even as grunts and rending groans and a shrieking symphony of squeals told him he was growing ears. Then all at once, the world spun and shook and came to a halt, amid shocking clarity.

Elminster was standing on warm, sharp rock, and his feet were bare. He had feet, and legs . . . and his own old, gaunt body, even to the beard. He was standing in a little hollow in a great waste of rock, with foul streams of gas curling around him, burning his legs as they sighed past. Atop the rocks, bare, thorny branches of stunted trees stabbed like despairing fingers up into the blood-red sky. The ground trembled. From somewhere near at hand a flame shot up, raged briefly amid scorched rocks, and fell away out of sight again.

El became aware that something was standing in the deep shadow at the far end of the cleft. It was strode forward, stepping around many teeth of rock. Flame-yellow eyes met his with the force of a striking serpent, and held him in thrall as their owner advanced leisurely, giving Elminster a smile that was a long way from pleasant—and at the same time promised many things.

An eyebrow lifted, mirroring curving horns above, and a softly hissing voice asked almost gently, "Don't know me, little cringing wizard? I favor a more splendid shape, these days!"

Magic curled around Elminster's throat, choking any answer he might have wanted to make, and the devil's smile widened. "Like my gentle talons spell? Nothing to touch the great and mighty magics you're wont to hurl, of course, but it serves me . . . aye, it serves."

The horn-headed devil turned its head and smiled, those flame-yellow eyes still transfixing Elminster like the tines of a gigantic fork. "Still know me not, Old Mage? You *must* be tired."

Elminster gazed at the burly devil, wondering just when he'd become, in this unholy creature's eyes at least, any sort of expert on the diabolical.

His captor was a naked humanoid whose skin was seal-smooth and mottled gray, shot through with hues of brown and darker gray . . . very like the shadowed stones of Avernus that rose around them both.

A few scales glinted on the fiend's neck and ankles. Its humanlike head sported two curving horns. What had seemed at first glance to be a cloak drawn around the devil could now be clearly seen as a necklace of tentacles. One shot forth to curl around Elminster's bare shoulders, thrusting like a vengeful eel through tatters of drifting vapor—a good thirty feet or more—as the eyes that held Elminster's became a little redder.

"Know, then," the devil said with grotesque formality, sketching a little bow—and forcing, with his tentacle, the dazed and exhausted Old Mage to match it—"that you are the guest of Nergal, most mighty of the outcast Lords of Hell." His smile broadened, and his eyes were now as red as old coals. "You may greet me."

El struggled to speak, finding his throat dry and stiff. Nergal's smile became a smug, crooked thing. "Body a mite rebellious, great wizard? How sad. You will already have noted that my poor and paltry magics have served to return you to your true shape, and you've already felt my gentle talons. They ensure that any magic you cast or unleash is drained to strengthen my bonds upon you—oh, you may see them not, but bound you are, and shall be for as long as it's my pleasure to keep you so. You're wrapped in spell bindings linked to my mind; you'll never escape me unnoticed."

Nergal's lips curled in a sneer as he added, "None have broken my mind yet, Elminster, though you're welcome to try. Attaining freedom is a laudable goal for any sentient being."

The ground trembled again, and a flame shot up over their heads, searing a squalling imp. Nergal's smile broadened as he withdrew his tentacle—and the shuddering of the rocks beneath Elminster's baking feet made him stagger and almost fall.

"Laudable," the devil added gloatingly, "but nigh impossible. You see, I've spent much time observing your exploits, Old Weirdbeard—and I have uses for you. Oh, yes."

The archdevil's tentacles were suddenly writhing above his shoulders, like the limbs of an excited and gigantic spider.

"You will, of course, attempt to escape, perhaps even to harm me. Such failures will make little difference to your torment—and they *will be* failures."

Tentacles stretched forth almost lazily, and a diabolical smile widened.

"You see: You're in *my* cozy little dale now, wizard."

And wearing that same welcoming smile, Nergal reached out with a tentacle and tore Elminster's right arm off.

FORGOTTEN REALMS

For five hundred years,
Elminster has fought evil in the Realms.

Now he must
fight EVIL in HELL itself.

Elminster in Hell

By
Ed Greenwood

An ancient fiend has
imprisoned the Old Mage
in the shackles of Hell.
Bent on supreme power,
the demon is determined
to steal every memory,
every morsel of magic from
the defender of the Realms.
As the secrets
of Elminster's mind are
laid bare, one by one,
he weakens unto death.

August 2001

But Elminster won't go down without a fight.
And that is one instance for which his captor may be woefully unprepared.

FROM THE DARKEST REACHES OF
FAERÛN'S PAST COMES A NEW ENEMY.

Return of the Archwizards

AN EXCITING NEW FORGOTTEN REALMS EPIC

BOOK I: *The Summoning*

TROY DENNING

A new evil returns to Faerûn after millennia spent in a shadowy hell.

March 2001

BOOK II: *The Siege*

TROY DENNING

The world-spanning schemes of Shade begin to take shape,
along with a new empire in the heart of the Great Desert.

December 2001

FROM BELOVED AUTHOR
ELAINE CUNNINGHAM...

FOR THE FIRST TIME TOGETHER AS A SET!
SONGS AND SWORDS

Follow the adventures of bard Danilo Thann and his beautiful half-elf companion Arilyn Moonblade in these attractive new editions from Elaine Cunningham. These two daring Harpers face trials that bring them together and then tear them apart.

Elfsong
Elfshadow
Silver Shadows (JANUARY 2001)
Thornhold (FEBRUARY 2001)
The Dream Spheres

AND DON'T MISS...
STARLIGHT AND SHADOWS

Daughter of the Drow
In the aftermath of war in Menzoberranzan, free-spirited drow princess Liriel Baenre sets off on a hazardous quest. Pursued by enemies from her homeland, her best hope of an ally is one who may also be her deadliest rival.

Tangled Webs
Continuing on her quest, drow princess Liriel Baenre learns the price of power and must confront her dark drow nature.

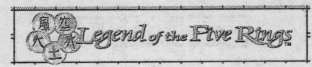

Legend of the Five Rings™

The Phoenix
Stephen D. Sullivan

The five Elemental Masters—
the greatest magic-wielders of
Rokugan—seek to turn back the
demons of the Shadowlands. To do so,
they must harness the power of the
Black Scrolls, and perhaps become
demons themselves.

March 2001

The Dragon
Ree Soesbee

The most mysterious of all the clans
of Rokugan, the Dragon had long
stayed elusive in their mountain
stronghold. When at last they emerge
into the Clan War, they unleash a
power that could well save the
empire . . . or doom it.

September 2001

The Crab
Stan Brown

For a thousand years, the Crab have
guarded the Emerald Empire against
demon hordes—but when the greatest
threat comes from within, the Crab
must ally with their fiendish foes and
march to take the capital city.

June 2001

The Lion
Stephen D. Sullivan

Since the Scorpion Coup, the Clans
of Rokugan have made war upon
each other. Now, in the face of Fu
Leng and his endless armies of
demons, the Seven Thunders must
band together to battle their
immortal foe . . . or die!

November 2001